COGNAC VILLAIN

PUSHKIN BRATVA
BOOK 1

NICOLE FOX

Copyright © 2023 by Nicole Fox

All rights reserved.

No part of this book may be reproduced in any form or by any electronic or mechanical means, including information storage and retrieval systems, without written permission from the author, except for the use of brief quotations in a book review.

❦ Created with Vellum

MAILING LIST

Sign up to my mailing list!
New subscribers receive a FREE steamy bad boy romance novel.

Click the link below to join.
https://sendfox.com/nicolefox

ALSO BY NICOLE FOX

Viktorov Bratva
Whiskey Poison
Whiskey Pain

Orlov Bratva
Champagne Venom
Champagne Wrath

Uvarov Bratva
Sapphire Scars
Sapphire Tears

Vlasov Bratva
Arrogant Monster
Arrogant Mistake

Zhukova Bratva
Tarnished Tyrant
Tarnished Queen

Stepanov Bratva
Satin Sinner
Satin Princess

Makarova Bratva
Shattered Altar
Shattered Cradle

Solovev Bratva

Ravaged Crown

Ravaged Throne

Vorobev Bratva

Velvet Devil

Velvet Angel

Romanoff Bratva

Immaculate Deception

Immaculate Corruption

Kovalyov Bratva

Gilded Cage

Gilded Tears

Jaded Soul

Jaded Devil

Ripped Veil

Ripped Lace

Mazzeo Mafia Duet

Liar's Lullaby (Book 1)

Sinner's Lullaby (Book 2)

Bratva Crime Syndicate

Can be read in any order!

Lies He Told Me

Scars He Gave Me

Sins He Taught Me

Belluci Mafia Trilogy

Corrupted Angel (Book 1)
Corrupted Queen (Book 2)
Corrupted Empire (Book 3)

De Maggio Mafia Duet

Devil in a Suit (Book 1)
Devil at the Altar (Book 2)

Kornilov Bratva Duet

Married to the Don (Book 1)
Til Death Do Us Part (Book 2)

Heirs to the Bratva Empire

Can be read in any order!

Kostya

Maksim

Andrei

Princes of Ravenlake Academy (Bully Romance)

Can be read as standalones!

Cruel Prep

Cruel Academy

Cruel Elite

Tsezar Bratva

Nightfall (Book 1)

Daybreak (Book 2)

Russian Crime Brotherhood

Can be read in any order!

Owned by the Mob Boss

Unprotected with the Mob Boss
Knocked Up by the Mob Boss
Sold to the Mob Boss
Stolen by the Mob Boss
Trapped with the Mob Boss

Volkov Bratva

Broken Vows (Book 1)
Broken Hope (Book 2)
Broken Sins *(standalone)*

Other Standalones

Vin: A Mafia Romance

Box Sets

Bratva Mob Bosses (Russian Crime Brotherhood Books 1-6)
Tsezar Bratva (Tsezar Bratva Duet Books 1-2)
Heirs to the Bratva Empire
The Mafia Dons Collection
The Don's Corruption

COGNAC VILLAIN

One wardrobe malfunction.

Two people who don't belong together.

Three awful words: "Be my wife."

Everyone else is at this party to marry the host.

I'm only here until I can get a ride home.

When my dress rips in the world's worst-timed wardrobe malfunction,

I go find somewhere quiet to fix it.

So I'm standing there in nothing but my heels when,

As my luck would have it, the door opens…

And the man of the hour walks in.

I wish I could say I played it cool.

But it's been a looong time since anyone has seen me in my birthday suit…

Much less the hottest man I've ever laid eyes on.

All I want to do is fix my dress, click my heels three times, and be back on my couch in fuzzy slippers.

But Ivan has other ideas.

He's decided who he's taking to the altar…

And I don't have a choice but to say "I do."

COGNAC VILLAIN is Book One in the Pushkin Bratva duet. Ivan and Cora's story concludes in Book Two, ***COGNAC VIXEN!***

1

CORA

I can't believe I let my friends drag me out tonight.

After an endless shift waiting tables at the diner, dishing out lukewarm enchiladas to ungrateful senior citizens who tip like it's still the Great Depression, the last thing I wanna do is put on a fancy dress and go to a party.

But Francia and Jorden, my fellow Quintaño's waitresses, insisted. And worse yet, Francia is refusing to let me wear any underwear with this gown I'm borrowing from her.

"Visible panty lines in Vera Wang is, like, a sin against God," she says in a horrified gasp, as if I'm going straight to hell for even suggesting such a thing. "Under no circumstances are you allowed to wear any. Over my dead freaking body."

I don't even get to argue back, because almost immediately after, she gets nauseous and runs to the bathroom to be sick. I would've called it a night, but party animal Jorden isn't letting anything stop her from getting shmammered.

"Nuh-uh. Francia got a stomach bug, but I've got the dancing bug," she proclaims. "I'm going *out* and I'm getting *drunk*. And you, my lovely lady companion, are coming with me."

Dammit.

So Jorden and I call an Uber from the apartment after we finish getting ready. At first, we're bopping to music, laughing, feeling like Disney princesses on our way to the ball. We both worked doubles at the diner every day this week in order to splurge on a rare night out, so we are determined to live it up.

Fun. That is the mission.

But the closer we get, the queasier I become.

It's not that Francia's stomach flu was contagious, either. It's the line of cars parked along the road that first gives me that nasty stomach drop feeling. Mercedes G-Wagons, Rolls Royces, and Lamborghinis as far as the eye can see.

It reminds me too much of my old life.

I ran from that life for a good reason. I hated the condescension, the fakeness layered on top of everything like glitter sludge. When I left, I swore I'd never be back in places like this.

Yet here I am. Lucky me.

The feeling only gets worse as we approach the house. But then we turn the corner…and there it is.

The mansion is lit up like a jewel in the night. All glass everything. Beautiful people lounge everywhere: on the steps, in the rooms, in little groups of four and five spread out across the back lawn.

"We're only staying 'til midnight, Jor," I warn my friend as we totter up the front steps in high heels. "I'm opening the diner tomorrow and I do *not* want to be hungover for the Saturday morning rush."

"Yeah, yeah, whatever," she sasses back. "In bed by midnight or Cora the Explorer will turn into a pumpkin. Roger that."

Then she hooks her arm through mine and brings us up in front of the bouncer. "Hi," she purrs.

He glances down at us over the edge of his clipboard. "Names?"

Jorden elbows me hard in the ribs. "Say it," she hisses under her breath. "Like we practiced."

I sigh. "Francia Delacour and guest." We rehearsed that little white lie enough times on the ride over that it comes out more or less natural.

The bouncer takes a long time perusing his list before nodding and stepping aside. "Enjoy your evening, ladies."

Then we step through the door and into another universe.

Everything gleams white and golden, with bold hints of black marble where you least expect it. There's an honest-to-goodness fountain in the center of the living room and I'm fairly sure I saw a peacock roaming the grounds out front.

"Is this a house or a palace?" Jorden asks me, dumbfounded.

"Better question," I reply. "If Francia can get into parties like this, what on Earth is she doing waiting tables at Quintaño's with us?"

It's not the only thing about Francia that doesn't quite make sense. She randomly showed up to work one day with a diamond Cartier tennis bracelet on, for example. When I asked her where she got it, she just laughed and smiled and changed the subject—then it was gone the next time I saw her. She never invites us to her apartment; whenever we hang out, it's at my place or Jorden's. Truth be told, I'm not even sure what part of town she lives in.

"Champagne, ladies?" comes a voice from my left. I turn to see a server offering us a selection of glittering flutes of champagne on a silver tray.

"Yes, *please!*" Jorden chirps. I get one; she snatches up two. "One for me and one for my, uh…other friend."

The man bows his head and whisks away without another word. Jorden promptly downs the first glass in a single go and sets the empty flute on a nearby pedestal.

"Thirsty?" I tease her.

"Girl, I get, like, one night out per year to enjoy myself. So I'm gonna enjoy myself. Mama deserves to have fun. And," she adds, bumping my hip with hers, "so do you."

"Yeah. Fun. Totally."

But that gut-churning feeling is still alive and well in the middle of my belly.

We meander through the house, snagging hors d'oeuvres off of circulating trays and gawking at the insane architecture. We pass more knots of people, too, congregating on every surface and talking intently.

Someone told me once that background actors in a movie are taught to whisper "watermelon watermelon watermelon" over and over again to pretend like they're having actual conversations. That's what this feels like.

Except instead of whispering "watermelon," they're whispering two words. It takes a while for me to make them out, but when I do, something in the phrase makes me feel like there's a cold breeze rushing over my skin.

Ivan Pushkin.

Again and again, everywhere we go, that's what I hear.

Ivan Pushkin.

Ivan Pushkin.

It rises up from every single group we pass without fail. There's a strange sort of skittishness in the air, too. Every female between the ages of eighteen and forty keeps checking over their shoulders like they know something we don't. Like something important is coming and they want to look their best when it gets here.

We find ourselves stepping out onto the back lawn. It's festooned with fairy lights branching out from a stage at the far end. A jazz band plays classy music to a crowd of people intent on looking cool by ignoring it. No one dances at parties like these.

Correction: *one* person dances at parties like these.

"Uh-oh," Jorden warns with a wicked grin. She points down at her hips, which are starting to shimmy from side to side like they have a life of their own.

"Jor…"

"Uh-oh!" she repeats in a delighted cackle. "I can't help it, Cora! It's—I'm—*They're aliiive!*"

"We've been here for twenty minutes and you're already wasted?"

"No," Jorden claps back, "I'm having *fun*. You should try it sometime."

I love her, I really do—I just can't match her energy all the time. Definitely not without significantly more alcohol in me.

She, on the other hand, doesn't need a drop of the stuff. Even when she's sober as a judge, Jorden is a ten out of ten. She laughs loud, loves loud, lives loud.

It's miraculous, honestly, because she's been busting her butt to make ends meet for as long as I've known her. She was raised by a single mom off food stamps, working in diners like Quintaño's long before she was actually old enough to do so legally.

She's right: she does deserve a break. Life is hard.

"You go dance," I say sheepishly. "I'm gonna go find another drink first so I can keep up with you."

She shrugs and flips her hair over her shoulder. "Fine. But if you find me grinding up on some hot young thing when you get back, it'll be your loss!"

I grin and kiss her on the cheek. "I hope I find you grinding up on *two* of them."

"Don't tempt me, girl. I just might. I really just might."

Laughing, we separate and I go back inside the house in search of a bathroom. I put on a brave face while Jorden was watching, but as soon as I find a bathroom, I shut the door behind me, lock it, and draw in a huge, shuddering breath.

This is too much. It was a bad idea to come here. Back to a place like this, around people like this… I turned my back on this world. I never wanted to return.

As soon as I get out of here, I'm going to double down on that vow.

When I touch the back of my neck, my palm comes away soaked with clammy sweat.

"Midnight," I swear to my reflection in the mirror. "Just a couple more hours, then the clock will strike midnight and you can say goodbye to these people forever."

Midnight.

We're almost there.

I rinse my sweaty neck and step out of the bathroom, ready to brave the rest of the party. Through the distant double doors, I catch a brief glimpse of Jorden in the crowd. But before I can even get a step in her direction, I feel an unexpected hand on my waist.

A voice accompanies it. "Hey there, gorgeous."

I follow the sound of the slurred greeting to a rumpled man with a damp forehead. He's swaying from side to side.

"Hi." I give him a tight smile and retreat towards the wall.

"I came over because you look lonely." His words are breathy, arriving on a cloud of alcohol fumes. "Thought I'd keep ya company."

I wrinkle my nose. "Oh, that's nice of you. I'm fine, though. But thanks!"

If he understands the implied goodbye, he doesn't show it. He steps closer, his belly pressing against me. "Who are you with?"

"My boyfriend," I lie reflexively. "He's getting me a drink right now."

He hesitates for a second and then cackles. "Bullshit."

That throws me for a loop, mostly because he's so certain. "I don't—I mean—How would you even know?"

"Because you're here to meet *him*. Just like the rest of them." He says it with more of that same finality. Like he knows something I don't.

I have lots of questions, but none I want to sit and discuss with this charming fellow. I try to edge past him. "I'm just going to—"

"He isn't that great, you know." He shifts with me, blocking my path. "Everyone is here for Ivan, but I'll show you what a real man can do for you. There's no line to get to me."

"Gee, I wonder why," I mutter to myself. To him, I say, "I have literally no idea what you are talking about. You probably don't, either. You're drunk. So if you could just let me go—"

Suddenly, his sweaty, meaty hand slaps my ass.

Distantly, I hear threads of my dress popping. But it's like paying attention to a dripping faucet when your house is on fire. I have bigger fish to fry.

Anyone who's ever worked in the food service industry knows that customers do jaw-dropping things. Married men leave their phone numbers on the receipt; friendly-looking grandpas pinch your ass; their wives hiss that you're a slut beneath their breaths.

And anyone who's ever been *stuck* working in the food service industry, even when they're so sick of all those things, knows that there are two choices: you can take it all on the chin and keep your job—or you can live out the fantasy of every server ever and show the motherfuckers who crossed the line that they messed with the wrong person.

Today, I'm the wrong person.

And this is the motherfucker who crossed the line.

2

IVAN

I'm bored out of my fucking mind.

Everywhere I look at this party, I see the least interesting person I've ever met. And the next, and the next. For a bunch of scumbags and criminals, you'd think they would have something engaging to discuss.

But they don't. The furthest thing from it, in fact.

Because just about every soul under my roof tonight is here for the same irritating reason.

To get me to marry.

Whether it's them I'm meant to be marrying, or their daughter, sister, cousin, mother, whoever, they aren't too particular. They just want to get closer to me. To my empire. By any means necessary.

I don't even blame them. The Pushkin Bratva is the biggest shark in a sea full of them. We have the money. The power. We decide who gets what and when, and the usual answers to those questions are "us," "all of it," and "right fucking now."

"These things will be the death of me," I mutter.

"So why are you here?" asks Yasha, my best friend and right-hand man, as he snares a toothpick of cheese from a passing waiter.

"Because Anya will be the death of me if I bail."

He snorts through a mouthful of brie. "True. That sister of yours owes you one for what she's putting you through tonight."

"That she does," I agree.

But even that is a massive understatement. I wouldn't be here, subjecting myself to this bullshit, for anyone but her.

If it weren't for *me*, though, she'd be going through hellfire right now. Our father was furious enough when he found out what she'd done. Rebuffing half a dozen decent marriage proposals in order to elope with a lowly Bratva foot soldier? It's blasphemy in the eyes of the old bastard who birthed us. Daughters, in our father's mind, are pawns to be moved around the board as he sees fit. God forbid they should marry for love.

I think she should do whatever the hell she wants. That being said, I'm not exactly big on the concept. Marry for love: fine, if that's what Anya desires.

But I will *not* be doing the same.

If I'm going to be forced to marry, I'll be marrying for *business*. Nothing more. I'm marrying to take the heat off my sister's transgressions. I'm marrying to solidify the Pushkin Bratva as the preeminent force in the American underworld.

Love has nothing to do with it.

A sudden sound from behind me draws my attention. Yasha and I turn as one, conditioned by years of fighting alongside one another to be ready for whatever comes next. It wouldn't be the first party we've attended that ends in gunfire and bloodshed.

But there's none of that to be seen.

Not yet, at least.

A woman I've never seen before is baring her fangs at the drunken nephew of the Greek Genakos mafia don. Stefanos is his name, I think. He's coarse and sloppy, which matches his reputation. Even now, his eyes are rolling in their sockets, loosened by too much of the free booze on hand. His claws are reaching out toward the girl.

"Keep your *fucking* hands to yourself," she spits at him.

"Aw, c'mon," he mutters through clumsy lips. "I was just tryna be friendly."

"By grabbing my ass?"

"Tryna appreciate you, too," he mumbles. "You don't gotta be a bitch about it."

Her jaw drops. "I *know* you did not just call me a bitch."

"I said you're *bein'* a bitch, not that you are—"

He doesn't get to finish the sentence before she cracks him across the face with a vicious slap. Those freewheeling eyes of his go blank and he stumbles backwards. He bumps into a wall and wobbles.

Then he rights himself and his unkempt smile twists into something far meaner.

Cognac Villain

"Listen here, you fuckin' whore…" He advances on her. Those hands of his suddenly don't look so limp and harmless. He goes to paw her again. She tries to bat him off, but he's bigger and stronger than her, so he just swallows her up with his bulk as he backs her into the corner by the bathrooms.

And with that, I've seen enough.

I'm not here to be anyone's white knight. But I'll be damned if this inebriated moron is going to go around groping unwilling women in front of me.

When I was a boy, I saw my father do far too much of that. I couldn't do anything to stop him then.

But now? Now, I'm perfectly capable of ripping this motherfucker to pieces.

I cross the distance, find the back of Stefanos's collar, and rip him to the ground. He shrieks and hits hard enough to shake the nearby sculptures on their pedestals.

A champagne flute crashes to the floor and shatters in a million directions. One of the jagged pieces cuts Stefanos's ear. His blood starts to pool out onto the white marble.

I plant a knee on Stefanos's chest and bend down close enough for him to hear every word I breathe in his face. "I think you are the one who ought to 'listen here,' my friend. The lady told you no. She asked you to keep your hands to yourself, but you did not. So now, I'm putting my hands on you, and I won't stop when you ask me to. I won't stop when you beg me to. I won't even stop when you scream and plead and cry for me to please God just *have some fucking mercy*."

Stefanos's eyes are wide and still now. His lower lip quivers. The cold fear sweat beading in his mustache disgusts me. "P-p-plea—"

"Shh." I press a finger to my mouth. "I just told you that begging won't help." Then, sighing, I release my weight from off his chest and stand again. I pull my tuxedo cuffs into place as I look down on him from above. "But I don't feel like getting your blood on my suit tonight. So for now, I'll let you go. Get the fuck out of my sight."

He doesn't have to be told twice. He scrambles away on his hands and knees, leaking blood, until he can gather himself back upright. Then he goes bumbling away, down the corner and out of sight.

When he's gone, I turn to the girl.

3

CORA

I'm still standing where that asshole left me backed into the corner. My hair is mussed and sweaty and my jaw is aching from biting down so hard. I'd like to get out of here, but I'm stuck for two main reasons.

One is that the man who just rescued me from Mr. Handsy Douche Bag is currently smoldering down in my direction. He looks like if testosterone had a face. Pure, rippling masculinity. Eyes like preserved honey. Hands that, even now, are flexing and unflexing like they're capable of doing so much more.

The second reason is that, if I move out of this corner, Prince Testosterone and all the rubber-necking onlookers will get an eyeful of my bare butt.

That's because, when the douche bag tried to paw at me, he ripped my dress all the way up the back seams. I can feel the cold breeze of the air conditioning blowing where I really wish it wouldn't.

Not good.

So that's my predicament in a nutshell: hottest guy I've ever seen plus one hell of a wardrobe malfunction. I'm a waitress, not a mathematician, but even I know that that doesn't add up to anything great.

"Relax," he rumbles. "You don't have to worry. I handled it."

"Yep. Relax. Working on it." It's difficult to talk, given how hard I'm trying not to move for fear of ripping the dress further.

I have a delirious mental image of just staying planted right here for the rest of the night. They can use my arms like a coat rack. The clean-up crew will have to get a crowbar to pry me out of the corner in the morning.

"I'd advise you to start by inhaling," he suggests. "In through the nose, out through the mouth. That sort of thing." There's an undercurrent of dark laughter in his voice.

I wrinkle my nose. "Which part of this is funny to you?"

He doesn't seem bothered in the least by my sharp voice. "The part where you look like you're about to have an aneurysm if you don't take a breath in the near future."

He's right—I really am clenching dangerously hard. For medical reasons, if nothing else, I sigh and take a big sip of air.

As I do, I feel another stitch in the seam give way.

Things are going well.

"You know, you look like a busy, important man," I say, doing my best to keep my ever-growing desperation out of my voice. "I'm sure other busy, important men and women would very much like your attention somewhere else in the party, right?"

Cognac Villain

He shrugs. "Maybe. Hard to say."

"But easy to find out! You could go…over there, maybe!" I jut my chin in the direction of the back lawn. "Or there. Or there. Anywhere, really. Lots of people are no doubt extremely eager to ask you about, uh, world politics or the economy or who you think is gonna win *Naked & Afraid* this season."

Unfortunately, Prince Testosterone doesn't take any of my suggestions. "Then they can wait." He inches closer, which I really, really wish he wouldn't do. "What's your name?"

"Who, me?"

"No, the *other* girl cowering in the corner."

I force a laugh. "Oh, I'm nobody. Not busy or important in the least, and I don't even watch *Naked & Afraid!*"

It feels like the walls are closing in. I'm making silent oaths in my head and hoping that some deities above are listening and will take mercy on me. *I'll wear only pants for the rest of my life if you get me out of this mess. Just please, for God's sake, help me!*

If anyone up above hears, they show no sign of it.

He edges closer still. I can smell his cologne now. Cedarwood and sage. It's making my head spin.

Over his shoulders, most of the other attendees have turned back to their conversations, though I still feel a few stray eyes drifting in our direction here and there. It's hard to look anywhere but at him, though. He's just got this confidence, this magnetism, that brings me back to his gaze again and again.

For his part, he doesn't seem to have any problem blocking out the whole world to focus on just me. "You're a strange one."

"You don't even know the half of it," I promise him. "Seriously. I'd run if I were you."

I'd run if I were me, too, I add silently.

He still doesn't smile or show any signs of a departure in the near-future. "I'll ask you one more time: what's your name?"

I'm scraping the bottom of the barrel as far as lies and distractions go. Between that and the tickle of cold air on my bare skin and the *tick-tick-tick* sound-slash-sensation of more stitches giving way and my ever-growing terror that somehow, some way, this terrifying man knows who I am—who I *really* am—I'm about this close to just telling him the truth.

Or maybe I'm just sick of lying. Of hiding. Of running. It's been years of it now and it's starting to get old.

So I open my mouth. My real name is right on my lips. "I'm—"

Then someone taps the man on the shoulder.

He straightens and turns with a scowl on his lips. The person interrupting us is slender and tall, with a wiry frame and a shock of brown hair. He's got the same kind of serious composure in his face that Prince Testosterone has. A *do-not-fuck-with-me*-ness.

The new man whispers something urgent in his ear. Both their scowls deepen. Their eyes flit out to the lawn.

I see that for what it is.

A window of opportunity.

With one last prayer to the heavens above just in case any of those celestial assholes have decided to tune in, I clamp the ruined halves of my dress together as best as I can, pirouette on my heel, and take off waddle-running down the nearest hallway before the two men turn back to realize I'm gone.

My plan is simple: I'm going to find somewhere quiet to fix my dress. Then I'm going to find Jorden and we're going to get the hell out of here.

With any luck, I'll never see that man again.

4

CORA

Bad news: this place is a labyrinth. I feel like I've been running for hours, twisting and turning down hall after hall. The one silver lining is that at least I'm leaving the super Hulk behind.

I shiver at the thought of him. He was too perfect to be real. His bone structure was brutally sharp. Those lips had a cruel slant to them. And those *eyes*—Lord have mercy, those amber eyes could hypnotize a girl if she's not careful.

He hadn't laid so much as a finger on me, but the way he looked at me was a physical touch in and of itself. It stroked the deepest parts of me.

As if I didn't already feel plenty naked with a gaping rip in the backside of my dress.

I shake off the memory just as a door with a thin slice of light at the bottom beckons. It looks like a bathroom, so I push through—

And come to a screeching halt.

Cognac Villain

A trio of girls is clustered around a hand mirror balanced on top of the sink. Their hair is expertly curled, their dresses flawless, their manicures glistening in the candlelight.

Two of them don't notice me enter. The third looks up from where she's bent over the mirror with a straw pressed to her nostril. Her face is reflected on the surface below, although it's broken up by five or six neatly arranged lines of white powder.

When she sees me, she frowns. It's not a frown of surprise at being barged in on, though.

It's a frown of *recognition.*

"Cordelia?" she says in shock. "Is that you?"

Cordelia. A dead name. A nobody name.

My heart jumps into my throat. One thought blares through my head like a tornado siren: *run.*

This time, I hold nothing back. I run and run and run. High heels be damned. Ripped dress be damned.

I keep running, down hallways and up stairs, until my breath burns in my lungs. Then I burst through the nearest door I see and slam it shut behind me.

Inside the darkened room, I keel over, elbows on my knees, and try to inhale. I'm so tired I don't give a rat's ass about the fact that anyone who comes up from behind me could get a high-def view of where the sun don't shine.

I stay there for a while. Even when I catch my breath, though, my heart continues to pitter-patter in my chest.

She saw me. She *knew* me.

I shudder again. *Cordelia.* God, I hate how that sounds.

I'm *Cora* now.

Cordelia is dead.

Eventually, my heart calms down, though the tang of fear never truly leaves my mouth. When I'm as at ease as I'm gonna get, I look around the room.

I'm in an office of some sort. Very masculine, dark palette, brooding. It's shadowy in here, though there's light coming through a set of French doors. When I walk over, I realize the attached balcony looks out over the rear lawn. Most of the crowd has shuffled outside, so it's a maze of bodies. The sound of laughter and clinking glasses rises up to meet me. There's no sign of Prince Testosterone or his friend.

I turn my back on the balcony and fish my phone out of my purse. I press Jorden's contact and hold it up to my ear. It rings and rings, and then:

"Heeeey! Girl, where'd you go? This party is crazy!"

Oh jeez. Jorden is blitzed beyond belief. I know that looseness in her voice, that cackle. The girl is D-R-U-N-K. She isn't coming to save me.

I'm all on my own.

"Uh, never mind," I mumble into the phone. "Butt dial. I'm coming to find you. One sec." I hang up and drop my phone onto the nearby couch.

I find a lamp in the corner and click it on. The rip is in the back, so I need to get this dress off and try to finagle some kind of safety pin stopgap solution good enough to get me out of here without mooning every partygoer in attendance. With a grimace and a prayer, I start trying to peel off the dress while doing the least damage possible.

The back where the drunkard's hands went is pretty ruined, but if I can just wriggle out of it carefully and find a safety pin around here somewhere, there's a chance I'll be able to—

Riiiiip.

Never mind. I'm screwed.

My oh-so-careful efforts have just extended the rip even further. As soon as I let my hands go limp, the dress parts in two like wilted flower petals and pools around my feet. I'm left standing there, in the middle of some stranger's office, in nothing but high heels and nipple pasties.

Which, of course, is when the door opens.

For a second, I hold out hope that it's Jorden, here to provide backup.

But it's not Jorden.

It's not Jorden at all.

5

IVAN

It'd be a mistake to call her the girl in the green dress—mostly because she's not *in* the green dress anymore. It's puddled around her feet and she's not wearing a stitch of anything. Just high heels and nipple covers.

I close the door behind me. "No one is supposed to be in here."

"I'm hiding," she blurts, trying her best to cover herself up, not that it does much good. I'd have to be Mother fucking Teresa to keep my eyes off of her body.

Fucking hell, she's stunning.

I swallow down the rush of desire. "Stripping, hiding, I don't give a shit what you call it—but you can't do it here."

She levels me with a glare that rivals the one she gave the Greek mutt outside. "And who are you? Security?"

"You must be joking."

She doesn't know who I am? I call bullshit. Everyone here knows who I am.

She's blushing from head to toe—I can see every inch of flushed skin—but she doesn't shy away. "So, not security, then? Probably some trust fund baby who thinks you own every room you walk into."

"Big words from someone skulking through a stranger's house naked."

"Hiding!" she yelps again. "And believe me, I would give anything to be clothed right now. Preferably in sweatpants and a hoodie with a parka on top, but beggars can't be choosers. I'd accept that strappy, skin-tight monstrosity on the ground right now if it would just *cooperate*."

She hates this party, she doesn't know who I am, and instead of bragging to me about who designed her ruined dress, she's longing for sweats.

She can't be real.

A breeze blows through the open doors and the woman in front of me shivers. Before I can second-guess the instinct, I shrug out of my jacket.

"What are you doing?" she asks.

Good question. It might be the first time in my life I've voluntarily asked a woman to put on *more* clothes.

Her eyes are wide and shockingly green as she shrinks away from me. Like a dog that's been kicked so many times it's sure that the only thing the future could hold is more pain.

"Beggars can't be choosers." I dangle my jacket in the air between us. "Take it or leave it."

She watches me warily for another long breath before she lunges for the jacket and slips it on.

Her skin disappears beneath the long sleeves and broad shoulders. The jacket absolutely swallows her, but I'm not laughing. Somehow, the image of her swimming in my jacket is even more tantalizing than her taut, naked skin.

She tucks the material around her middle and crosses her arms to secure it. "Thanks. For a second, I thought you were going to parade me out of here naked as punishment."

"Don't tempt me."

"Don't threaten me," she retorts.

"Don't act like it would be all bad. You'd be the center of attention."

"Don't act like all women want the same thing."

I arch an amused eyebrow. "Don't they? You got all dolled up and marched in here to sell your soul to Ivan Pushkin. Just like the rest of them."

"Not you, too?" she murmurs. "*Ivan* this, *Ivan* that. Everyone can't get enough of the guy. Who even is he?"

I join her at the window, gazing down at the partygoers below. "Everyone is here because they want to marry him."

"I'm sure *he* thinks so." She wrinkles her nose and points at a paunchy man standing by the shrubs. "What about that one?"

I clock the person she's pointing at immediately. My mind whirrs and conjures up the relevant facts. Valmor Shundi. Albanian underboss. Likes his whiskey aged for seventeen years and his women for less than that.

"Him, too. The poor bastard has a nasty drug problem and is about to get caught for stealing money from his clients. He needs his daughters to secure a good match now before his name turns to shit."

"How do you know that?"

"I know everything." I point out the scrawny Italian man next to the stage. Again, my mind hums and pulls up what I need to know. Alfonso Marciano. A Rossi family underboss. Cokehead. "That one is into group sex with his boss and his wife."

"No way," she giggles. "He's wearing a pink polo with a popped collar. How is he having threesomes?"

"Foursomes, actually. He brings his own wife along." I point out the woman in the brown bedazzled dress who is scanning the lawn like a vulture. "Though I'm not sure you can criticize anyone else's appearance, all things considered."

She glances down at my suit jacket and winces shyly. "Fair enough. But I looked better before that asshole ripped my dress."

"Agree to disagree," I murmur.

I didn't actually intend to speak out loud, but that slipped out before I could stop it. Her blush is bright enough to see in the gloom.

"What about that one?" she asks, obviously changing the subject.

I follow her finger to see her singling out the emaciated blond hair of the one man I would have most preferred not to think about. The laughter disappears from my voice. "Konstantin Sokolov," I say quietly.

"You don't have any dirt on him?" she teases. "He's not, like, a terrible poker player or secretly into dressing up like a furry in his free time?"

No, I think to myself. *He's the father of the woman I was supposed to marry.*

"He's no one," I said out loud instead. "No one at all."

"Hm. Okay." She turns her head to the side, dark hair spilling over her shoulder. "Final question: what's *your* name?"

I have to admire her tenacity. She is really claiming she doesn't know who I am. I'm still not sure I believe her, but it is nice to be anonymous. If just for a few minutes.

"Tell me yours first."

"Or what?" she challenges.

"Or I'll kick you out for trespassing."

She narrows her eyes. "Are you sure you aren't head of security? You're on a real power trip."

My gaze doesn't waver from hers. The world shrinks around us. "I'll answer when you tell me who you are."

She hesitates for only a second. "Francia Delacour."

I flip through my mental rolodex of names and contacts and allies and enemies, but there is no Delacour as far as I can remember.

Frowning, I turn to the bar cart and grab two glasses. "Care for a drink, Ms. Delacour?"

"God, yes. But you don't get off that easily. You're supposed to tell me if you're the head of security or not."

I hold up my glass and take a sip. "If I was head of security, would I be drinking on the job?"

"If you were bad at your job, you might."

I pass the second glass to her. "I'm not bad at anything."

"I hate that I actually believe you." She tastes the drink and winces. "I also hate cognac."

"That's a three-hundred-dollar bottle."

"Ah. Well, in that case, it's the best thing I've ever tasted." She pastes on a big, fake smile. "Better?"

I'm sure I'll never see her again after tonight, so what the hell? Marriage is looming, and after everything that happened with Konstantin and Katerina Sokolov, I'm positive it will be an absolute fucking hellscape. Might as well enjoy myself while I still have the chance.

I clink my glass against the edge of hers in a toast to wherever this night is going to take us. "Much better."

6

CORA

The draft in this jacket is unbearable. It's made even worse by the bedroom eyes the owner of the jacket keeps tossing my way.

Come to think of it, those bedroom eyes are exactly *why* the draft is so unbearable. No underwear, arousal, a draft—it's a bad combo.

As I see them, the problems are several-fold. One, I'm butt-naked in a borrowed suit jacket. This is not what we in the female empowerment business like to call "the command position."

Two, I don't know this man. He could be head of security, he could be a clown out of costume, he could be a spy on a secret mission from the Kremlin. Who knows? Not me.

Third, and most importantly, I am butt-naked in a borrowed suit jacket. I think that point bears repeating.

My brain keeps drifting to how much Francia's Vera Wang must've cost. Every time it does, I make myself take another sip of disgusting, expensive cognac and wonder how on earth I'm going to pay her back.

"More?"

The man's huge hand is already halfway around the glass when I realize what he's asking. His fingers brush mine and I jerk my arm back like I've been electrocuted. The only reason the glass doesn't crash to the floor is because the man has Superman-like reflexes and snatches it out of mid-air.

"No, that's okay." I shake my head, cheeks burning. "Thanks, though. For the drink. The first one."

And for sending my groper off with his tail between his legs. And for the jacket. And for not kicking me out the door in my birthday suit.

The debts between us are piling up. I should thank him for everything he's done, but I can't bring myself to do it. Because I could have gotten myself out of this mess.

I *should* have, anyway. Sitting back and letting a man swoop in to rescue me is so not my story anymore. No Prince Charmings. No Happily Ever Afters.

Admittedly, I do have one too many evil stepparents, but that's as far as the similarities go.

Prince Testosterone is tinkering around behind me at the bar as I step over the destroyed dress and further out onto the balcony. The evening air is warm and balmy. A babble of cross-talking voices rises straight up from the crowd below.

"Where is he? I heard he might be watching in from the security cameras. Do I look okay?"

"I haven't seen Ivan once since I got here. I doubt he's even here. Men like him never come to their own parties."

"Portia got her boobs done. As if *that* is why Ivan has never looked twice at her. Forget her horse teeth and beige personality; she thinks it was the boobs. Get fucking real."

The Ivan talk is really blowing my mind. It's like he could snap his fingers and give every female on the property an instant G-spot orgasm. I've been around plenty of pompous, overstuffed peacocks in my time, but none of them have ever drawn *this* kind of devotion.

Maybe I should stick around and find out who this guy is.

No sooner does the thought cross my mind than do I see a man separate from the crowd below. He steps out, then cranes his neck to look up at the string lights hanging overhead.

"Boris must be hoping he can liquor Ivan up enough to convince him to marry. Why else would there be endless trays of champagne without a bite to eat in sight?"

I duck back out of sight and hold my breath. I hope to God I hid in time. Saying my heart is in my throat isn't a metaphor. I can taste the blood. The iron tang of *fear*.

Because I'd recognize that voice anywhere.

And if my monster of a stepfather sees me here, there's no telling what he'll do.

"Either that," he drawls, "or he's hoping a respectable woman will get drunk enough to forget that Ivan is a fucking sadist."

My stepfather's voice fades away as he moves through the crowd, but I stay put. I can't move. I can barely breathe.

It's been years since I've been that close to him. Could he sense how near I was? Did his skin crawl with disgust like mine did?

I doubt that very much. Why would it?

Monsters never run from their prey.

7

CORA

"You look spooked."

The voice behind me upsets the delicate balance I'm striking in these heels. I fall forward, catch myself on the railing, and then jerk myself right back to make sure my stepfather doesn't catch sight of me. The breeze is cold in all the wrong places.

I sort myself into something resembling stability. "Huh?"

"That look on your face. Like you just saw a ghost."

"I'm fine. No ghosts. I'm just having second thoughts about that drink." I've already had a bit more than my usual night out allowance, but I'll do anything to spend a few more minutes in this room, safe from the boogeyman of my past.

I need time to come up with an escape plan.

"Alcohol is not going to improve your situation," he remarks as he turns to the bar to pour me a second drink anyway.

"What situation is that?"

He looks back over his shoulder, dark eyebrow arched. "Do you actually need me to explain it?"

I grit my teeth. "You wanna know something? You play the hero type—saving me from a drunk man downstairs and offering your jacket—but you're kind of an asshole."

"Only 'kind of'?

"Oh, I'm sorry. Would you rather be a full-blown asshole?"

He walks over with a smirk and a fresh drink. "If you're going to do something, you might as well commit."

I grimace, but I take the drink and throw half of it back. The alcohol burns going down. It still tastes terrible, but I'm not in this for the flavor profile. If I'm going to walk out of this room with my bits and bobs hanging out of a borrowed suit jacket, I need a little liquid courage.

"Now," he continues, "are you going to keep trading barbs or are you going to tell me why you looked so scared just now?"

I shake my head. "I'm not scared."

Not anymore, at least.

I have no desire at all to see my stepfather or relive any portion of my past, but I'm not *scared* of him. I escaped and he hasn't caught me yet. As far as I'm concerned, that means I've won.

"You saw something. Or someone. I want to know who it was."

"No one. It was nothing. I just, uh…tripped." I lift one leg to show off my heels. "It's what I get for wearing impractical footwear. I should always remember to wear shoes I can run in."

"You say that as if you're always getting ready to run."

I turn. He is so much closer than he was a second ago. The world fades away as he shifts into stark focus.

His lips are curved and gorgeous. I didn't notice it before, but black ink marks swirl out of the collar of his shirt, whirling around his thick neck. "You have tattoos."

"You're changing the subject."

"So did you. Earlier. It makes me think you're hiding something."

"I am," he admits freely. "But I'm not lying to you. Are you lying to me, Francia?"

The false name lands with an awkward clunk between us. "No."

He moves even closer. "Did you see your boyfriend down there in the crowd? Maybe a husband? You have a guilty look about you."

"You recognize that look, hm? Maybe that's why you know so much about everyone else's affairs—because you're the one causing them."

"I don't know a thing about you or yours." His gaze drips down my face like honey, slow and sweet. "Who are you?"

I bite my lip and turn back to the doorway. I take a slow step forward. Then another. My stepfather is gone, so I can let myself relax against the doorframe like I don't have anything to hide. "I'm no one's wife or girlfriend, I can promise you that. And unlike everyone else here, I have no desire to be. I'm okay on my own."

"I don't believe you."

I snap my attention to him. "Excuse me?"

"I don't believe you. You saw someone in the crowd. But if you don't want to tell me, so be it. I don't care who it was."

I should deny it, but he can see straight through me. "Why not?"

"Because there's not a single person at this party who can stop me from doing what I want."

The thrill that races down my spine is reason enough on its own to get the hell out of here. I'm supposed to be having fun, not falling into devastating lust with a handsome stranger.

But I can't leave. Because for the first time in…well, maybe forever, I feel *safe*. I feel like, if my stepfather walked through this door, this man would put himself between him and me without hesitation.

"I don't need you to protect me."

He drums his finger on the side of his glass. "I saw you try to fend off Stefanos downstairs. You did your best, but it wasn't quite enough, was it?"

"I don't like to whip my kung-fu out on civilians," I joke lamely. "I prefer to handle things nonviolently."

He chuckles. "As you should. Me, though? I have a different approach." He fingers the edge of his lapel, which would normally be fine and dandy, but since *I'm* the one wearing the jacket, those fingertips are venturing just a little too close to my bare chest. "I think some things should be handled right to the point of breaking. Again, and again, and again. And then—only when they've proven they deserve it—*then* you give them the little bit of violence they've been asking for."

"Oh…well, that's…certainly something." I swallow past a massive knot in my throat. "But I can handle myself just fine."

Considering the heat brewing inside of me, I'll definitely be *handling myself*, alright. Maybe two or three times in a row.

I formulated my opinion on men like this one a long time ago. Rich, powerful men in expensive suits who drink aged cognac. They are used to getting what they want in life and nothing less. When it's denied to them, they aren't afraid to take it by force.

Standing here in nothing but a jacket, a gentle buzz brewing in my veins, I should be terrified. He could take advantage of me. He could force me out of this jacket if he chose.

But he won't.

I don't know how I know that, but I do.

"You know, I should probably go."

The moment the words are out of my mouth, I know it's the right choice. Get out of here before I do something—or some*one*—I'll regret. Plus, I haven't seen Jorden. I'm sure she has downed several more flutes of champagne since I left her. She's going to be drunk and she'll need my help getting her sloppy self home.

"After all that, you're going to leave without saying goodbye?"

His voice is warm molasses in my ear, smooth and rich.

I look to my right and see the door. The exit.

And I know immediately that I'm not going to take it.

Dammit. I was so close to doing the right thing for once.

"For a head of security, you're awfully presumptuous," I croak.

He arches an eyebrow and laughs. "For a naked woman in my office, you're awfully feisty."

"I'm not—Wait." The words freeze on my tongue. Every inch of me ices over until I'm a glacier in this man's strong arms. "Did you just say *your* office?"

Prince Testosterone's grin ticks one notch wider. "I did. I'm Ivan Pushkin. It's a pleasure to meet you."

8

CORA

His name is ringing in my ears. He is Ivan. Ivan is him. I'm in a room alone with the man everyone else wants to be alone in a room with.

Holyfuckingshit.

"Wow. Uh, okay. Well, it was great to meet you as well, but like I said, I really should go. This isn't my scene."

"No? Then tell me what scene you prefer."

"I know you can't imagine a world beyond these palace walls," I say, sarcasm oozing out of every word. "But some of us don't live in a fairy tale. Some of us live in the real world. With bills and 9-to-5 jobs and…and…and we have to wash our own dishes."

"So washing dishes is your scene?"

"Maybe!" I cross my arms and take a step away from him. "Not all of it, obviously. I have… I have other stuff, too."

"Do tell."

He draws closer to me. The rest of the world blots out instantly. It's like a cone of silence has descended over us. It's me and Ivan. Ivan and me.

Nothing else exists.

"I have…friends."

He nods, waving me on.

"Jorden and F—" I stop myself, remembering my lies. "Jorden. I work with her."

"One friend. Quite the scene."

Now, I know I'm not imagining it—that's *definitely* judgment.

"I'm sure you and your oh-so-close group of hundreds of vague acquaintances here can't relate. It's so *normal* to have a party where everyone in attendance is only there because they want to marry into your family fortune. Is that what I should strive for?"

He shrugs. "Strive for whatever you want. You said you weren't here to marry me, but if you've changed your mind, you're welcome to join the queue."

"That's not what I—oh, for God's sake, I'm not talking about wanting to marry you! That's not why I'm here."

"Then tell me: why *are* you here?"

I can't help but feel like he already knows what I'm going to say before I even say it. Maybe that's why I try to throw him off with something unexpected.

"To get the scoop on you and sell it to the gossip mag with the highest bid."

I deliver the line with as much confidence as I can muster in my suit jacket ensemble. He immediately laughs right in my face.

"No, you're not."

I bristle. "It wouldn't be that hard if I was. Everyone here is whispering about you."

He leans in close. I catch a hint of sandalwood. *Rich people soap,* I think. My mom kept sandalwood hand soap in her and my stepfather's master bathroom. Weirdly, the smell doesn't bring back bad memories now. I just want to lean in closer.

"Everyone is *always* whispering about me," he says softly. "It comes with the territory."

"The territory of being as rich as God?"

"That," he agrees. "And also the territory of looking like one."

"Oh, gross. Were you this cocky a minute ago? I don't remember feeling this constant urge to roll my eyes."

He smiles, not bothered in the least. "You came here with your friend."

"Is that a question?"

"No. I'm just trying to understand if this is a dual investigative operation you're performing." He flicks a finger in my direction. "And if your dress mishap was some kind of distraction. If so, it was…thorough. I was quite distracted."

My body flushes. I'd give anything to be in sweatpants on my couch right now. Far from this world and this man and his intoxicating attention.

"Did you check with the security at the gate to see who I came with? Or were you watching me on camera?" I look around the hallway ceiling. "How many cameras are in this house?"

His face remains perfectly neutral. "I like to learn more about who I've invited into my house. I'm sure you can understand."

I'm sure I absolutely cannot. If someone is in my house, I already know who they are. Mostly because my apartment is only five hundred square feet, not five hundred rooms.

I could tell him I'm not Francia Delacour and I only used her name to get inside, but then he'd ask my real name, and that would open up a can of worms I'd really prefer to stay closed.

I'm still fumbling for what to do and say when he suddenly places a hand on my hip and pulls me into him.

"You seem on the fence about whether you're interested in me," he muses.

"Then let me clarify for you: I'm not."

He presses a palm to his chest. "A weaker man would be hurt by that."

"It's a good thing you're not weak, then."

"A very good thing." He looks at me. "You're not weak, either. When Stefanos grabbed you, you didn't hesitate to put him in his place."

"He put his hands on me, so I put my hands on him."

Ivan's dark brow arches. "Is that all it takes?"

I gulp. There's no missing the dark flirtation. "You're the star of the show here. I'm sure you have ways of getting what you want out of people."

"I'm not sure a woman like you will fall for my usual tricks."

Oh, how wrong he is. I think I'm falling for them right now.

I bite the corner of my lip to hide a smile. "It really bothers you that I'm not interested, doesn't it? I'm sure you aren't denied things you want very often. This must be a new experience for you."

"Nothing has been denied yet," he says, his voice a low rumble.

He's right. With every word spoken, I feel like I'm walking towards the edge of a cliff. The wind is whipping through the open doors and my stomach is cratering.

Ivan takes another step towards me. We're only a few inches apart. "How did you get an invite to this party?"

I open my mouth and close it, fumbling with the clumsy truth. "I, uh…"

"This isn't your scene," Ivan cuts in slowly. "You didn't recognize me earlier. Now that you do, you still have no interest in marrying me. I'm a smart man, but I can't figure out what you're doing here, *Francia*."

"I'm here for…for…for fun."

"How convenient." His eyes gleam. "I have an idea in that regard."

Then he pulls me in the final distance and presses his lips to mine.

9

CORA

He tastes like cognac and bad decisions.

I curl my hands through the dark hair at the back of his neck. His mouth parts and dares me in. The suit jacket slips wide as our bodies slide together and Ivan works his knee between my legs. I gasp when his thigh drags across my bare flesh.

"I thought you weren't interested," he taunts.

My eyes are still closed, my head spinning. I feel drunk, but I know I haven't had enough to drink for that.

"I'm not interested in *marriage*," I correct. "But this is…"

This is reckless.

This is crazy.

His hands slip down to my hips and he grinds me more against his muscular thigh until I'm quivering. "You've got me on the edge of my seat, princess. This is what?"

He called me "princess," but I'm not that. I'm not the girl who gets Prince Charming and rides off into her happily ever after.

But I can have *this*, can't I? Stolen moments with a dark prince all my own. A peek into the glittering world of the youth that I fled from.

"A fairytale," I tell him. "It's a fantasy."

Ivan walks me backwards until I'm flat against the wall. His hands skate under the lapels of his own jacket and tease along my heated skin.

"Lucky for you, fantasies are what I'm good at."

Desire coils in my chest, eager and demanding. "Is that so? Have you been fantasizing about this?"

He nods shamelessly, his stubbled cheek rasping against my face. "Since the moment I walked in and saw you standing in my office. It was the perfect plan, if I'm being honest."

"Get naked and throw myself at you?"

"Get naked and tell me you don't want me. It leaves me with no choice but to prove you wrong."

He drags a finger up my inner thigh and through my wetness. When I spread my legs apart for him, he works that finger into me one fraction of an inch at a time. My whole body rocks with every pulse. I'm clamping my teeth down as hard as I can, but the pressure is building and building and I'm terrified it might tear me apart when it finally erupts.

His lips are hot on my neck. Beneath my earlobe. His other hand teases my nipple into a painful peak, then squeezes my hip and encourages me to ride his palm as the orgasm intensifies inside of me.

My breath catches. I'm tight from head to toe, tight enough to snap, tight enough to crumble. And then: "*Oh,* fucking God," I gasp as it explodes inside of me. I'm glad he's here and he's strong, because if I didn't have him to hold onto, I'd be a puddle on the floor.

And he's not done yet.

"Now," he murmurs in a dark, steely snarl, "let me show you just how wrong you are."

He reaches between us and frees himself from his pants. I have to stifle a gasp when he springs to life in my hand. He's hard against my palm and so unbelievably big that I feel a twist of fear in my gut. Surely that's not about to go inside of me…

Right?

My body is shaking. It could be from the chill on my nakedness, but I know better. This is a bone-deep shiver. Adrenaline is coursing through my veins and my vision is going hazy.

I wrap my hand around his cock and press him against me. He teases my opening and I can't help but buck against him. He slips an inch in, then retreats again. He pauses there.

So close to nirvana.

So close to salvation.

So close to a very, very bad idea.

Should I be doing this? Ivan Pushkin is dangerous, or so I'm told. Nothing about this is smart. Anyone could walk in on us and I don't want to be known as the easy girl who fucks billionaires in the dark corners of parties.

But I also don't want to be the dead-inside girl who works nonstop and lives paycheck to paycheck. For just a few minutes, I don't want to be the scared little kitten who is running from her past and doesn't have a plan for her future.

I want to be the woman that Ivan thinks back on long after he's married to whatever brainless bimbo he's going to choose. I want to be the woman who surprised him and challenged him.

Tonight, I want to be the heroine of this story.

So I bite his neck and pull him the rest of the way into me.

Ivan thrusts in as I tighten my legs around his waist. We crash together in one smooth stroke and I arch my back as an involuntary gasp rips out of me.

"Oh, God," I whimper.

He's everywhere. With every thrust, the pressure inside of me grows and shifts. It's like I'm being ripped apart at the seams, stretched beyond the normal limits of what a human should be able to handle—and my God, it feels *so freaking good.*

"What is this?" I whisper. "Why is this… This is so good."

It feels silly to be shocked by good sex. But in my experience, sex is more of a formality. Sure, it can occasionally be nice, but it isn't earth-shattering. It doesn't tear down everything you thought you knew and rebuild it.

Sex shouldn't make you question the purpose of life.

But *this* sex does.

Ivan shifts my hips, leaning me back to take me at a new angle. He hits something deep inside of me and I cry out.

"There it is," he growls. He presses me against the wall and clamps the flat of his hand over my mouth. "Scream for me. Scream for me, baby, and let me swallow up every bit of it."

He drives into me again and again. Whoever said men moaning isn't hot didn't know what the hell they were talking about, because every time a new breathless snarl passes Ivan's lips, I get another notch closer to exploding.

He bends down and pulls my breast into his sinful mouth. His tongue flicks over my nipple until I'm practically bent backwards from how good every inch of him feels.

"Come for me," he commands. "Let go."

That's all it takes—another orgasm tears through me. Ivan's hand is still over my mouth. I bite down on his skin to stop from crying out.

"Fuck!" he spits, but he doesn't pull his hand away; he just drives into me harder. Punishing me with more, more, *more* of him.

Until I clamp around him, pulsing and shaking from head to toe. The never-ending orgasm.

"You're so fucking tight," he grits out.

Then Ivan comes, too.

He pulses into me, spilling his own pleasure until we're both panting and limp on the side of his house.

I want to soak up every second of this fantasy. I don't want to let a moment slip away unenjoyed. But the sounds of the party on the lawn below are starting to break through our little bubble. Someone in the crowd calls out Ivan's name.

"Where is he?" a woman shouts.

Ivan pushes his jacket off of my shoulder and presses a kiss to the bare skin there. "Incredible. Fucking incredible."

"Acceptable," I correct. I try to sound nonchalant, joking, but my voice is trembling. I can feel my thighs shaking still.

He opens his mouth to say something, but then a different loud voice booms out instead. "Ivan Pushkin, you are wanted."

For a second, I think it might be God Himself breaking in from the heavens to remind me that Ivan Pushkin is this party's most eligible bachelor and I don't stand a chance in snaring him.

Then I realize it's just the DJ making a formal call through the speakers.

He presses his forehead to mine. "Fuck this party. Let's go to my room and see if you can scream any louder than that."

I'm tempted. The desire to stretch this fantasy into an entire night—to tangle up with him until morning—is strong. But it would be a mistake.

"You have guests," I demure.

"I don't care about my guests, Francia," he says simply. "I'm more interested in you."

The wrong name washes over me like a bucket of ice water. It rinses away whatever is left of the fairytale moment we just experienced.

He doesn't know me. He doesn't even know my real name.

None of this is real.

More cries of "Ivan!" rise up from the crowd.

"The natives are growing restless," I say with a small smile. I shove away from his chest on shaky legs. "Go appease them. I'll meet up with you later."

His jaw works back and forth. Then he grips my chin with his thumb and forefinger, angling my face up to his. "Don't you dare run off on me."

"I won't," I lie. I point down to the high heels I'm still wearing. "I'm not wearing the right shoes to flee, remember?"

His eyes trace over my body as he takes a step back. "Later."

That single word holds a dirty promise. One I desperately wish I could keep.

But I can't.

With one final nod, Ivan disappears through the door.

As soon as he's gone, I follow.

I see Jorden quickly. She is lounging against a pillar, a drink in hand, chatting with a handsome young man with way too much product in his hair. As I pass her, I don't even break stride; I grab her hand and pull her along with me.

"Hey!" she yelps, dropping her glass.

I hear it shatter against the pavement, but I don't let go.

"Cora," she complains. "What are you doing? Where are we going?"

I pull her through a side gate and around to the empty front yard. I hold firmly onto her hand. "Back to reality."

10

IVAN

I can still feel Francia's heat wrapped around my cock when Yasha steps in front of me.

"I've got bad news."

"I don't want to hear bad news." I wave him away. "Talk to me about it later when—"

"Konstantin wants to talk to you," he blurts.

I spin around, glaring at him. He's gesturing behind me, but I ignore him. "Then tell him that he can f—"

"Hello, Ivan."

I wince. The robotic voice behind me can only belong to one man.

I turn around and face Konstantin Sokolov. He looks even paler up close. His blue eyes are washed out in the warm glow of the string lights. Instead of offering his skin a warm tint, he looks sallow. Almost sickly. Nothing new for him.

"You made it," I drawl. "What a treat."

I would have preferred not to put him or the rest of his sour-faced brood on the guest list. But excluding them would have invited even more drama I didn't want.

He laughs without a drop of humor in it. "I'm too old for events like this. These parties are for the young."

"So then why are you here?"

I feel Yasha prod me in the back. *Careful*, he's warning. *Play nice.*

But I'm not throwing Konstantin out on his ass. As far as I'm concerned, that *is* playing nice.

"We've been friends for a long time," Konstantin says. When he sees my face, he corrects himself. "Our families have been allies, rather. I've known your father for many years. He's a good man. An honest man. He is a man of his word."

I have to stop myself from spitting on the floor at Konstantin's feet. Anyone who thinks my dad is honorable deserves nothing less than that.

"It's a shame he isn't the one on the auction block," I reply. "The way you describe him, he'd be snatched up in a minute."

Konstantin isn't amused. He never is. In all the time I've known him, I've never seen him smile.

Except the day he looked me over like he was inspecting livestock and then shook my father's hand to seal a deal I never wanted.

"It looks like the 'auction,' as you call it, is going well enough for you. Plenty of women showed up. Do you plan to accept the highest bid?"

It's a simple enough question, but I know what he is really asking.

"I don't intend to announce my engagement tomorrow, if that's what you mean."

"So you haven't met a woman special enough to turn your head yet?"

Francia's face comes to my mind. A not-insignificant part of me hopes I'll find her in my office when I finally get away from Konstantin.

But maybe it's best if that's not the case. It could never last. Konstantin may not think so, but I'm a man of my word, too. I've made promises I have to keep. Promises someone like Francia could never fit into.

"No one I plan to marry," I answer simply.

He nods. "Smart man. You're waiting for the right woman. As you should. But you don't have to wait. I have plenty of daughters."

Immediately, I feel Yasha tug gently on the back of my shirt. He knows what I'm thinking before I can even say it. But nothing can keep the disgust off of my face.

"Your oldest isn't even thirteen," I hiss.

"Then be patient. Your father and I worked out an alliance. There is still time to make it happen. Katerina can be replaced."

What a loving father, swapping out his daughters like pawns on a chessboard. Maybe my own father has a use for someone like Konstantin Sokolov, but I don't. Our families' alliance will end when I am *pakhan*.

I lean in. "*Everyone* can be replaced."

He stiffens, but I brush past him, headed back into the party to look for the only person who might be an exception to that statement.

I can't imagine replacing the woman I met tonight—Francia, if that is even her real name. That's why it's even more important that I find her. The moment we shared tonight was exactly what she said: a fantasy.

But real life is no fantasy.

Nothing and no one is ever as good as they seem.

11

IVAN

People call out to me from the crowd as I wade through. Others say my name in hushed whispers, giggling with their friends. I ignore them all and slice through the grass towards the stage. The band is softly playing, but they fade out as I mount the steps. By the time I grab the mic, they've gone quiet.

There's a sharp shriek of feedback through the speakers. Then every eye is on me.

I didn't have a plan for what I was going to say when I started walking this way. But now, there's only one thing worth mentioning.

"The party is over."

Disbelieving, unfamiliar faces stare up at me. People wait for a punchline that will never come.

"Thanks for coming. See yourselves out." I point towards the gates. "Now."

I drop the mic, sending a resounding thud and another screech of feedback through the party.

As I make my way back to the house, no one approaches me. For the first time all night, I'm given a wide berth. Like I'm suddenly contagious.

It's a fucking relief.

Yasha is standing by the patio doors, his lips pressed into a firm line. "Your dad is going to be *pissed*."

"Tell security to stop Francia at the door."

He frowns. "Who?"

"Francia Delacour," I snap impatiently. "She's wearing my suit jacket. *Only* my suit jacket. I want to talk to her. Don't let her leave."

"Oh, shit," Yasha laughs. "Sounds like you already did more than talk to her."

"*Now*, Yasha."

Yasha senses the urgency in my voice and holds up his hands in surrender. He pulls out his phone to relay my order to the security team. In the meantime, I turn back to the departing crowd.

Forlorn faces slathered in makeup glance my way. But I don't see Francia among them.

She shouldn't be hard to catch. Dark hair. Nude except for my suit jacket. Someone will spot her. Surely someone will spot her.

That assurance fades as the crowd thins.

"No one has seen her," Yasha tells me fifteen minutes later. "She might have left before you called the party off."

"I don't want to hear where she *'might'* have gone. We don't spend hundreds of thousands on security for *'might.'* Fucking find out where she went. *Now.*"

"What's the deal with this girl? Do you know her?"

I undo my tie and throw it at the stairs. "No. That's the problem."

"You didn't know half of the people here, and you could care less."

"Those people didn't break into my office and…" My voice trails off. I didn't intend to share that tidbit. There are no cameras in my office, despite the way I made it sound to Francia. Our moment will forever remain private.

Yasha stands tall. "You think she was sent here to gather information? Who sent her?"

I consider the question. If Francia was a spy, I would have known. I would have realized. She told me she was a reporter, which was clearly a lie.

But I don't have any other reason to care this much about where she went.

"That's what you're going to find out. Track her down. Tell me when you have."

Yasha nods solemnly. "We'll have her by morning."

Damn right we will.

No one can hide from me.

12

CORA

I'll never take panties for granted again.

Even working the early shift at Quintaño's with a horribly hungover Jorden can't bring me down. I'm clothed and far, far away from the influence of Ivan Pushkin.

Life is good.

"How is there *more* gum under this table?" Jorden is doubled over, head under booth thirteen. "I just cleaned it, like, two days ago."

"Middle schoolers," I call.

A regular group of scrawny middle-school boys always claim that booth on Sunday mornings. They buy nothing but soda and one appetizer to share and they always tip in pennies. I wouldn't mind so much if they didn't also leave their chewing gum plastered under the table.

Jorden stamps her foot. "I'm not letting them in today. They can find somewhere else to eat."

"Right," I say, sarcasm thick. "And you'll say that even when they tell you you're the prettiest waitress they've ever seen? Or when they ask for your phone number and slip you little love notes on the back of their napkins?"

Jorden smirks. "Maybe I wouldn't be so starved for attention if you hadn't dragged me away from Hot Athlete."

"The fact that you're calling him 'Hot Athlete' instead of a name doesn't bode well for the strength of that relationship."

"Screw the 'strength of the relationship,'" Jorden says. "He was an *athlete*. That means stamina, Cora. Power. *Flexibility.* Are you hearing me? Are you understanding?"

I wrinkle my nose. "Everyone understands. You're gross."

"Says the skank who came home in nothing but a man's suit jacket!"

I hiss and spin towards the swinging kitchen doors. They're still closed and I can hear the kitchen staff clanging pots around, so Francia probably can't hear us. But still—better safe than sorry.

I whirl back to face Jorden. "We're *not* talking about that," I say through gritted teeth. "I'm going to repair that very expensive dress and get it back to Francia. No one will ever know it happened."

That's the plan, anyway. I shoved the dress in my purse before I left Ivan's office. By the time I got home last night, I was too wound up to think about it. Then I woke up and came right into work today. I'll check the damage when I get back to my apartment after my shift.

"So what happened? Did it just rip or—"

"I told you: that drunk guy grabbed me."

She snaps her fingers. "I do remember you saying that. I think. It's hazy."

"Because you were barely conscious on the ride home last night."

"No judgment," she reminds me with a scolding finger. "We were having fun. I wouldn't have seemed so drunk if you'd also been drinking."

I hold up my hands in surrender. "You're right. No judgment. But that goes both ways."

Jorden considers, her mouth twisted to one side as she cleans off the six-top in the middle of the dining room. "Okay, but…"

"No exceptions!"

She winces. "Okay—except you came home with no panties, so I want to know—"

"La la la la la! I can't heaaar you!" I sing over her, drowning out her voice.

Jorden groans. "Fine! Don't tell me. You probably hooked up with a bazillionaire, but why would I want to hear that story? It's only my entire life goal."

"Dating a guy like that is *not* your life goal."

"You're right," she deadpans. "My goal is to be a waitress here until I die. Because I'll never make enough to retire. Pension? Who needs it! I'll pay for a nursing home with my middle-school boy tips and $2.13 an hour."

I replace the salt and pepper shakers on the tables with fresh ones and check the clock hanging above the fake ivy wreath. We open for the brunch crowd in ten minutes. Joy, oh joy.

"No thanks," Jorden says, continuing her rant. "I plan to find me a sweet little sugar daddy. That party was chock full of them."

If Jorden knew what having a "sugar daddy" was really like, she wouldn't want it so bad.

I could tell her. I could walk her through my mom's life. Through what was supposed to be my life. But I didn't run away just to dive back into that cesspool again.

Clean break. That's what I want. Which means I can't tell Jorden that I've seen her fantasy up close and personal, and it doesn't look anything like the advertisements.

"Guys like the ones from last night want girls in ballgowns who are eternally tipsy on champagne. They aren't interested in working class girls like us," I say. "And it's their loss! We're awesome."

"I never would have thought of you as a snob, Cora."

"I'm not a snob! I just…"

"You just judge people based on how much money they have." She smiles and shrugs when I turn to look at her. "It's fine. Be a snob if you want. I'll still love you even when I'm rich beyond belief."

I throw a damp towel over my shoulder and lean against the corner of the booth. "It's not that they have money. It's that none of them know what it's like to work for it. They look down on people who don't have money and they think they should be in charge of them just because they were born with a perfect credit score and a trust fund."

Jorden wrinkles her nose. "Sorry, babe. But I've been working for as long as I can remember. If a man with deep pockets wants to take me away from all of this gum scraping, then I'll gladly let him."

"You want to be dependent on a man?"

"If it means I can finally breathe, then yeah." Jorden winks as she passes, bumping my hip with hers. "But until then, I'll sign on for the brunch shift with you and accept compliments from middle schoolers."

Just then, Francia swings through the kitchen door with a heavy sigh. "We have *got* to hire more kitchen staff. I'm not getting paid enough for this." Her hair is frizzed out around her face and her cheeks are red.

"Just tell Dino you won't help him with the pastries anymore. It's his job," I tell her.

She puffs out a breath, blowing her bangs off of her forehead. "I know. I will. It's just that, when I don't help him, we run out of pastries. And you know who customers yell at when I don't bring them a cinnamon roll? I'll give you a hint: it isn't Dino."

"In a perfect world, customers wouldn't yell at anyone. But if they have to," I say, mulling over the way Dino swats at waitresses' asses with his dishtowel, "it should always be Dino."

Francia brightens. "Speaking of a perfect world, how was last night?"

Jorden squeals. "Girl, you missed out. That place was wall to wall with beefcakes."

"Ew." I wrinkle my nose. "I don't remember seeing any beefcakes."

"You probably just remember seeing one." She wags her brows. "You were all over—"

"The snack table!" I interject. "There was a croquembouche."

Jorden stares at me blankly. "A what?"

"A tower of cream puffs with caramel. It's a French dessert. They're like—"

"Boring!" Jorden blares. Her hangover is still lingering, so she winces at the sound of her own voice. "I didn't eat a thing."

"Hence the drunken stupor when I dragged you out of there."

She looks at Francia and rolls her eyes. "She's exaggerating. It was so much fun. I met this amazing guy. He's an athlete and—"

Jorden rambles on. I listen in only so far as I need to make sure she doesn't mention Ivan.

"—biceps like you wouldn't believe." Jorden is still talking a mile a minute. "He picked me up and carried me like I was nothing. I felt like I was on the cover of one of those historical romance novel covers. You know, with the ripped bodices and flowing hair? It was hella romantic."

Francia turns to me the moment there's a break in the conversation. "Who did you talk to, Cor? These things can be kind of snobby. Hopefully, everyone was nice."

Jorden snorts. "Oh, they were more than nice. Cora was busy entertaining all night."

I'll kill her. I swear to God I will. I love her, but I'll kill her.

"Entertaining who?" Francia asks.

I smile and wave her away. "Jorden was enjoying the free champagne too much to know what was going on. I just wandered around and observed."

"You had to have talked to someone," she presses. "Did anyone ask who invited you? What did you tell them?"

She seems oddly interested in my evening. But she's probably just wondering what she missed.

"I only had to tell the security at the gate your name. Otherwise, no one asked," I lie.

She frowns, her mouth opening to say something. But the bells above the front door jangle, cutting her off.

"Oh!" Jorden spins around and looks at the clock. "Wow. We are open already."

I hurry and finish wiping down the last two tables while Francia slides all the chairs onto the floor.

"Come on in, boys," Jorden calls to our customers. "We just opened, so give us a second to get ourselves sorted." She plucks the rag out of my hand and slaps a stack of menus against my chest. "I need some more concealer and a vat of coffee before I can serve *that* table."

I'm not sure what she means until I turn around.

"Brawny" doesn't begin to cover it. The men at the table are huge in every direction. Thick necks, even thicker biceps. Three of them are decked out in all black like they're stopping for a bite to eat before they continue on to their day jobs as top secret ninjas.

Except one man with his back to me. He's narrower than the others, leaner in a way that I've always found more appealing. I can't determine much from the back of his head, though.

The pull of attraction brings with it a thread of guilt. As if I owe the man I spent last night with at least twenty-four hours of emotional monogamy. It's ridiculous, of course; I can guarantee Ivan Pushkin isn't thinking about me right now. So I can be attracted to the back of whoever's head I damn well please.

With that, I plaster on my best people-facing smile and slide menus across the tacky surface of their just-washed table.

"Welcome to Quintaño's. We're serving brunch right now, so you lucky gentlemen get our full breakfast *and* lunch menu. Let me know what you're in the mood for and I can point you to the right page in the—"

I'm halfway through my spiel before I even look up at the men.

My mouth falls open in what has to be a very unattractive gape. But I can't summon the energy to close it.

All of my energy is directed at remaining standing.

At not turning and fleeing into the kitchen.

At not throwing myself directly into Dino's fresh vat of frying oil.

Because a set of molten amber eyes I never thought I'd see again are blinking up at me. There's not a single drop of surprise in the rest of his granite expression.

"Good morning, *solnishka*," Ivan Pushkin says. "Did you miss me?"

13

CORA

Oh, shit.

A crazed, manic laugh bubbles out of me and, even when it fades, I stay grinning like a clown on party drugs. "Wow. The world is so small. I can't believe you're here right now."

"That's the only thing you've said in the last twelve hours that I know is true," Ivan Pushkin says darkly. "I can tell you weren't expecting me."

My heart is a hummingbird, flapping uselessly against my ribcage. "No. No, I wasn't. But I—Well, I'm, uh, Francia." I introduce myself to the rest of the stone-faced men at the table. I hope the real Francia is in the kitchen by now so she doesn't hear me play-acting as her, but I don't have time to turn around and check. "It's nice to meet you all."

The men don't respond. Ivan does, though. With just one word. A single word that shatters my lie into a million pitiful pieces.

"Cora."

On instinct, I turn towards the sound of my name. Towards Ivan.

And just like that, the game is up.

He smiles, the edges as sharp as broken glass. "It's nice to meet you, too."

I sag into myself, eyes pinned to the floor. "Okay, so…I'm not Francia. You know that, obviously. She was the one invited to your party, not me. I was a guest. But I needed her name to get inside. Then I met you and I kept using her name. I don't know why I did it. Well, I kind of know why. But it's complicated. I shouldn't have—"

I'm in the middle of a rambling explanation when the three men slide out of the booth in unison.

I stumble back, eyes darting from one goliath to the other. But they don't pay attention to me. They split up, moving in three different directions.

One goes to the front door, one pushes through to the kitchen, and the other checks the long hallway that leads to the bathrooms and the manager's office.

"What are you doing?" I call out.

No one bothers to answer.

The kitchen door swings open. Francia and Jorden are at the front of a very confused procession of line cooks and busboys.

"You're closing early today," Ivan announces. There's no threat in his voice, but it's impossible to miss the authority. "Enjoy the day off."

Dino scowls at Ivan. "And who the fuck are you?"

Ivan's eyebrow gives a subtle arch. "No one."

"No one?" Dino parrots back.

Ivan nods. "Exactly. Keep practicing that. I'm no one. You saw nothing. Say it until you believe it if you don't want any trouble."

It's almost worse that he's talking softly. Almost warmly. There's a quasi-friendliness to the way he is laying down exactly what is going to happen.

The fear lies in the unknown of what happens when he *stops* being quite so friendly.

Francia raises her hand like she's in school. "We can't leave. We'll be fired."

Ivan turns to her. "There are worse things than being fired. Just worry about doing what I say, Francia."

Shame coils up my spine. He knows her name. He knows my name.

What else does he know?

"I don't care about being fired," Jorden spits. "What are you doing with Cora?"

I shake my head at her. I appreciate the concern, but I don't want her involved in whatever the hell this is.

Another man steps forward and ushers Jorden and Francia towards the front door. "Cora will be fine. Don't worry about her."

Jorden turns her disgruntled gaze to the man. "Who are you?"

He keeps herding her to the exit. "My name is Yasha. Not that that matters to you."

Yasha and Jorden disappear. Francia is already outside with one of the big thugs. Another shepherds the rest of the kitchen staff out with nothing more than brief, confused glances in my direction. As soon as they see Ivan watching them, they snap their attention away. As if even looking at me might be crossing a line.

I could cry out for help, but it wouldn't make any difference.

Ivan Pushkin always gets what he wants.

And right now, for whatever reason, he wants me.

When we're alone, Ivan flips the open sign to "Closed" and turns back to me. I'm frozen in place and flushed from head to toe as he saunters closer. "You lied to me. You're not Francia Delacour."

"I'm also not an investigative journalist." I throw my arms wide, gesturing to my polyester waitressing uniform. "In case you couldn't tell."

He snatches my wrist out of the air. My breath catches in my throat. "What is your aim?"

"I don't have an 'aim.'"

His eyes narrow. They're dangerous eyes—predatory eyes. "You loathed every single person at my house—myself included—yet you used your friend's name to get inside and find me."

"*You* found *me*," I correct him. "I told you to leave me alone, remember?"

"And then you stripped naked in my office." As if remembering the scene, his eyes slip down my body.

My skin prickles with awareness. "My dress fell apart. I didn't have a choice!"

"Someone coached you well. You have an answer for everything."

"I wasn't coached. I'm not—" I groan in frustration. "I'm the one who left you, remember? You told me to stay and wait for you, but I left."

"Maybe you left because you got what you wanted."

"Oh, that's right." I snap my fingers. "Don't you remember reading off your debit card and PIN number between orgasms? That was my dastardly plan and you fell right into my trap. If you see a suspiciously high Target charge on your credit card statement, you'll know which villain is responsible."

I'm not sure where this confident, feisty streak has come from, but it's the only thing keeping me standing.

"I don't take you for a woman who is so easily satisfied."

He's wrong about that. I was *very* easily satisfied last night. Several times, actually.

I squeeze my thighs together, desperately trying to keep as much blood flowing to my brain as possible.

"I was at your party to have a good time and let loose. That's all. If I'd known who you really were, I wouldn't have gone anywhere near you."

"You knew who I was when we were fucking," he growls. "The scales were unbalanced, it seems. You knew who I was, but I didn't know who you were."

"And now, you're the one breaking into my place of work to threaten me. If I had to make a bet on which one of us has suspect motivations, I wouldn't put money on me."

All at once, he draws back. The storm cloud on his brow clears to a faint overcast. "I'm not threatening you."

"What do you call this?" I scoff.

Through the front window, I can see Jorden's ponytail swishing back and forth as she sways from one foot to the other. I hope she's okay. I hope they're all okay.

Ivan shifts in front of me, blocking my view of the window and forcing my eyes back to him. "I call this a fact-finding mission. I'm here to find out who the fuck you are and what the fuck you want."

"Well, when you ask so nicely…"

His growl is a deep rumble of thunder in his chest. "I'm not going to hurt you—unless I have to. The choice is yours."

I stare at his chest to avoid being sucked into the sexy vortex of his eyes. "It's up to me whether you hurt me or not? Okay, great. Then count me as a loud and proud member of Team 'Don't Hurt Cora.'"

Ivan could crush me underfoot if he wanted. He could make me disappear with the snap of his fingers. But I refuse to back down. I refuse to shrink away the way I know he expects me to.

I can feel him staring holes into me. After steeling myself, I finally look into his eyes.

But I'm still not ready.

Instantly, I'm taken back to the inky shadows of his party with every reason to leave, but I can't force myself to move. Because I'm tangled up in him in a way I don't know how to undo.

Does he feel this, too?

In answer, his gaze drops to my chest. Then his eyes widen, shock etching into the lines of his face.

I'm about to make a joke about how my polyester-clad cleavage has never made anyone look so haunted before. But before I can, without an ounce of warning, Ivan Pushkin drops his shoulders and tackles me to the floor.

14

IVAN

For a woman who thinks I'm here to hurt her, Cora is being awfully mouthy.

At this point in most of my business dealings, people are pleading. There are bowed heads, clasped hands, and bent knees involved. Tears aplenty. Maybe some unintentional pants-wetting on a particularly pathetic day.

But Cora lifts her chin and plants all one hundred and thirty pounds of herself firmly in front of me.

"It's up to me whether you hurt me or not? Okay, great. Then count me as a loud and proud member of Team 'Don't Hurt Cora.'"

I'm about to tell her I'd rather be on Team 'Make Cora Scream Again.'

Then I see a light.

A red sniper's dot in the center of her chest.

I act before I even realize what I'm doing. I dip my shoulder, charge forward, and wrap an arm around her waist. My other hand cradles instinctively around the back of her head.

She starts to scream, but the air whooshes out of her as we hit the ground. I take the worst of the fall. My knuckles bite into the hard tile floor and split open.

"What in the hell are you doing?" she shrieks. "Get off of me! Let me up—"

"Don't fucking move!"

I band my arm across her chest to hold her down…

Just as the room implodes.

Large windowpanes advertising dulce de leche crepes, southwest egg scrambles, and enchiladas as big as your head shatter in their frames and then explode inward. Glass shards and dust rain over us. I throw myself over Cora, shielding her from the eruption even as my back is pelted with glass shrapnel and pain skitters across my skin.

For a few moments, it's mayhem.

Then it stops. The world goes eerily quiet.

Cora is tucked into my chest. She was afraid of me a second ago, but now, her face is buried in my shirt, her hands fisting the material like she's floating out to sea and I'm her life preserver.

"I think it's over."

My voice seems to shake her from her stupor. She peeks her head out from under my arm and stares wide-eyed at the glass-covered floor. "Was that a bomb?"

"Sniper."

She chokes on the word. "A sniper. A sniper was going to… Holy shit. You saved my life."

"Don't get too far into your 'thank you' speech. The shooter is still alive."

That realization sends her curling against me once again.

I rise up on my aching knee and offer her my hand. She takes it, slipping her fingers into mine, and we crawl around the bank of booths in the middle of the room so we are further from the windows.

She leans against the seat next to me. She isn't weeping and crying the way she should be. The way most women would.

Without the adrenaline and the feel of her body against me as a distraction, anger rises up in my chest. "What the fuck are you involved in?"

She turns to me. "You think this was because of *me*?"

"No one targeting me would look in a shithole like this. I'm starting to think you could be lying to me about a whole lot more than your name."

I have plenty of enemies, but none of them so desperate and sloppy that they'd shoot up a restaurant full of innocent civilians in the middle of the day. There's a missing piece of the puzzle here.

"I lied about my name, but I'm not lying about this. No one is after me."

She's lying or she's wrong. I don't have time to figure out which one. Not until I solve the problem facing us now.

"Are you okay?" I finally ask.

She turns to me, eyes narrowed. "What?"

I repeat the question slowly, as if she might need time to understand each individual word. "Are. You. Okay?"

"I heard you, but... Yes." She runs a hand over the back of her head like she's checking to make sure. "Yeah, I'm okay. Are you?"

"I'm perfect."

"Don't we all know it," she mutters.

I ignore her and flip onto my knees just as the back door opens. My hand moves to the gun on my hip, but then I hear Yasha.

"Ivan?"

Good. He's alive.

"Over here. Do you have eyes on anyone?"

"Working on it," he says. "Whoever it was, they didn't go after anyone standing outside. They were aiming for the windows. Stay put; we're clearing the perimeter." Then he disappears back outside again.

"*We* were the targets?" Cora is still resting against the side of the booth. Her knees are tucked against her chest, her arms wrapped around her legs. She's looking to me with wide, green eyes.

If she was anyone else, I'd kill her. There's something she isn't telling me and she's putting me at risk.

But she isn't anyone else. She's...

Well, I have no fucking idea who she is. Not really.

I rest my elbow on my knee and look into her eyes, leveling with her. "Now is the time to bare it all, Cora."

Her cheeks flush. "We already played that game."

I roll my eyes. "If you have enemies, tell me now. Your life could depend on it."

"I don't have any enemies," she retorts. "Unless you count yourself."

Good point.

I haven't decided what I am to her yet.

15

IVAN

Yasha crashes through the back door fifteen minutes later with a thrashing man in his arms.

"Enough with the resisting," he barks at the poor bastard. "You're captured. Give it up already."

The man falls to the greasy tile floor and rises to his hands and knees. Dark eyes bounce from face to face in hope and desperation.

"There's nowhere to go," I inform him coldly.

The door leading out to the alley slams closed with finality, rattling the stainless steel shelves. I moved Cora into the kitchen to get away from the windows in the dining room. But with the numerous sinks and drains in the floor, this will make a nice kill room, too. Blood cleans up about as easily as tomato sauce.

The man starts to say something, but I hold up a hand and he immediately clams up again.

I pace across the floor towards the man and gesture for him to sit up. He's small with stocky arms and legs. His neck is thick and his head is balding. When he sits up, he glares at me, lip curled.

I promptly slug him in the face.

He collapses forward again, wheezing out a curse. Cora gasps from somewhere behind me, but I can't think about her now. I have to stay focused.

I crouch down in front of the man with a sneer on my face. "Why did you shoot at us?"

The man's eyes are dark. He turns his head and spits on the floor before facing me again. "I wasn't shooting at you."

"Oh, so it *was* the windows you were after. Well then, nice shot. They never stood a chance."

"I was aiming for *her*," he hisses.

"Ah." I frown. "Then I stand corrected. You're a fucking terrible shot."

"It was a warning. I wanted to draw you outside." He leans around me to see Cora. "I wanted a clear shot at her."

My fist connects with his soft jaw before I can stop myself.

"Fuck!" he complains as he spits out a bloody, broken tooth fragment. "If you're going to kill me, just kill me."

"You sound surprisingly eager for death."

He spits blood and shrugs. "I'm dead either way. I failed the mission."

I feel Cora inching closer. I hold out an arm to stop her and she lays her hand on my wrist. It's a small gesture. Just a light touch. But it is far more distracting than it should be. Same goes for her strawberries-and-cream scent poisoning me more and more with every breath.

"Who sent you here?" I grit out.

He shakes his head. "I can't tell you that."

"You're dead either way," I remind him. "No point in being shy now."

"*I'm* dead, either way, yeah. But my family is another matter. If I tell you who sent me, they're dead, too. Unless…"

In the corner of my eyes, I see Cora's brows draw together. There's a small scrape along her jaw from the glass. I barely stop myself from reaching out to dab the blood away.

The man swallows. Then before I can say anything else, the man lunges forward at her.

She doesn't even have time to react before I grab the assassin by the throat and throw him back on the stainless steel countertop.

"I'm sorry!" Cora gasps as she lunges backward. "I didn't—I thought—"

"Don't apologize." I squeeze the man's throat. He wraps his hands around my wrist, but it would take three of him and a fucking miracle to make me loosen my grip. "That's his job. Come on now, *mudak*. Apologize to the lady."

His mouth opens, a wheeze leaking out of his collapsing windpipe.

I hold him tighter. "Hurry. Apologize before it's too late."

His tongue looks swollen in his mouth. His eyes are bulging. He looks like an overripe tomato ready to pop.

"Ivan," Cora breathes in warning.

She has mercy for the man who lunged for her, who shot at her—but I don't. If he doesn't do what I ask, he'll die right here. Right now.

No one is going to touch Cora before I get the chance to figure out what is running through that gorgeous head of hers. What secrets are hiding behind those green eyes and pouty lips.

"S-sorry," the man finally rasps out. His eyes are rolling back in his head as the word oozes out of him.

"There. That wasn't so hard, was it?" I let go and he sucks in air in great wheezing gulps. "Now, tell me why you shot at her."

He hacks up a phlegmy cough. If he was going to live to see tomorrow, he'd be sore.

As it is, that won't be a problem.

"Target practice."

I growl in frustration, my hand itching towards his neck again. "Don't fucking play with me, *mudak*. You know what I want to know."

He presses a hand protectively to his neck and nods. "I was sent here to make sure she died…so you two couldn't get married."

Fuck. Cora is indeed involved—but it's not because of anything she did.

It's because of me.

"*Married?*" Cora spits. "We aren't—Why would anyone think we were—Who sent you here?"

I lean forward, looking into the man's bloodshot eyes. "Answer her question."

He clenches his jaw. "I can't. My family… They'll all die. Every one of them. I can't—"

I hold up a hand to silence him. "I understand family loyalty. You're protecting them. There's honor in that."

Yasha shifts into view, an eyebrow raised. A question in his expression. *Should I take Cora away first?*

Probably. I don't usually offer outsiders a front row seat to my criminal dealings. But I don't want her any farther away from me than she is right now. Not until I know who is after her and why she might be after me.

I give a quick shake of my head and turn my attention back to the wannabe assassin in front of me.

"All I've ever done is for my family," he says. "I needed the money. I don't want to kill people, but I have to eat. You know?"

I nod. "I know. I understand. We all have to make tough choices."

He sighs, relief rolling off of him. "I'm so glad you—"

"We also have to face the consequences of those choices."

There's a beat of hesitation. A blissful second where he doesn't yet understand.

And then he does.

He stiffens, but it's too late. The gun is in my hand and pressed to his temple before he can plead for his pathetic life.

The shot rings out.

Cora screams.

And the man who dared to hurt her goes slithering to the ground.

16

IVAN

"Calm down."

Cora's panic is natural. But it's an inconvenience. There's no time for it.

I turn back to look at Yasha. "I need you to—"

"I'll clean this up." He inclines his head in Cora's direction. "Take care of her."

We've been working together so long that we have a natural rhythm. Yasha sets about dragging the man's body onto the floor. I turn back to Cora. She's pressed in the corner of the greasy kitchen, her face a sickly shade of white. It's a mirror of how we met last night, but the stakes are ten times higher.

"Come with me."

I grab her arm, but she flinches away from me. She cowers against the steel appliances. Her knees start to give way, her body sinking toward the floor.

I hold her just above the elbows and pin her against the wall with my hips. She tries to fight, but she isn't even looking at me. She has no idea what she's fighting against.

"Cora." She is blinking past me, watching Yasha do his work. I shift into her line of sight and grab her chin to bring her gaze to me. "*Cora.*"

The name suits her so much better than Francia. The way it rolls off of my tongue is familiar. Lyrical. Almost sweet to the taste.

Her lashes flutter. Finally, she's looking at me. Her green eyes clear and focus. "You killed him."

"He tried to kill us first. I think it was justified."

"You…" She shivers. "You shot him in the head."

"It's a better death than he would have gotten elsewhere. He failed his mission. Whoever hired him would have killed him, but much more slowly."

Cora blinks again, her mouth opening and closing. Then, without warning, she slams a fist into my chest. "Who are you?"

"You stole my line."

Her jaw sets as color returns to her face, her lips turning a soft shade of petal pink. "You killed a man, Ivan. At my job! What the fuck is happening?"

She raises her hand to hit me again, but before she can, I pin her wrist to the metal oven above her head. I press forward so we're flush, my face no more than a couple inches from hers. I can feel the warm exhale of her shock on my chin.

"Don't ever raise your hand to me, Cora."

"Oh, so you can dish it out, but you can't take it?"

"I killed him, but I haven't touched you. Not without your eager and express permission." I hold her steady with my hips, refreshing her memory in case she's forgotten about last night. "I'm being gentler with you than I should be. Don't test me."

Her eyes search my face. Whatever she finds there makes her ease back. Her body goes slack beneath my weight, until I'm satisfied enough to release her hand.

"Good. Now, come with me."

This time, when I say it, she listens. Cora walks with me out of the kitchen and into the dining room. Glass cracks under our feet. I have to sweep shards off of a booth before we can sit down.

Cora sinks into the flaking maroon vinyl and drops her face into her hands. "This is the worst day ever."

"First time being shot at?" I ask conversationally.

She scowls at me from between her fingers, unamused. Then she drops her hands. "Can I leave now? I don't want to be a part of…of whatever this is."

"That man was sent here to kill you. You're already a part of this."

"Yeah, but…" She lowers her voice and leans closer. "He's dead now."

I lean in, mocking her whisper. "The person who hired him isn't. He'll come for you again."

That realization hits her like a physical blow. She snaps back against the booth, eyes wide. "Someone is after me?"

"All signs point to yes." I flick a few shards of glass off the table. "You've pissed someone off in a major way."

"How? Why? Is this because we…because we…"

"Fucked?" I offer up.

She grimaces. "Because we slept together? Is one of those women coming after me because they think I want to marry you? If so, just tell them I have zero interest."

I press a hand to my chest in faux offense. "Ouch, Cora. Words are weapons, too, you know."

She rolls her eyes. "We shouldn't be joking right now. This is serious!"

"If I stopped joking every time I had to kill a man, I'd never joke again. What a terrible place the world would be without a little humor."

She stares at me, disgust mingling with her horror. "People at the party said you were a criminal, but I didn't really believe them. I thought you were involved in, like, financial crimes. Embezzlement or something like that."

"I am."

"Of course you are," she mutters before continuing. "But this is… This is more than I bargained for. I should have left last night. I should have walked out of your office and disappeared."

"But you didn't. It's just like I told your would-be assassin back there: everyone makes choices and everyone faces consequences." I hold out my arms. "I'm your choice and this is your consequence, princess."

"Don't call me princess,'" she hisses. "I'm not your *princess*. I'm not anything to you. We slept together one time. I'm not going to let that ruin the rest of my life. I'm leaving."

"No, you're not."

She stares at me, a silent battle of wills. Then she starts to slide out of the booth.

Before she can reach the edge, I lift my leg and plant my foot on the seat, blocking her path. "Don't mistake my sense of humor for weakness, Cora. Don't test me. You will not win."

"And what are you going to do? Chain me up?"

She says that as if it isn't a distinct possibility. I just killed a man in front of her. Chaining her up barely registers on the spectrum of terrible things I've done.

But just as I start to answer her, an idea comes to me.

A bad idea. Possibly the worst one I've ever had.

I could chain Cora up. That would be one way to handle things. But the assassin admitted he shattered the windows to try drawing Cora outside so he could get a clear shot. I'm not going to draw out whoever is coming after her by keeping her locked away.

She needs to be visible.

She needs to be with me.

"Actually, I believe *you'll* be the ball and chain."

Her nose wrinkles. "What are you talking about? What does that mean?"

The woman is difficult already. This plan won't make her any easier to handle. But until I can guarantee her safety and figure out who she is, I don't see that I have another choice.

Choices and consequences. Consequences and choices.

I'm making a choice. I'm more than ready to suffer whatever follows.

"It means you and I are getting married."

17

CORA

He's kidding. He *has* to be kidding. Right?

Right?!

Ivan leads me back through the kitchen. I keep hold of his hand only because I'm not sure I can navigate the restaurant by myself right now.

I've spent too many hours here to count. I've worked opening shifts and stayed long after closing. Any other day, I could do cartwheels down the hallways with my eyes closed.

But right now, my mind is a complete and utter blank.

As we walk into the kitchen, I look to the counter where Ivan killed the man. Five minutes ago, it was a stomach-turning bloodbath.

Now, though, it's spotless. No blood. No body.

"Your guy does quick work," I say softly.

Ivan looks towards the counter and shrugs. "He's had practice."

Goosebumps sprout across my shoulders and down each arm. *Who is this man?*

He saved my life and then turned around and took another ten minutes later. I've always known people aren't black and white. My mom was a perfect example of that. There are no angels and demons. No clear delineations between the good and the bad in the world.

But Ivan Pushkin lives in the gray space like no one I've ever known. I can't make sense of him.

"We're getting married." I say it more for myself than anyone else. I'm not anywhere close to actually processing or accepting it. I'm mostly just checking to make sure that I do in fact understand what that series of words means, just as a general concept. As for what it means *for me in particular?* That will take lots of time yet (and maybe a therapist) to unpack.

Ivan only nods in answer, holding open the back door into the alley.

I step through it and into the cool shade between the buildings. The cement is damp the way it always is, condensation trickling from the air conditioners and pooling on the ground. There's the sickly sweet scent of food rot emanating from the dumpsters at the mouth of the alley.

It's all so normal. So mundane. I could almost believe everything that just happened was some kind of twisted nightmare.

Then Ivan steps in front of the daylight coming from between the buildings. He's all too real.

"I need my stuff," I blurt.

"Yasha will grab whatever belongs to you inside and bring it to my house later."

"Not that stuff. My stuff from home."

"Like?"

"Like…normal stuff!" I snap. "Human stuff. Clothes and my phone charger. I need a toothbrush."

"I can replace all of that," he says dismissively.

The walls seem to close in tighter. I feel my freedom shrinking, evaporating like it was nothing. Like it was never there to begin with.

"I don't want to replace it," I grit out. "I want *my* stuff. I'm going to my apartment."

Ivan checks something on his phone and shakes his head like he's bored. "No, you're not."

"You can't stop me."

He blows out a breath. "I just made it clear that I can do whatever I want."

"And you want to hold me against my will?" I challenge. "You want to kidnap me and force me to marry you?"

I don't really think there's any hope that I'll appeal to some deep reservoir of morality inside of him. But then he stiffens. He pockets his phone and turns to me with rigid, careful movements.

"I want to keep you alive. I want to keep you *breathing*." He stalks closer to me. "You don't have a single fucking clue how much danger you're in. A sniper just tried to shoot you in the chest and you want to parade back into your apartment for a goddamned *toothbrush*."

It sounds ridiculous when he says it like that.

"This isn't about a toothbrush. It's about my freedom."

"Take that up with whoever has a hit out on you."

"Feels like semantics," I mutter.

He stands tall, looking down his nose at me. "You have no concept of the danger you're in or the saving grace I'm offering you."

"You're offering me a gilded cage," I say. "But I'm supposed to be okay with it because you're going to buy me whichever toothbrush my heart desires?"

"A gilded cage is a lot better than a coffin, wouldn't you say? That's where you'll be if you go back to your apartment. It isn't safe."

I shake my head. "My apartment is safe. It's in a nice neighborhood. I'm on the—"

"Fifth floor," Ivan finishes. "You have a balcony overlooking a flower stand and you live across from an elderly couple with two cats."

Angela and Geoff open a new bottle of wine every Friday night and bring me a glass. When I make brownies, I take them a pan. They're Geoff's favorites.

But I've never told anyone about them. The only way anyone would know any of this is if they'd been watching me.

"How do you—"

"It was easy for me to find you, Cora. Your neighbors were willing to tell me anything I asked. If that sniper knew where you worked, he sure as fuck knows where you lived." Ivan reaches out and taps the center of my forehead where the killer's bullet might've gone. "Think it through. You'll see that I'm right."

The fight in me vanishes all at once.

I thought I was safe. But Ivan knows everything about my life and we only met twelve hours ago.

Who else knows?

He is still standing in front of me when the door swings open. It's the man who escorted Jorden outside and cleaned up the body. Yasha, I think he said.

"The inside is clean and the manager scrubbed the tapes. I got the backups, too, and everyone else is clear on the story," he explains. "When the cops come asking, they'll say the robbers were wearing masks, no discernible features, nothing noteworthy to share as a description. Same ol', same ol'."

How many times have they done this before that it has become a routine? They have a built-in story that they feed to witnesses.

"Tell the kitchen staff to wait half an hour before they call the police," Ivan orders. "That will give me time to get Cora out of here and somewhere safe. There's no way to know how many hitmen have been sent to—"

"My friends!"

Guilt hits me hard. I'm a terrible person. How has it taken me this long to think about my friends?

"They're fine," Yasha dismisses. "All the shots went through the windows. I got them to safety while the shooting was still going on."

I spin to Ivan. "They have to come with me. You said it isn't safe here, right?"

"Let me take care of this."

"Sure, 'cause you've done a fan-fucking-tastic job taking care of things so far. You show up, and within minutes, my work is in literal tatters. I don't even know if I'll have a job after this. You might have just gotten all of my friends fired. How are any of us supposed to survive when—"

"If your friends are in danger, it has nothing to do with my choices and everything to do with yours," he growls.

"Mine?" I yelp. "You're telling me that all of this is my fault? Are you serious?"

"What the fuck did you expect to happen? Everyone else at that party would have killed to be in that office. Did you think the other ladies-in-waiting would give you a polite golf clap and congratulate you on a job well done?"

Yasha is biting a knuckle to hold back a laugh, but I ignore him. I have to; my entire body is burning with shame.

"I never would have touched you if I'd known—"

"But you did. Choices and consequences, Cora."

"Stop saying that!"

He steps closer, but doesn't touch me. It doesn't matter, though. I feel his presence like a finger stroke down my spine. My body shivers closer to him. Parts of me remember what it felt like to be this near. To smell him. Feel him. Taste him.

"Don't pretend you would have walked away from me if you'd known who I was. You *did* know," he chides. "You knew who I was and you still decided an orgasm from me was worth whatever trouble might come."

He's right. I knew who he was when he touched me. When I asked him to make me scream.

Ivan takes my silence for agreement. "Good. So we're agreed. You'll play my wife and I'll take down whoever is after you."

"I haven't agreed to anything."

He grimaces. "On second thought, maybe I should get an actual chain."

"I appreciate your help, but this is my life on the line. I don't even know you. Either of you!" I rub my throbbing temples. "I'm not going to marry someone I don't love. I ran from that fate once before and I'll do it again if you make me."

The words tumble out of me before I can stop them. Ivan leans back and looks me over.

I should learn to keep my mouth shut. Ivan knows too much about me already. I don't need to hand him more ammo.

"Unlike whoever you ran from before, I have the power to drag you back," he says after a long, strained silence. "I'll do it as many times as it takes."

"But why do you even—"

"This isn't forever, Cora. It's for now. Until we catch whoever is after you."

I huff out a breath. "But why do you even care who is after me? Who am I to you?"

He raises his hand and grazes a calloused finger across my cheek. "No one. You're an empty vessel I can use as I please.

As bait. As a wife. That's what makes you perfect for this, Cora."

His words shouldn't hurt. I don't know him. I don't want to know him.

"I'm not going to be your bait."

"Then you and your friends will die."

He says it so bluntly that it steals my breath away. Like any good predator, Ivan notices the weakness and moves in for the kill.

"You told everyone at that party your name was Francia. Whoever is after you might not know any better. They could go after the real Francia, too."

I chew on my lower lip. "So her apartment…"

"Compromised," he says. "You both need protection. Unlike our deal last night, my services now come with a price. Cooperate with me and I'll make sure your friends stay alive."

I've heard a million different versions of this compromise before. I've seen them play out.

My mother crying in her walk-in closet, surrounded by a designer wardrobe she wore with pasted-on smiles.

Girls I grew up with making "good matches" with men who sent them on tropical resort vacations so they could fuck another woman in their bed.

Marriage in Ivan's world is an exchange, a sacrifice. Life isn't a fairytale. Every good thing comes at a price.

The question is whether I'm willing to pay it.

"So if I pretend to marry you, you'll protect Francia and Jorden?" I ask.

"You're going to *pretend* to marry me either way," Ivan clarifies. "But if you cooperate and make it easier for me, then yes, I'll help your friends."

It's almost as if I don't have a choice at all. So I might as well make the best of it.

"As soon as I know my friends are safe, I'm gone."

He nods in agreement. "If your friends are safe, that means the threat is dead and I have no further need for you."

Slowly, I extend my hand.

Ivan's envelops mine. Warmth and too many memories flood through me. Memories of his hot breath on my neck. His fingers exploring other parts of my body. As soon as we shake, I jerk my hand back.

He watches me wipe my palm on my pants and smirks. "This should be fun."

18

IVAN

The drive from the restaurant to my house takes over an hour. I stay quiet because I said all I needed to say in the alley behind the restaurant. Cora has to come with me either way, but I'd rather her come willingly. Which she did…though "happily" is apparently not on the table.

She spends the first chunk of the time in a broody silence, her hands folded tightly in her lap. But as the drive drags on and the engine lulls us into a sense of calm, she eventually leans her head against the window and lets out a weary sigh.

Ten minutes later, I'm parked in front of my house with a sleeping Cora in the passenger seat.

"I have no clue what to do with you," I mutter.

Fake or not, I must be out of my fucking mind to think this was the best course of action. I don't know how to be married. I don't *want* to be married.

Yet…

I look over at Cora—my fake wife. Her dark hair is painted mahogany in the light streaming through the window, her pale skin dappled in mid-morning sun. Being with her feels more right than it should. Especially since I still don't know why she was at my party or in my office.

She looks so vulnerable. The disdain she's worn since she learned my name is gone in sleep. She looks younger. Innocent.

But no matter whether Cora is innocent in all of this or not, killing the sniper with a single bullet is a mercy I won't extend to whoever is responsible for putting a hit out on her.

When I catch who's hunting her, I'll make him fucking *suffer*.

The garage door opens and Niles appears. He stops on the three steps down to the garage, eyeing me in the driver's seat and the unfamiliar form asleep against the window.

As the Pushkin estate manager, he's good at anticipating my needs. He's been working with our family for generations. How many exactly, no one knows. But his pale, gaunt face has a haunted quality that can take some getting used to.

When I step out of the car, he waves. "I didn't know you'd be returning with company, sir. Would you like the usual guest suite made up?"

Niles knows exactly how to make my female guests feel welcome. Clean linens, fresh bouquets, and a complimentary bottle of champagne on ice when I show them to their temporary room.

Cora would see right through a ploy like that.

I can imagine her sneering as she took in the neutral decorations and lack of personal touch. *"How many women have you taken to this bed?"* she would ask.

"No, actually. I want the second master suite prepared."

Niles is speechless for a long moment until he clears his throat. "Of course. Whatever you need, sir." He moves towards the passenger side door. "I can call one of the guards to carry her—"

"No." The word tears out of me before I can stop it. "I don't want anyone to lay a fucking finger on her, understood? No one touches my woman but me."

Niles blinks again. It's the only sign of his shock. Then he bows his head. "I'll strip the bed and remake it myself. It will be ready by the time you get her inside."

Without another word, he turns and hurries into the house.

I don't enjoy stressing him out. He does good work and I appreciate his loyalty. But if people are going to buy that Ivan Pushkin is getting married, I have to sell it. To everyone.

Myself most of all.

Cora has shifted slightly, her temple resting against the crossbar between the doors. I'm able to pull her door open without any trouble and slide her out of her seat.

It's only when I scoop her into my arms that I realize the mistake I've made.

She's too close. I can feel the soft curve of her hip against my stomach. Each inhale draws between her lips like a whisper. Long lashes flutter against her cheeks and her strawberry scent radiates.

I remind myself of the facts. Cora and I are pretending. I looked her in her face and told her she meant nothing to me. *Bait. An empty vessel.*

I need to remember that.

Grimacing, I carry Cora inside the house and up the stairs. I pass by the office where I met her and the image of her standing in front of me perfectly naked rises to the forefront of my mind.

Fucking hell. This might be harder than I thought.

I pass by my bedroom and walk to the room next door. I push it open and find Niles adjusting the comforter.

He hears me coming and pulls the blankets down to make space for her. "I'm going to bring up fresh towels and toiletries. I assume the rest of her belongings are in the trunk?"

Gently, I nestle Cora onto the mattress and pull the blanket up to her chin. She shifts. Her lips part. Then she exhales deeply and sinks back into sleep.

I back away from the bed, not taking my eyes off of her. "She doesn't have any belongings."

"They haven't arrived yet or—?"

"She has nothing," I explain. "I'm putting you in charge of ordering her whatever she needs: a new wardrobe, jewelry, shoes, anything. Whatever she asks for, she gets. No questions asked."

"Of course," Niles says. But his eyes are burning with excitement. The man has been trying to dress me since I was a teenager. It's Christmas fucking morning for him.

In Niles's hands, no one will question whether Cora belongs here or not. She'll look made for the role.

She'll look made for *me*.

19

IVAN

Yasha is leaning against the wall next to the bedroom door when I step out into the hallway.

"Did you get your lady love all settled in?" he croons.

"Shut the fuck up."

He holds up his hands and shrugs. "That sour attitude must be why Niles just tore through here like he was on fire. I've never seen him so flustered."

"If we want people to believe Cora is my wife, *everyone* needs to believe it. No exceptions."

"You don't have to convince me."

I look to Yasha, brow raised. "What does that mean?"

"It means I knew from the start there was no way in hell you were going to marry some ditzy daughter of a don and be happy. Those girls exist in the safe little snow globe worlds their daddies build for them. But this girl?" He hitches his thumb towards the door and blows out a breath. "I can see the two of you working well together."

I snort. "You must have missed when she insinuated she'd rather chew off her own leg than marry me."

"And you must have missed when you went all caveman on that sniper for trying to touch her."

"He didn't try to touch her; he tried to kill her," I snarl.

Yasha snaps and points at me. "That's what I'm talking about. If that's part of your husband act, then you're nailing it. Very believable. *'The Oscar goes to… Ivan Pushkin!'*"

I blow out a deep breath and walk past him towards my room. "Sort out the protection teams for her friends and meet me downstairs in half an hour."

I think Yasha says something about me "sorting out my hard-on for Cora," but I slam my door before he can finish.

My clothes smell like gunpowder and sweat. I peel my shirt off and kick my pants into the pile next to the hamper.

Yasha was just being an asshole, but he wasn't entirely wrong about the hard-on. A fight always gets my blood pumping. Usually, I call up a sure thing afterward. Someone who knows it won't ever be more than an hour between the sheets.

But I can't think of a single other woman I want to call right now.

Because the only woman I can think about is only one wall away.

"A shower. I need a shower." I stomp into the bathroom and turn the handle to searing heat. I hiss as the hot water pelts my back and then sink into the comfort.

Trace bits of blood I didn't notice swirl down the drain. Bit by bit, my muscles relax in the heat.

But no amount of steam and scrubbing can cleanse my mind of Cora.

My cock is hard, almost throbbing with the need to release. And she's so close. One room away. There's even a door connecting us.

But I don't want her in a separate room. I don't want her out of my sight, period. I want to feel her body against me, her delicate hand stroking over my skin, her mouth letting loose those delicious little gasps…

I wrap my hand around my cock.

"Fuck," I rumble. I can't remember the last time I was this turned-on.

Actually—I can.

Last night.

I hear her voice in my head. I feel her silky skin on my tongue and wrapped around my waist.

I stroke my hand to the feverish pace I set last night. It was almost impossible to hold off my pleasure when Cora felt so good coming around me.

I press one palm to the cold tile and work myself with the other. Pleasure twists low in my gut, tightening the way they did last night when I could feel her orgasm pulsing through her, through both of us.

She was so tight…

"So fucking tight," I whisper.

I squeeze my eyes closed and see her body, naked beneath the lapels of my suit jacket. Her breasts bouncing with every thrust.

Ivan…

Then I come.

"Fuck."

I spill down the drain, pump after pump after pump until I sag against the cold shower wall.

But even when I'm done, I don't feel relieved. The tension is still right where I left it. So is the need.

Goddammit.

This woman might be a bigger problem than I thought.

20

IVAN

"Did a cold shower help?" Yasha asks. He's sitting in my office with his feet kicked up on the coffee table, a shit-eating grin on his face that makes me think he knows exactly what I was doing upstairs.

"It would be great if you could at least pretend to be professional for once in your godforsaken life."

"Do you mean *actually* pretend? Or do you mean the way you're 'pretending' to marry Cora? 'Cause I think I can manage the first one." He places his feet flat on the floor and sits tall with a faux-serious scowl on his face. "How is this? *Yes, sir, Mr. Pushkin, sir. Right away, sir. Very good, sir. Pip-pip cheerio, tally-ho, sir.*"

I learned years ago that it is better to ignore Yasha when he's in a mood like this. Mostly because it's usually a good sign. If things are going to plan, Yasha is a goofy jackass. When shit hits the fan, he turns grim.

I glare at him until he holds up his hands and slouches back into his seat. "Fine. I'm here, I'm professional, I'm ready to talk business."

"Then talk," I deadpan.

He sighs. "Francia is under guard. I moved her out of her apartment, since Cora was using her name last night at the party and her place might become a target. Did you ask her about that, by the way?"

"Ask who about what?"

"Cora," he says. "About why she was using a fake name with you. Was she trying to keep a low profile or—"

"Business," I remind him.

Chastised, he ducks his head and carries on. "Francia is in the apartment complex in the Valley. If the risk on her increases, she can be moved to a more lowkey safehouse, but for now—"

"The apartment is fine. I don't need anyone knowing about our safehouses unnecessarily. Dear old Dad wouldn't appreciate me divulging family secrets."

"Speaking of…" Yasha lowers his voice and leans in. "What are we telling Don Pushkin about all of this?"

"I'll handle my father."

"Right," he nods. "I know. But if he asks me—"

"Then you tell him to talk to me."

Yasha looks unconvinced. Probably because he knows as well as I do that not answering a direct question from my father is a surefire way to end up with a knife in your belly.

Cognac Villain

Otets is not one for subtlety or mixed messages.

"Until then, I want answers," I say. "I need to know who is after Cora and why."

"I gave you everything I had this morning."

I snort dismissively. "You gave me her work address, her apartment number, and a useless interview you conducted with her neighbors."

He shrugs unapologetically. "Angela and Geoff were really nice. They said Cora is like the daughter they never had. They asked if I was her boyfriend. They said we would make a handsome couple. What do you think?" He laces his fingers under his chin and smiles like a debutante.

My stomach twists. "I think you're proving with every passing second that I should get someone else on this job, too."

He frowns. "Hey. Low blow."

"You're the one flirting with senior citizens," I snap. "We have fucking work to do, Yasha. I need to know where Cora came from and who her parents are. Anything at all that might connect her to anyone at that party."

"You want to know if she has a boyfriend, you mean."

The possibility that Cora was in my house to meet another man has indeed occurred to me. I just hope it isn't true.

I can't guarantee that hypothetical man would survive my questioning.

I run my tongue over my teeth. "I want to know who is in my house. If she's some kind of spy or a plant—"

"Or taken, or in an 'it's complicated' relationship," Yasha adds on, not missing a beat.

My hold on my composure snaps. "This isn't a fucking game, Yasha. Someone thinks this woman is my fiancée and they are trying to kill her. That is an attack on the Pushkin family. It can't stand."

"I know." Yasha dips his head like a pouting puppy. "I am taking it seriously."

"Then stop cracking jokes and make sure Cora's security detail is airtight."

He sits up with a frown. "But she's staying in the mansion."

"So?"

"So she's in one of the most secure locations on the entire West Coast. Nothing can touch her inside these walls."

"Then it should be easy to find trustworthy men willing to take on the job," I say. "They'll be patrolling her twenty-four hours a day, seven days per week, until whoever is after her is caught. If she so much as sniffles, I want to know about it."

Yasha stares at me for a few seconds, his eyebrows raised in surprise. Then he wheezes out a laugh and shakes his head. "It might be easier to just put a dog collar on her and leash her up. Keep her close to you so you can make sure she's being a good girl."

"I don't need a collar for any of that," I tell him. "That's what the wedding ring is for."

21

CORA

I jolt awake.

My chest is heaving and my eyes can't seem to settle. I look for something, anything, to ground me. To remind myself that this has all been a dream. The party, Ivan, the shooting... all of it.

But I don't see my bright yellow alarm clock with the googly eye stickers over the buttons. I don't see the stack of CDs I've thrifted over the years even though I don't have a working CD player. I don't see the framed photo of me and Mom from when I was seven, the only one I have without my stepfather in it.

Instead, I see a four-poster bed with cream-colored silk curtains tied around each post. There's a long wooden dresser topped with an ivory vase filled with blood red roses. The frames on the walls are gilded and the carpet is plush.

The last thing I remember is climbing into Ivan's car. I closed my eyes at one point. I must've fallen asleep. Now, I'm here.

What happened in between?

There's a large window on the wall to my left. The curtains are drawn, but a sliver of daylight peeks through a crack. It's not much, but at least I know it isn't nighttime.

That's something.

"Hello?" My tired voice is barely more than a whisper. I clear my throat and try again. "Hello?"

There's a door a few feet to my right. It's open, but I don't hear anything beyond. Slowly, I slide out from under the impossibly silky sheets and walk to the door.

A massive bathroom stretches out in front of me. There's a single sink set in a long vanity. The mirror is framed in gold; so is the glass shower door. The tiles are iridescent, a pearly white that changes colors as I move from side to side. A fresh stack of towels sits on the counter.

Suddenly, I feel filthy.

My hair smells like gunpowder and I have the metallic tang of blood in my mouth. Without a second thought, I strip out of my clothes and start the shower.

Steam swirls in the air, warming the bathroom to a toasty temperature my drafty apartment bathroom has never been capable of.

Money can't buy happiness, but it can buy a really incredible shower.

It can also buy soap and hair products that smell like manna from heaven. I scrub and rinse off and, once my skin is clean and pink, I kill the flow and dry off with a fluffy white towel.

The fairytale shatters when I realize I have to step back into my work uniform. No fairy godmother to magic me into a clean pair of sweats.

I pull my panties free of my pants and wince at how damp they are. I vaguely remember dreaming while I slept. Ivan's hands on me in dark corners. His voice in my ear. The tension inside me building and building and…

"What the fuck is wrong with me?" I mutter.

I toss my shamefully soiled panties into a small trash can to hide the evidence and grimace as I pull on the polyester uniform over my bare skin.

Once I figure out where the hell I am, my first order of business will be a change of clothes.

It takes a few minutes for me to work up the courage to leave my room. When I finally crack the door open, I recognize the hallway immediately.

The maroon carpet runner and the beige walls with warm wood trim.

This is where Ivan hosted his party last night. It makes sense that he actually lives here, I suppose. I just can't imagine it. Throwing lavish parties here? Sure. Padding around in holey flannel pajamas and watching Hallmark movies? Not exactly.

Though I doubt Ivan even has holey flannel pajamas. Picturing him in pajamas at all is a stretch. He is probably one of those hyper masculine guys who sleeps in the nude.

The thought sends heat burning to my face, and I quickly redirect my train of thought.

What a horrendously gaudy wall sconce. Only a real asshole would pick that out.

I'm still staring at the sconce, trying to think of anything except Ivan's bare, muscled body, when I feel a presence behind me.

I spin around, arms held in some confused form of a fighting stance.

Yasha just arches a brow, his mouth pinched in an amused smile. "Hello to you, too."

I lower my fists. "You shouldn't sneak up on people."

"I didn't think I was. I've been standing out here since you creeped out of your bedroom. You should be more observant."

I don't have a snarky comeback for that. He's right—if I'm going to live in this house, I have to pay attention.

"What time is it?" I turn in a circle until I see an intricate gold clock resting on a narrow table. Delicate flowers are painted on the face. It looks like an old granny clock. Nothing Ivan Pushkin would buy.

But I'm more surprised by the time.

"It's twelve noon?"

"It's not twelve midnight," Yasha chuckles. "I'd be getting my beauty sleep if it was. Not all of us can afford to snooze the day away."

I can't afford it, either. Not usually, anyway. I can't remember the last time I took a nap in the middle of the day. Definitely not since I moved out of my stepfather's house.

"Why were you waiting for me?" I ask. Yasha hesitates, and I'm pretty sure I know the answer already. "Or did Ivan ask you to guard my room? Because our deal requires me to cooperate. It's not as if I'm going to make a run for it and let Francia fend for herself against trained assassins."

Yasha holds up his hands in surrender. "First of all, that guy was pathetic. Second, relax. I'm here to give you a tour. The estate is large. Ivan doesn't want you getting lost."

In a normal house, that would be a joke. But in this mansion, it's a distinct possibility. Maybe a tour wouldn't be such a bad idea.

I agree, and Yasha leads the way, heading towards the stairs.

"Aside from Ivan's office, which I hear you've already seen—" He glances back at me, and I'm sure my face is as red as a stop sign. "—this wing is just the two master suites and then some additional bedrooms. Maybe kids' rooms someday."

The idea of Ivan having kids—of some other woman carrying his children—is an insect buzzing around my head. Inconsequential, but annoying.

Whoever he chooses to have kids with, God help her. That's all I have to say.

But I catch on another detail.

"*Two* master suites?"

"One." He points to the door I just walked through. Then he rotates forty-five degrees and points to the door next to mine. "Two. This one is Ivan's. The rooms are connected by an interior door. It's more of a double master suite, I guess."

I try to hide the panic clawing up my throat at the realization that Ivan is going to be sleeping one wall away. One door away.

A single twist of the handle and I could be in his room. I could find out what kind of pajamas he wears—if he wears any at all.

A bolt, I think. *I'll install a bolt.* Or lock it with a wedged chair under the handle so he can't infiltrate my room while I'm sleeping. Maybe I'll call Jorden and ask her how to burn sage to keep demons at bay.

Yasha doesn't notice my agitation as he continues downstairs.

Last night, the interior of the house was dark, lit only by selective lamps and candles. Today, sunlight streams through large windows. I notice a lot of details I missed.

"All rich people must use the same interior decorator," I mumble.

Yasha chuckles. "Have you been in a lot of mansions?"

Just my stepfather's, I want to say. But I chide myself quickly. *Pay attention. Don't let anything slip.*

"I, uh…watch a lot of HGTV."

"Yeah, well, Ivan is in the process of taking over the place from his parents. Redecorating hasn't ranked high on the to-do list."

Yasha leads me through a den, a meeting room, then back through another set of doors into a kitchen.

"That's basically everything," he sums up.

"This house has a million rooms. There's no way that was the full tour."

His eyes glimmer with mischief. "Everything you need to know about, anyway. If you get lost, it'll be because you were sticking that little button nose of yours where it didn't belong."

He reaches out to tap my nose and I slap his hand out of the air. "Don't touch me."

From the other side of the kitchen, there's a stifled laugh. I turn to see who it was—and have to bite off the beginnings of a scream.

An elderly man is standing next to the pantry. His face is long and gaunt with bushy eyebrows. His eyes seem to be sunken into the sockets, hooded yet perceptive. If Yasha told me he couldn't see him standing there, I wouldn't doubt it. The man looks like a ghost.

"And this is Niles." Yasha sweeps an arm towards the man. "He may look like the cryptkeeper, but he's actually the caretaker."

Niles turns to me with a polite smile. "Keep putting him in his place, Mrs. Pushkin. Master Yasha needs a firm hand."

"Oh, no, I—" I shake my head. "My name is Cora. I'm not Mrs. Pushkin. I'm not—"

"Married yet," Yasha interjects quickly. "She's still Ms.... What's your last name again?"

"St. Clair. But you can call me Cora." I smile at Niles. "Please."

He bows his head respectfully. "Is there anything I can get for you, Cora? I apologize that your room is nowhere near ready yet. I wouldn't have put you in there today, but it was at Mr. Pushkin's request. He wanted to keep you close."

Oh, I'm sure he did.

"But if there's anything I can get you in the interim, something to eat or drink...?" He looks at my outfit and grimaces. "Some clothes, perhaps?"

I nod gratefully. "Clothes! Yes. Clean clothes would be amazing."

Niles nods again. "The guest room directly across from yours isn't being used right now, but there are plenty of things in there that should fit you. You can have your pick until your things come in."

A room full of women's clothes isn't being used right now? As in, it has been used in the past? When? How frequently? By whom?

The jealousy is stupid. Ivan isn't my husband. He isn't my boyfriend. He isn't anything to me.

You're no one. You're an empty vessel I can use as I please. As bait. As a wife. That's what makes you perfect for this, Cora.

I need to remember that.

22

CORA

The guest room is as bland as the rest of the house. So are the clothes in it. Neutral basics, jeans, jackets. I slip into a pair of camel-colored joggers and a white tank top. It feels so good to be out of my waitressing uniform that I don't care who they belong to.

When I get back down to the kitchen, Niles redirects me outside. "Yasha is waiting for you on the veranda. I'll have lunch sent out shortly."

Someone else preparing food for me will never be normal, but I thank him and step through the French doors.

Yasha waves from a circular table across the patio. Flower boxes brimming with marigolds and periwinkle outline the edge of the patio behind him. A soft breeze blows across the lawn, lifting my hair. It's such a picture-perfect setting that it's almost impossible to think I was being shot at only this morning.

The thought fractures the moment. Cracks of panic bleed through the lovely scene. I look up at the blue sky above, white wispy clouds burning away in the sun, and all I see is *danger*.

Could someone attack us from above? What about the hills surrounding the compound? Are there any snipers up there? What if—

"You're safe here," Yasha calls.

I turn back to the table and he's watching me. His feet are kicked up on the chair next to him, crossed at the ankle.

"We're exposed."

He shakes his head. "No one comes within three miles of the fence without someone on staff knowing about it. They won't get close enough to take a shot. You're safe."

"I thought I was safe at the diner." I pad over and drop down into the chair opposite him. "That was in public."

"Yeah, well a sniper can blend in better in public. They can disappear into the crowd. Out here?" He shakes his head. "They don't stand a chance. Plus, no one with even half a brain would try to break onto the Pushkin estate. It's a death sentence."

"And Francia has this same kind of protection?"

"She's covered. Don't worry."

I wrinkle my nose. "I'm always going to worry when my friends' lives are at risk."

"Speaking of friends." Yasha drops his feet to the ground and folds his hands on the table. "Is there anyone you need to alert about your whereabouts?"

I'm used to Yasha being kind of a smart ass, but he's being serious now. This is what he's like in his official role as…uh, whatever it is he does for Ivan.

I'm embarrassed by the lack of names coming to mind. "Jorden and Francia already know. Maybe I could tell my neighbors."

"I left a note for Angela and Geoff." I arch a brow and Yasha shrugs. "They're nice people. They seem to care about you."

"They might be the only ones," I mutter.

Yasha turns to the side and plucks a marigold out of the planter. He twirls it around his finger, stripping the leaves from the stem one gentle tug out a time. "Do you have any family?"

"None that would care if I went missing."

You'd think I'd get used to my family's dismissal of me. That, at some point, the ache of their indifference would stop hurting. But the wound reopens again and again, as fresh as the day I first left.

"Are you an only child?" he asks.

"How did you know?"

He smiles knowingly. "I recognize my own kind."

Talking about myself is one of my least favorite pastimes, so I jump at the opportunity to shift the focus to Yasha. "What about your parents?"

He moves from the marigold stem to the petals. He plucks them one by one, making a pile on the table in front of him as he talks. "Addicts. They had other priorities. Getting high, mostly."

"It must have been hard growing up around that."

"It was. That's why I left when I was thirteen."

I gawk at him. "Thirteen? Like…ten plus three? That thirteen?"

"Is there another kind?"

"I just can't believe it," I breathe. I was on the streets at thirteen, but I was with my mom. That was scary enough. I can't imagine doing it alone. "Where did you go?"

"Wherever I wanted. I started out as a thief." My thoughts must be written on my face because Yasha waves me off. "Don't judge me. Growing boys get hungry and I needed to eat. Stealing was easier than anything else. My parents were hopeless and shelters always tried to call the police and have me put in foster care. It was easier to be alone. I got good at it."

"You got good at being alone?"

He gives me a sad smile. "No. I never got good at that. But I was great at picking locks, taking only what I could carry, and then finding the right buyer. By the time I was seventeen, I was getting hired by grown men for high-level jobs. Serious shit. That's how I met Ivan."

"Ivan hired you?"

"No." Yasha grins. "Ivan was my target."

"Oh." I remember the way Ivan dealt with the assassin this morning. He claimed that was merciful. What would no mercy look like?

"I know better than to cross him now," Yasha chuckles. "At the time, I thought he was just some useless rich kid. I broke into his car and stole his phone. I didn't make it three blocks before he charged out of an alley and tackled me."

"And you survived?" I blurt.

"Yeah. But only because that was Ivan's plan all along. He's the one who hired me."

I frown. "That's what I said, and you said—"

"There's an artform to storytelling, Cora. It wouldn't be interesting if you guessed right away. I was building suspense." He sighs and continues. "Anyway, apparently, I'd hit one of the Pushkin warehouses a couple weeks prior. Ivan was tasked by his father to shore up security. He figured the best way to do that would be to go straight to the thief who broke in. I started out on the security team and worked my way up."

"You stole from him…and he rewarded you with a job?"

"And a house," Yasha adds. "We roomed together for a while, actually. Ivan moved out on his own for a few years once he was eighteen. He wanted some space to…*roam*, shall we say. We had an apartment in the city."

I don't even want to ask all the many ways Ivan *roamed* during that period of time. I'm going to take an "ignorance is bliss" approach to much of Ivan's personal life.

"Ivan is…" Yasha shakes his head like he can't find quite the right words. "A good man. He's a better man than he likes to let on, at least."

Every time I blink, I see him pressing a gun to that man's head this morning. I hear the deafening bang of the discharge. I see blood on the expo counter.

Ivan saved me. But a "good man" would have called the police, wouldn't he?

Yasha sweeps the golden marigold petals onto the patio and stands up with a groan. "Well, good chat."

"Where are you going? I thought Niles was going to bring us lunch."

"He'll bring *you* lunch. I have work to do."

I subconsciously glance towards the stone fence again.

"You're safe here, Cora. I swear it." Yasha digs into his pocket and then places a phone on the table. "This is yours. Some numbers are programmed in there. If you're in trouble and no one is around, you can call for help."

I lunge for the phone like it's a lifeline. My own phone is still in my locker back at Quintaño's. I navigate to the contacts and feel my chest ease at the site of my friends' names. Ivan's name listed right next to theirs gives me a jolt of something I don't quite understand and don't want to.

"Thank you." I give Yasha a sincere smile. "Really. Thanks."

He nods. "It was Ivan's idea."

My smile fades. "Okay, so where's the catch?"

"There's no catch. Just don't tell anyone your exact location. And play up the story that the two of you are madly in love and getting married. If it's going to work, everyone needs to believe it."

"But my friends—"

"Are depending on your acting skills," he finishes. "If you blow your own cover, we'll know. Your calls will be monitored by the Pushkin security team. Before you get all offended, they do that for every call that originates inside the compound. It's another security feature to make sure we don't have a rat." Yasha arches a brow. "So you'll be fine…as long as you're not a rat."

"I'm not a rat. I'm here against my will, remember?"

Yasha runs a hand through his light hair and glances around. "Don't let Ivan hear you say that."

"What?"

"Nothing. Just…I think you should try to make the best of things while you're here." He gestures around to the meticulously landscaped yard and blue sky. "It's nice."

"Prisons can be nice," I mutter.

"It's not a prison, Cora."

"Okay, then can I leave right now? What if I want to go for a walk or head to the mall? I'm sure I can just pop over with no problem, right?"

I didn't think it was possible for his good humor to flag, but Yasha looks genuinely exhausted by me. "You'll have to talk to Ivan about that."

I roll my eyes. "Right. Talk to the warden, not the jailer."

"It's really not going to be so bad, Cora. If you give it a chance, you might have a good time."

Yasha walks inside and I slouch down in my chair. "That's exactly what I'm scared of."

23

CORA

I eat lunch—an incredible pork taco that I would give my left nipple to have the recipe for—and then experiment with a stroll around the yard.

I pace back and forth, slowly making my way further and further from the house as a kind of test.

If I move twenty paces out, will a guard appear to escort me back?

What about thirty paces? Maybe a drone will buzz overhead, a tiny gun aimed and ready to fire.

But nothing happens. The sky remains clear except for the sun, which turns my shoulders pink. I kick off my sandals and drag my toes through the lush grass.

More and more, I think Yasha is probably right. Life here in Ivan's mansion won't be so bad…

Which will make things even worse when I'm ruthlessly kicked back to the dirty curb of my normal life.

I don't want to sound ungrateful. My life is good. It's better than living in abject poverty and it's certainly better than the bedazzled cell my stepfather had planned for me.

Still, it's nice to have a hot meal delivered to my table. It's nice to freely spend an afternoon without counting down the hours until my next shift at the diner.

I have a feeling, when all is said and done, it will be hard to walk away from this.

I make it all the way to the back fence and turn around to face the mansion. It's breathtaking that people live like this. That *I'm* going to live like this, no matter how briefly.

The house is a stunning three levels with balconies draped from some of the windows. A mezzanine level winds halfway around the top floor. Endless windows and doors and rooms and secrets tucked away in what can only be described as a castle.

Except the man inside is no Prince Charming.

And I'm sure as hell no princess.

My mind is making its fifth pass over my long list of worries when I finally pull the phone Yasha gave me out of my pocket and tap in Jorden's number.

She answers immediately. "Hello?"

"Hey. It's me."

There's a pause before she shrieks. "Cora! I've been blowing up your phone all day. Where have you been? What happened? The windows blew out. Someone said a gas explosion, but I don't know. I thought I heard gunfire. Are you okay?"

She's talking so fast that she's panting by the time she pauses.

"I'm okay. I'm fine."

"You sure?" she asks. "Was it an explosion? Or a shooting? That hot guy who took me outside wouldn't say anything."

I frown. Ivan didn't take her outside. Then I realize who she is talking about. "Yasha?"

"Right. Yasha. He told me not to worry about it. But guess what? I'm worried! Where have you been?"

"I've been…" I imagine Ivan sitting in some dark room somewhere, headphones on and a monitor with my face splashed across it in front of him. "I've been with Ivan."

There's a long pause before Jorden speaks again. "Ivan… Pushkin? From the party last night?"

"Yeah. He came into the restaurant this morning."

There's another long pause. Then Jorden screams.

"What?" I gasp. "What is going—"

"You fucked Ivan Pushkin at the party last night and then he showed up to see you the morning after?!" Jorden squeals. "Holy shit! I can't believe it! But…wait. Was the explosion this morning because of Ivan?"

"No. It was…" I try to quickly sort through what I can and can't tell Jorden, but in the end, it's easier to lie. "It was all a case of mistaken identity. A drive-by shooting, I think?"

"Shit. Really?" She blows out a long breath. "That's a relief. I mean, it's absolutely batshit, bananas, bonkers, totally off the rocker. But still a relief, I guess."

"Yeah, it is. But I'm still kind of shaken up. I'll probably take a few days off of work."

"Usually, I'd be pissed because I cannot be covering all of your shifts, but the restaurant is closed for repairs, anyway. Come over. Or I can come to you?"

I wince. "I'd love to, but…I'm not at my apartment right now. I probably won't be for a while."

"Oh. Where are you?"

Yasha told me not to give away my exact location, but I'm assuming it's safe to say… "I'm with Ivan."

This time, when there is a long pause, I know to pull the phone away from my ear. Through the speaker, I hear a tinny shriek.

"No way!" Jorden squeals. "He invited you back to his house?"

Invited, abducted. To-may-to, to-mah-to.

"Yeah. That's why he came to the restaurant this morning. He was there because I ran off last night without giving him my number."

Jorden is making all kinds of giddy noises from the other end of the phone. I wouldn't put it past her to be literally jumping for joy right now. Then she stops. "Wait! That whole party last night was for Ivan to find a wife, right?"

I chew on my lip. I hate lying to her. "Uh, yeah. Right."

"And now, he wants your number?"

"Correct."

A third silence stretches. I wince in preparation for what I know is coming in three, two, one…

"HOLY SHIT! IVAN PUSHKIN WANTS TO MARRY YOU?!"

I let Jorden calm down to a decibel safe for human ears before I put the phone back to my ear. "That seems to be correct."

"Oh my God! I thought this kind of thing could only happen in fairy tales, but you've got yourself a real life prince."

Sure. Prince of darkness, maybe.

"How did this happen?" Jorden badgers me. "I mean, obviously, he met you and was enamored with your beauty and wit and cleavage and other incredible qualities. But what happened last night?"

Now, *this* part I can tell without any lies.

I run through the drunk man ripping my dress to shreds and Ivan walking in on me naked in his office. "I had no clue who he was at first," I admit. "When I found out, I tried to leave— but I guess I didn't quite get that far."

"Insane," she breathes. "This whole thing is insane. If you need me to get out there with my voodoo shit and lay a curse on his ass and bust you out *Ocean's Eleven*-style, you just say the word. But if not, I'm happy for you. If you're happy, that is."

"I…think so, yeah. Thanks." I try to sound the part, but I can feel exhaustion creeping back in. Lying is hard work. "But I have to go."

"Of course. So much sex to have and money to spend. You're a busy woman now."

I snort. "I'll talk to you soon, okay?"

"Lunch!" she demands. "We will have lunch. It will be a long lunch. Very thorough. No detail too small, do you hear me?"

Now, my smile comes easily. Jorden is so quintessentially Jorden in this moment that I can't help but love her. "I hear you. It's a deal."

And I really mean it. One day, I'm going to sit down and tell Jorden everything. The truth.

I just have no idea when that will be.

24

CORA

On my long trek back across the lawn, I decide to call Francia. I already have a stomachache from lying to one friend. I might as well go for a double header.

But she doesn't answer. I try to tell myself that doesn't mean anything. Ivan's men are watching over her. She's safe. He wouldn't let anything happen to her.

I fire off a text instead.

Today was insane. I don't know what you know, but...yeah. Call me when you get a chance. I'm okay. I want to make sure you are, too.

Since she didn't answer my call, I don't expect a quick response. But before I can even pocket my phone, it buzzes.

FRANCIA: *I'm okay. But apparently my apartment isn't safe? These people are telling me they know you, and I should trust them? WHAT IS GOING ON?*

Lying to her is going to be significantly harder. Jorden was easily roped into the faux romanticism of the whole thing.

Danger amid a whirlwind romance and all that jazz. Francia has always been more practical.

CORA: *You can trust them. There's too much to explain, but hopefully this will be over soon and you can go home.*

FRANCIA: *Did something happen at the party?*

I nervously tap my thumbs on the edges of the phone. Ivan should have given me a script for this. Or he should have handled these conversations himself. I have no idea what I'm allowed to say, but I know one small slip-up could mean Francia no longer has the protection she needs.

CORA: *What do you know about Ivan Pushkin?*

FRANCIA: *I know he showed up at the restaurant this morning to talk to you. Did something happen last night?*

Everything happened last night. More than I want to explain to her over text.

Before I can formulate a response, another text from Francia vibrates in.

FRANCIA: *If you're getting married, tell me now.*

She knows more about the party last night than I thought she would. She didn't mention it was some matchmaking thing when she sent me off under her name. Probably because she didn't think it was important. What would someone like Ivan Pushkin want with someone like me?

The question echoes around all of the deep, dark places of my brain.

What does he see in someone like me?

Nothing, apparently. I'm just the bait.

CORA: *I can't explain everything right now. I'm safe, and I'm making sure you are, too. I'll tell you more when I can.*

Before the guilt can slither under my skin, I silence the phone and slide it back in my pocket.

As soon as I set foot on the brick patio, the door from the kitchen opens and Niles steps outside. I can tell he has been waiting for me.

"Mrs. Pu—Cora," he corrects himself deftly. "A few of the things I've ordered for you have arrived. I wanted to let you know in case you wanted to unpack them yourself."

"Already? It's only been a few hours."

His smile is slight, but proud. "I have a wonderful working relationship with many designers and boutiques. They were happy to put something together on short notice for Mr. Pushkin's new bride."

Bride. I'll never get used to hearing that word. Certainly not when it's aimed in my direction.

"You really didn't have to go to all the trouble for me, Niles."

"Of course I did," he says. "It was my pleasure, but more than that, Ivan insisted."

Appearances, I tell myself. *This is just about appearances.*

Everything we're doing is for the charade. It will be more believable that a man like Ivan could be slumming it with a girl like me if I'm wearing the right clothes. As a bonus, a whole slew of shopkeepers and designers now know Ivan Pushkin is engaged. The word is spreading.

All part of his plan.

I swallow down my panic and force a smile to my face. "Thank you so much, Niles. I'll be inside in a minute."

He bows and slips away.

I go back and forth for a few moments on what I want to do, but in the end, exhaustion wins out. I'll unpack and then take a nap. Everything will feel more manageable after a bit of rest.

I take one long look at the backyard and then steel myself as I walk through the doors into the kitchen.

Niles has disappeared and the kitchen is empty. There's a tray of fruit and cheese left on the counter. It reminds me of going to open houses with my mom, back before she married my stepfather and after my biological dad left. I can't count how many stale chocolate chip cookies, tiny pickles, and lukewarm finger sandwiches we pilfered from real estate agents who would never get our business.

I take a cheese square for old times' sake and nibble on it as I walk out of the kitchen.

I cut across the formal living room and am almost to the entryway when I hear heavy footsteps on the stairs. I freeze. It's too late to run back to the kitchen—whoever is coming would see me retreating. But I can't force myself to keep walking into some unknown social situation.

Then a set of strong thighs come into view. Followed by a devastatingly tapered waist wrapped in a tight gray t-shirt. I don't need to keep looking to know this body is topped with a square jaw and molten amber eyes.

Ivan jogs down the stairs.

He looks like he's in a hurry. Maybe he'll breeze right out the door. Maybe he won't see me.

I stay still, watching him descend the stairs and start to turn in my direction. But before he can see me, a female voice cuts through the quiet.

"Why haven't you called me?"

A woman steps into the doorway. Her back is to me, but she has an hourglass shape and dark, wavy hair that falls to her mid-back. She's in a tall pair of wedges and a breezy summer dress. It doesn't take a detective to recognize that she is gorgeous.

Nor to see how Ivan's face lights up when he sees her.

The sight of his genuine smile nearly knocks me backwards. Straight, white teeth behind full lips.

My God in heaven above, is that a dimple in his right cheek?

The heat stirring in my core is immediately doused when the woman throws herself into Ivan's arms…and he hugs her back.

"I've been busy," he murmurs into her dark hair. "But I'm fine."

"And how the hell was I supposed to know that?" She pulls back and squeezes his elbows as if she's making sure they're still properly attached. "Yasha told me there was a shooting and then immediately stopped responding. You need to talk to him about his phone etiquette."

Ivan rolls his eyes. "I need to talk to him about a lot of things. I had it all handled. He shouldn't have worried you over nothing."

Her hand reaches out to stroke his cheek. Ivan ducks away, but she forces the contact, patting his face. "I'm always going to worry about you, Ivan. I love you."

I swore to myself that I didn't care how many women Ivan had been with or would be with. It's none of my business. He is going to get married one day and have children with another woman. None of that is my business.

Because this is *pretend*.

We are *pretending*.

No matter how many ways I explain it to myself, though, it doesn't change the fact that my jealousy is very, very real.

"Oh," the woman says. "And who has been in my room? There are clothes on the bed and my closet is a mess. Niles is slipping up with the cleaning around here."

Her room? I turn to leave before I do something I'll regret, but Ivan's voice stops me in my tracks.

"That was Cora. She's in the living room, if you want to meet her."

I mouth a curse and spin around, screwing my face into a smile.

Ivan swoops into the room, his arm around the woman's shoulders. Even from the back, I knew she was beautiful. Now, there is no doubt.

She has a heart-shaped face and rosy apple cheeks. Her lashes are long enough that they might still be attached to the goddess who must have bestowed them on her.

I can handle a lot, but being introduced to my fake husband's mistress is pushing me a wee bit beyond my comfortable limit.

"Cora," Ivan rumbles. His voice is deep and casual. He doesn't sound guilty at all. "I'd like you to meet—"

"I'm Cora," I interrupt, holding my hand out to the woman. "I'm Ivan's fiancée."

What in the hell has come over me? Who am I?

I glance at Ivan. His mouth is a tight line. The dimple in his right cheek is making an encore appearance for a very different reason.

Screw it. He didn't want me to tell her? Then he shouldn't have brought her here.

I expect the woman to be upset, but she's smirking. Actually…she's shaking like she wants to laugh, but is holding it back.

"Nice to meet you, Cora. I'm Anya." Her hand is silky smooth in mine. She's never done a day of work in her life. "Ivan's sister."

My running list of "Reasons Why This She-Devil Is The Absolute Worst And Deserves A Fiery Death" freezes mid-scroll. If this was a cartoon, my eyes would bug out of my head.

"Sister," I breathe. "You're his…sister. You're siblings."

"And you're his fiancée!" She elbows Ivan in the side. "That would've been nice to know, too."

Ivan mumbles through a half-hearted excuse, but I'm so overcome with relief that I'm not paying attention.

The guest room wasn't for a harem of sexual partners. It was for his sister.

The knot in my stomach eases. My chest doesn't feel as tight. But the relief is chased by a bolt of panic because I shouldn't feel relieved at all.

None of this is my business and I can't afford to care about my fake husband.

25

IVAN

"When did all *this* happen?" Anya wags a finger between me and Cora.

"When do you think? You were at the party last night," I grumble.

She elbows me again. "Yeah, I was. Which means I had to talk to dozens of women who thought the best way to you might be through me." She turns to Cora. "I never saw *you*, though."

Cora tucks a strand of hair behind her ear. Her face blushes pink, matching the new color on her shoulders.

She spent hours outside. I watched her walking around the lawn and thought about going to join her.

But after my weakness in the shower, I decided that keeping my distance might be for the best.

Anya sighs when both of us remain awkwardly silent. "Really? Is this some big secret? I want to hear about your meet-cute. Now!"

"Don't be a brat."

Anya spins to elbow me again, but Cora interrupts. "She's not being a brat. I think it's nice that you care about what is going on in your brother's life."

Anya presses a hand to her chest for a stunned moment and then, before I can stop her, she pulls Cora into a bear hug. "I knew my brother would find the perfect woman for him some day. I just knew it."

Cora meets my eyes over Anya's shoulder for just a second before quickly looking away. She pats my sister on the back and manages a smile.

Anya whips out an arm to rope me into the hug. She squeals. "I'm so happy for you two!"

Cora is pressed against my arm. The warmth of her body sears into me. She smells like...like *me,* actually. Like sandalwood. Niles must have stocked her shower with my body wash. It sparks some possessive part deep inside of me.

She is mine.

"Okay. That's enough." I slide out of the hug and put some distance between us. "Why are you here, Anya? I'm sure your husband misses you. You should be getting back."

I start to steer her for the door, but she dodges me. "Are you trying to get rid of me already? I just got here."

Exactly. Anya has only been here for three minutes and I'm already questioning everything.

This fake marriage plan seemed like a good idea before Cora shook my sister's hand and introduced herself as my fiancée. Anya has always wanted me to get married for love. It's been important to her since she got married.

"Lev and I are so happy. I want that for you, too," she said on her wedding day. "Whatever it takes, I want you to be this happy, Ivan."

She should know better than most that it isn't possible for me, but she still held onto hope.

Now, I'm toying with those hopes. It's for her own good—for the good of the Bratva—but it doesn't make me feel any better.

I'm about to tell Anya that she should leave because Cora and I want to be alone, but then Cora swoops in and delicately loops her arm through Anya's. "No one is trying to get rid of you. We'd love to have you. Niles made some snacks in the kitchen."

Again, Anya's mouth falls open. She turns to me, sheer delight written all over her face. "Do you see this hospitality? I can't believe I've put up with your brutish ways for so long."

I flip her off and she blows me a kiss in response.

"I don't want to overload you," Cora teases, "but I was thinking about making coffee, too."

Anya groans. "Cora, you and I are going to get along famously."

That's what I'm worried about.

The two of them sashay into the kitchen. I trail along irritably. Cora gets plates down out of the cabinet and passes them out. Anya grabs a handful of cheese and crackers and then leans in, a grin on her face.

"Tell me everything. Full details of the meet-cute."

I expect Cora to buckle under my sister's insistence. When people aren't used to Anya, she can be a lot. "TMI" is not part of her vocabulary.

Instead, Cora smiles with ease and doesn't even look at me as she answers. "I know it probably sounds crazy, but we met for the first time last night."

"So the party worked then?" Anya claps her hands. "Were you introduced, or—"

"Enough with the inquisition," I snap.

This time, Cora is the one to reach out and lay her hand over mine. Electricity buzzes in the space between our skin.

"I don't mind answering her questions." Cora gives me a practiced smile and then focuses her attention on my sister. "I think Ivan is trying to protect me."

Anya frowns. "Protect you from what?"

I have no idea what Cora is about to say. I have half a mind to interrupt her. I don't know how I'm going to explain to my sister that this entire thing is bullshit, so I sure as fuck don't want Cora doing it for me.

But I'm also fascinated by the way she is taking control of this situation. I want to see what she does with it.

"Last night didn't go exactly the way I planned," Cora admits. "I first met your brother when he saved me from being groped by some drunk man."

"Stefanos Genakos," I explain when Anya looks to me for an explanation.

She grimaces. "Oh. Gross. He backed me into more than one corner before I got married. He should be banned from these parties."

"I would second that. He was not a gentleman. Your brother, however, was. He stepped in and protected me." Cora reaches over and grabs my hand again. She takes it easily, curling her fingers around mine like we've done it a million times before.

Anya stares at our intertwined hands like she might be seeing things. "Well, brother, will Stefanos live to tell the tale?"

"He'll live to tell the tale of how he got his ass kicked."

Anya silently cheers as Cora continues. "But before Ivan swooped in, the guy—Stefanos, I guess—*ripped my dress.*"

Anya gasps. "No! Where?"

"Right up the backside." Cora drops her face into her hands with the perfect self-deprecating chuckle. "The material was really delicate. By the time your brother found me, the entire dress had shredded apart. I was standing in nothing but my birthday suit trying to fix it somehow."

"No!" Anya claps both hands over her mouth and looks at me. "What did you do?"

"I gave her my suit jacket."

"Which I thought was very chivalrous of him—until I showed up today and found out there was an entire closet of your clothes just a few doors down the hall I could have changed into," Cora says.

Anya lunges across the island and slaps my arm. "All men are creeps! Especially the ones I'm related to."

"I could have let her leave naked," I point out. "So I think the suit jacket was a fair compromise."

"Pig!" Anya accuses even as she has to bite back a laugh.

Cora slips off of her barstool and turns to the coffee pot. While she's away, Anya silently pulls on my sleeve. *She's amazing*, she mouths, jabbing a finger in Cora's direction.

I wave her away without a response. I won't dare open my mouth on the topic. There's no telling what I might accidentally say.

"This coffee pot is like a spaceship." Cora stands back and bops the side of the stainless steel machine like that might help. "I need a PhD just to get my caffeine fix."

I move behind her, sliding an arm around her back to flip the switch on the side. My forearm grazes over her hip bone. Her hair tickles my chin. It's an ordinary kind of contact that feels somehow a billion times more intimate than what we did in the shadows last night.

Cora turns. She's blushing from head to toe, but she raises her chin with dignity. "Thank you."

"My pleasure." My voice is little more than a rasp.

She blinks and slides past me. "Coffee will be ready in a few minutes. Do you take cream and sugar, Anya?"

"Ungodly amounts of both," Anya replies.

This hostess act is throwing me for a loop. At the drop of a hat, Cora is operating with the nonchalant grace that most women earn after countless tutors and too many reprimands to count.

Who is this woman?

I'm still mulling over Cora's possible origins when I realize what Anya is saying.

"I've been hoping Ivan would find someone nice for literal centuries." She grins over at me. "He may not like to show it, but Ivan is a champion of love."

Cora practically chokes on a cracker. She calms herself down and schools her expression. "Is that so?"

"It is! Ivan wants the people around him to be happy. He goes to great lengths to ensure they are."

Shit. Anya thinks Cora and I are the real deal. She has bought into our lie so completely that she is about to spill our family drama to her. I'm trying to come up with a casual way to tell her to shut the fuck up and leave when the front door bangs open.

"Hello!"

Cora sits taller. "Are you expecting anyone else?"

"No, I—"

"Etot chertov dom morg? Where the fuck is everybody?"

My sister and I share a pained expression as my father's voice rings through the house again.

I drag a hand down my face. "Guess it's a family fucking reunion."

26

IVAN

"Ivan?" My father's voice echoes through the house, growing closer. "Ivan!"

Cora is staring back and forth between Anya and me. "What don't I know?"

I hear his heavy footsteps on the tile and my chest clenches up with anger, same as it always does when the old bastard intrudes where he isn't wanted.

Anya is the first one out of her seat. She meets him in the doorway, her arms around his middle. "Hi, Daddy."

I bow slightly. "Hello, Fath—"

"What the fuck did I just hear about a shootout this morning?" he snaps. "You were in a shitty part of town taking down a mercenary?"

Anya pulls away from Otets and gawks at me. "You told me it was nothing!"

"I handled it. There was nothing to tell."

"That's not nothing, Ivan!" she gasps. "That's a huge steaming pile of something!"

"This is why I didn't tell you. I wasn't almost killed. The sniper was going after Cora."

If possible, Anya's face pales even further. She turns to Cora. "You sat here and told me all about your meet-cute, but didn't mention the *assassination attempt* you dodged this morning?"

I slip between the two of them, feeling oddly protective of my pretend future wife. Anya takes a step back, catching the hint.

My father isn't so easily defeated.

He doesn't even have to look at her to cut her down to size. "Why were you even there, Ivan? I don't understand what in the hell an attempt on the life of a waitress has to do with you."

"Daddy," Anya whispers, "she is Ivan's fiancée."

Fucking hell. This is not how I wanted to announce any of this.

Without even glancing at me, he shakes his head and laughs. "No, she isn't." My father waves Anya out of the way and moves in on me. "I want to know what is going on, Ivan. I want to know right fucking now."

I sigh. "Cora was attacked because someone believed she and I were going to get married. I decided the best way to smoke out who authorized the attack would be to continue the ruse."

My sister drags herself back to the island and drops into a barstool. "So…you aren't getting married?"

Cora hasn't said a word since my father arrived, but she leans in close. "I'm sorry, Anya. For what it's worth—"

I interrupt. "I thought the best way to ensure no one found out we're pretending was to lie to everyone."

"I'm not *everyone*," Anya hisses. "I'm your sister. Just because I'm not in the inner circle doesn't mean I don't deserve to know what the fuck is—"

Otets slashes a hand through the air, silencing her instantly. "Enough, Anya! This is bigger than your hurt feelings."

Anya opens and closes her mouth. Ultimately, she decides to stay quiet. She crosses her arms and leans against the island while my father changes course, closing in on Cora.

Cora looks to me. Every bit of the ingrained politeness I saw from before is gone. She could handle Anya, but she is way out of her depth with the man who birthed me. Her green eyes are wide, searching my face for a way out.

"Who are you?" he asks her.

Cora's full lips part and close. She clears her throat and sits tall. "My name is Cora St. Clair."

He frowns. "I don't recognize it. Are you somebody?"

Cora doesn't understand the question. Who would understand a question like that? Isn't everybody somebody?

Not in our world.

I move to stand next to her. "She told you who she is."

"I don't know any St. Clairs."

"Oh." Cora looks down at her lap, her head shaking. "You wouldn't. It's my father's name, but he…he left us. It was just me and my mom. She's not—Well, I'm not really from—I came to the party with a friend last night."

"Fucking hell. You really are just a waitress." He spins on his heel, pacing back and forth. Then he stops in front of her again. "How much of this plan was your idea?"

"What?"

"You go from waiting tables to being waited on. It's a nice deal for you," he accuses. "Did you set this up with one of your friends to play rich and fuck my son?"

"Enough," I growl.

He ignores me. "I bet the assassin was one of your friends. Maybe a brother? A boyfriend?"

Cora is too shocked to even speak.

"I killed the assassin," I tell him.

"Wonderful." He snorts. "So now, she's a loose end with leverage. This just keeps getting better and better."

"I'm not—" Cora lets loose a shaky breath and tries again. "I'm not going to tell anyone anything. Ivan saved me."

"Yes, but *why?*" He leans in close, the word hissing between his teeth. "Why are you worth his time?"

"Daddy," Anya tries to intervene.

He turns to her. "What? Am I supposed to believe *both* my children have a fetish for the lower classes?"

Anya's face flames. I can see her clenching her teeth to keep quiet.

With her cowed, he turns back to me. "I don't know why I'm surprised. You love putting women on my payroll who do absolutely nothing to benefit the Family."

Usually, I'd let my father run out of steam before stepping in to be the voice of reason. Stepping in now, however, keeps him from revealing to Cora far more than a civilian like her should know about who we are and what we do.

It also has the added benefit of deflecting the barbs he meant for my sister and Cora. He's made it no secret that he thinks Anya and her husband are nothing but a drain on the family. They've argued about it until they're both red in the face. It does no good. Anya doesn't need to sit through that lecture again.

"I do what I have to do to fix the fucking messes you insist on creating for us," I snarl.

"The only thing I did where Katerina was concerned is arrange a perfect match for you. You're the one who threw it all away for—" He flings a disgusted hand in Cora's direction. "*This.*"

"This isn't about Katerina or Cora," I say with preternatural calm. "This is about protecting our family from someone who wants to hurt it."

Ten years ago, I wouldn't have needed to explain this. But time and age has worn on my father's abilities to see situations clearly. He is all instinct and rage now. Logic takes a backseat.

His flabby jaw works back and forth. "The girl is useless. She doesn't have any connections. What good does she do for us?"

I want to point out that ninety-eight percent of the women my father hand-selected to be at my party last night are undeniably useless. They are little more than pretty lawn ornaments perched in front of their family estates. *Look at where I come from. Stop and admire me.*

Cora is nothing like that.

It doesn't ultimately matter, though. Because I have a very good use for Cora. My father is just too blind to see it.

"Cora helps me draw out the identity of the person bold enough to attack our family."

"We can do it without her. Without you taking yourself off the market and ruining the potential of a suitable match being made."

"Cora is going to be a litmus test for who amongst our allies is trustworthy and who is trying to manipulate us. If you think that's useless, perhaps it's time for you to retire."

He scowls. "You'd love that, wouldn't you?"

I give him a tight smile. "I only want what is best for the family."

We stare at each other for a few seconds. He's deciding whether to push. Whether to fight.

I don't have to decide: I'll die on this hill.

Finally, he takes a step back, nodding. "You think you are ready to lead? Fine. Prove it. Handle this before it becomes a problem I have to fix. I have a feeling you won't like *my* solution."

With one last scowl tossed in Cora's direction, he turns and leaves.

27

CORA

That could not have gone worse.

As soon as the front door slams closed, Anya blows out a breath. Ivan doesn't move. He stares in the direction his father left like he expects him to return and wreak more havoc. Like the villain in a slasher movie coming back to life after you're certain he's dead.

I look over to Anya, but she won't meet my eyes.

I lied to her. I get it. But someone needs to break this silence, to clear the air.

I guess that someone is me.

I step forward. "Thank you, Ivan, for…" I swallow. "I'm sorry that didn't go well, but thank you for defending me. I'm sure he'll come around and—"

"Anya." His voice is icy rage as he looks over my shoulder at his sister. "Take Cora upstairs."

Anya stands up. "I have to go and—"

His breath comes out in a low growl that silences whatever was going to be Anya's excuse. Then he turns and stomps out of the kitchen.

I cross my arms over my chest, wishing I could sink into the floor beneath my feet.

Anya and I sit in silence for a second, both of us dumbfounded as to how to move forward.

A few minutes ago, Anya had her arm wrapped around mine and the same wide, dimpled smile I've seen on her brother's face only twice. Now, her mouth is a thin slash as she tips her head to the left. "Let's go."

"Anya, I'm sorry about—"

"It's fine," she snaps. She ascends the stairs. I trail behind her until we get to my room, where she sits on the tufted bench at the foot of the bed.

I close the door and lean against the dresser, too nervous to sit down. "It doesn't feel fine. I don't feel fine about it. I don't like lying."

"You sure did a convincing job."

I sigh. "Today was a lot. I was just doing what I thought I—"

"I know." Anya sighs and waves a hand through the air. "I'm being a bitch. You didn't have any more choice than the rest of us do. I understand. I guess I'm just… Usually, I'm the person who is in on Ivan's plans. I'm the one he tells—well, not everything, but he tells me a lot. Usually."

Ivan being close to his sister… I never would have imagined it, but I can see it now. Anya is light and warm in the same way Ivan seems to stay shrouded in darkness and mystery. They balance each other out. Two sides of the same coin.

"I'm sure he would have told you the truth," I offer. "This all happened so fast. I mean, eighteen hours ago, I didn't know your brother existed. Now, we're married. Fake married. Actually, fake engaged. I doubt there will even be a wedding."

Anya huffs out a laugh. "I see you all have really planned this out."

"Hardly," I mumble. "We've barely even spoken. Everything I told you downstairs was true, though. About how we met. That all happened just last night. The only thing that was a lie was the marriage part."

She gives me a tight smile. "Thanks for your honesty."

I toe at the plush carpet. "You can go if you want. Ivan told you to take me upstairs and…" I gesture around. "I'm upstairs. You don't have to stay."

She arches a brow. "I'm not a servant, either. I don't follow my brother's commands."

My mouth opens and closes uselessly. "Right. You just said… It seemed like you wanted to leave, but he asked you to bring me here. You said you don't have a choice, so I thought you'd want to—"

"I'm being a bitch again." She sighs and rearranges her hair. "Everyone does what my brother commands. It comes with the territory of being Bratva."

Bratva. Hell if I know what it means, but it can't be good. Ivan shot a man in the head a matter of hours ago, for fuck's sake, and his family acts like this is any normal day for them. How deep does the rabbit hole go for the Pushkin family?

"Are you going to work for your brother one day then?"

"I already do."

"But I thought your dad was—"

"It's complicated." She shrugs. "He's stepping down and Ivan is taking over. But I'll still be the second-born daughter who married a disappointment. No birthright, no penis, and no rich, well-connected husband. I might as well be an STD on the family jewels for all the good I do."

I've got a million and one questions. *What does a Bratva do? What does Ivan do? What exactly is he 'taking over'? Does that mean he's—*

But just as the words come to my lips, Anya claps and stands. "Anyway, I'm just being a drag. Don't mind me. Ivan always says I throw a pity party better than anyone. That's all this is."

"Everyone has family drama. I get it. I know we aren't really going to be sisters-in-law, but you can still talk to me if you want. I'm sure Ivan will bring me an NDA or something similar soon enough. I'll be legally bound to keep your secrets."

"An NDA," she repeats with a soft chuckle. "How quaint."

That sends a shiver down my spine. Who are these people who seem to operate entirely outside of the law? These people with their guards and mansions and secrets and their implied threats swimming behind every single word?

"Your brother saved my life. He's saving my friends' lives. I owe him, is what I'm saying. You can trust me."

Anya tips her head to the side, sympathy written all over her face. Then she grabs her purse from the end of the bed and walks towards the door, stopping for only a second to lay a hand on my shoulder. "First rule of surviving in our world, Cora: don't trust anyone."

Before I can say anything else, Anya closes the door behind her.

28

CORA

My phone rings not long after Anya leaves. "Hi," Jorden says when I answer, her voice surprisingly sharp. "Do you have a second?"

I sit on the window seat and tuck my feet under me. "I have nothing but seconds."

"Has Ivan said anything to you?"

I chew on my cheek. "He's said a lot of things." *You're an empty vessel I can use as I please. As bait. As a wife. That's what makes you perfect for this, Cora.* "Like what in particular?"

"Like…I don't know," she mumbles. "Something about what is going on. You said everything is fine, but these two massive men are standing outside my apartment right now and I'm kinda freaking out."

I'm on my feet before she even finishes the sentence. My heart is in my throat, thundering away, making it impossible to breathe.

"Are you okay?" I choke out. "Who are they?"

Maybe I can yell for Ivan. He'll know what to do. He could get someone to her faster than the police could, surely.

"Guards, I guess."

I frown. "Guards?"

"Yeah, that's what Yasha said."

I close my eyes and try to calm the storm of panic in my chest. "You talked to Yasha?"

"He called me an hour ago and told me he was sending guards to watch my apartment."

I drop my face in my hands and blow out a long breath. "Okay. Lead with that next time. I thought you were about to be kidnapped."

"What? Is that a possibility? Is that why I have the guards?"

This Jorden is a much different version than the one I spoke to a few hours ago. Before, she was wrapped up in the charm of my whirlwind romance. Now, she sounds terrified.

"No. You're not going to be kidnapped. The way you said that just scared me."

"That makes two of us, Cora! What the fuck is going on?"

Which is precisely the title of this chapter of my memoir, for sure. ***What the Fuck Is Going On?: Why you shouldn't hook up with billionaires at an arranged marriage party. By Cora St. Clair.***

Wait, no—Cora Pushkin.

I shiver.

"What did Yasha tell you?"

"Nothing. Well, almost nothing. All he said is that I was going to have guards outside my apartment. But why? He wouldn't answer any of my questions. Obviously, something is going on that I don't know about."

I keep chewing on the inside of my cheek until the coppery taste of blood fills my mouth. "There's a lot going on that I don't know about, too," I say finally. "But Yasha is just trying to keep you safe. Marrying Ivan is… It's a risk. When word gets out, my friends could become targets."

There's a long pause before she speaks again. "And this has nothing to do with him being in a Bratva?"

For the second time in as many minutes, my heart lurches uncomfortably. "What?"

Ivan monitors these calls. Someone is going to overhear Jorden making accusations. She'll become a target—a "loose end," as Ivan's dad said. Will they cut her?

"I don't know. I've been looking online ever since the guards showed up and there are some weird stories out there about Ivan. Like that he is some kind of crime boss or something. It's all rumors, but it's starting to feel possible."

Rumors available to anyone with a Google search bar. They can't kill her for that, right? Surely not.

"You know what kind of shit is on the internet these days. Conspiracy theories and what not. This is probably just more of—"

"So you haven't heard anything weird since you've been there?" she interrupts. "You just met him last night, Cora. Maybe it isn't safe that you're staying with him."

"It's safe here. I promise. Ivan is protecting me."

I hope.

Jorden hums nervously. "I want to be happy for you. I *am* happy for you. But I also love you, girl, so I want to make sure you're going to be okay and I have a weird feeling about all of this."

Tears fill my eyes. "I know. I love you, too. All I want is for you to be safe. That's why you have guards there. It's all because I panicked and wanted to make sure our engagement wouldn't put you in any danger. You know, since you were at the party with me last night, and then everything that happened at the diner this morning…"

It's also why I'm lying now: because telling her the truth isn't safe. Yasha and Ivan and Anya have made it clear that the less people know about what is going on here, the safer they are.

Ignorance is bliss.

"That doesn't make any sense. Why would anyone care that you're getting married to Ivan Pushkin?" she asks. "I'm starting to wonder if the shooting this morning was actually a random drive-by. Has he said anything to you about it? Are we sure it wasn't someone he is in, like, a turf war with or something? I just don't want—"

My phone buzzes. I pull it away from my ear to see that Francia is FaceTiming me.

I'm not sure a call from Francia is really the saving grace I wish it was, but right now, it's all I've got to escape Jorden's incredibly accurate line of questioning.

"Hey, Francia is calling me. I have to go, but I'll call you back," I say, interrupting Jorden mid-speech. "Bye!"

She's still talking when I end our call. Then I take a deep breath, paste on a smile, and answer Francia.

29

CORA

"Hi, Franny."

The screen is black for a second longer before Francia appears. She's holding the phone out in front of her, but as the call connects, she leans it against something on the table in front of her and sits back. "Can you talk?"

"Yeah. I was just—" *Dodging Jorden's questions and lying to our mutual friend.* "I'm free. What's up?"

"I talked to Jorden."

"When?" I ask. "I was just talking to her."

Are the two of them talking and putting the pieces together? Maybe I should find a way to tell them the truth if it will mean they stop looking for answers.

"A few hours ago. She told me what you told her. About the wedding. It would have been nice if you'd mentioned it to me."

"I was going to tell you, Francia. I was. I just didn't want to do it over text. It's all happening so fast and I needed a second to process it. I'm sorry."

"No, it's okay." She sags slightly. "I was freaking out earlier."

"Probably because strangers were telling you you weren't safe in your own apartment."

She chuckles humorlessly. "That might have been part of it, yeah."

"Are you okay now, though?" I ask. "I haven't completely ruined your life, have I?"

"You haven't ruined anything. This is not—" She frowns and leans towards her phone. "Where are you?"

"I'm in my room."

"That's not your room." Francia shakes her head. "Turn the camera around. Give me a tour."

I stay seated and quickly circle my phone around the room, too fast for her to really process. "It's just a room. A nice room."

"A really nice room," Francia corrects. "When is the wedding going to be?"

"I have no idea. We haven't really talked about it."

We haven't talked about anything. I've barely even seen my husband-to-be since we got here.

"I'm sure it will be soon. Ivan was looking for a wife, which means he's ready to get married. Now that he's chosen you, what's the point in waiting? This kind of thing usually leads to a short engagement."

"'This kind of thing'?" I ask. "You make it sound like this happens a lot."

"It isn't so unusual for people in his tax bracket. It *is* unusual for someone like Ivan," she says softly. "He's the type who can marry whoever he wants. But I guess it took a special kind of woman to make him settle down."

My face flushes. Not because Francia is right—but because some part of me wishes she was.

I wish I could be the kind of woman that would turn Ivan's head. The kind that might make him think twice about settling down.

But this is all fake. I'm no one. All of this is nothing.

"How do you know Ivan, Francia?"

"I don't know him."

"Well, you were invited to his party," I remind her. "How did you get on the guest list?"

"Oh…" She waves a hand dismissively. "That's just one of those weird things. My family knows his family going way back. We still get Christmas cards from the Pushkins. I'm sure they invited everyone they know who had daughters."

What I want to ask is: *Do you know what a Bratva is? Is your family part of a crime syndicate? Have you ever seen a man die right in front of your eyes?*

Instead, I ask, "How does your family know the Pushkins?"

"My parents have this, like, boutique firm and Boris Pushkin hired them years and years ago to represent him. He won his case and they stayed friends. More like acquaintances, really."

"Your parents are attorneys?" I can practically feel the back of my neck tingle thinking about Ivan's guards listening in on this conversation. Every detail feels like something they can use against my friends, some tally they can make as yet another reason to dispose of them.

"My dad is. My mom is a legal assistant. I am, too, actually," she says. Then she tips her head to the side. "Technically."

"Wait—you could work at a law firm, but you're a waitress at Quintaño's?" As soon as the question is out of my mouth, I try to back track. "I mean, It's a good job. I love it. I am just surprised. Don't your parents need you at the firm?"

She shakes her head. "Not really. My position is in flux. If I was anyone else, they'd probably fire me. Since I'm their daughter, they keep me on retainer and pay me a reduced rate. It's enough to live comfortably and the tips from waitressing are a bonus."

"Oh. Well, that's nice."

"It has its moments," she admits. "But they have a lot of… expectations of me. I'm not quite ready to meet them all yet. When I am, I won't have time to pick up odd jobs and meet new people."

All the hours I've spent working with Francia and even meeting up for drinks after work or at her apartment, I never realized how much we have in common. Or how much we *could* have in common.

I know what it's like to be in the shadow of your family with no way out.

"I can't believe we've never talked about any of this before," I say.

It's not that I haven't asked. It's that she has this amazing ability to wriggle out of any line of questioning.

She fidgets with the edge of the table. "Yeah, well, there isn't a lot of time to talk when you're waiting on a full dining room for five-percent tips."

I groan. "Don't even remind me."

"Why not? It's not like you're going back to waitressing anytime soon."

"Oh—Er, I guess not."

"You guess not?" she asks.

I chew on my cheek before I remember I'm on video and slap on a smile. "Probably not. I just hadn't thought about it yet."

They are going to hate me when I waltz back into work in a few days and tell them this whole thing was a ruse. If I can even tell them that. To explain what Ivan and I are doing… It would reveal a lot about who he is, who his family is.

Maybe I'll never be able to tell them the truth.

"Hmm. Well, if you're as bored as I am, you probably have nothing but time to think."

I wince. "I'm sorry."

"It's not your fault," she says quickly. "I just don't have a big, strong man to keep me company in here the way you do. I'm actually looking forward to going back to work."

I don't have a big, strong man to keep me company, either. So far, it seems like Ivan is doing his best to avoid me as much as I've been avoiding him.

"I'll live vicariously through you two. What have you been doing? Do you have any plans?"

I want to make something up, but I can't. Because I want it too much. A safe place, someone to love me, a world away from the running and scraping by I've been doing. I've seen enough to know Ivan Pushkin isn't the knight in shining armor girl's dream about, but for a broken girl like me, he feels awfully close.

My throat is closing up. Francia is staring at me expectantly, waiting for me to answer what should be a simple question, but I can't find a single word.

Then there's a knock on my door.

My salvation.

"Oh, sorry, Fran—someone is at the door."

"I'll let you go, then." She waves. "Talk to you soon."

I close out of the call. It feels like stepping off stage. The lights are off of me, the curtains are closed. The performance is over and I can breathe again.

The lies are for their own safety, I tell myself. *I'm doing everyone a favor.*

"Just a second," I call out. I straighten my shirt and pinch my cheeks, trying to force some color back into my face. I feel exhausted and frail, but I don't want to look like it, too.

Someone knocks on the door again. Harder this time.

I have a feeling I know who it is.

30

CORA

Ivan is leaning against the door frame, his arms crossed. "A wife should never make her husband wait."

He's wearing short sleeves. For the first time, I can see his arms. The black tattoos that peek out of the collar of his shirt and snake up and down his muscled biceps and thick forearms.

I suppress a shiver and turn to saunter back across my room as if I could care less that he's standing in my doorway.

"I knew we were pretending to be engaged. I didn't know we were pretending to live in the Dark Ages."

He chuckles. "What happened to the woman who was thanking me profusely in the kitchen only a few hours ago? I saved you from my big, bad father, if you recall."

"Your father didn't seem so big and bad to me." I sit on the bench at the end of my bed. Sitting on a bed with him in the room feels like opening the door to a very bad idea.

"Tell me how you feel if you're ever in a room alone with him. You might change your mind."

He closes the door behind him and faces me.

If it's even half as scary as being in a room alone with his son, then no thank you. Every nerve in my body is on high alert.

I thought this mansion would be more than big enough for the two of us. Now, I'm not sure there is such a thing. This *planet* might not be big enough.

"He seemed like an asshole."

Ivan laughs humorlessly. "That's because he is. A dangerous asshole, though. One you should avoid when you can."

"Are you worried he doesn't approve of your fiancée? I guess he was hoping for a Fortune 500 heiress or the princess in line for some foreign throne. Sorry I'm 'just a waitress.'"

"I don't give a fuck about his approval. It's my time now. His reign is over."

I shudder at the thought of King Ivan on the throne. Crown on his head, all hail, all peasants bow before him.

He's a nightmare now. What will he be like when the coronation comes?

"Well, I guess it doesn't matter what he thinks of me much anyway." I shrug.

"What makes you think that?"

"I'll be gone in a few days." Ivan stares at me. I squirm under his gaze. "What?"

"This isn't going to be resolved in 'a few days,' Cora."

"But..." I lick my lips and twist towards him. "But I have to get back to work soon. I have a life."

"A life you won't have if you stroll back into that restaurant like you weren't shot at this morning." He gestures to the room. "You're safe here."

My voice shakes as I respond. "I know I'm safe here. And I appreciate that, I really do. You've gone above and beyond to make me comfortable. That doesn't mean I want to live here. I can't just quit my job."

"Yes, you can. The restaurant is blown to bits anyway. They'll close for repairs."

"Okay, but that—That doesn't mean—I still need—" The half-formed sentences stick in my throat. I can feel pressure building in me. My grip on control slips as the well-decorated walls of my cage close in. "You can't lock me up in here."

Ivan goes deathly still and his voice drops an octave into a raspy rumble. "Need I remind you that you agreed to our deal?"

"To save my friends," I point out. "It was under duress. You threatened me."

His amber eyes turn molten. "If you're waiting for me to apologize for refusing to let you go back to your apartment and get yourself killed, don't hold your breath."

He stalks closer. I resist the urge to shrink away.

I ran before. I ran away from my stepfather, from the life he thought he could chain me into—and yet here I am, back in the lion's den.

Clearly, running isn't an option.

If I want freedom, I have to fight.

He's close enough for his breath to whisper over my heated face. "I've done you nothing but favors, Cora. Since the moment we met. I could have left you naked and alone in my office," he growls. "I could have let fucking Stefanos Genakos have his way with you. He would have, too. No one else at that party would have done a thing to stop it."

"If that's how you feel, then God help your real wife someday. How will she be useful to you?"

He arches a dark brow. "Careful, Cora—or I may start to think you're jealous."

I laugh a bit too suddenly for it to sound real. "Why on earth would I be jealous?"

He walks around me, forcing me to spin like a top to keep him in my line of sight. "Maybe my father wasn't so far off. Maybe, when all is said and done, you'll be sad to leave the comforts I've provided."

I gasp. "I'm not some gold-digger! I work for my own money and I make my own way in life. I don't need a husband. I don't need you or anyone else taking care of me."

His head tilts to one side, assessing me. "Good. Because I won't be your husband. This deal isn't the two of us playing House. I'm going to put up with you as long as I have to until I figure out who is coming after my family. Then you'll be gone and we'll both be free."

"I won't stay here if you think you get to control my entire life. I'm not your little whore."

He's in front of me before I even realized he moved. His chest is pressed to mine, and he's looking down his nose at me, rage rolling off of him in hot, violent waves. "You agreed to the job and you'll do it. You'll do it if I have to drag you back here screaming every day. You'll do it if I have to cuff you to my side every second of every hour. You'll do it if it hurts, if it feels good, if you love it, if you hate it—I don't give a damn, Cora. No matter what happens, you are going to *do as I say*."

My hands tremble at my side. I clench them into fists so he doesn't see them shaking.

"I am your boss, your judge, jury, and executioner," he snarls. "I am the sun around which your world revolves. Do you understand?"

At the party, I caught glimpses of a man I recognized. Someone who was forced to play a role against his will. Someone who had to bow to the whims and wishes of his family and forfeit his own desires.

That man is gone. Or maybe he never existed.

Maybe, like me, Ivan was wearing a mask the night we met. And maybe the monster beneath is worse than anything I could've imagined.

But if he thinks that means I'll submit to him, he's very fucking wrong.

"What are you going to do?" I spit. "Kill me?"

Without even a second of hesitation, Ivan leans in. I feel his hot breath on my face. "It wouldn't be the first time."

Before I can find the words, he storms out of my room and slams the door closed.

31

IVAN

Breathe. I need to breathe.

Or else I'm going to fucking explode.

My chest is tight. Rage crawls up my throat and tenses across my shoulders. Worst of all, my cock is achingly, infuriatingly hard.

"Fuck."

Cora St. Clair is a nuisance. Her arguing gets in the way of me doing what needs to be done to save her damned life.

It also makes me want her far more than I ought to.

She was right—the women who usually want me don't have a thought in their pretty heads. They are lifeless dolls who have been born and bred to obey. They don't cause a scene or stir up trouble. The only dream they have for themselves is to marry rich and live easy.

But Cora is fire and sass. She fights back. I want to stoke the heat inside of her, not douse the flames.

Unfortunately, I don't have a choice. Because I don't need a queen.

I need a pawn.

"That went really well," I hear from behind me. I turn and see Yasha coming up the back stairwell. "You two are the picture of wedded bliss. The definition of holy matrimony."

I frown. "What are you talking about?" I would've noticed if he was anywhere within listening range.

He hitches a thumb towards her door. "Quite the spat you two just had. You had to pull out the gravelly *pakhan* voice on her. Very nicely done, by the way."

I frown at him, a question in my eyes. Finally, he taps his ear. "I did what you asked and had a mic placed in her room. I was in the control room listening to her conversation with Francia when you knocked."

"I didn't ask for you to put fucking spyware in her bedroom. We have security cameras and her phone is tapped. The mic in her room is redundant. I want it removed."

Yasha nods without hesitation. "I'll have them disabled immediately." He strokes his chin. "What will we do for entertainment, though? The two of you were like a reality TV show. Very tense stuff."

I swipe out at him before he sees me coming. He yelps as my fist thwacks into his shoulder. "She's not here for your entertainment. She's here to do a job."

"One she'd clearly rather be executed than do." He straightens, keeping his arms in front of him as a shield. "Who knew being married to you was such a chore?"

I glare at him. "It's just because she doesn't understand the threat she's under. If she knew how dangerous it could be, she'd be happy to be here."

At least, that's what I tell myself. Because I refuse to think for even a second that I'm actually imprisoning her.

That's my father's prerogative, not mine. I don't want an unwilling bride, no matter how temporary. Which reminds me…

"I want her on the payroll," I order.

Yasha stares back. "Have you talked to Don Pushkin about this?"

I hear my father's voice echoing in the dark recesses of my mind. *You love putting women on my payroll who do absolutely nothing to benefit the Bratva.*

"No."

He won't like it, but I don't care. I'm not going to give Cora any room to make herself out as a prisoner here. Not when I'm saving her life.

Yasha runs a hand over the back of his neck. "Well, if you want my opinion—"

"I don't."

In typical Yasha fashion, he carries on anyway. "Cora is independent, but she also wants to feel needed. She won't do well if she feels like some porcelain doll on the shelf. You should give her some tasks and responsibilities, things she'll excel at. Let her prove to herself and to you that she can be useful. It will help her to take ownership of her role here."

I draw back, blinking at my second. "Why do you think you know more about my fiancée than I do?"

"She's your *fake* fiancée. Getting to know her will help sell the story, right?" Yasha tiptoes around me. "The more comfortable she is around you and me, the better the optics."

I want Cora to be comfortable here.

With me.

I want her to find a place here.

With me.

It's just because she's my "wife," though. I feel possessive of her because it's part of the act. That's all this is.

Yasha leans in, eyes wary. "Are we cool?"

I run my tongue over my teeth. "We're cool."

"Okay," he sighs. "Great. For a second, I thought—"

"So long as you do what you're asked and leave matters involving *my wife* to me, then we're fucking dandy."

Before Yasha can come up with some smartass thing to say that I'll have to kill him for, I turn into my room and close the door in his face.

32

CORA

I'm not sure what I'm hoping for as I press the phone to my ear.

Comfort, maybe. Normalcy. Some sign that the world beyond this estate is still spinning. Because right now, my universe has stopped.

"I am your boss, judge, jury, and executioner. I am the sun around which your world revolves. Do you understand?"

There's no mistaking it for what it was: a threat. But a threat shouldn't make my thighs quiver. It shouldn't force me to press my legs together and fight off memories of when that power was thrusting into me.

I squeeze the phone tighter with every ring.

"Please pick up," I beg. "Please pick up."

I'm desperate for any connection to society outside of this mess. So desperate my standards have hit rock bottom and kept going south.

Cognac Villain

After too many rings, the voicemail picks up.

"This is Shondra, Mr. St. Clair's assistant. He is out of the office this week, but I'll be monitoring his messages. If it's urgent, please leave your name and number. Mr. St. Clair will get back to you as soon as he can. Thank you."

Does being held against my will by a man who may or may not be a criminal so I don't get killed by an unknown assassin qualify as "urgent"?

I hang up before the beep. I haven't spoken to my father in years. I'm not going to let the first time be a voicemail. A voicemail that will probably be transcribed by Shondra.

In some ways, this is a sign that the world is still turning: my father remains a disappointment.

Jorden and Francia are in enough danger as it is. There's so much I can't tell them, but they have so many questions. Rightfully so. I don't even blame them.

I just can't answer them, either.

With every blink, I see Ivan's scowling face in my mind's eye. I hear the hiss of his voice as he tells me I'm no one. As he reminds me that I'll be kicked to the curb the moment he's done with me.

I know this isn't like the last time. This isn't like Mikhail—my stepfather's big plan for how my future would end.

Still, the resemblance between now and then is uncanny. So uncanny I'm having a hard time not throwing myself from the window as a means of escape. Running is an instinct, and I've honed mine to precision over the years. Sitting still is torture.

I throw my phone on the bed and pace to throw open the window. Partially for the fresh air and partially to remind myself that I'm twenty-five feet off the ground and I'd break my neck if I jumped.

"How did I get here again?" I mutter to nobody in particular.

I've never spent much time thinking about destiny, but now that I'm trapped in yet another loveless engagement—real or not—I have to wonder whether this isn't just my fate. To end up forcibly married to someone who couldn't care less about me.

There's a bang on the other side of the wall. I turn towards what I know is Ivan's room.

He's so close. I could call out to him and he'd be here in a second. I could talk to him and say…

Well, I don't know what. I'm not sure if I want to scream at him or apologize. It's not that I think I was wrong, but I want this situation to be tolerable, if nothing else. For both of us.

I press the heels of my hands into my eyes and grit my teeth. "That's giving up. It's giving him what he wants."

But maybe it's what I want, too. Ivan's dad wasn't entirely wrong, after all. With some concessions, I could make this arrangement work for me. A mansion, around-the-clock protection, and gourmet meals whenever I want? If that's prison, then I know a lot of people who would love to sign up.

My conversation with Jorden from what feels like a lifetime ago resurfaces.

Sorry, babe. But I've been working as long as I can remember. Well before it was legal. If a man with fat pockets wants to take me away from all of this gum scraping, then I'll let him.

You want to be dependent on a man?

If it means I can finally breathe, then yeah.

I get that. I really do. But there has to be more to life than just the absence of struggle. There has to be hope for something beyond not-terrible-*all*-the-time.

And I just need to know I'm not alone here.

I don't need Ivan to love me; I'm not that delusional. I'm aware that this isn't a real marriage. It isn't even a real relationship. But still, I need to know I'm more than just the burden that cruel fate or terrible luck stuck him with.

Again, I see the simmering rage in his gaze, the curl of his sneering lip as he glared down at me.

Maybe a burden is exactly what I am.

Before I can think about what I'm doing, I grab my phone off the bed and tap in a familiar number. Unlike Dad, Mom answers on the second ring.

"This is Evaline."

I could hang up. I'm calling from a new phone. She'll never know who it was. She'll probably just assume it was a spam call or a wrong number.

But her voice is a lifeline floating in the water and I'm slipping below the surface. On sheer dumb instinct, I lunge for it.

"Hi, Mom."

She inhales sharply. "Cordelia? Is that you? Are you alright?"

I sigh. It's the first time I've called her since I left. I should have expected she'd suspect something is wrong.

To be fair, something *is* wrong.

"I'm fine," I tell her. "I just wanted to see how you're doing. Check if you're okay."

It's more than she's done for me. At one time in my life, she was my everything. It was the two of us against the world.

"You and me, me and you," she used to whisper over whatever dinner we managed to scrabble together.

I believed her wholeheartedly. She was my mom. Why wouldn't I?

Then someone better came along and I became an afterthought.

"Who is it?" a muffled voice in the background asks.

It's the same voice I overheard at Ivan's party. The same cruel voice that still plays in my nightmares from time to time. Alexander McAllister.

My stepfather.

"Don't tell him," I beg her in a desperate whisper. "Lie."

"Evaline, who is it?" he asks again.

I can hear her hesitation. She's probably chewing her lower lip and glancing over her shoulder at him. I get my inability to lie from my mother. My father was always remarkably good at it. You don't start a secret second family without a few gnarly lies up your sleeve.

"Mom," I rasp.

Still, she says nothing. But with that, she has said more than enough.

I hang up the phone and blink back the tears burning in my eyes.

My mother chose my stepfather over me years ago. When we moved into his mansion and she let him auction me off to the highest bidder, to Mikhail—that was her choosing him. I don't know why I expected anything different today.

My own parents don't love me. Why do I think anyone else should? Maybe a loveless marriage built on mutual convenience is the best I can hope for. If I was smart, I'd get on my knees and beg Ivan to make this official.

He at least seems to despise this world of masks and false facades as much as I do. It might be that the only thing that exists between a lifetime spent alone and a loveless marriage is a business arrangement.

I guess the devil next door knows he's going to get what he wants.

33

CORA

I awake from dreams I don't remember with a sticky, pulsing ache between my legs.

Ivan Pushkin is a hard man to escape.

Even in my subconscious.

I slide out of the sheets and pull the comforter over the evidence of my shame. Niles is probably far too decent to say anything, but I know he'll notice that the bedding smells like sweat and God only knows what else.

Shower. That's what I can control right now. I need a shower.

I pad into the bathroom and my plans change immediately when I remember the tub my en suite is outfitted with. It's big enough for two people. Even me and someone as big as Iv—nope. No. No. *No.* I won't let him ruin this for me.

While I don't appreciate being trapped here—correction: while *conscious* me doesn't appreciate being trapped here, although Dream Me seems to disagree—I have no intention of turning my nose up at the amenities. I spent too many months living on the street without so much as a toilet. I know the joy of a hot bath.

Steam swirls from the faucet as the tub fills with scalding water. All the better to burn away the remnants of last night and the last few days.

I vow not to think about where Ivan's hands gripped me two nights ago at the party as I slip out of my borrowed clothes and kick them into the corner of the bathroom.

I'm so focused on not thinking about him that I'm also not thinking about the unlocked door that connects our rooms. I'm certainly not thinking about the fact that the bathroom door is wide open.

So when I hear a latch click and release, I spin around just as Ivan walks through that door and looks through the bathroom doorway.

At me.

At *all* of me.

He slides his gaze down and back up, then one more time for good measure. "I'm having déjà vu," he rumbles at last. His voice is raspy and low.

I should find something to cover myself with. Slamming the bathroom door closed would also be a normal response to a man standing in front of you while you're naked.

But Ivan isn't just standing in front of me.

He's standing in front of me *shirtless*.

If I thought his bare arms were a temptation, the full expanse of his chest is a full-on seduction. The tattoos that swirl across his biceps and creep out of the collar of his shirts also delve down, down, down.

I'm seconds away from actually walking towards him to try and step through it, when he clears his throat.

"See something you like, *moya zhena?*"

His deep velvet voice snaps me out of my thoughts. I jerk back and do a pitiful job of trying to cover up my more delicate bits.

"I could ask you the same question. You're the one who keeps barging in on me while I'm naked."

His eyes trail down my body again, dripping over my skin like honey. "I made it abundantly clear the night we met that I liked what I saw just fine. As did you."

My face flushes. I cross my arms over my chest to hide the evidence of exactly how much I like what I see. "What do you want, Ivan?"

Delicious amusement curls in the corner of his mouth. "I think I've made that abundantly clear, too."

"Do you have something to tell me?"

"You need to get ready."

"That's what I was doing before you barged in here. *Without knocking*, might I add."

"What were you getting ready for, looking like that?" He drops his chin, his amber eyes looking up at me through lashes far too pretty for a man so brutal. "I had my own plans for how to legitimize our marriage. But if you want to get a head start on the consummation… well, your adoring husband would never deny you something like that."

His words ooze sarcasm, but I burn up with them anyway. My body is on fire from the inside out, and I'm sure he can see it written in the blush coloring every inch of my skin.

"You and I have very different priorities."

He nods in agreement. "My priority is to keep you alive; yours is to make your own life as difficult as possible."

He isn't wrong. I could have stayed home the night of the party.

I could have left after Ivan offered me his jacket.

I could have told him who I really was and *not* begged him to fuck me until I scream.

Again and again, my choices make my life more complicated.

But Ivan isn't helping, either.

"You can't just walk into my room. We may be pretending to be a couple, but we aren't. I'm a guest in your house, according to you."

He strolls closer and leans against the bathroom door. "I say if we're playing the part, we might as well get the perks."

I gasp in disgust and snatch a towel from the cabinet behind me. I wrap it around myself and my "perks."

"I say we need ground rules," I fire back.

"Okay, ground rule: you do as I say, and I keep you and your friends alive."

I clench my teeth. "That's the deal we made, but we need to set expectations for how we treat each other. If I have to stay here—"

"Which you do."

I bristle but I don't let him throw me off-course. "*If* I have to stay here, then I need to know what to expect."

I need to be able to prepare, on some level, for encounters with him. I need to know what's expected of me when we're in public—and, more importantly, what's expected in private.

Living in this gray space of desire and disdain is not an option. I'll burn to ashes.

Ivan continues to stare, waiting.

I blow out a breath. "First, I want privacy in my room. You can't come in here whenever you want."

"Our rooms are connected."

"Then unconnect them," I snap back. "You control everything and everyone, right? Lock the door."

His jaw shifts back and forth. "No need for a lock. I can control myself if you can."

What if I can't? I stiffen my spine and nod. "I can, too."

He adjusts his arms. The muscles flex and shift beneath his smooth skin. I chew on my lip as a lightness fills my chest. *Connected door or no... I don't stand a chance.*

Ivan arches a brow. "Is that all, or do you have more—"

"No sex," I blurt.

His mouth snaps shut, his amber eyes narrowing. "I thought you could control yourself?"

"This is a business arrangement, right? That's what you called it."

"I'm aware of what I called it," he growls.

"Okay. So do you regularly have sex with business associates? I'm guessing not. So I'll do what needs to be done when we're in public to sell the story. But behind closed doors, no sex."

"Fine," he barks. "I agree to your terms so long as you hold up your end of the bargain. You have to sell the story, Cora. When I need a smitten wife at my side, you need to be there."

"Fine."

"Then be ready in an hour," he says.

I tighten my towel around my chest. "Where are we going?"

He half-turns on his way out and drawls, "What kind of husband would I be if I didn't get my wife a ring?"

Then he strolls out of my room and into his, his back rippling with power and definition all the way. It's only when the door between our rooms snaps closed that I blink and break out of the trance.

I turn and drain the tub I just filled.

I need a cold shower instead.

34

IVAN

I look across a sea of glittering diamonds and gold and see my fiancée. That's what I called her when my family's long-time personal jeweler asked why I needed the last-minute appointment. The first person beyond the circle of my own family who knows.

"I wanted to let my fiancée hand-select her engagement ring," I told Kieran. "Whatever she wants, it's hers. No questions asked."

At those words, Kieran looked like he wanted to marry me. He's an incorrigible gossip, too, so I'm sure that the second we're gone, he'll take out a billboard saying that the new Pushkin bride is wearing his jewelry.

Which is why I chose him as one of our first stops.

Kieran immediately turned to Cora, peppering her with questions about size and preferences. She gave him a blank stare in return. Overwhelmed by all of this, no doubt.

"I'll leave you two to browse as I prepare some custom mockups I've been saving for a special occasion." He winked at me and disappeared into his office in the back.

Cora and I have been perusing the display cases ever since. We're circling each other in tense silence. Every time she tucks her dark hair behind her ear and twists her full lips in concentration, I get rigid.

I can't seem to decide what I hate more: being close to her or not being close enough.

God, the way she looked standing in that bathroom...

My office had been dark the night we'd met. She kept my suit jacket on, kept the curves and edges of her concealed under wool.

This morning outside of the tub, she was illuminated from every possible angle. I saw the soft swell of her breasts and the curve of her hip. I'll never scrub the image from my mind. Not that I'd want to. Especially after the way she looked back at me, her green eyes going dark with desire as they trailed over my tattoos.

We're alike in that way: I also love the allure of something I'm not supposed to have.

"This one," Cora says suddenly.

I snap my attention up. She's pointing to a case at the front of the store.

"Not good enough. Pick something further back."

She glares at me over the glass. "You haven't even seen it."

"I don't need to. It's directly in front of the doors. I'm not going to let you walk around with a cheap ring on your finger. You're mine. Act like it."

She mutters something that sounds an awful lot like "snob," but she walks deeper into the store—which brings her closer to me.

As she passes by the display case I'm standing next to, she points into it. "That one is nice."

I follow her finger and then scowl. "That's a plain band."

"An *expensive* plain band," she points out.

I check the four-digit price tag and snort. "Hardly."

"I don't care about jewelry. I never wear it. When I do, I don't want it getting in the way. I'd rather have something simple."

Niles did a good job with Cora's wardrobe. She's wearing a pair of high-waisted tweed trousers with a silk cami tucked in. She looks sleek and classy. She looks like she belongs here.

The trouble, it seems, will be teaching her to *act* like she belongs here.

Kieran chuckles as he walks back into the showroom. "In all my years as a jeweler, I've only heard one other woman say something like that. It was a couple years ago and—"

His eyes catch on Cora and widen.

She snaps her head back down, her hair falling between them like a shield.

"And anyway," Kieran pivots, trying and failing to make a seamless transition, "I have the mockups if you'd like to see them."

Cora mumbles a "yes" and we meet at the back display case. Kieran spreads digital renderings across the glass surface, never once meeting Cora's eyes.

I don't miss the spark of recognition.

They know each other.

She's been here before.

Yasha told me Cora's mother and stepfather are rich. She told me herself that he was at my party the other night. I'm sure she's been here with her mother, maybe getting a piece cleaned or having something resized.

And yet...some primal part of me chafes against the suggestion that she might've come here with another man. The beast in my chest growls.

"I have an array of options," Kieran begins. "If you're looking for something on the simple end of the spectrum, we have solitaire engagement rings. Though I would highly recommend an accompanying band after the ceremony. I can keep it understated, but a beautiful woman such as yourself should have a beautiful ring to match."

There will be no ceremony. This may very well be the only ring I ever buy Cora. I want it to count.

"That sounds nice," she starts.

But I swipe the renderings of the solitaire settings into a pile. "I want something bigger."

Cora leans in close. "What about what *I* want?"

I turn and grip her chin gently. "I want everyone within a ten-mile radius to know *you are mine.* Isn't that what you want, too?"

If she wants to keep her part of the bargain, there is only one answer she can give me.

Her throat bobs. "Yes."

I brush my thumb over her lower lip and release her. "Good girl." Then I tap the pile of papers. "Pick something else."

Kieran and Cora take over the conversation, discussing thousands of different options and customizations. There are no additional signs that they've had this same conversation before with another man standing at Cora's side. But the feeling that I'm filling another man's absence weighs heavily.

It shouldn't matter. It doesn't. Cora and I are not in a relationship. This is a business arrangement. We have ground rules and well-outlined roles and expectations.

But I can't stop imagining her wearing this ring. *Only* this ring. On her knees before me with her hand wrapped around my—

"That one," Cora says definitively. "I want that one."

The rendering is of a simple diamond setting in the center with a crown of diamonds around it, opening as if they're petals of a flower in bloom. The band is made of delicately molded gold leaves.

Kieran beams, telling me all I need to know about the price of it. "Impeccable choice. Any customizations?"

"No, I like it just the way—"

"I want the center diamond twice as big," I say.

Kieran and Cora both turn to me, one of them looking far more delighted than the other.

"That can be arranged," Kieran assures me greedily. "I'll need to make some adjustments to the surrounding stones, but it's nothing I can't handle. The extra size will increase the price, of course."

"I don't give a fuck."

I sign where he tells me to do, then put my hand on the small of Cora's back and escort her out to the waiting vehicle.

I silently hold the car door open for her. I don't say anything until I turn away from the direction of the estate. When she realizes we're headed a different way, she sits up. "Where are we going?"

I bite back a smirk. "We've got one more stop to make. You're going to love this one, I promise."

35

IVAN

From the outside, the shop looks like any other boutique on the street. *"Le Plaisir?"* Cora frowns at the gilded letters above the door. "We're shopping? I thought Niles bought me everything I'd need."

The thought of Niles walking into this shop is enough to tear a laugh from me. "There are some things that I prefer to handle myself."

I open the door and usher her inside. The bell above the door chimes our arrival, but Cora doesn't make it more than two steps in before she slams to a stop.

A long table runs down the center of the small space. Mannequins in barely-there lingerie perch on top of it. Underneath them, in lit shelves that ring the shop, are countless sex toys. Every shape, length, kink, color, and voltage imaginable.

I close the door behind me. Cora shrinks back into me, itching for escape. "We made rules, Ivan. We can't—"

"I said I'd keep my hands to myself. But if you're going to demand celibacy, you'll need something to take the edge off."

The idea came to me fully formed. I didn't question it. Partially because I want to prove to her now that there is no checkmate with me. I always win. *Always.*

But a deeper, darker part of me wants to see what Cora will do in a luxury sex shop. The part of me that has always craved a bit too much trouble wants to know what she'll be drawn to, what she likes.

I know how she looks and sounds when she comes on my cock.

What about when she's tied spread-eagle on a bed while I tease her with whips and vibrations and soft kisses between her thighs?

Her face quivers. She's too stubborn to show me what she's really thinking, but I can guess at the tensions rippling inside of her right now.

They probably look a lot like my own.

Finally, she turns away from me, looking out over the store. "What's my budget?"

I run my thumbs along the suddenly tense column of her neck. "Do your worst."

Cora leans back into my touch, rocking against the pressure of my fingertips into her muscles. Then, as if remembering who I am, she jerks away and heads for the nearest display.

A red-headed woman in a dangerously low-cut top appears from the back. She glances at Cora and then turns her attention to me, a wicked smile on her lips. "Hello. Is there anything I can help you with?"

"We're just looking," Cora calls over her shoulder. She's huddled over the shelves like she's worried the woman might see what she's buying.

"Of course. Take your time." The woman takes a step closer to me. "If you see anything you like, be sure to let me know. I'd love to personally assist you. My name is Madison."

The flick of her tongue over her red-painted mouth is hard to misconstrue.

She retreats toward the back. Cora watches her leave with a scowl on her face.

"See anything you like?" I ask. "The associate would love to *personally* assist you."

"Madison would love to personally assist *you*." She snorts. Cora thinks for a moment, then she waves down the saleswoman. "Excuse me, miss? We're going to need a basket over here. Maybe two. I have quite the shopping list to get through."

My wife-to-be gives me a wicked grin that has a powerful effect on everything below my belt.

Cora will never be able to one-up me.

But *fuck*, the woman fights dirty.

Dildos, vibrators, clitoral stimulators—you name it, Cora grabs it. If I hoped to narrow down her interests in the bedroom, I'm out of luck. Cora unceremoniously dumps her haul into the basket without a word and then goes back for more.

"Are you interested in any lingerie today?" Madison points to a lacy black set on a mannequin in the back corner. She speaks in Cora's direction, but keeps her eyes on me. "I have this set for myself and I can't recommend it highly enough. I've tested it *thoroughly* and it has stood up to whatever I've put it through."

I gesture to Cora. "Whatever she wants, she can have."

"How generous of you," the woman purrs. "Not all men are so understanding of a woman's needs."

I glance over and catch Cora staring daggers at the redhead. Then she snatches up three lingerie sets and practically hurls them at the saleswoman. "Do you have a dressing room?"

"Sorry, we don't. We've had too many incidents." She winks at us both. "Some people can't wait to get home. They find the allure of something new a little too exciting."

Cora's jaw practically grinds her teeth to dust, her tongue running over her teeth when she's able to relax enough. She's not missing any of Madison's clumsily obvious hints. "How am I supposed to know if these fit me then?"

Madison waves towards the back of the store. "There's a mirror in the back to hold things up to yourself, but we have a generous return policy. Sometimes..." She looks to me, eyebrow arching. "Sometimes, things don't work out and you need to exchange for something new. We understand that and we are happy to accommodate our customer's needs. No matter what they might be."

"Thanks," Cora bites out. She stomps off to the back of the store.

Madison steps closer to say something to me, but I breeze past her without a word and follow Cora.

The back room is a lounge with a leather sofa and a tall mirror in the corner. I can see the reflection of Cora leaning against the corner, her eyes closed. Her full lips are pursed in an exhale.

"You're not taking this seriously."

She stiffens at the sound of my voice. One eye opens narrowly. "*I'm* not taking this seriously? You're not exactly leaping to help. Or are you too distracted by Miss Obvious over there? Shall I give you two some privacy?"

"There it is again," I remark.

"There *what* is again?"

"Jealousy. It's an interesting look on you. Not as good as" —I glance at the pile in her arms— "sheer pink lingerie, but still interesting."

I can see her teetering on the edge of an explosion. The wise voice in me says to defuse the situation. What good can come of stoking her fire?

But the voice in me that said, *"Follow her into the office"*, the voice that started all this shit, now says, *"Light the match and watch it all burn."*

Do it, I'm daring her silently. *Flash that fire. Stake your claim. Be bold enough to say you want something that's right there for the taking.*

What I'm really asking my fiancée is, *What are you made out of?*

I already know the answer.

I just need *her* to see it for herself.

She chews on her cheek as she thinks. Finally, she shakes her head. "This is a sham of a marriage anyway. Why should I care if some woman flirts with you? Why should I care if you take her home and dress her up in lingerie, then take her right back out of it?"

Because I want *you to care.*

"Because you want your friends to be safe," I say instead. "Because you want to catch the person who tried to kill you yesterday. That won't happen if you don't play your part to perfection. This may be a sham to the two of us, but it's real to everyone else. We have to make them believe it."

"I don't know how." She presses a hand to her face. "I don't know how to do this, Ivan. I'm in so far over my head. Two days ago, I was a *waitress.* Now, I'm…I'm…"

I can't hold myself back anymore. Seeing her here, in this place, with that confused flush in her cheeks matching the flush on her collarbone…

I want her every bit as badly as I did the night we met.

I stride closer and pin her against the wall. *"Mine,"* I finish for her in a breathy growl. "You're fucking *mine.*"

Her pupils eat away the green of her irises. "What? I can't. We're not—"

I press my lips to the curve of her neck just below her ear. "It's all pretend, Cora. Settle back and enjoy the charade."

She shivers when I grip her hip. I let my fingers spread out across the swell of her body, claiming as much of her as I possibly can. I hike up her dress and shove those panties roughly aside, then brush my finger through her arousal. She's already slick for me, dripping.

I want her—no, I *need* her—to start embracing her position at my side and the power it brings. The best position is whichever one allows me to bury my dick inside her sweet body, but there's far more to it she hasn't even begun to tap into.

"You're mine," I remind her, rubbing my thumb over her clit. She sucks in another trembling breath and I feel her grind against my hand. She tries to do it subtly, but there's not a chance in hell I'm missing the way she's desperate for more. "Stop worrying about other women trying to steal what they can't have. Show them why it's you. Show them why you're mine…and why I'm yours."

When her eyes meet mine, glazed with lust and need, I plunge two fingers deep inside her.

She arches her back against the wall, pushing her into me even more. Fuck, how could I even begin to notice another woman when she's already so fucking perfect?

I whisper exactly that to her as I start to rub that sweet spot inside her. She shudders and clutches my arms as I nip her skin and continue to murmur all the reasons why she shouldn't take bullshit from anyone. Least of all some pathetic, thirsty sex store clerk.

Our bodies are pressed together, my erection hard against her thigh. Cora drags her leg against me and moans my name in a frazzled, strangled rasp. "Ivan…"

Suddenly, a voice breaks through the sexual haze. "How are things going back here? Do you two need any…" Madison's voice trails off as she enters the room and sees the two of us.

I have no intention of pulling my fingers out of Cora's slick heat, but she grips my wrist anyway. Her fingers are cold, but her gaze on the saleswoman is suddenly fiery. Whether the woman returns it or not, I have no idea. I'm too distracted by how Cora's glare looks even better with her flushed skin.

"We're fine," she says sweetly. "Thanks, anyway."

Madison clears her throat. "You can't do that here. You have to—"

"*You* have to sit down and shut up." Cora's voice is laced with irritation, but it's the rumble of her fury that makes me so fucking hard. She glares at Madison and, at the same time, rolls her hips to fuck herself on my hand. "And show me some fucking respect instead of eyeing my man like some dick-hungry slut. He's *mine*."

Holy fuck. If she's not careful, I might actually end up fucking her hard right here, right now.

I'm halfway convinced Cora wouldn't mind that at all.

The woman behind me practically chokes on her shock. "You can't—"

"My wife just told you what you're going to do," I growl. Cora clenches around me. "So sit the fuck down and shut the fuck up."

An amused smile curves my lips when Madison takes a trembling seat on the edge of the couch. Cora gasps and I don't know if it's because of the thrill that throwing authority gives—or if it's because I'm working my fingers inside her faster and massaging her clit more with my thumb.

She deserves this. She's a fucking queen waiting to be crowned. She just has to be willing to see it—and accept it.

Her nails dig into my wrist, begging me to keep going. "How did that feel?" I ask, nipping at her ear. "To show her who you belong to?" A whimper works between her bee-stung lips. She clings to me just to stop from crumbling to the floor.

"Good," she moans. "It felt… It feels so damn good."

Madison might still be sitting where I ordered her to or she may have run for the hills—I have no idea. Nothing exists beyond this woman and the way she feels in my hands.

I lose myself in her pleasure, driving her to the edge so I can greedily watch her spill.

"Ivan!" she grits out, her body clamping down on my fingers. "I'm—fuck…fuck…Ivan…" She tries to tell me, but I already know. And I bask in the way she shatters in my arms, her lashes fluttering as her toes curl and she bucks herself on my fingers, soaking them with her release.

She floats down, sighing and holding onto my neck for dear life. I keep her there, pinned between the wall and my hips.

The bride I never asked for.

The queen I never saw coming.

36

CORA

I sit on the edge of my bed and stare at the black bag in my closet. Scarlet tissue paper peeks out of the top, a scandalous hint of what's tucked away inside.

In the sex shop yesterday afternoon, I felt powerful. With Ivan's fingers stroking all the places where I ached for him, his entire focus on my pleasure, I realized all at once how intoxicating control can be. How a person can come to crave it.

Then we left the shop.

The orgasm faded and Ivan retreated behind the icy walls of his mask. The man who, just minutes before, had been whispering soft commands in my ear, urging me to come apart for him, turned into a mute stone pillar.

The silent treatment carried on the rest of the day and through the night.

Even still, I woke up from a dream sweaty and panting and shamefully wet. I threw my covers back and stared at the door connecting our rooms, willing it to open.

Needless to say, that didn't happen.

Now, I've moved on to staring at Plan B. The bag.

I drop my face into my hands and scrub at my tired eyes. "Pathetic. You are pathetic."

And horny. That shoe fits, too.

We're barely a full day into this celibacy arrangement and I've already creeped as close as physically possible to breaking the rule that *I* insisted on.

I don't think we fully broke it, though. Ivan got me off, but he left with a visible bulge in his pants. He was not satisfied. It's probably a technicality, but at this point, a win is a win.

I glance at the door again, wondering if he took care of himself last night. Maybe at the same time I was lying in bed thinking about him, he was holding himself and thinking about—

My face flames. I shake my head at my own thoughts. "Yep. Absolutely pathetic."

If Ivan is taking care of himself—or having someone else take care of him, though I absolutely *cannot* let myself think about that—then why shouldn't I work out my own tension? That's what these toys are for, right? Ivan wouldn't have bought me half that sex shop if he didn't want me to use it.

I stand up, edging towards the bag of sex toys like maybe I can sneak up on them. I won't have to admit I'm having dirty, sexy thoughts about my fake husband if the toys don't see me coming.

I snort at my accidental pun and take another step closer to the bag.

It's not breaking the rules if I only *think* about having sex with Ivan. I can ease the yearning in my core and make sure something like what happened in the back of that sex shop never happens again.

"This is what he wants," I whisper to the dark, needy side of myself. "He wants me to think about him." I blow out a breath and snatch the bag off the floor. "But there's no harm in trying them out."

I dig into the bag and grab the first thing I feel. Whatever it is, I'll carry it into the bathroom with me, burn off some of this energy, and be done with it. With Ivan.

But as soon as I pull a toy out of the bag, the door between our twin bedrooms bursts open.

I yelp and drop the bag, but I tighten my grip on the toy like I might be able to wield it as a weapon.

As Ivan stomps toward me in flagrant violation of one of the two rules I requested—*knock before you enter*—he opens his mouth to say something.

Then he sees what's in my hand. I glance at it, too, and wince.

I'm holding a rather long, quite girthy purple dildo.

"Sorry to interrupt you two," he drawls.

I hurl the toy back in the bag and face him, my arms crossed over my chest. "You aren't interrupting anything. I was just finding somewhere to put all this stuff."

His other brow joins the first. My body burns with the awareness of what I've just said.

"Not somewhere to put it, like—" I groan. "A drawer or something! So Niles doesn't see. What do you even want?"

He steps over the bag of toys and walks into my closet. "You need to get dressed."

I follow him, pausing in the doorway. Being in confined spaces with Ivan Pushkin is my undoing, apparently.

"Despite what you think, I have managed to get ready on my own every day of my life up to this point. I don't need you barging in here and—"

"We have an interview today." He throws a bright green dress at me and then spins around and digs through my top drawer. "It came up last minute."

"What kind of interview?"

"An engagement announcement." He turns around, a pale pink strapless bra dangling from his fingers. "Wear this and that," he says, pointing to the dress. "Nothing else."

He looks through my shoe options with authority. I would have assumed he'd be lost when it came to women's fashion, but he quickly dismisses a pair of chunky heels, a wedge, and a loafer in favor of a nude heel with a fabric tie around the ankle.

Much to my irritation, it will go perfectly with the dress.

"I don't need your help choosing an outfit." I edge around him and pull out the top drawer again, digging for the underwear that match the bra.

Ivan slams the drawer shut and leans against it. His biceps bulge against the sleeves of his black t-shirt. "I said 'nothing else.' Was that not clear?"

"I thought you meant I shouldn't wear a jacket or something."

"Obviously not. A jacket would look ridiculous with this dress." He pinches the ruffled chiffon sleeves. "I meant what I said. *Nothing else.*"

My eyes widen as the meaning sinks in. "What part of an engagement announcement requires me to go commando?"

"The part where I required it of you," he says coolly. "The car leaves in thirty minutes. Don't be late."

He swoops out of the room as quickly as he entered, but I swear his pants are fitting him tighter in the crotch area than they were when he first walked in.

The door closes and I look down at the clothes in my arms. The outfit Ivan chose for me, sans proper undergarments.

Maybe he wants to avoid panty lines for the photos, I think.

Then I hold the dress up and realize that won't be an issue. The dress has a fitted bodice, but the skirt and sleeves are light and airy. Layers of tulle and chiffon that flounce and dance as I swing the dress.

I hook on the bra and am tempted to grab the panties anyway. How would he know if I followed his orders or not? It's not as if he is going to check…right?

Ivan has told me he does nothing without a reason. Is it possible that the reason behind this outfit choice is simply that he likes it?

He plays cool. He plays aloof. He plays distant.

But maybe Ivan Pushkin is spending his nights the way I am: tossing and turning and wondering what's going on on the other side of the adjoining door.

I pull the dress on and delude myself into thinking that this is all part of some plan. If Ivan is more attracted to me, then it means he'll be a better fake husband. Knowing I'm not wearing anything under my dress will make him more… attentive to me. It's pure business. Pure strategy.

As strategic as the flirty, innocent dress he has me dolled up in. Between my hair twisted into a side braid and the silhouette of the dress, I look like I jumped straight out of the 1940s. It's oddly wholesome for the fiancée of the notorious Ivan Pushkin.

As far as anyone can see, I'm innocent and naive. The perfect target. What they don't know—what I'm finally starting to figure out—is that I'm in on the plan, too.

On my way out the door, I swipe on a bold red lipstick.

It fits how I'm beginning to feel.

37

CORA

This interview is a trainwreck.

The interviewer is a middle-aged woman in an ill-fitting pantsuit. "I love love," she informed us the moment she walked through the door. "You have no idea how fast I jumped at the opportunity to share your story. I'm so honored to be here."

Now, half an hour into what feels more like an interrogation than a fluff piece, she is sagged in her seat with a weary grimace on her face.

"Was there anything about the other person that stood out to you immediately?" she practically begs. "Anything at all?"

At first, I tried to let Ivan lead the interview. He's had more practice at this kind of thing than I have. Between the two of us, he is the charmer.

But thirty minutes into this torture, it is a race to respond before he can continue to kill what is already a thoroughly dead vibe.

"It's hard not to notice Ivan when you walk into a room." I press my palm against his bicep, and he goes rigid under my touch. "He rescued me from a pretty embarrassing wardrobe malfunction. My dress ripped, and he offered his jacket. Between the chivalry and his good looks, I was smitten."

Hope floods the woman's face. She sits up, leaning in. "Oh my goodness! What's the story there?"

"A drunken asshole tried to assault her," Ivan growls.

"How heroic of you, sweeping in to save her!"

"It's my duty to control guests at my own party. Once I saw what was going on, I didn't have a choice."

Oh yes, *duty*. The readers will swoon to hear about how it was Ivan's unwilling obligation to protect and then marry me. Truly the stuff of which romances are spun.

I paste a smile on my face. "And once we realized how much we had in common, we didn't have a choice but to get married."

It's not actually untrue. And yet Ivan somehow manages to look even less approachable. He scowls, his jaw flexing like he's trying to crack his own molars.

Is he doing this on purpose? Are we trying to blow this interview?

The interviewer looses a sigh and reaches for her camera bag. "Well, let's get a close-up of the ring, shall we?"

I don't know how much Ivan paid Kieran to overnight this custom job, but the exact ring from the mockup he showed me yesterday is now perched on my finger. Ivan unceremoniously tossed it to me in the car.

"Put this on," he grumbled.

Again—just a touch shy of a storybook proposal.

I had to bite back my shock at the sheer size of it. He might as well have put a diamond-encrusted softball on my finger.

"That is gorgeous!" She snaps a photo. "Can you hold hands?" she asks, nervously eyeing Ivan. "And move closer together. I'll take a shot with your hands in focus and your bodies blurred. I think it will look nice above the fold."

I inch closer until our thighs are pressed together. The heat of him burns through the thin fabric of my dress. Then he slides his hand under mine, his fingers curling around my knuckles.

It's the first time today I've seen his cold facade start to defrost.

As the woman lines the shot up, her face tucked behind the camera, his thumb strokes the side of my hand. I feel that touch everywhere from head to toe.

"Got it!" the woman says, springing up like she's fleeing a fire. "I think we're done here."

Ivan drops my hand like it stung him. I wrap my arms around myself to hide the shiver moving through me.

The woman pauses in the doorway. "It was lovely to meet you both. Good luck."

I wait until she leaves the room before I sag in my chair. "She wished us luck like we're going to war."

In a way, I suppose we are.

He stands up and checks his watch. "Let's go. I have things to do."

"Ivan," I breathe, "that was…not great."

"She took some notes; she snapped our photo. People are going to read it and now, they'll know we're together."

I chew on the corner of my lip. "Right…"

"What the fuck do you want?" he barks suddenly. "Should I have fingered you during the interview to prove to her that we're *in love?*" He spits out those words like they're poison.

What happened between us yesterday has existed within a bright, shiny bubble in my memory. Ivan has wasted no time in popping it.

"It would have been better than whatever surly, standoffish B.S. you just pulled! She probably saw right through the act and thinks I'm in a hostage situation."

His nostrils flare as he spins towards me. "No one was holding you hostage yesterday. You begged me to make you come."

"I didn't mean that. I just meant—"

"As long as people find out we're married, nothing else matters," he spits. "This is all a means to an end."

"Thanks for the reminder," I whisper under my breath. "For a second there, I almost forgot."

38

CORA

I'm on the back patio, twirling the diamond planet around and around my ring finger, when I hear the doors open.

I whip around hopefully. Then I'm forced to face the disappointment that floods me when I see it is Anya standing in the doorway rather than her brother.

I haven't seen Ivan once since we got back from the interview. When I saw Niles coming out of his office a couple hours ago, even he looked frightened by whatever he'd seen in there.

High Lord Ivan is in a foul mood, it would seem.

"Howdy." Anya sounds friendly enough, but I can see the wariness in her eyes as she approaches.

How am I supposed to behave around my pretend sister-in-law after lying to her about loving her brother? I settle for a stiff wave. "Good to see you again, Anya."

She stops in front of me and lifts her huge designer sunglasses up into her wavy hair. "Is it? Because you look miserable."

Whatever nonsense I was about to say falters.

"Easy." Anya eases into the chair across from me. "I know the truth, remember? You don't have to pretend to be happily in love in front of me. What has my brother done now?"

The last couple days rise up like bile in my throat. The need to tell someone—*anyone*—what is going on is almost overwhelming.

But I can't tell Anya about my dirty dreams or the sex shop or the way I can't decide if I want to smother her brother with a pillow or drag him beneath the sheets with me.

"Nothing. Everything is great. We're doing fine."

Anya arches her brow and doesn't say a word.

It doesn't take long before my paper-thin resolve gives way. I sag in defeat. "We had an engagement announcement interview this morning. I'll be shocked if the reporter doesn't also announce our imminent divorce at the end."

She winces. "That bad?"

"Worse. He barely spoke to me all morning, which is fine. I get it. It's not like we're really… I mean, this isn't real." I'm not sure if I'm reminding myself or Anya. "Ivan doesn't owe me anything. But it almost felt like he was sabotaging his own plan. All we had to do was hold hands and smile and tell a few pretty lies, but he hung me out to dry. I just don't know what I'm supposed to do with that."

Anya reclines back in her chair and slides her sunglasses back down on her nose. "Oh, my brother. He's a funny one."

"'Funny' is not the word I'd use to describe Ivan."

"Unique, then," Anya amends with a smirk. "He can be hard to pin down if you don't know him very well."

I'm not sure if she means it as a jab or not. Either way, she's right. I don't know Ivan very well. At all.

"Does that mean you can pin him down? Because I would love some tips. One minute, he's this smooth, effortless man who can charm the panties off of—" Anya gives me a look and I clear my throat. "He's charming, is what I'm trying to say. Then the next, he's a block of ice. When we had to hold hands for a photo op, I thought I was going to lose my fingers to frostbite."

Lies. Despite how terrible the interview had gone, heat had still pulsed through me.

That's the real trouble with Ivan. If anyone else treated me like he does, I'd run as fast and as far as possible in the other direction. But even when he tries to push me away, my body draws closer.

"I guess..." I take a deep breath. "So much of what we're doing is pretend. So I guess I just don't know which side of him is real."

"They both are."

I frown. "I don't see how that's possible."

"He has a lot on his plate. He's responsible for everything." Anya sits up and folds her hands in her lap. "Part of it is my fault. Things were different before I got married. Ivan had the freedom to—" Her eyes cut to me and she shakes her head and lets the sentence linger unfinished. "Things changed after that."

I know her father doesn't approve of her husband. She told me as much. Their father also made it clear he would never approve of me, either.

"Just a waitress" echoes through my head. It's not the kind of thing you forget easily.

Anya reaches over and pats my knee. "He just needs time to adjust."

"I don't know how much longer I can put up with this. The hot and cold moods are a lot to navigate."

Especially when the hot is so obscenely hot. It would almost be easier if he was always the sexy, flirty Ivan I met that night at the party. I can prepare for that. But when he goes from one extreme to the other, I just get lost in the mix.

Anya frowns at me, her full mouth reminding me far too much of her brother for my liking. Then, suddenly, she jolts upright. "I know exactly what you need."

"A mood ring?"

She smiles. "Even better. You need a date night."

I can't help but snort. "I think it would be easier to get Ivan into a mood ring wedding band than it would be to get him to agree to a date night with me."

"Yeah, right," she dismisses. "Have you seen yourself? Unique my brother may be, but underneath it all, men are the same. The promise of you in a little black dress will be all the encouragement he needs."

"You do remember this is a fake relationship, right?"

"Oh, I remember. Believe me. But the attraction is real. I know my brother well enough to know that you are every bit his type."

I tell myself I don't care if I'm his type. It doesn't matter. It certainly doesn't change anything.

We're still not getting married.

We're still not having sex.

We're still faking this insanity 'til the cows come home.

"You two just need to get to know each other," Anya continues. "You can't plop down in front of cameras and act like a couple if you haven't practiced."

That almost makes sense. How are we supposed to easily touch and play if we've never done it before? Performing in front of other people is way harder than doing it in private.

Although Madison from the sex shop might disagree.

She points at me. "I can tell you're on board."

"I'm only on board if Ivan is on board. I'm here to do what he says, and—"

Anya groans. "My brother needs a kick in his pants. You can't just roll over every time he asks, Cora."

I turn my face towards the sky to hide the flush warming my cheeks. She has no idea exactly how eager my body is to roll over under Ivan Pushkin.

"Dinner," I mutter. "That's it. If Ivan agrees, we can do dinner. *Just* dinner. Not a date, but a night to…to practice."

She claps her hands. "Yes. Okay, I will totally make this happen. Tonight."

She seems oddly confident as she marches away from me and into the house on what I'm sure is a doomed mission.

Ivan was a wall of ice this morning. There is no way even Anya, as sweet and bubbly as she is, can melt him down by tonight.

But if she does, I suppose a little practice won't be the worst thing in the world. I'd love to endure the next few days, weeks, or however long this takes with something akin to a friendly ceasefire. I'm sure that's possible without blurring the already very muddy lines between us…

Right?

I groan and sink down into my chair. It's fine. Anya's plan will probably fail, anyway.

39

IVAN

Anya doesn't even bother knocking. She strolls into my office with a tux draped over her arm. "You and Cora have a reservation at Boulon in ninety minutes."

I don't bother looking at her. "Not interested."

Before I can even pretend to be reabsorbed in my work, Anya throws my tuxedo on my desk. It lands across my arms just as she leans over the desk and jabs a finger into my chest.

"Your wife is *mis-er-a-ble*," she claps. "I could see it written all over her face. She tried to play it off, but that girl looks like death warmed over."

I grimace. The interview this morning didn't go as well as I hoped it would. Turns out, even a facade with good intentions rubs me the wrong way. Sitting there next to her, pretending to be something we aren't…

It reminded me too much of everything I swore I'd never become.

"Then tell her to be a better actress."

Anya groans. "She could be the best actress in the world and it wouldn't matter. No one in their right mind would look at the two of you and think that you're in love and on your way to getting married."

"*You* believed us."

She narrows her eyes. "I was in shock. I give it two hours and I would have untangled your entire deceitful web."

"Cora's happiness isn't my priority. I'm saving her life. I'd say that's enough."

"Your plan to catch whoever is after her only works if they think Cora is an *actual* threat. That means you need to look like you enjoy being around her."

That's precisely the fucking problem. I *do* enjoy being around her. Too much, actually.

"Then talk to her about—"

"No, *you* talk to her about it. Over dinner," Anya says. "You're her husband."

"Fake husband. Fake fiancé, actually. We aren't fake married yet."

She rolls her eyes. "Don't you want to actually catch whoever is threatening our family?" she asks. "You almost act like… like you don't want this thing with Cora to end."

I can feel Anya's assessing eyes on me, waiting for any sign of a crack in the facade.

"Of course I want it to end," I snarl.

And why wouldn't I?

My life is amazing. I'm rich and powerful. I can buy whatever I want and have whoever I want. Meanwhile, Cora is a waitress.

Even as I think it, the words chafe. They sound far too similar to something my father would say.

They also don't ring particularly true.

Cora is a lot more than a waitress. She's loyal to her friends and willing to sacrifice to protect the people she cares about. She's fierce in everything she does. In kindness and fury and fucking.

That ferocity is just another reason it is high time Cora got out of my house and out of my hair. I need someone who can do what I ask and stay out of my way.

Cora is not that woman.

So the sooner she gets out of my life, the sooner I can find a woman who respects my need for those things.

"Just talk to her," Anya presses. "Please?"

I meet my sister's eyes. "Fine. I'll talk to her. Dinner."

~

I'm pretty sure my sister is the only person in the world who could get me into a tux against my will.

Then I look up the grand staircase and see Cora.

I'd put on a suit for her. *I'd take it off, too.*

I silence my dirty thoughts and drink in the sight of her.

She's wearing a midnight blue gown that makes her skin shine like starlight. The neckline plunges low across her chest and a slit rises along her right leg to nearly the top of her thigh. Her hair falls in loose waves around her shoulders that I want to gather up with my hands. I imagine myself shifting her hair to one shoulder and pressing my mouth to the hollow of her throat. Suckling. Biting. Claiming.

Suddenly, my sister's long, loud whistle cuts through the thought.

"Holy shit," she catcalls. "You look amazing!"

Cora turns to her, a pleased smile brightening her face. "Thanks, Anya."

Anya elbows me in the side as Cora reaches the bottom step. "Doesn't she look nice? Tell her she looks nice. Tell her. Say it. Say it now."

I love my sister. But right now, I want to strangle her.

"You look nice." My voice sounds robotic. My movements feel robotic, too, as I shift to the base of the stairs and hold an elbow out. Just the way I was taught.

In the same easy, well-trained grace, Cora curls her arm around mine and stands beside me.

Anya circles us like a judge, taking us in from every angle. "You two look like a real couple to me. A beautiful, real couple."

"Then maybe we don't need to do all this practice, after all," Cora jokes. "Maybe I can just go back upstairs and—"

She starts to let go of my arm, but I hold tight.

When she looks over at me, a question in her eyes, I ignore it and lead her towards the door.

Anya trails behind us. "Your reservation is in half an hour."

"I know."

"Make sure you smile," she calls.

I wave a hand over my shoulder to bat her away like the irritating little fly she is.

"Hold hands!"

"Goodbye, Anya," I bark.

When the front door is closed and Cora and I are on the porch, I blow out a breath.

"We don't have to do this," Cora says softly.

I look down at her. At the curl of her lashes and the pink shimmer of her lips. "I know."

"And just for the record, this was Anya's idea. I didn't tell her to do this. I didn't want to—Well, I don't mean—"

"I don't do anything I don't want to, Cora."

She stares up at me. I can see her trying to puzzle out the meaning behind what I said. Honestly, I'm not entirely sure, either.

With Cora next to me, the idea of dinner doesn't seem like such a waste of time.

What a fucking disaster *that* is.

40

IVAN

Every time she moans, I clench my teeth. My body locks up purely so I don't do something I'd regret.

"This is incredible." Cora slides her plate towards me. "Take a bite. Seriously."

"We each got our own, you know. We don't have to share."

She cuts off a slice of cheesecake and holds it out for me. "Just be quiet and try it."

She's got that look in her eyes, that infuriating, intoxicating, *I-won't-quit* spark. So with a growl, I pluck the fork out of her hand and take the bite.

Shit. It is good.

"Who even came up with putting lemon curd on cheesecake? What genius?" She snatches her fork back and eats another bite, her eyes fluttering closed as her lips wrap around the fork. "I'm in love."

And I'm rock hard.

I had no idea a three-course meal could be a sexual experience, but Cora is an... enthusiastic eater. It's hard for my mind not to imagine that same energy in other, much less innocent scenarios.

"If you can look at me like you're eyeing your dessert, Anya will be proud of our progress."

She grins, narrowing her eyes. "In your dreams."

She has no fucking idea.

The night has flown by. I imagined we'd have a tight, sixty-minute dinner where we rehashed our rules and practiced holding hands. But everything happened naturally.

I guess I should have known after the first night we spent together: being with Cora is easy.

She finishes her dessert and leans back, wrapping her arms around herself. She rubs her hands along her biceps to stay warm. There's a heater blowing behind me, but she's closer to the draft coming off the balcony ledge.

"Here." I start to shrug out of my jacket.

"Thanks, but I'm okay."

I slip it off and stand up. "You have goosebumps. I can see them from here."

I can also see the points of her nipples through the dress, though I keep that detail to myself.

I drape the jacket around her shoulders. The memory of the last time I offered her my jacket hangs heavily between us.

She looks up. "What's this going to cost me?"

I slide my chair closer and sit down, blocking some of the wind coming from the balcony ledge. "What do you mean?"

"If I know anything, it's that nothing good in this world comes without a price." She grips the lapels and pulls them tightly around herself. "So, what do you want?"

Her face is flushed from the wine and the cold, but Cora is burning. Her eyes are a vibrant green, shimmering in the twinkle lights. But it's deeper than that, even. I saw it the night we met when she told Stefanos exactly where he could shove his jackassery. When she told me that she had no interest in marrying *anyone*, let alone someone like Ivan Pushkin, whoever the hell he was.

She isn't just burning—she's incendiary.

She's asking me what I want, but surely she already knows. Surely it's obvious.

I'm about to tell Cora exactly what I want—and where and when I want it—when the waitress reappears with a silver wine bucket in her hands.

"A gift," she says, taking the empty bottle from the center of our table and replacing it with champagne.

I'm content to ignore the waitress and the bottle. My gaze is still locked on the pulse thrumming in Cora's neck. On the curl of hair against her collarbone. On the swell of her breasts in the shimmering fabric.

"Oh, how nice," Cora exclaims. "From who?"

The waitress shakes her head. "I'm actually not sure who it came from. We don't usually carry it, but I know it's a very expensive bottle."

"If anyone asks, we're overcome with gratitude." I wave the waitress away. "Thank you."

Cora pulls the bottle free, studying the label. I want to shove it and the entire bucket off the balcony. It's all a distraction.

Then Cora goes pale.

I see the shift in her. The way the color drains from her cheeks and her eyes turn wary. She glances up at me and whispers my name, a hollow sound. "Ivan…"

Instantly, alarm bells sound in my head.

This was all a distraction. The wine, Cora, the conversation. She's in danger, and I let myself become distracted.

I snatch the bottle out of her hands and turn it around. A word on the label has been scratchily underlined in red ink.

Francia.

41

IVAN

"Ivan," she whispers again, "what's going on?"

I fucked up, that's what. I got sucked into a ruse of my own making. I forgot what we're doing here in the first place.

I plunge the bottle back into the ice bucket and press my hand to her leg. "You're okay."

She's shaking under my touch. "Who sent us that bottle?"

"I don't know." I look around, but the other tables on the patio are empty. There are no direct windows into the dining room downstairs. If anyone knows we are here, they must have seen us come inside or been following us since we left the house.

And I didn't even fucking notice.

Stupid. So, so stupid.

"Could it be a coincidence?" Her hand wraps around my wrist the same way it did yesterday in the sex shop. Except this time, she's not clinging to me in ecstasy. She's clinging to me in utter fear.

"No."

I pull out the phone I all but forgot about for the last two hours and text Yasha. ***Send a driver to pick up Cora. Someone knows we're here. Alert all security and bring in reinforcements.***

"Who are you texting?"

I pocket my phone and wave down the waitress from where she has been watching in the stairwell.

"Is everything to your liking?" she asks, a cheery smile on her face.

"Where did you say this bottle came from?"

"It came from the Champagne region in France. We work with a local—"

"I know where fucking champagne comes from. I mean this specific bottle," I growl. "Tonight. You said you don't usually serve it, so who brought it in?"

She swallows nervously. "I'm afraid I don't know. It was in the kitchen. They told me to bring it to you."

"Who?"

"The kitchen staff. No one told me who delivered it. I might be able to ask the chef, but these kinds of things aren't usually written down anywhere. We only know what is written on the cards, and this bottle didn't come with a card."

Because it didn't need to. The sender made their message crystal clear with one stroke of their red pen.

"I'm sorry," she adds. "If you don't like the champagne, I can take it away and replace it with something else. I can—"

I wave her away. "Give yourself a fifty percent tip and close my tab. We're leaving."

My hot-and-cold act is doing a number on our waitress, but she stands a bit straighter. She scans the table as if to remind herself exactly how much money we spent here tonight. "Thank you, Mr. Pushkin. It was a pleasure to meet you. I hope you two have a good rest of your night."

The woman finally leaves. I grab Cora's hand. "We're leaving."

"Do you think we're in danger?" Cora stands, my jacket slipping from her shoulder. "Is it safe to leave?"

This threat is a bit more subtle than the red laser point of a sniper in the center of her chest, but I can't take it any less seriously.

I pull her close and slide my jacket back into place, covering her shoulders. "I told you I'd take care of you. So do as I say and let me."

I can tell there is so much more she wants to say, but she presses her mouth into a tight line and nods. "I can't believe I'm saying this, but…I trust you."

I keep hold of Cora's hand as we take the stairs back down to the narrow hallway. This time, however, instead of cutting across the dining room, I sneak through the camouflaged door beneath the staircase. It's painted black to blend in with the shadows.

The hallway is dim, weaving through the narrow space between the public dining room to the left and the private dining spaces to the right. Doorways open into quiet chatter and candlelit dinners, people completely oblivious to the threat we're under.

We're only twenty feet from the secondary entrance to the restaurant—a blacked-out glass door next to the women's restroom—when a harsh male voice cuts through the white noise of restaurant conversation.

"A deal is a fucking deal and he knows that," the man hisses.

Cora stiffens. I tuck her behind me, twisting towards the voice.

It's coming from the men's restroom.

"He made a deal, but the details have changed since it was agreed upon," a second voice says. "I think maybe that gives him—"

"He swore to marry a Sokolov daughter, and that is what he will do," the first man says. "Konstantin won't be made a fool of."

The fucking Sokolovs.

Cora tugs on my arm. "Ivan? What is it?"

I don't have time to explain before I hear footsteps moving towards the door.

In any other situation, I'd gladly confront whoever is in the bathroom right now, get the answers I need, and leave them for dead. But Cora...

She's clinging to my hand with trembling fingers. She's scared, and I have to get her out of here. I won't put her in harm's way again.

The bathroom door starts to swing open. In a single move, I spin Cora towards me and tuck us both into the small, shadowy alcove between the men's and women's restrooms.

We need a cover. A distraction. An alibi of sorts.

So, as the men's voices grow louder and emerge only a few feet to my right, I grip Cora's chin and claim her mouth with mine.

42

CORA

I have no clue what is going on.

Champagne, fleeing, mysterious voices, and now... *kissing?*

I don't have even a second to make sense of it all before Ivan whips me into a corner, presses every inch of his muscled body against mine, and kisses the hell out of me.

I hear male voices grow louder and then retreat, but I'm not sure if they're actually gone or if the thrum of blood through my veins is drowning everything else out.

All night, I've felt a buzz under my skin. A sense that I'm too big for my body. Now, with his soft lips on mine and his hands sliding along my waist, I've been unleashed. The monster crawling under my skin takes over, fisting the collar of his shirt and hauling myself up because no matter how close I am to him, it isn't close enough.

He loops a hand around my waist and presses me more firmly into the wall. I can feel every inch of how much he's enjoying this against my inner thigh.

His tongue flicks across the roof of my mouth and I shudder with animal pleasure. I bite his lower lip and curl my fingers through his hair, holding him against me, trying to stretch this moment on and on and on.

But I can feel him retreating. His hands have gone still over my ribs like he doesn't dare move another inch higher. He's drawing back, putting space between our bodies that leaves my flushed skin cold.

One last brush of tongues and lips. Then it's over.

"Cora," he murmurs in a husky snarl.

If he's trying to stop this, then he shouldn't say my name like that.

Reluctantly, I let him go and slide to the floor on shaky legs. He's looking down at me with glowing amber eyes. Then he glances up and down the hallway, and it hits me…

This kiss was a cover.

A strategy.

Ivan didn't want us to be seen, so he kissed me until those men left.

And I turned feral. I practically sprayed him in my attempt to devour him in a dark hallway between public restrooms.

I'm grateful for the dark because it hides the shame that burns across my face as I back away from him, straightening my dress.

He starts to say something. "Cora—"

"Anya would be proud of that performance," I say, slapping on a cheery smile to keep the tears from welling in my eyes.

"I don't know about you, but I think we made this fraud of a relationship look pretty real there for a second."

His expression doesn't change, but the light in his eyes flickers and dims.

"I don't think chemistry is our issue." Ivan steps back and shoves his hands in his pockets. "If I could fuck you in front of everyone, there wouldn't be a soul on Earth who could doubt that this marriage is legitimate. It's everything else that is the problem."

Well, then. That's certainly one way to put it.

My lady bits applaud the idea enthusiastically. The rest of me tells them to zip it.

I try to come up with something—anything—to say. But there isn't time. I'm still in danger, and Ivan still swore to protect me. Which he is doing, even though I was content to risk my life to get in his pants.

He leads me through the exit door and onto the sidewalk. I see someone leaning against a lightpost and I jerk back, only to realize it's Yasha.

"Evening, lovebirds," he croons.

"What are you doing here?" I ask him. Then I turn back to Ivan. "I thought we were leaving."

He reaches around me and opens the back door of a black car. A driver is sitting in the front seat. "*You're* leaving. We're going to look more into the champagne bottle."

I want to argue with him. But what would I even say?

Our date can't end like this. You were supposed to drive me home and kiss me on the front porch. I was going to invite you inside.

The fairytale version of this night blooms in my mind and then withers in a single second.

Reality is a lot uglier.

I let him help me into the backseat. But before he closes the door, I reach out and grab his hand. "Be careful, okay?"

He stares at me. I see a flicker of that light come back. A small spark of hope in his eyes that makes me wonder if there isn't something else going on here.

Then he slams the car door closed and walks away.

Yasha gives me a small wave and follows him.

43

CORA

It's been hours and he still isn't home.

I want to ask Ivan what he found out at the restaurant and figure out who might be after me. But just as urgently, I want to ask if that kiss in the hallway melted his bones the way it did mine.

It's been *hours* and I'm still vibrating from the force of his lips on mine. I can still feel the singe of his hands across my skin and the warmth of his breath on my neck.

And I don't even know if he's alive.

"Of course he's alive," I hiss at myself, shoving away from the door.

I pace the well-worn path I've made in the carpet, cutting across to the bathroom and then spinning right back to that door.

I can't sit still. I certainly can't sleep. All I've done for hours is wait to hear even a whisper of noise on Ivan's side of the door. Anything to let me know he is okay.

I'm considering calling the number Yasha programmed into my phone. Maybe he'll answer and I can talk to him. But as the thought crosses my mind, I realize that Ivan could have called me at any point in the last couple hours. Or texted. Hell, he could have sent Niles up with a Xanax and a note to let me know everything is fine and that he had a nice time on our "date."

But he didn't.

Because it wasn't a real date and this isn't a real relationship.

I'm not his girlfriend and he isn't anything to me. Why should I care what he's doing right now? What difference does it make to me?

Then I remember the feel of him between my thighs. The way his hands gripped my ribs. The way he tasted on my tongue, like lemon curd and champagne.

It matters to me because I got a hit of Ivan Pushkin.

All I want now is *more.*

"No," I whisper, backing away from the door. "No, I don't need him. I don't *need* him. I can take care of myself."

Unlike this morning when I tiptoed around the bag of sex toys like they might explode, tonight, I grab the bag and overturn it on my comforter. I spread the toys out, carefully selecting the wand I want, and march into the bathroom.

I need to relax, so I will.

This is what Ivan wanted, anyway. For me to learn to take care of myself. Right? Right.

The hot water does nothing to ease the fire in my blood, but the heat focuses between my thighs as I press the wand to my aching center.

There's no need for a warmup. I've had hours of anticipation. Now, I just need release.

I slide the wand deep inside of me and roll my hips. The tiles are cold on my back, but this is the position I need to be in. The cold wall behind me, the heat of the water streaming down my front...almost as hot as the heat of Ivan's body pressed to me.

I close my eyes and work the toy in and out, my pace growing feverish. I don't have time to wait. All I've been doing for hours is waiting. Now, I need release. I need...

"Ivan," I rasp.

Heat shudders through me as his name tumbles from my lips. It's a tantalizing shame, acknowledging what I want, but knowing I can't—shouldn't—have it. But here, in this shower...I can have whatever I want.

Whoever I want.

I smooth a line from my neck to my chest, kneading and stroking. I imagine calloused fingers over my skin, strong hands taking what they want. What we both want.

I don't do anything I don't want to, Cora.

Ivan has fucked me. Saved me. Kissed me. Dated me.

Does he want this, too? Is his desire a gnawing hunger low in his gut the way mine is? A sinkhole of need yawning open, consuming every other thought?

I arch off the tile wall as the pleasure builds. I imagine strong hands on my lower back, holding me up. Soft lips sucking in one nipple and then the other, lavishing my body with attention.

"Ivan." I moan his name like a prayer, chanting in breathy gasps before the dam inside of me cracks under the pressure.

The orgasm almost takes me to the shower floor. I have to catch myself on the shelf. Shampoo and conditioner bottles go flying in the process.

Eyes still closed, I feel the desire pull out like the tide. Receding back into the place where I need to hide it, but where it will never fit. Not entirely.

Whatever I feel for him, it's too big to stay tucked away.

But I have to try.

I start to lower the toy to the edge of the shower when the same calloused hand I just imagined slides over mine, holding the toy in place.

Then I hear a voice.

"Do it again," Ivan growls. "I want to watch."

44

CORA

Am I still imagining this?

I look over to see Ivan standing just outside the glass partition. His shirt is off, the lines of his tattoos dark against his skin. He's watching me carefully. His eyes are almost black with wanting.

I should be scared. My heart is thundering, but it's almost like some small part of me expected him to be here.

"You didn't knock," I say softly. As if that matters. He could have blown through an entire wall to be in here now and I still wouldn't kick him out.

He steps into the shower wearing nothing but a pair of black briefs. My eyes snag on the impressive length tenting the material before I whip my attention back to his face.

Ivan moves close around me and gently pulls the wand from my hand. He flicks the switch on, then presses it back between my fingers. I jolt and bite my lip to stop from crying out.

"I came to check on you," he whispers against my neck. "I heard my name."

Any embarrassment I might feel is burned away in the inferno that roars through me as Ivan situates his length between my thighs.

His other hand grips my hip. I look down just as a streak of pink water flows down my leg. I frown at it, confused. Until my gaze slides up to Ivan's arm.

"You're bleeding." Even as the words leave my mouth, I know they aren't true.

It isn't his blood.

I've seen him kill before. I watched him pull the trigger. Now, he's here, covered in blood... and all I want is to lick him clean.

Fuck, I'm sick.

"Tell me what you're thinking," Ivan orders.

I lay my head against his shoulder and close my eyes. "Are you as dangerous as everyone says?"

"No." He turns and kisses my throat before his lips move to my ear. "I'm worse."

I should stop this. If I was smart, I would tell Ivan to leave. I would hold firm to the boundaries I set, let him save me from whoever is after me, and then go back to my normal life without a single glance in the rearview mirror.

But maybe... maybe this is all my imagination. Maybe this is a vivid fantasy. A pocket of time where I can have what I want and not be punished for it. Where I can be the damsel and Ivan, as bloody and dark and wildly wrong for me as he is, can be my knight.

"Ivan?"

I whisper it so softly I'm not sure if he can even hear me over the shower. But of course he does. He slides his hand up my stomach, his thumb brushing the underside of my breast.

"Fuck me. Please."

His amber eyes flare bright. "My pleasure."

45

IVAN

I was in her room listening to the shower run. I planned to walk away. It was late and being there after everything that happened tonight was a mistake.

Then she said my name.

No—Cora *moaned* my name like a fucking siren call.

Now, I'm coiled around her, her breath on my neck and her wet skin sliding against mine. She's begging me.

Fuck me. Please.

I will. Of course I will. I don't have a choice.

But first…

I want to watch her fall apart.

I work the wand against her, buzzing the absurdly expensive machine over the bundle of nerves between her gorgeous thighs. I bought her the toys to use, but when I walked in the bathroom and saw it in her hand as she moaned my name, I've never wanted to snap a device in half more in my life.

It should have been me.

"Is this what you want?" I growl.

Cora wraps her arm up and around my neck, hanging from me as she writhes against the pressure. "It's good enough."

I bite her earlobe and tug until she bends back, her throat exposed. "You deserve more than 'good enough,' Cora. *Is this what you want?*"

She's panting now. Her body is twitching, fracturing apart bit by bit. I'm so hard it hurts. The friction of her thighs isn't helping me focus.

"Ivan," she gasps. Her throat bobs as she swallows another moan. "I'm—I'm coming."

Then, before I can even give her permission, that's exactly what she does.

I feel her stomach tense under my hand. She trembles with the release, sucking down lungfuls of air. Tiny splutters pass her lips and she jerks and spasms in my arms.

It's fucking beautiful.

But it isn't enough.

Not for her. Certainly not for me.

She's still coming down when I throw the wand on the shower floor and spin Cora against the glass. Her eyes are wide and searching as I band a gentle hand around her throat.

"Tell me you're satisfied. Tell me that was enough for you."

Tell me you don't want this so I can walk away.

Water clings to her lashes and streams between her breasts. She's flushed and breathless from two orgasms. It should be enough. If not, the fact I'm covered in another man's blood should be reason aplenty for her to walk away.

And if she won't, I should. I can't have her. I can't want her.

But fuck me, she is the only thing I want. Everything else can burn to ashes. I want *her*.

Her hand reaches out, stroking lightly over my abs. "Ivan…"

Whatever scrap of control I had left cracks apart at the quiver in her voice.

I grip her thigh with crushing force and wrap her leg around my hip. Cora should be screaming for help, but instead, she tugs down the waistband of my briefs.

"It wasn't enough for me," she breathes. "I want…"

She doesn't finish the thought before I slam into her.

"Fuck." I brush my thumb over her pounding pulse and push her head back. I pin her to the cold glass wall with my hand and my cock and my body.

Then I pull out and crash into her again.

Each retraction is an opportunity to leave. To end this. To sever whatever connection exists between us.

But the pull is too fucking strong.

Cora claws at me. Her nails scrape at the bits of dried blood on my arms as she drags me closer to her, rising to meet every thrust with the same desperation I feel burning in my bones.

Cognac Villain

"Take me." She wraps her arms around my neck and lifts her other leg to hook around my back. "Take me, Ivan. Like this."

I watch her body fall onto mine. The way she tenses with every thrust. Her lips are parted, and she draws close. Closer. Close enough that I feel her breath on my face and smell her toothpaste.

She's going to kiss me again, and I know it will unleash whatever is lurking under my skin for her.

Just as her eyes flutter closed, I slide out of her and pull away.

Her feet slap against the shower floor. "What are you—"

"Turn around." I spin her and claw at her hips. Red marks map all the places where I've touched her, like living tattoos.

She presses her palms to the tile at the very moment I fill her from behind. A long moan works free from her throat.

I press the heel of my hand hard to her lower back, bowing her in front of me. Taking exactly what I want.

This isn't about her. This is about me.

I lie to myself again and again, thrusting into her as if it has nothing to do with who she is to me.

"Don't stop," she begs. "Keep going. Like that."

I hook a hand around her throat and haul her body up. Her shoulder blades crash into my chest, but she's still trembling against my body. She's still straining for the exact right angle.

"Yes, yes, yes." She punctuates each slap of our bodies with a cry of pleasure that electrifies me. Finally, she gasps. "I'm coming. I'm—"

Her body tightens like a vice around me and, when that happens, I don't stand a fucking chance.

I spill into her. The leash on my self-control is gone, missing, destroyed—if it ever even existed in the first place. I grip the base of her throat, bite her shoulder, palm her breasts. I explore every remaining inch of her body, milking every possible second of this moment for all its worth.

Cora just rests the back of her head on my shoulder and hooks her hand around my neck as I explode.

Finally, reality comes swimming back to the forefront and I can inhale again. She looses a breathy laugh. "Oh my God… That was… Ivan, that was…"

She can't finish the sentence. She doesn't need to.

I know what it was.

I also know exactly how dangerous it's becoming.

46

IVAN

I sit on the bed as Cora finishes her shower.

The water turns off and, a few seconds later, she pads into the bedroom with nothing but a towel wrapped around her. Considering what we just did, it shouldn't send such awareness through me. But it does.

Every side of Cora is something new, something I want to collage and keep for myself.

Cora in my suit jacket.

Cora in a dress for date night.

Cora in the shower.

Cora in a towel.

Every single image is seared into my retinas. When will I finally have enough of her?

She falters when she sees me, hesitating for just a second before she walks over to the dresser.

"I didn't expect you to still be here." She frowns and turns away, digging through her top drawer and pulling out a black pair of panties. "Did you need something from me?"

Yes, I almost say. *I need the rest of your life to be spent at my side, doing what we just did again and again.*

But of course I can't say that. And I don't have a good excuse for being here.

So I push to standing, half-expecting to walk past her into my room and slam the door closed. But I'm drawn into her orbit as I get closer. As I pass, I open the drawer and pull out a silk pajama set.

"Wear these."

She wrinkles her nose. "I get why you picked out my outfit for the interview, but I don't see how what I wear to bed is part of our business arrangement." She fingers the blush pink material.

I'm about to tell her that there is a whole hell of a lot going on between us that has nothing to do with our arrangement when I notice her arm. Her throat.

Bands of red wrapping around her, turning dark on the edges.

I reach out a hand and run my fingers over her throat. She goes taut like a violin string. One pluck and she could be in my control.

"I left marks," I murmur.

"Oh." She eases back, gesturing towards her throat. "It's okay. I'm not hurt. Don't feel bad."

"Did anything I do hurt you?" I ask.

She blinks up at me, obviously confused. Her face flushes pink. "No."

"Then why would I feel bad?"

The truth is that I fucking *love* these marks. I want them to stay. I want to look at her and always remember the moment when she begged me to fuck her.

I grab her towel. Cora doesn't try to stop me as I tug it away from her.

It pools around her feet when I drop it, the rest of her blissfully naked.

"I touched you there." I gently grip her hip over the marks I left behind. Then I smooth my way up to a few small bruises on her ribs. "And here."

She's staring down at where my hand is pressed to her skin, her green eyes blazing. "Do you always take stock of the collateral damage like this?"

No. Hell no.

In every other case before Cora, I'm long gone by the time anyone is in the shower. I certainly don't stick around afterward and pick out their pajamas. That was the objectively better way to do things.

Even now, I should leave. But I can't. Not yet.

Instead of answering, I grab the clothes from Cora's arms and begin to dress her.

"I know you've seen me naked a lot, but I can dress myself," she protests weakly. Her voice is thick and her nipples are pinched into sharp points.

I pull the silk camisole over her head, loitering around the soft swell of her breasts. "I told you I'd take care of you. So that's what I'm doing."

She swallows and nods, allowing whatever this is to continue. Both of us caught in the tangle of something we don't fully understand.

I pull the shorts over her long legs, already itching to take them off again. But no. We shouldn't.

And maybe that's what this is. As I'm dressing her, I'm layering on my own armor. I'm taking back my self-control and giving this story a natural end.

As I settle Cora into the mattress and pull the blankets under her pointed chin, I tell myself this is over.

I can't afford to lose control.

I can't afford to be distracted.

I can't afford to have anything that means too much to me. Anything someone else can take away.

She smiles up at me, those bruises glowing like jewelry around her wrists and throat. "I waited for you."

"You were in the shower."

"No." She shakes her head. "I mean earlier. After our—After dinner."

Date. She was going to say "date." Is that what it was?

I want to know how the night would have ended if the champagne hadn't shown up. In some ways, it feels like all roads will always lead back to this. Like we can't help ourselves.

"I was worried about you," she adds.

I remember the way she grabbed my hand as I put her in the backseat of the car. *Be careful.*

No one aside from Anya and Yasha has ever said that to me. No one has ever cared. Then she sat up at home waiting for me…

She's looking at me like she's still waiting. For what, I don't know. But I know it's something I can't give her.

I adjust the blankets, then rise and turn away, walking towards the shared door between our rooms.

If Cora is waiting for me, she better get used to it.

She'll be waiting forever.

47

IVAN

"It's good, right?" Anya is bouncing from foot to foot in front of my desk, eyebrows wagging in impatience. "Isn't it good?"

I scowl up at her. "Shut up and let me read. Then I can tell you what I think."

But she's right. The interview Cora and I did two days ago is good. Great, actually.

Which begs the question: *How the fuck did that disaster of an interview turn into this?*

"You two sound so in love!" Anya snatches the paper away, her eyes seconds away from turning into cartoonish hearts. She points to a paragraph. "This part. I love this part. Listen. *'Ivan and Cora admit their relationship is a bit of a whirlwind, but it doesn't feel that way from the inside. 'My whole life has been a series of experiences and disappointments that have made me ready for someone like Ivan,' Cora said. 'Someone dependable and loyal. I know that he'll always take care of me.'"*

She sure as hell never said that. Not when I was around, anyway.

Anya tosses the newspaper at me and throws herself down into a leather chair, practically vibrating with glee. "Oh my God, I *knew* sending the two of you out on that date would work."

"So much for that being 'strategy.'"

She snorts. "You know me too well to think I was serious about that. I wanted the two of you to get loosened up and then—" She winks suggestively.

"As my sister, you're supposed to be repelled by that kind of talk."

"As your sister, I'm supposed to want what is best for you. If you have to get some in order to see that, then that's fine by me. It's all part of the process."

Nothing about what is happening between me and Cora is part of any normal process. We're doing everything backwards, or sideways, or inside out. Whatever direction we're going, it isn't a straight line, and it doesn't make any fucking sense.

That's probably why I haven't talked to her since I dressed her in those sinfully small pajamas and tucked her into bed.

I fold the newspaper and drop it into the top drawer of my desk. I'll read it later when Anya isn't breathing down my neck.

"I know what is best for myself."

Anya stares at me for a few seconds…then she bursts into obnoxious laughter.

I've learned that it is best to let her run her course, so I go back to working until she can breathe again.

"The—*whooo*, that was a good one; I'm tearing up—the fact that you believe that is really cute, brother. I mean, you were going to let that interview run without any intervention. It doesn't speak well to your judgment."

I frown. "What the fuck does that mean?"

"Did you really think this is what that interviewer wrote about the two of you?"

My stony silence is answer enough.

Anya shakes her head and continues. "The first draft read like a medical report. It was fucking bleak. The writer was afraid of upsetting you, but it was obvious you two gave her nothing to work with."

"Because there *is* nothing to work with. We aren't a real couple," I spit.

Anya slouches down in her chair and rolls her eyes. "Thank God your fiancée has a good head on her shoulders, at least."

"What does Cora have to do with this?"

"With the interview?" she asks. "Everything. She wrote it! The reporter said she couldn't pull it because they didn't have a backup article and her editor would have killed her, so Cora begged her to let her take a shot at rewriting it a bit."

Cora did that. On her own. She reached out to the interviewer and took action without me ordering her to. Without any prodding. She just…saw a problem and fixed it. She didn't even ask me about it.

"She's pretty amazing, isn't she?" Anya is smirking far too smugly for it to be safe.

I wave her away. "Some of us have work to do. Go be a nuisance to someone else."

She stands up and tosses her hair dramatically. "Maybe I'll go hang out with my future sister-in-law."

"She isn't real."

Anya simply blows me a kiss and hurries out of the room.

I try to get back to work, but a few minutes later, I find myself kicked back in my chair with the newspaper in my hands.

The article is good. Really good. Even people who don't know a damn thing about me or my family would read this and root for us. Cora softened me in all the right ways, making me approachable, desirable. She also made me sound like the luckiest fucker in the world for having a woman like her on my arm.

I could call her up and thank her. It would be the right thing to do after ghosting her for the last two days.

I tap the edges of my phone, considering.

Finally, I pick it up and text Kieran. ***Have a simple gold bracelet sent to my house for Cora. For the note, just write, 'Thanks.'***

She won't be able to wear the wedding ring once our sham marriage is over, but she can keep a bracelet if she wants to.

For some stupid reason, I find myself hoping she will.

Yasha walks into my office ten minutes later with a breakfast sandwich in his hand. I scowl up at him. "You're late."

"I was hungry. Oh, shit." He winces. "I can go grab you one."

"I'm not hungry; I'm impatient." I point to the chair across from my desk. "Sit. Tell me what you found out."

He sets the sandwich on the edge of my desk and blows out a breath. "Well, not much, honestly. Your dad had never heard of the St. Clairs because there isn't much to hear. Cora's dad is pretty well-off, but he makes his money the boring, legal way. He also dipped out when she was a kid and has a whole new family now. Cora isn't in any of the pictures I could find of his 'family' online."

That's reason enough for me to hate the bastard. I don't need to know any more.

"And her mother?"

"Her mom, Evaline, married Alexander McAllister almost ten years ago."

I frown, scouring my mind for any mention of that name. "Do I know him?"

"It's possible. He moves in some of the same circles, but he keeps a low profile. No one really has him nailed down."

"That's why I asked you to look into it. To nail him down."

"And I did!" He lounges back, his hands raised in defense. "I tried, at least. He's just some generic rich guy as far as I can tell."

"It just doesn't make any sense." I growl in frustration. "Cora was at that party under her friend's name. But why? If her stepdad moves in the same circles—even a tangential circle—she would have been invited, too."

Yasha shrugs. "Maybe her invite got lost in the mail."

"Hm." There's more, too. "When we were shopping for her ring, Kieran acted like he'd seen her before."

He feigns shock. "A rich woman in a fancy jewelry shop. How scandalous."

"He acted like she'd been there before—with someone else," I grit out. "I think Cora might have been engaged before this."

He frowns. "Nothing about a previous engagement came up anywhere."

"You're running into a lot of dead ends where Cora is concerned."

"Maybe because there isn't much to find."

I shake my head. "Or because there's something someone doesn't want you to find."

"Like what? Cora seems nice. I can't imagine her having some dark, sordid history."

"That doesn't mean she doesn't have one. Look into it more. Interview people, follow leads, dig for dirt. Whatever you need to do."

Yasha sits up and blows out a breath. "Man, I—I know you like this girl, but—"

"I don't *like* her," I snap. "I'm letting her into my house and I need to know who the fuck she is. This isn't any more personal than that."

Yasha arches a skeptical brow for a moment before he clears his face. "Okay. Either way, we have bigger shit going on. Don Pushkin called us in for a meeting tonight. He wants to know who tried to assassinate Cora."

"I'll deal with my father," I tell him. "Look more closely into Cora."

He takes another bite of his sandwich and flops back in the chair. "If you're sure."

Hell no, I'm not sure. Since Cora showed up, I haven't been sure about a fucking thing.

But I shove that uncertainty down and nod. "I'm positive."

48

CORA

You'd think living in an adjoining room with the guy would have us tripping over each other several times per day, but no. Since the night of our not-a-date, he's been a ghost.

I wake up early in the morning and he's already gone.

I wait up at night and he stays out even later.

For all I know, he might be a bat sleeping upside down in a tree somewhere. Because he certainly isn't getting enough sleep in the bedroom next door to mine.

The thought of where exactly Ivan might be sleeping—*who* he might be sleeping with—has me burying my nose even deeper in the historical romance novel I found tucked away in the lowest, dustiest shelf of the library.

Angst and confusion aside, all this free time to kick back and relax has been nice. It's been so long since I've had time to read a book or contemplate my relationship with a man. Even having a relationship with a man to contemplate, fraudulent and temporary as it may be, was a luxury before all of this.

Now, I'm lousy with time to ruminate on all things Ivan Pushkin.

I try to focus on the text in front of me. On Jessamine trying and failing to climb atop her horse, so the scandalous rake Duke Andrew has to help her. He grabs her waist and she tenses all over. A man in Victorian England has never touched her like this. She's aflame.

"Relatable," I groan, slamming the book shut.

I don't know why I'm surprised. It's hard to escape thoughts of Ivan when I'm living in his house. Especially when we can't talk about what happened the other night.

He found me in the shower and proceeded to raise my standards for all future sexual encounters so impossibly high that I might as well not even bother dating anyone else.

I've been ruined on all men who are not Ivan Pushkin.

Yet I have no clue if that was a one-off born out of our undeniable chemistry or if he'd like to repeat it again. Right now. And then an hour from now. And many times more in the future, maybe until we both die from overstimulation.

"Oh, God." I sink down into the velvet lounge chair and cover my burning face. "What is happening to me?"

The only reason I'm here is because someone wants to kill me, but I'm spending ninety-five percent of my energy wondering if Ivan thinks I'm cute.

It's pathetic.

I'm lying on the chaise, the book flat on my chest and my gaze stuck on the ceiling, when my phone rings.

I jolt out of the chair and fumble for my phone in my back pocket like my life depends on it. But when I see the number, my disappointment is visceral.

I drop back down into the chair and answer. "You shouldn't be calling."

"You called me first," my mother says. "I can only hope it's because you're ready to come home."

I bite back a humorless laugh. "I called because I thought you could talk to me. I thought things could be..." *Like they used to be.* "I just wanted to see how you were doing."

When I called the other night, my mom was stunned. Now, she's had time to prep for this call. She's playing her part perfectly. "You know how I'm doing, Cordelia. I do miss you."

I shiver at my old name. It's like passing through a ghost. The air around me seems to drop twenty degrees.

"I miss you, too."

Truth is, I've been missing her for years. Way before I left. I've missed my mom since the day she got married to my stepfather.

"Then come home," she pleads. "Call off this engagement or whatever it is with Ivan Pushkin and come home."

I freeze, my heart hammering against my ribs. "Where did you hear about that?"

"It was on the front page of the society section."

"You read the newspaper?"

"No, but your grandmother does. She sent me the article."

Ivan's entire plan hinges on us going public with our engagement. But I was too busy running from gunfire to really think about what that would mean. About precisely who would see it.

"Does he know?"

I don't need to specify who. She knows who I mean.

"Not yet." She sighs. "But I have to—"

"Don't tell him!" I hate the shakiness in my voice. How quickly the memories come flooding back. Feeling trapped and alone, terrified of what my future looked like. Whether I'd have a future at all.

"Cordelia, I can't keep this—"

"Don't tell him," I repeat. "Mom…please. I'm not ready to come back."

I'll never be ready, but maybe, if she thinks there's a chance, if she thinks there is a possibility I'll come back… Maybe she'll keep this secret.

I just need a bit more time to figure out what I'm going to do once my stepfather knows where I am.

Because the moment he finds me, he'll try to haul me back to his house and marry me off again. If things with Ivan end and I don't have a job lined up, I might not have another choice.

The silence on the other end of the line is deafening.

"Mom…"

"Okay," she says softly. "I won't say anything. But I can't control if he finds out."

A tiny ray of relief bursts through the gloom hanging over me. "Thank you. I just need—"

"You'll be home one way or another," she interrupts. "The sooner you do it, the better off we'll all be."

She hangs up before I can say anything. Not that there is anything to say.

I should have known he'd never *actually* let me go.

I'm so deeply entrenched in my pity party that I don't hear anyone come into the library. Which is why I shriek the moment Anya starts talking.

"Ivan loved the article."

I almost flop off the chaise in my panic, but I manage to catch myself on the arm of the chair. "When did you get here?"

"Just now." She raises her brows. "Are you okay?"

I sit up, hand pressed to my racing heart. "You scared the bejeezus out of me."

"It's probably because you're sitting in this dank old room in the dark. Open some windows. Let the sunshine in."

Anya walks around me and does just that, throwing back the thick curtains. Sunlight comes streaming in and I feel the urge to hiss like a scalded vampire.

She strokes the windowsill to inspect for dust. "Niles really is remarkably good at his job," she comments. "No one comes in here and yet it's still spotless."

"The Pushkins aren't big readers?"

She shrugs. "So many enemies to kill, so little time to read."

"Is that common? The… the killing of—"

"I was joking." She says it a bit too quickly and waves a hand as if to dismiss the conversation. "What are you doing here, anyway? Niles said you haven't been downstairs all day."

"I've been relaxing."

I didn't realize Niles was paying such close attention to my movements. If he's telling Anya what I'm up to, it's probably safe to assume he's telling Ivan, as well. I don't know why it bothers me, but I'd rather him not know that I'm just hiding away in the library with a book while he's out there, doing whatever it is he's doing.

Anya snorts. "You don't look relaxed. You almost shot through the roof when I walked in."

"I'm used to living alone. It's still new to have other people around."

My apartment is probably already gathering dust. It's only been a few days, but it feels longer. Like I've gone down the Wonderland rabbit hole and time is passing out of order.

She shifts towards the shelves, running her finger along a row of leatherbound books. "That makes sense. Ivan is still getting used to me popping in unannounced and it's been years. He says he hates it, but I know he secretly loves the company."

"He definitely does. It's obvious the two of you are close."

She smiles to herself. "Do you have any siblings?"

"No. It's just me."

"Are you close with your parents, then?"

I chew on the corner of my lip. "Nuh-uh. My dad left when I was little and my mom got remarried. We aren't close anymore."

She winces. "I relate to problematic parents, believe me. But I'm sorry."

"It's okay. That's life."

"Yeah…" She sighs and then seems to come alive again, sitting up tall. "Speaking of parents, would you want your parentals invited to your wedding?"

"Invited to my—My future wedding, you mean? Or are you talking about… Ivan and I aren't really getting married."

Or are we? How far is he planning to take this charade? The image of me in a white dress standing in front of Ivan in a tuxedo… I mean, I can barely handle living next door to him. I cannot vow before God. I'll be smote by divine lightning for my dirty thoughts alone.

Anya shakes her head. "I know, I know. This is all about appearances. If things take a little longer than expected, I'd love to have a guest list ready for Save the Dates. Just to keep up the charade."

My heart rate eases back to something resembling normal. "I guess that makes sense."

"So, on the parent front, is that a yes or—"

"No!" I say sharply. "No. Especially if it isn't real. I'd rather keep them out of this. There's enough going on without digging up the past."

Anya leans in close. "You said *if*."

"What?"

"If," she repeats. "'*If it isn't real.*' Do you think it could be real?"

"What? No. No, that's not what I meant. I didn't say it like—I just meant that since this isn't real, I won't say anything. One day, when it could be real, with someone else, then maybe—"

"After reading that interview you rewrote, I thought I heard wedding bells." Anya shrugs, a smug smile pinching her lips tight. "You never know how things might turn out."

The interview. I almost forgot about that.

"Has Ivan read it?" I ask. "What did he think?"

Anya grins and reaches behind her. I didn't notice the black box before. Probably because I was too busy screaming bloody murder.

"Niles said this arrived for you a few minutes ago." Anya shoves the box into my hands and hovers over me. "Go on. Open it."

Slowly, I peel open the lid. There's a white piece of cardstock sitting inside. A single word typed in the center: **Thanks**. When I pick it up, I see what it's covering.

"Oh wow, that's—" Anya tips her head to the side, assessing. "That is kind of plain, but still a nice gesture. Ivan has clearly never bought a woman jewelry before."

I pick up the plain gold band, running my thumb over the polished edge.

No frills. No gaudy gems or diamonds. No over-the-top detailing.

Just a simple gold band. Like the engagement ring I wanted.

The same one I wanted when Mikhail and I were in Kieran's shop, a lifetime ago. I hoped Kieran wouldn't recognize me. He sees so many customers that there was no way he'd remember me, right?

Wrong, as it turned out.

"It's perfect," I murmur under my breath.

"Really?" Anya inspects it a bit closer and then shrugs. "Then Ivan knows what he's doing. That's another good sign."

I close the lid and tuck the box carefully in my lap. "A good sign for what?"

Anya's brows shoot up innocently. "What? Oh, nothing. I'm just talking. I do that a lot. You'll get used to it."

Ivan was right: when it comes to loving Anya, she really doesn't give you a choice.

"Anyway," she chirps, "I'm thinking we need to get you out of the house and do some wedding planning. You need to see and be seen if we want this plan to work."

I'm beginning to wonder whose plan she's executing: Ivan's or her own secret agenda.

"Every time I've gone out in public, I've been threatened."

Or absolutely ravished by her brother.

Either way, it's a bad idea.

"Which is why I've booked private appointments, duh! Your dress fitting and cake tasting are going to be exclusive. No one will be allowed in or out without some extensive vetting and there will be security everywhere. No one will touch you."

"Maybe someone could just come to the house and I could look at dresses here. Then we wouldn't need all of the guards and security measures."

She swats away my idea. "There is no way in hell that my brother's wife is trying on wedding dresses in her walk-in closet. Not gonna happen."

"Have you seen the closet, though? It's amazing."

"It's still a closet. This has to be extravagant. It's like royalty getting married," Anya says. "That's what you and Ivan represent to people. It's a way of life that has to be maintained and flaunted."

I squeeze the box in my lap until my knuckles turn white. "I don't want to be royalty."

"We aren't really royal," she laughs. "But our family has a lot of responsibilities. *Ivan* has a lot of responsibilities. We need to exude strength and normalcy right now until this threat is under control."

I hear the words Anya is saying, but I can't make sense of them. She's talking like we're spies in the midst of some foreign war. Like this is an espionage movie instead of my real life.

I blink at her, mouth hanging open for a moment. "Who *are* you people?"

Anya's smile falters. "We're ungodly rich; that's who we are. This all comes with the territory."

Assassins. Executions. Armed guards.

I know rich people. I've *been* rich, no matter how briefly. None of this comes with the territory.

This is *mafia* stuff.

Maybe that's what Ivan's dad was talking about when he mentioned a Bratva. I mean, it fits. Who else aside from career criminals can murder people with no remorse the way I watched Ivan kill that sniper?

It obviously wasn't the first time he'd killed someone. And given the blood I saw wash down the shower drain two nights ago, it probably wasn't his last.

Anya jumps up and backs towards the door. "Well, I better go. I have some things to get in order before our cake tasting tonight. Come hungry, okay?"

I nod and wave, a plan of my own taking form.

If no one is going to tell me what is really going on here, I'll just have to figure it out for myself. And tonight, at a secure location away from the WiFi I'm sure Ivan is having monitored, I'll be able to do just that.

Answers are long overdue.

49

IVAN

"Well?" Otets barks. He slaps a hand on the desk that was once his. He likes to reclaim his throne whenever he visits my home office. A reminder of who he thinks is really in charge. "Tell me what you know."

I sprawl in the armchair across from him. "Two Sokolov guards were at the restaurant when Cora and I had dinner the other night."

"What did you find out before you killed them?"

I glance at Yasha where he's standing in the corner. He ducks his head.

I look back to my father. "We didn't kill them."

"You let them go?" A vein in his neck throbs.

"The Sokolovs are an ally. I didn't want to make trouble."

He snorts. "Too fucking late for that, isn't it? You and Katerina caused enough trouble for a lifetime."

"And killing two guards who were guilty of nothing beyond gossip in the men's room could start an all-out war. Is that what you want me to do?"

"Don't be smart, son." He wags a finger at me in warning. "You say the Sokolovs might be involved in going after our family. I assume that is a crime worthy of death. How important is the family to you?"

I grit my teeth. "Important enough that I'm not going to run headfirst into a war if I can avoid it."

Yasha steps forward. "We questioned the two men, sir. We bloodied them up. They didn't have anything to say."

"Because they knew you were weak." Otets ignores Yasha entirely, his disdain focused on me. "They knew they were going to walk away with their lives. If anything, getting a beatdown from the future *pakhan* of the Pushkin Bratva is a badge of honor they will wear with pride. You probably earned them a promotion."

"I made it clear that I am onto them. Now, Konstantin knows that. He might slip up and—"

"He won't be able to attack your supposed bride even if he wants to. I happen to know she hasn't left the house in days." He scoffs. "You know how you catch a predator? *With bait.* This girl is a worm on a hook. You don't catch anything by yanking her away any time someone gets close. You have to let them get a taste or this is all for fucking nothing."

I take a deep breath, biting back a thousand cutting words I'd rather say. "It's not for nothing, Otets. We have a lead."

"If you'd had the guts to take a risk, you could have the person who is targeting us."

"Or," I counter, "I could have lost Cora and the person responsible still would have gotten away. Then I'd be left with fucking nothing."

I meant it in terms of the plan, but the words ring true somewhere in my hollow chest.

When this is over and Cora leaves, what will all of this be for? So I can safely marry some stand-in wife I don't give a shit about?

Otets narrows his eyes. "Have you fucked her?"

I tense, fighting the urge to strangle him for even asking. "That doesn't matter."

"It matters to me," he spits. "It matters to the Bratva. If you're wasting time, money, and resources so you can shack up with this fucking waitress, that matters a whole hell of a lot to all of us."

"Does it look like I'm playing House to you?" I fling my arms wide. "I haven't even seen her in two days because I've been busy tracking down information."

"I saw the bill for the engagement ring. We'll be lucky if she doesn't pawn it for a down payment on her new life."

"I had no idea we were short on cash," I drawl. "If you're worried about our finances, I'll get it back from her and re-gift it to the next woman."

That's a fucking whopper of a lie. I'll melt it down before I see it on any finger aside from hers.

But it doesn't matter. This isn't about the money for my father.

It's about control. His loss of it, specifically.

"I'm worried that you're getting lost in your own con, Ivan." He leans forward, his fingers drumming slowly on the tabletop. "When the time comes, you need to be able to cut the bait and reel it in. You need to be able to get out of this unscathed, whether your little slut does or not."

"Don't call her that."

I'm shaking with the force required to stay sitting. To not drag my own father out of his chair by his throat.

Yasha edges towards the door, but Otets doesn't move. Doesn't blink. "What did you say?"

I look at him, my voice louder now. "I won't sit here and let you disrespect her."

My father smirks at me, but there is no warmth in it. No joy.

Only a sense of retribution.

"I won't let this game go on much longer, boy." He waves another warning finger, his nostrils flaring. "Get your shit together and be prepared to cut that girl loose for the greater good. If you can't, I'll do it for you."

He stands and storms out, leaving me sitting there with a single thought burning in my head.

I'd like to see him fucking try.

Yasha escorts my father out, then returns and collapses into the leather chair across from me with a sigh. "Fuck."

"What? I thought that went well."

He scowls at me. "Be serious, Ivan."

"That's usually my line."

"Because you're usually being an uptight ass about nothing," he says. "This is not nothing. The *pakhan* is pissed."

I wave a hand in the air. "You don't have to be afraid of him."

"I'm not afraid of him; I'm afraid for you," he says. "There's a difference."

I hear Cora's voice in my head. *Be careful.*

For all Yasha's fuckery, I've always known he cares. I know I can count on him. The fact that Cora has now joined ranks with him in bothering to worry about me is something I can't quite grasp.

"Don't waste your time with either. I'm fine."

"You're fine right now," Yasha counters. "What I'm worried about is what happens when this is over. I'm worried what will happen when—*if*—you have to cut the bait."

My father took his rainclouds with him, but I feel another storm brewing as I turn to Yasha. "I won't have to do that."

He holds up his hands in surrender. "I hope not. Cora is good for you. I don't want to see anything bad happen to her."

Even the suggestion has me tightening my fists. "Then let's make sure it doesn't."

"I'll try. I really will. But you know as well as I do that we can't control everything. Especially when Don Pushkin thinks Cora is expendable."

I flex my jaw, trying to drum up the words I know I need to say. Finally, I spit them out. "Isn't she?"

"That's what I'm asking you." His voice is soft, solemn. "You like being around Cora. I can tell. Even Anya likes her, which is a small miracle. Your sister hates any woman who even looks at you. But I think she can see it, too: that Cora fits in here. With you. In our world."

It's strange, hearing my private thoughts spoken out loud by someone else.

Cora *does* fit in here.

Cora *could* hold her own in my world.

She belongs.

"None of it matters," I say with finality.

"How can none of it—"

"None of it matters because this is a temporary arrangement," I say, cutting him off. "This is a mission. Feelings can't get in the way of a mission. Not mine. Not yours. Not Cora's. This thing between me and her was always meant to end."

Yasha sighs. "But it doesn't have to. Not if you don't want it to."

"What I want is to do my job. That means I can't have Cora falling in love with me and fucking things up." I drop my feet to the floor. "This is all an act. A good one, if even *you* bought into it."

Yasha is quiet for a few seconds before he speaks. "Are you sure, Ivan?"

"I'm sure that I have a responsibility to the organization and my father and my sister," I tell him, "to marry someone who is actually suitable. Someone who can be what I need to do my job. And that person isn't Cora."

I sit tall and turn towards him…only to see someone else in the doorway.

"Cora."

She blinks at me. Her eyes are glassy, filled with tears she is refusing to shed.

She lifts her chin and looks at me. "We're leaving for the cake tasting in ten minutes. I just wanted to let you know."

I start to stand. "Cora—"

Before I can get another word out, she turns and leaves.

50

IVAN

Slices of every imaginable cake combination are laid out on the glass counter in front of us, but Cora hasn't touched a single one.

I lean in close, voice low and tight. "You basically made love to a lemon curd cheesecake two nights ago. Maybe drum up a fraction of that energy for this cake."

She doesn't move. She is a glacier next to me. "Things were different two nights ago."

"We were pretending then and we're pretending now. Nothing has changed."

I know the words are a lie. Cora knows it, too. Two nights ago, we were out on a date, with the possibility of something swirling alluringly between us.

Now, I've gutted those hopes. One cruel word at a time.

I saw her in the doorway to my office. The shock etched into the lines of her face. The hurt. I thought the gut punch I felt then was the worst it could get.

Until now. The fire in Cora has gone dormant, replaced by an icy indifference I can't seem to thaw.

That hurts worse.

The baker emerges from the back. "How is the happy couple?" The woman is beaming at us, too thrilled with her good fortune at having been chosen as our baker to even notice the schism widening before her eyes. "Are there any flavors you particularly love? I can bring out more samples or whip up different combinations if there is something you want to try that isn't here."

Cora keeps her eyes on me. "Order whatever you want, *dear*."

What the fuck did she expect? She told me the night we met that she had no interest in this world. Even if I had told Yasha what I was really thinking, what I was really feeling, what would have changed? Sure, I could have said that Cora is *different*. That she brings color to the monotone drudgery that is my day-to-day life. That my pulse quickens when she enters a room and when she leaves it. That I fucking *dream* of her.

But even if I told him all that, nothing would have changed.

We still wouldn't have a shot in hell of being anything more than what we are now: two people pretending they have a future that doesn't exist.

I hold her gaze for one second, two, five, ten. Then I spin back to the baker. "Leave. Come back when I call for you."

The woman's smile fades. "Oh. I—Do you need—?"

"I need you to leave," I grit out. "*Now.*"

Even as the baker stumbles back towards the kitchen door, Cora doesn't move. Doesn't react. The only sign she's even conscious of what is happening around her is the way she flinches as I spin back to her.

"If you're mad, say so."

She lifts her chin. "I'm not mad."

"Like fuck you aren't. For someone who hates masks, you sure love to hide behind one."

She snaps her attention to me, eyes flaring. "I'm not hiding anything."

"Since when?"

"Since always!" She throws her arms wide. "The only reason I'm here is because *you* demanded it. Because otherwise, my friends and I would be killed and you wouldn't do anything to stop it. I never had a choice."

I'm looking at Cora, but I don't see her; instead, I see Katerina Sokolov standing in front of me, hands shaking around a champagne flute as we toasted.

I see my mother, head bowed as she over and over again resigned herself to her fate.

This is not like that.

I'm *not like that.*

"You think you don't have a choice?" I spit.

She lifts her chin. "I *know* I don't."

I slide a plate of lemon raspberry cake between us and swipe my finger through it. Pink buttercream and berries drip down my finger as I hold it to her lips. "Try it."

"No."

I lean closer. "I thought you said you didn't have a choice."

"You know damn well that's not what I was talking about, Ivan."

"So you have a choice in some things but not others?" I press. "It's a wonder you have freedom at all if I'm such a monster. That must be why you were trembling in the shower the other night. You were *afraid* of me."

Her jaw clenches. Color rises high in her cheeks. She's remembering exactly what happened.

The way she begged me to fuck her. How much she wanted me to touch her.

Suddenly, she sits forward on her stool and wraps a hand around my wrist. Her green eyes are locked on mine as she leans forward and parts her lips.

The moment she wraps her full lips around my finger, I see my mistake.

I feel my cock growing in my pants. Achingly hard. Painfully hard.

We've shattered through the wall of ice, but now, we're at the other extreme. Heat burns between us, scorching every other thought and worry out of my head.

I shift closer and palm her thigh. I just need to ground myself to something real, something tangible. Because with every second that Cora's mouth is on my fingertip, the likelihood that I throw her on the counter and devour her like the cake we're supposed to be tasting grows exponentially larger.

Her lashes flutter closed. She tightens her hand around my wrist, twisting as she swirls her tongue slowly around my finger. It's impossible not to think about where I wish her tongue was instead.

Then she moans.

Holy fuck, she actually moans. I feel the vibration in my bones.

Her cheeks hollow out. She sucks every possible drop of frosting from my finger. Her tongue flicks the end of my finger once and then again.

I'm shaking with lust. Stuck in a trap of my own making.

Then her eyes open.

And the moment shatters apart.

The house lights come on. The curtain parts. The fantasy we've been living in for days dissolves like the paper dream it is, and I force myself to pull my finger free of her mouth.

Her mask is gone. All that's left is stunned fear and crushed hope.

Cora blinks at me, her eyes darting around in hopes of some kind of escape. Then she jolts up, almost knocking her stool back in the process. "I need to use the restroom."

As she sprints away, I adjust my pants and consider the choice now before me: do I pretend I don't give a damn and let her go?

Or do I follow her into the bathroom and show her exactly how much I care?

51

IVAN

I glance at the bathroom door again and again. As if the answer to the question circling around my mind will appear there.

Just as I decide Cora has been gone too long—a whopping five minutes—and I should go after her, my phone rings.

I answer the call and squint through the front window to the dark world beyond where I know Yasha is standing guard. "What do you want?"

"I want to know if I should give you two some privacy. Things are heating up in there."

I honestly forgot Yasha was watching over us. The moment Cora wrapped her lips around my finger, I forgot the rest of the world fucking existed. My universe narrowed to one very specific point.

"We're playing our parts, Yasha."

"Uh-huh," he says, unconvinced. "My part, apparently, is to be your voyeur. That's what I feel like out here. Like some creepy perv being turned on by cake."

I flash a middle finger at the glass even though all I can see is my own watery reflection. "Fuck off."

Yasha laughs. "Is that an order? Because last I heard, your wifey is still under threat."

I spin back towards the still closed bathroom door. Maybe she's going to hide in there until our cake tasting is over.

"Have you seen any movement out there?"

"Nope. Nothing beyond the two of you getting cozy."

I roll my eyes. "I can handle the interior. Why don't you keep your eyes out there and far away from Cora?"

I hear the possessiveness in my own voice. The claim I'm laying on her, even though I don't have a claim to lay. Not after what I said in my office—what Cora overheard.

I'm waiting for Yasha to call me out on it. He and Anya seem set on making this arrangement permanent for some reason.

But he doesn't say anything.

I wait a few more seconds, sure I'll hear his cackling laugh any second.

"Yasha?"

Nothing.

I check my phone and the connection is gone. Silent.

Everything is silent, actually. The kitchen was bustling with movement and clattering pans when we arrived, but I don't hear a thing now. No footsteps. No muffled voices.

I turn back to the bathroom door and it's still closed.

Something is wrong.

I walk to the bathroom and pound on the door. "Cora!"

Nothing. Not a sound beyond my own breathing.

"Shit." I kick at the base of the door, the wood rattling in the frame. "Cora, open the door!"

Wrong. Wrong. Something is very fucking wrong.

That thought thrums through me like a second heartbeat as I step back and then throw all of my weight into the bathroom door.

The trim rips away from the wall and the door flies open, revealing Cora…

Sprawled out on the floor.

For one heartstopping second, I think she's dead. *I let her walk away from me, and now, she's dead. I didn't take care of her. It's all my fault.*

Then she lifts her face.

She's alive, but so pale. So fucking pale. Her eyes are half-closed and her head keeps bobbing up and down like she's fighting to stay awake.

"Cora." I drop to my knees next to her and grab her hands in mine. "What happened?"

She blinks, trying to focus, but there is a glaze over her expression I've never seen before. She's right in front of me, but she might as well be a million miles away.

"My…phone," she mumbles.

I shake her gently. "Can you hear me?"

Her head flops in my direction like it's too heavy to hold up. "Ivan." Her fingers twitch around mine. She moans. "Ivan."

She's been drugged. Someone slipped her something.

I tense up. Not only did someone attack my fiancée, but they did it on my watch. After I promised Cora I would take care of her.

After I swore I'd keep her safe.

From the world.

From myself.

"We have to go," I tell her. "*Now.* Can you stand?"

Her hand flops into her lap. Onto her phone. I don't know if she's trying to tell me something or if that's all the movement she's capable of, but there isn't time to figure it out. I pocket her phone and scoop her into my arms.

Her head is heavy on my shoulder as I carry her out of the bathroom and through an emergency exit.

The door opens into a dark alley between buildings. There should be a guard positioned here, but the alley is empty. The fact Yasha hasn't called to ask what the fuck I'm doing breaking down the bakery's bathroom door is also a bad sign.

Right now, Cora needs me to get her out of here. She needs me to stay focused.

Which is getting harder with every raspy exhale I feel against my neck.

Her hand is swaying limply at her side, her body jostling with every step. I have no idea what she was given. I don't know how much longer she has to—

"No."

I say it out loud to myself. To Cora's fluttering lashes and parted lips.

She won't die. I won't allow it.

Slowly, I slide her body down mine and set her on her feet. She manages to lock her knees enough that I can hold her up with one hand around her waist.

"Ivan," she moans. "Am I—"

"Let me get you out of here. We'll talk then."

It doesn't end here. It can't. There will be a later.

I pull out my phone and dial Yasha's number, but the call doesn't go through. There's no service. If there was any doubt at all about whether this is an attack or not, it's gone now.

We're being targeted.

Which means we have to get out of here before—

"Don't fucking move," a voice growls from behind me.

At the same time, I feel a gun press against the back of my head.

52

CORA

The next time I open my eyes, I'm outside.

A cool breeze whispers across my overheated skin. I feel marginally more coherent. Coherent enough to recognize the strong arm around my waist, at least.

"Ivan." It takes real effort to say his name. I try to stand on my own feet, but I fall more firmly into the hard cliff of his chest. "Am I—"

"Let me get you out of here." He pats my waist, his hand spread across my ribs like armor. "We'll talk then."

He seems to think there will be a "later." That whatever is happening to me isn't permanent. That's nice. I let his confidence seep into me, ebbing away the panic my weak body is trying to muster.

Then I feel him stiffen. A voice I don't recognize echoes through the alley. "Don't fucking move."

I turn my head. The world in front of me swirls like watercolors before crystallizing into shape. When it does, I frown.

A man in black. A mask pulled over his face. Standing behind Ivan. With a gun to his head.

That's not so nice.

There isn't time to think or plan. Without hesitating, I stumble out of Ivan's embrace. "D-don't. Don't shoot. Don't —Please don't hurt him."

Ivan is glaring at me. Rage is rippling off of him like living shadows, crowning him in darkness. It's probably whatever I've been drugged with, but I feel the darkness reaching towards me like vines, trying to pull me closer.

"Cora," Ivan growls in warning.

The man readjusts his weapon. "Shut up. Both of you."

But I can't stay quiet. Not when the truth has been laid so bare before me.

I know, in this moment, that I'd rather die than see something bad happen to Ivan. I'd rather hand myself over than let him get hurt.

This might all be a game for him. But I'm not playing. Not anymore.

"Please." I look past Ivan to the man behind him. To the gun pressed to his head. "Please don't hurt him."

The man tilts his head to the side. I can't see his mouth, but I can sense a smile in his dark eyes. Then he turns the gun on me.

The world explodes. Sound and movement and color. I see the flash of the shot. Then something hits me. *Someone*, rather.

Ivan throws himself into me and shoves me out of the way. A feat that doesn't take much effort considering my legs are little more than poorly stacked building blocks.

I collapse into the side of the building, the wind whooshing out of me.

I need to get up. I need to fight. I need to help Ivan.

The thoughts are wisps of smoke. I reach for them, but they dissolve in front of me.

I *can't* get up. I *can't* fight. I *can't* help Ivan. I can barely even keep my eyes open.

Between long blinks, I see him struggling with the shooter. They're fighting and grunting. I can't tell who is winning or what is going to happen. But as I slip into inevitable sleep, one thought rises to the surface of my muddled mind.

I trust him.

53

CORA

Ivan has his arm around my waist. His hand fits so perfectly against me. Like we were made for this.

We're in the jewelry store, diamonds glittering all around us. Ivan is watching me slide ring after ring onto my finger. Every time he wrinkles his nose and shakes his head.

"I've tried on the entire store," I laugh.

"None of them are good enough. You deserve the best."

I press onto my toes and kiss his cheek. "I already have the best. I have you."

I should feel awkward and uncomfortable. We're only pretending, after all. But there's no sense of that here. This all feels...real. Normal.

Like we're an actual couple.

Ivan smiles down at me. Amusement dances in his amber eyes. "Much to my dismay, you can't wear me all the time."

"I can try," I purr.

He leans in, his lips close to my ear. "Tell me what you know."

I press my nose to his neck, breathing him in. He smells like gunpowder. Like dust and blood and...

I pull back. "What are you talking about?"

But he's gone.

∼

Ivan is now kneeling down a few feet away from me. He's talking to a man who is curled on the ground.

"Who sent you?" he barks. "What did you give her?"

The man on the ground is dressed in all black. I can't see his face, but I see his hand. He pulls something out of a pocket in his jacket.

A gun.

I try to lunge, but my body is frozen. I can't move as I watch the horror unfold in front of me, powerless to do anything to stop it.

But the man doesn't shoot Ivan.

He points the gun at himself. He wedges it under his chin and—

∼

The car door bangs closed. Ivan is in the backseat next to me. Camera flashes from the paparazzi light up the window. I understand why. He looks incredible in his tux.

His mouth is pulled into a devilish smirk. A smile that promises nothing but trouble. When he turns to me, I feel my insides melt.

"We aren't going home," he tells me. "We're going out on the town."

I laugh. "After all the cheesecake I just ate, you'd have to roll me out on the town."

"I'll roll with you." *He arches a brow and slides a hand over my stomach.* "On the town, in our bed—either one is fine."

Our bed. We share a bed.

Of course we do. Why wouldn't we?

"I'm stuffed, but if you try really hard, you might be able to convince me to roll into bed with you."

He snorts. "You think I'd have to try?"

"Really hard," *I tease.* "Just because you wine and dine me does not mean I'm a sure thing."

"You're going to be okay," *he says suddenly.*

I laugh nervously. "I assumed I would be. Should I be nervous?"

His smile fades. He leans across the back seat towards me. Someone —Yasha, I think—is in the driver's seat. He's bitching at traffic and swerving all over the road.

"What is going on?" *I ask.*

Ivan doesn't answer; he just loops his arms under my knees and around my back. He hauls me into his lap, curling me into his chest like I'm a child.

"You're going to be okay," *he says again.*

My heart is beating a lopsided, unsteady rhythm. "I wish you'd stop saying that. I know I'm okay. I trust you."

It's the words I thought before. The words I thought when...when I was on the damp, cold ground in the alley.

The alley behind the bakery.

The gun.

It hits me all at once.

This is a dream.

I'm curled against Ivan's chest, but the gauzy filter of the dream is gone. The car is dark, but streetlights paint the interior yellow every few seconds as Yasha flies down the road.

I look up in a moment of light and catch a glimpse of Ivan's face. Blood is splattered across his cheek. I don't think it's his.

It's hard to think of anything. My thoughts feel faraway, disjointed. Maybe I'm still dreaming. But this doesn't feel like a dream.

My head is pounding and my bones ache. It feels like they're grinding together with every bump of the car. My stomach swirls. If I'd eaten more than one bite of cake, I know I'd be throwing it up right now.

The worst part is, all I want to do is go back to sleep.

Back into my dream.

As if he can sense my discomfort, Ivan smooths a hand down my spine. He draws me close to him, encircling me with his arms and his scent. It's not the gunpowder and dust of the alley, but something quintessentially Ivan. It makes me think of warm nights beneath the stars. Of crisp breezes and moonlight.

My eyes flutter closed, and I feel his breath on my cheek.

Soft words spoken in Russian, whispered like a promise against my skin.

I don't know what he's saying, but I sink into the words and his arms. I let them carry me away.

54

IVAN

Yasha skids to a stop in the driveway. "Hold on, and I can get the doors for—"

But I'm already in motion.

I've been watching Cora every second of the drive, counting her breaths. Waiting for them to grow shallow, to stop coming altogether.

I can't sit still for another second. There isn't time to wait.

I fold her against my chest and run for the front doors. Per my orders, Dr. Popov is already here. He opens the front door as I mount the steps and ushers us inside.

"I have my things set up in the sitting room." He starts to lead the way, but I brush past him.

Faster. Everyone needs to move faster.

Dr. Popov is nearing eighty. He's been a Bratva doctor since well before I was born. One day, he'll need to be replaced. But for today, he keeps pace with me just fine.

"Lay her on the couch." He slides his stethoscope into his ears and lays a hand on my shoulder. "You can wait in the kitchen until I'm—"

"I'm not going anywhere," I growl.

I let her out of my sight once, and someone attacked her. Somehow, without me noticing, someone got to her.

I refuse to let it happen again.

The doctor stares at me, not in defiance, but in question. I've never overseen his work before. There's never been a need to. I know he'll always do his best to take care of any patient in front of him.

This is different.

Cora is different.

I jab a hand at her too-still body on the couch. "Examine her. *Now.*"

Dr. Popov jolts at the authority in my voice. He bends his already-hunched back over her and begins his examination.

Cora stirred a few times in the car. Her eyes would roll in my direction or her lips would form around nonsense sounds, almost like she was trying to speak to me. Once, I even thought I saw her smile. But she hasn't so much as batted an eyelash in the last fifteen minutes.

She doesn't look quite as waxy pale as she did when I found her on the floor of the bakery's bathroom. The fluorescents in there were harsh, giving her a deathly pallor. But the near-permanent blush she usually sports is missing from her cheeks.

Dr. Popov presses against the pulse point in her neck and checks her blood pressure. He draws blood from the delicate blue vein on the inside of her arm.

Through all of it, Cora doesn't move an inch.

It's bizarre, watching him work on her when, in every conceivable way, she looks perfect. Her pointed chin is tucked against her chest. Long lashes brush the tops of her cheeks. Her lips are slightly parted, as if in exhale.

I have the sudden urge to lean down and kiss her. Like we might be living in a storybook and one kiss could awaken her.

But this is no fairytale. I'm no Prince Charming.

"You think she was drugged, correct?" Dr. Popov asks.

I nod. "It's the only explanation. She was fine, but when I checked on her a few minutes later, she was on the floor."

My fist clenches at my side. Hard enough I think my knuckles will burst through the skin. Rage boils inside of me until I'm sure I'll breathe fire.

Prince Charming doesn't seek vengeance.

Prince Charming doesn't sit by the princess's bedside and plot all the ways he will maim and torture the villain responsible.

In this fairytale, I'm no hero. I'm the monster.

And when I find out who is responsible for this, I will rain death on all of them.

55

IVAN

"Again."

With a sigh, Dr. Popov repeats himself for the third time. "The blood test showed signs of a common sedative. She received a high dosage, but it will wear off in a few hours. She will be fine."

"How did it get in her system?" Yasha growls. He sounds almost as angry as I am.

It was his job to make sure the bakery was secure. It was his job to watch the two of us, make sure nothing happened. This is as much a violation to him as it is to me.

"I was watching them both the entire fucking time." He looks to me, pleading with me to believe him. "When our phone call dropped and I lost service, I saw someone in all black running down the street. I followed them. I—I thought it was the right call."

I clap a hand on his shoulder. "It was a distraction. You made the right call with the information you had."

Dr. Popov clears his throat. "As far as the sedative, it could have been in something she drank. Something she ate."

"She didn't touch the cake. Well, just one bite." My stomach tightens, remembering her mouth wrapped around my finger.

Yasha curses under his breath. "The water. She had a water bottle. I made sure the cakes were clean, but I didn't—The water bottles were sealed. I didn't think they would be an issue. *Fuck.*" He rakes a furious hand through his hair. "It must mean they were planning to move her to a secondary location. The only reason they tried to shoot her instead was because—"

"I interrupted."

My stomach twists at the thought that Cora could be in enemy hands right now. I look down at her on the couch, still asleep, her chest rising and falling in slow, even movements. The fact that *this* is the best possible outcome is un-fucking-acceptable.

"Next time, we do better." I look at Yasha, my eyes boring into his.

He shakes his head. "There is no next time. This won't happen again."

Dr. Popov picks up his black bag and holds out his liver-spotted hand for a shake. "If there is a next time, you call me. You know I'm always here for your family, Ivan. Whatever you need."

I thank the man and have Yasha escort him out to his car.

Then I'm alone with Cora.

Alone with her for the first time since I found her in that bathroom. The dread that swirled in me then makes a sudden reappearance.

Before I can stop myself, I bend low and scoop her into my arms. I haul her against my chest and hold her so I can feel every breath. So I can feel the warmth of her skin and hear her every exhale.

She's alive. She's alive. She's alive.

I barely glance at her bedroom door as I pass by it, walking towards mine instead.

I need her in *my* bed. In *my* room. Where I can see her and watch over her.

My room is dark as I lay her on the mattress. Her head tilts gently to the side, her cheek cushioned against my pillow.

She looks peaceful. *At home.*

I shove the thought down and take in the rest of her. The blood splatter dotting her clothes. The dirt from the alley staining her pale dress.

I dig through a drawer for a large t-shirt and get to work peeling her gently out of her clothes.

She's gorgeous—beyond gorgeous. But there is nothing exciting about what I'm doing now. About seeing her helpless and unconscious. Unresponsive to my touch.

I can't sit down. I can't stop moving. So long as I keep moving, everything will be okay. If I stay busy, she will wake up and this will all be…

Pretend.

The gnawing ache in my chest doesn't feel pretend, though. The yearning I have to burn the world down just to see her open her eyes isn't casual or temporary or fake.

The way she looks in my t-shirt, between my sheets…

It's not something I'll forget anytime soon.

I stand next to the bed, watching her breathe until the door opens and Anya bursts in.

"Is she okay?" Her eyes are wide, frantic. She sees Cora asleep in bed and freezes in horror. "Oh God. How long has she been like this?"

I have no idea how much time has passed. It could have been minutes or hours.

She drops down by Cora's bedside and cups her hands, and all I can think is, *Cora fits in here.*

Cora fits. With me. With my family. In our world.

She fits, but that doesn't mean she's right. Not for this role. Not for this life. Not when she could be attacked or drugged or killed just for the crime of standing next to me.

I've seen that fire inside of her dim before. I know what the world feels like without it.

I won't let it happen again.

"Stay here." I turn to the door, pausing with my fingers on the handle. "Don't leave her alone. Stay here until I get back."

Anya nods. "I'll stay. But where are you going?"

"To do what I should have done from the beginning."

56

IVAN

I fling the door to my father's study open hard enough that it bounces off the wall.

All of the men inside jolt. A few of his more loyal lieutenants rise to their feet, hands on their weapons, ready for a violent intruder.

"We are in the middle of a meeting, Ivan," my father snarls when they see it's me. "Wait for me outside."

I stand my ground. "Whatever bullshit you're working on can wait."

"'Bullshit'?" His eyes narrow to slivers. "Don't condescend to me. While you're taking your girlfriend on dates, I'm keeping this Bratva running."

"While you're hiding away in this room with your advisors, I'm fending off direct assaults on our family," I snarl. "There wouldn't be a Bratva to run without me."

"If there was an attack on the Bratva, I'm sure I would have heard about—"

"There *was* an attack," I assure him. "Which is why Cora's safety is now our top priority."

Otets waves his lieutenants back, telling them to sit down. "Don't waste my time with this, Ivan. You brought this girl into the fold and I made it clear she was your responsibility. You clearly can't handle that. She has officially become a liability and a distraction. I want her gone as soon as—"

"Cora *is* my responsibility." I slam the door closed behind me and spin back to my father. "But she is the sole target of our enemies. The fact you refuse to take this threat seriously is a fucking joke. Which makes *you* a fucking joke, too."

He leans forward. "You don't come in here and tell me how to—"

"What does it say that the Pushkin Bratva can't protect one singular woman? The *pakhan's* woman, at that?"

"She's not your woman." His eyes flare. "And you are not *pakhan*. Not yet."

"And I never will be if I die trying to save her. Which I will," I vow. "Because if Cora dies, the credibility of the Bratva dies with her. No one will take us seriously if we can't keep her safe. It will tell our enemies that we are ripe for the taking. It puts all of us in danger and it makes our defenses look weak."

Dmitry and Vadim shift nervously in their chairs. I know for a fact they feel the same way Yasha does about their responsibilities. They've sworn to protect the Bratva with their lives. They take it seriously.

And right now, my father is making liars of them.

"The only thing that makes us look weak is that your head could be turned by this peasant woman," my father spits back. "Our credibility was never questioned before she arrived. Now, she's making you soft."

I clench my jaw hard. "You can't see it. You really can't fucking see it. Amazing."

"Don't tell me what I can and can't see!" he roars. "I see more than you realize."

"Then you must see that someone out there wants into our family so badly that they are willing to kill any woman I choose. They are going to tear down the empire we've built, brick by brick, until they can waltz right through the front doors."

"Bullshit!" His face is red and sweaty, his eyes almost bulging out of his head. "This is all bullshit. A story you're concocting to get out of your bargain with me. This is all because you don't want to get married."

That was true at one point: I didn't want to get married. The decision was little more than a bargaining chip for Anya's freedom.

Now, the problem is…

I want to get married to the wrong girl.

But I can't and I won't. Not if it puts her life in danger. So the least I can do is make sure she's safe. No matter the cost.

"I'm going to uphold my end of our bargain," I tell him solemnly. "I've always intended to do exactly as I promised you. But I'm going to do it my way. I'm not going to allow some outsider to threaten me into making a choice. And I certainly will not let the Bratva I am going to inherit be discredited by allowing the woman on my arm to be hurt or disrespected."

I turn to Dmitry and Vadim. I take in their stoic faces—faces scarred from years of protecting this bratva, from decades of fighting for my family.

"This family has always been protected," I say to them. "Our security and strength have never been doubted. I won't let it start now."

They both nod in subtle agreement.

That, more than anything I've said, forces my father's hand. He can't afford his men to unite behind me just yet.

"Fine," he barks. "Your waitress is our number one priority. Do what needs to be done to make sure she is secure. Run anything else by me before—"

"No."

He pauses and draws in a surprised, rattling breath. "No?"

"No." I shake my head. "I'm taking the fight to them."

He sighs. "What happened to avoiding war?"

"I'm done playing defense. It's time to make a move."

Fuck, it feels good to say that.

57

CORA

My head is encased in cement. Eyes sealed shut. Mouth stuffed with cotton.

I'm not awake, but I'm also not in a dream. I'm in some sluggish middle ground, trapped in my own body.

Then I feel a hand around mine.

Ivan.

His name rises through the muddy waters of my mind before I realize the hand is smooth and small. Nothing like the work-roughened, large hands I know.

Not Ivan, then.

"Cora?" a soft voice says.

Anya.

I struggle against my heavy lids.

"You're okay," she reassures me. "You're okay. Just take your time."

I lie back and let myself come awake piece by piece. I shake my feet and hands. I take stock of my breathing with deep inhales and exhales to ease the nervous fluttering of my heart.

Finally, I peel my eyes open.

I hiss like a vampire when a beam of light stabs me directly in the eyeballs.

"Oh, shit!" Anya yelps. "Sorry about the window."

She drops my hand and scurries away and, a second later, the room is dark again.

I try to say something, but my throat is raw.

"Oh, here." She grabs a water bottle from the bedside table and holds the straw to my lips. "It's water. No poison. I already checked." I frown, and she ducks her head. "Sorry. That wasn't funny. Too soon, probably."

I gulp water. Drop by drop, I start to return to the land of the living. When I've had enough. I hand it back to her. "Wh… what happened?"

She blows a strand of hair off of her forehead. "I'll give you the short version: don't drink or eat anything while in public that hasn't been checked by someone on the security team."

I clear the hoarseness from my throat. "Maybe give me the slightly longer version?"

"You were drugged. Ivan found you on the bathroom floor of the bakery and carried you outside, but he was stopped by a man with a gun."

Bits of my dream come back to me. The smell of gunpowder. A bang. Ivan—

"Is he okay?" I rasp.

Anya presses a hand to my shoulder and eases me back into the bed. I didn't even realize I sat up.

"He's fine. He was grazed, but it was nothing. The shooter was going after you, not him." She pulls the blanket over my legs.

As soon as she's done, I shove the blanket back down and stare at my legs. My *bare* legs. At the threadbare t-shirt that barely covers the tops of my thighs. "Where did I get this shirt? And—" I look around at the oddly familiar room. It looks so much like mine, but in reverse. "Is this Ivan's room?"

The furnishings are moodier. Dark blue wallpaper, velvet curtains, and walnut. It suits him.

"And Ivan's shirt." Anya nods. "He brought you here so you wouldn't be alone."

I fight the urge to bring the comforter to my nose and take a deep breath. "I could be 'not alone' in my room."

"He wanted you close. Very close." She gives me a warm smile.

I pull the blanket back over my bare legs and cross my arms over my chest. "Did you dress me?"

"Not exactly…" She winces.

"Then who *exactly* did, Anya?"

She laughs and runs fingers through her hair. "For someone who just woke up from being drugged, you're surprisingly coherent. I didn't think I'd be answering so many questions."

"Anya."

She holds up her hands. "It was Ivan. But it wasn't like that. He just didn't want you to wake up in bloody clothes and he didn't trust anyone else to do it."

"You! You could have done it."

"I wasn't here yet. Your options were Ivan, Yasha, or Niles. Take your pick."

I mull it over for all of three seconds before I realize there was no better option. I'd have to go into witness protection if Niles ever saw me naked and Yasha can't be trusted with that kind of information. He'd tease me about it for the rest of… well, the rest of however long I know him.

I sink down in the blankets, knowing full well Ivan has already seen me naked multiple times. That isn't even the problem; I don't care that he saw me naked.

I care that him taking care of me when I couldn't take care of myself feels far too intimate for this game we're playing.

"It's sweet, isn't it?" I look over to see Anya has stars in her eyes. "I've never seen him so protective of someone before. He made me swear I wouldn't leave you alone before he left."

"He left? Where did he go?"

If my dream is to be believed, the man who came at us with the gun killed himself. I blink and see him raising the gun to his chin. I hear the shot echo on the bricks.

I shiver.

Anya shrugs. "He didn't say. But he made me promise to stay here with you. He looked… Well, I've never seen him so shaken. Yasha called and told me what happened and he said the same thing. He said that this was different. That *you* were different."

Her words poke at the dried-up husk of hope in my chest.

"I just think…" Anya perches on the edge of the bed, her hands folded in her lap. "I think this thing between the two of you is real. More real than either of you will admit."

I hear whispers in my ear. Gentle words of comfort and care. I feel his arms banded around me, protecting me.

All of that was real. But a future? A life together?

That can't be.

When I look up, Anya is watching me. Her expression is guarded. Then, as if deciding something, she takes a deep breath. "You know, I was promised in marriage to the heir to a tech fortune. Millionaires on their way to billionaires."

"Lev?" I ask.

She busts out laughing. "God. No. Lev is…" She smiles, her cheeks glowing pink. "Lev worked for my father, actually. He was on the security team. Lowest level clearance. He couldn't even buzz himself through our front gate. The guards on duty had to let him in any time he came to see me. Which made it hard to keep our rendezvous secret from my father and my fiancé. As you can imagine, Daddy wasn't pleased."

"You cheated?"

She wavers back and forth, a shy smile on her face. "I'd argue that it's impossible to cheat on someone you never chose to be in a relationship with. I barely knew the guy, let alone loved him. But I loved Lev."

"Did your dad know that when he set up the engagement?"

She snorts. "Oh, hell yeah, he knew it. My relationship with Lev is why he set up the engagement in the first place. He wanted to force us apart. He actually fired Lev, but Ivan hired him for his personal security team."

"Why?"

"Because unlike my father, my brother just wanted me to be happy." Her eyes go glassy, but she quickly blinks the emotion away. "Anyway, that stirred up a whole big brouhaha. My fiancé was threatening to pull out of the engagement and my dad was seriously considering murdering Lev."

I can't tell if she's exaggerating or not, but I have a feeling she isn't. Based on the little I know of him, Boris Pushkin seems more than capable of senseless murder.

Anya sags, seemingly exhausted by the memory of it all. "Everything was falling apart and I was about to end things with Lev just to protect him. To try to keep him alive and my family from splitting apart at the seams."

I'm on the edge of my seat now. A happy ending? In *this* family? Surely not.

"What happened?"

She smiles. "Ivan happened. I went to my father's office to tell him I was going to break up with Lev and marry the boring billionaire, but Ivan was already there. They were finalizing the details of a new plan. A bargain. Ivan swore that he would take on my burden and marry well for the family if it meant I could marry the man I loved."

I don't think I'm breathing. "You're joking."

"Dead serious. He made that deal and made my father swear that I would never be disowned. He couldn't cut me out of the will or pull security from me and Lev. Ivan staked my entire life on one promise: that he would marry someone my father approved of in my stead."

My stomach hollows out. I hear Boris Pushkin's sneering voice. *Am I supposed to believe* both *my children have a fetish for the lower classes?*

"Ivan never told me that."

He told me this was all pretend. He told me we would never work. He told me the outcome, but he never explained the reasoning.

"He'd be mad I told you," she admits. "He doesn't want to talk about it, but this is *my* story. This is what I can tell you, even if he would hate that you know."

"Why would he care that I know?"

If anything, this is an easy out for him. This information makes sense of so many things between us. It's his *'Get Out of Jail Free'* card—not that he needs one.

"Ivan cares more than anyone knows. More than he shows." She lays a hand over mine, squeezing gently. "If he reveals even a drop of emotion to you, there's an ocean of feeling where that came from."

I'm on an emotional carousel, circling around and around the same thoughts again and again.

But it all comes back to the same place.

My eyes well with tears. Frowning, Anya leans in close. "What's wrong, honey?"

Before I can answer, the door swings open. Ivan is in the doorway, silhouetted against the hallway light like an avenging angel. He's as beautiful as he was in any of my dreams with his crown of dark hair and burnished gold eyes.

"You can go, Anya," he says firmly, never taking his eyes off of me. "Cora needs to rest."

Without another word, Anya stands up. She pats her brother's shoulder softly before she closes the door and leaves us alone.

58

CORA

The room shrinks around us. He's standing a dozen feet away, but he might as well be breathing down my neck the way my heart is hammering against my ribs.

I can't have him.

He doesn't want me.

This isn't real.

This.

Isn't.

Real.

I repeat the words to myself again and again as if my mind might be able to keep my heart in line. Like there's a chance I can wrangle the feeling running wild in my chest, the one mewling and pawing to get close to the man in front of me.

"You're awake." His amber eyes see everything. There isn't a molecule of me he doesn't examine and make note of.

"I woke up a few minutes ago. Anya was with me. She said you left."

"I had things to take care of."

"People to take care of, you mean?" I look him over for any signs of injury. For blood splatter or bruises. I don't see anything. But I can't imagine he'd let this sin go unpunished.

His fists clench at his sides. Bands of muscle flex and contract across his arms, shifting the dark tattoos that swirl over his skin. "The man who shot at you is dead. If there was anyone else working with him, I'll find them all. Every single one."

God help those people. Wrath clouds his expression. I'd hate to be on the receiving end of that look.

"Thank you. For… Well, I don't remember everything that happened."

With each blink, I see Ivan kneeling next to me in the bakery bathroom. I see him looming over the dark shadow of my attacker. I feel his warmth wrapped around my body. I smell his musk.

I have to shake my head to clear the bits of memory like rocks from my shoe. "Thank you for saving me."

"You shouldn't have needed saving," he growls. "None of this should have happened."

"We knew this was a risk. Getting nibbled is the fate of the bait, right?" I try to smile to lighten the mood, but it doesn't lighten the heaviness in my chest.

Ivan goes perfectly still. His jaw works back and forth, back and forth.

I sit up, clutching the comforter against my chest. "I'm okay, Ivan. I feel fine."

"You weren't fine," he spits. "You were practically unconscious on the bathroom floor. You almost—They tried—*He fucking shot at you.*"

"And you saved me. I'm fine."

"Stop saying that. Just stop." A deep growl rumbles through his chest as he stalks to the bed. He claims the spot Anya was just in, his body brushing against my thigh. "You should be upset, Cora. The last time we spoke, you were mad. Be mad at me. Be furious."

Our last interaction rises up between us like smoke, obscuring everything else.

I was mad that Ivan didn't want me. That he could so easily say I would never be the right woman for him.

Then I was livid that I could be drawn back in so easily. One touch—one taste—was all it took to make me forget everything else and give myself over to him again.

Now, thanks to Anya's story, I know a little about what it is costing him. What he has sacrificed for his family.

And I can't find it within me to be mad about that.

"The only thing you need to know," he says, "is that I'll die before I let someone hurt you again."

I'm afraid to breathe. This moment is tenuous, fragile. One exhale could send it fluttering away.

Then he takes his hand away.

It's instinctual—the urge to be close to him, to not let him draw back yet again. I don't plan to do it, but I find myself lunging for his hand. My fingers wrap around his wrist and I pull him close. I cradle his hand between mine, staring down at where we intertwine.

"What I know," I say softly, "is that you are a good man, Ivan Pushkin. No matter what anyone says."

His thumb circles across my palm, sending goosebumps up my arm. "I'm good to my family," he murmurs. "I'm good to the people who follow me. But to everyone else—to anyone beyond the scope of that, to anyone who threatens me or the ones close to me—I'm a monster. Because that's what is required of me."

"By your father?"

"By this life." Slowly, he withdraws his hand from mine. "If I'm going to keep the promises I've made, I don't have room to be good to anyone else. I don't have time to add anyone else's needs to my plate."

I feel the wall between us going up brick by brick. I want to cry. *We were so close.*

But Ivan made a deal with his father and he wants to see it through. He wants to take care of his sister and be a good son, even if his father doesn't deserve it.

He *is* a good man, which is exactly why he's trying to push me away.

But the way his head is hanging now and his eyes fix on everything except my face, I don't think he wants this wall between us anymore than I do. Soon, though, we won't have a choice. The clock is running out, and I can feel our moments together slipping away.

That doesn't mean I'm ready to let them go.

I want Ivan right now, like this, even if it's only for a little while.

So I shove the comforter back, rise to my knees, and climb onto Ivan's lap. When he looks into my eyes, I drag a finger down his square jaw. "What about *your* needs, Ivan?"

59

CORA

His hands settle on my hips, fisting in the material of my shirt. *His* shirt. "What are you doing?"

"You spend a lot of time talking about what everyone else needs. I want to talk about what you need."

"What I need is to be a man of my word."

"So be one," I say plainly. "I'm not stopping you."

His thumbs stroke over my ribs. "No, but you're making it really fucking hard."

I may have been unconscious half an hour ago, but my body is thrumming now. I feel like a livewire in his hands.

"You have secrets. I know that. But so do I." I wrap my hands around his neck and trace my fingers through his silky hair. "We both have good reasons not to be here—not to be together. But I can't think of a single reason why I shouldn't let you tear this shirt off of me right this second."

I feel his hard length pressing against my center. "For one, this is my shirt." He smirks. "I'd hate to lose it."

"Oh. Okay." I reach down and pull the shirt over my head in one smooth motion. I toss it at the end of the bed and turn back to him. "Is this better?"

Outside, I'm confident. On the inside, I'm a ball of uncertainty.

Until I see the way Ivan is looking at me.

Desire turns his eyes dark—feral. He groans as if in pain and presses his forehead to the smooth skin between my breasts. "Cora."

My name on his lips is an aphrodisiac. Fuel on the fire—not that it needed any.

I slide my hips forward and back, gently grinding into him. "Some cruel twist of fate has brought the two of us together and I say we make the most of it while we can. Until we bounce off each other and go our separate ways, why not enjoy the sexual chemistry?"

He lifts his head from my chest, looking up at me beneath heavy brows. "I didn't take you for the casual sex type."

"And I didn't take you for the monogamous type," I fire back. "You'll marry a *'suitable woman'* one day. But until then, you're more than free to fuck me."

He squeezes my ribs, his hands shifting ever higher until his thumbs brush against the lace material of my bra. "Things are going to get complicated fast."

"Things are already complicated. But this?" I grind into him again, trying not to moan. "This has always made perfect sense."

He grits his teeth and swipes his thumbs over the hard points of my nipples. A faint whimper sneaks between my lips. "Nothing about you has made any fucking sense. Not since the moment we met."

I'm not sure what he means, but I don't want to ask. Not now. I don't want to get sidetracked with anything else.

Not when he is alive and in front of me.

Not when, in a not-too-distant future, he'll be far out of my reach.

"This will sell our charade." I'm breathless already, half-lost to the desire pounding between my legs. "It will make us seem more realistic."

His hands slide down my waist and wrap around my lower back. I arch into his touch.

"Unless we're planning to offer webcam viewings of my bedroom, I don't see how what we're doing right now will help sell anything to anyone."

If he wanted to, I'd let him set up a webcam. If it meant he'd keep touching me, I'd do just about anything.

He growls again, a low rumble vibrating from him and through me. I force my eyes open—force myself to look at him. At his stubbled jaw. At the tattoos climbing up his neck. At the golden flecks in his amber eyes.

And for just a second, I'm forced to look at myself. At my own motivations for being here. For suggesting any of this.

This is more than a flimsy facade for the sake of "his mission." This is a facade for what I really feel. For the feelings I can't navigate and won't confess.

Despite it all, I want this man. Desperately.

This is just the only way I can have him.

For now, it has to be enough.

Ivan's eyes trail over my face and my body. Then, all at once, he pushes me back and prowls over me. He settles between my legs, his hands pressed into the mattress on either side of my head, caging me into his body, his scent.

"God, it's good to feel you like this," he murmurs between bites of my collarbone. He looks at me up the length of my body, his eyes hooded. "Seeing you the way you were was a fucking nightmare. This is…better."

Someone admitting they like you better conscious isn't exactly poetry, but Anya's words ring out in my head. *If he reveals even a drop of emotion to you, there's an ocean of feeling where that came from.*

This is sex. *Just* sex, I remind myself. Hoping for anything more is a waste of energy.

"I prefer myself conscious, as well." I slide my hand between our bodies and stroke the underside of his erection. "It makes it easier to do this."

He drops his head onto my shoulder and groans in my ear. "Fucking hell, Cora."

I slip inside his pants and grip him. "It's good practice, too. You said if people could see us having sex, they'd have no doubt about our relationship. Maybe we should give it a try."

A laugh hisses between his clenched teeth. "Reconsidering my webcam idea?"

"I'm toying around with it."

At the next slow pull of my hand, Ivan gently presses his teeth into my shoulder. "Keep toying with it, then."

His lips find their way to my neck again, but he moves slowly. As if we have all the time in the world to be here. To explore and touch and kiss. And laugh.

That's the funny thing: all it takes is one look at Ivan to know that he would be great in bed. But the easy banter, the laughter—*that* was unexpected. That, more than anything, makes it hard to keep the yearning in my chest in the box where it belongs.

He growls out a curse and then slides away from my touch. His eyes are near black as he kisses his way down my stomach and lower. He tugs at the elastic of my panties, dragging the lace down my thighs and then shoving them down to the floor along with his own pants.

I watch him with my mouth open. He's so fucking gorgeous. It still blows my mind that this man chose me.

Then he pounces again and all thoughts go flying out of my head.

When he hooks my legs over his shoulders and lowers his face to my pussy, I almost buck us both off the bed. He feasts on me, licking and sucking until my hands are fisted in the sheets and I'm thrashing. My thighs clamp down around his ears as the sensation becomes too much.

I thread my fingers through his hair and ride him while I come undone again, again, again.

When he finally lifts his head, a wicked smile on his lips, my heart stutters.

I want more.

More than his body. More than mind-blowing sex.

I want all of him. The warrior. The protector. The leader. The charmer.

I want every iteration of Ivan Pushkin, and as much as I try to push that inconvenient truth to the side, it's impossible to ignore when he's smiling up at me like this.

"Scream like that every time I touch you and we'll have everyone fooled."

"Did I scream?" I didn't realize it, but I'm not surprised. The orgasm is still ebbing away, aftershocks still shivering through me.

He nods, keeping my legs hooked over his shoulders as he crawls up my body. "Don't worry if you missed it. You're about to do it again."

Before I can answer, he fills me in one thrust.

I claw at his shoulders, trying to bring him closer. To bury my face in his neck so he can't see what this is doing to me. But with my legs over his shoulders, this is as close as we can get. Close enough that he can see every fleeting emotion as it crosses my face.

I can see the sweat glistening in the hollows of his throat. I watch his jaw flex with each thrust. Worse, I see him study me the same way I'm studying him.

And when Ivan looks, he sees *everything.*

"Take this off." I grab awkwardly at his shirt, pretending I care about it while he's filling me again and again.

Ivan deftly slides my legs off his shoulders and leans back, tugging his shirt off with one move.

I reach for him, grateful for the position change until I go to loop an arm around his waist and find a large bandage there. It's taped over his ribs and wrapped partially around his back.

"What happened?"

He glances down and then shrugs it off. "Nothing."

"That's not nothing. That's a huge—" I lose my voice as he slides into me to the hilt, our bodies slapping together. I press a hand to his chest. "Is that from tonight? Did you get hurt?"

Anya said he was grazed. I imagined it like a road rash. But his bandage is bigger than my entire hand.

"It was a bullet graze. I'm fine."

I press a palm to his side, and he winces. "That's not fine, Ivan! He shot you! You saved me, but he shot you."

He growls low in his throat. "It's a graze. And we can talk about it later."

To punctuate the point, he draws his hips back and slams into me again.

"You shouldn't have—You have so many people who care about you." It's a struggle to keep my voice steady when my body is fighting to get closer to him. "I don't want you to die to save me. My family isn't like yours. There isn't anyone who cares about me. You should—"

He hauls me against him in an instant, dragging me off my back so we are kneeling together, chest to chest. "For fuck's sake, *solnishka*. I've explained this to you over and over again."

"Explained what? I don't know anything. None of this makes any sense to me."

"Then let me clear things up for you."

He slides my body up and down his thighs, taking me in slow, steady strokes while he looks into my eyes. He brings his mouth nearly to mine, letting our lips brush with every word.

"I do whatever the fuck I want."

I start to argue, but he takes my lower lip into his mouth. His tongue swirls against mine, muddying my thoughts and my senses. I'm putty in his hands.

His hand slips between us, thumb circling between my legs. I tip my head back, eyes closed. "You can't die for me, Ivan."

"Of course I can."

His thrusts are shallow now, but I feel like he's touching the deepest part of me. I want to stay like this with him for as long as possible. Forever, if I had my way.

But I don't have forever.

We might not even have tomorrow.

So I cling to the bleeding edge of now. We rock together until I'm rolling my hips against him and crying out to the ceiling, dizzy with pleasure.

Slowly, Ivan lays me back on the mattress. He fists a hand in my hair as we collide together. Once, twice, and again and again until he pants out a curse.

I trace the swirling tattoos on his arms as he spills into me. His body flexes with release, then he lets out a long, exhausted sigh. He nuzzles his stubbled face against my neck and, when he talks, his voice is a hoarse whisper in my ear.

"I always get what I want, Cora. And what I want is you."

60

IVAN

This shit was supposed to be fake.

Every time I look over at her, the light cutting through the window at different angles as the hours pass, I can't wrap my head around it. How can something that is supposedly fake feel so devastatingly real?

My phone is God only knows where. Aside from a few plates of food Niles has left in front of the door, I haven't interacted with another soul in well over fourteen hours. We've been fucking and talking and doing nothing at all, but *together*.

It's miraculous. *She* is miraculous.

The fact that she is alive and breathing next to me is the only thing I care about.

All of which is fucking *terrifying*.

I sit up and drag a hand through my tangled hair. Cora's arm is thrown over her head. Her cheek is resting on her elbow, her lips parted like she fell asleep talking. I think she did, actually.

"I've never known a guy who wanted to use toys in bed," she said a few hours ago, still flushed from her fourth—maybe fifth, possibly sixth or seventh or twelfth—orgasm of the night. "They're always afraid they'll be replaced."

"Then you've only slept with lesser men."

She snorted. "You can say that again."

"No, you say it." I rolled over, a light hand banded around her throat. "Say I'm the best you've ever had."

Heat rose in her cheeks, turning her a gorgeous shade of pink that had me semi-hard again. But her green eyes found mine and stuck. "You're the best I've ever had, Ivan."

Some unspoken truth floated between us. Saying it would ruin things, so I didn't. Neither did she. I just stared down at her, watching as her blinks became slower and slower until her eyes stayed closed.

She's been asleep since then, catching up on the sleep we lost last night.

But I haven't slept at all. I don't want to sleep. I don't want to miss a second of this time where the only thing that matters is the sound Cora makes when I slide into her.

Because, as soon as we step foot outside this room, Cora becomes just another cog in the machine of my life. An asset in a mission. A pawn on the chessboard.

She inhales deeply, her chest rising and falling under the thin sheet covering her chest. It occurs to me, not for the first time, that she knows far more than she should about our family, but not nearly enough for my liking.

There's so much I can't tell her.

Murders, missing persons, billion-dollar handshake deals in smoky backrooms. She saw me kill the sniper who tried to hurt her. She knows what we're capable of.

But she doesn't know about Katerina. She hasn't seen the complicated tangle of my past and I can't even begin to unwind it for her. Not if I'm going to keep my promises.

So Cora can never truly understand me or my motivations, and I can't be with her without defaulting on the deal I made on behalf of my sister. Which leaves me…

"Fucking stuck," I mutter.

I reach out and run a finger over her shoulder. Her skin is golden in the late afternoon light. I feel like a demon clinging to the front gates of heaven. I trace the lean muscle of her bicep, tugging the sheet lower and lower.

Her eyes are closed, but her lips curl into a lazy smile. "I've never had to say this before, but please don't give me another orgasm. I now think it's possible to die from pleasure."

"What a way to go, though." I let out a low whistle and curl my hand around the underside of her breast. I cup the weight in my palm. She fits against me so fucking perfectly. "Death by orgasm."

Her nipples pucker into points. "I've never been in this kind of danger before."

I prop my head on my fist. "That's a shame."

"Go figure. The best relationship of my life is a fraud."

The interaction from the jewelry store rises to the forefront of my mind. I convinced myself it wasn't my business before so I didn't get distracted by unnecessary details. But this entire day has been a distraction. Might as well go for broke.

"You and Kieran had met before I took you to his shop."

Cora winces, then sighs and lets it go. She is still wearing my diamond on her ring finger. It's the only thing she's been wearing since last night. "I hoped he wouldn't remember me. I was in there once. And only for a few minutes."

"With who?" It's an effort to unclench my jaw.

"Someone I didn't want to be dating, let alone marrying." She rolls onto her side and flips my hand over so it's palm-side up. Then she traces the lines of my hand with a meticulous finger. "I won't pretend to understand all of the pressure you're under, but I know a thing or two about family expectations. I know a lot more about disappointing them."

"So do you regret it? Not marrying whoever this asshole was?"

She arches a brow. "How do you know he was an asshole?"

I arch a brow in return. "Well, was he?"

"Yes." She laughs. "He absolutely was. And no, I absolutely don't regret running away."

Pieces of Cora click together. Her refined manners and understanding of my world paired with her job as a waitress in that shit heap of a restaurant. She was *someone* in a previous life. She ran away from it...

And I dragged her right back in.

"Earlier, you said you don't have anyone who cares about you."

She wrinkles her nose. "All I wanted was to be free. Now, I am. Nothing else matters."

"'Free'? I seem to remember you told me I was holding you hostage here."

"Are you going to keep quoting my words back to me?" She pokes me playfully in the chest. "I was…*adjusting*."

"And now?"

She smiles so wide her eyes are almost closed. "I'd say I've adjusted."

She stretches her arms over her head and yawns. Her eyes are puffy with sleep and there are pillow creases on her cheek.

Lying next to her like this feels more intimate than sex. There's something vulnerable about waking up next to someone.

I never thought I'd like it this much.

"It's not the first time I've been held hostage," she explains. "It *is* the first time I'm not mad about it."

"How flattering."

"Telling you you're better than my stepdad isn't much of a compliment. He set the bar so low it's basically in hell." She gives me a wry smile. "I preferred living on the street to living in his mansion."

"I didn't know you lived on the streets."

"Only for a year," she explains. "My real dad left and my mom was struggling. She married him without a penny to her name. When he left, he took everything."

"Fuck him."

She snorts. "That's exactly what his new wife did...while he was still married to my mom. She got pregnant and he bailed."

When Yasha told me Cora's dad had abandoned her, I was pissed. Now, I almost feel bad for him. He gave up Cora.

What a fucking idiot.

"So, yeah," she continues. "We bounced from shelter to shelter until Mom was able to get a job as a secretary at this accounting firm. My stepdad walked into her work one day and that was that. It would be a romantic story if he wasn't such a prick."

"Does he have kids of his own?"

"No. But don't worry, he viewed me as the daughter he never had." She rolls her eyes. "He reminded me of that often. Usually when he was trying to pimp me out for money."

I go rigid. "He didn't—"

"No." She lays a hand on my arm, soothing me back down into the mattress. "Not literally. But he made sure I met the sons of every rich friend he had. The sons of men he wanted to work with. I was the sign-on bonus."

"Welcome to the club," I say. "I was born understanding that the only reason I existed is because my father couldn't figure out how to make himself immortal. Someone had to take over everything he'd built."

"Do you think that made it easier? Being born into it?" She sighs. "I mean, it's fucked-up either way. But sometimes, I wonder what my life would look like if I'd been born into this world. If I'd been raised knowing that I was going to marry rich and spend my life being some millionaire's arm candy, maybe I would think it was normal. Maybe I'd be married right now. Pregnant, even. I'd spend my days shopping and supervising household staff and warming his bed every night."

She frowns. I'm positive images of her next to her asshole ex-fiancé are flashing through her mind right now. Some possessive part of me snarls at the mere idea of another man daring to set foot in her head.

I grab her chin and bring her eyes to mine. "That would never be you, Cora."

"How do you know?"

"Because you would roast those poor bastards alive, no matter how many they tried to set you up with. Some people just can't be contained. You are one."

"You make me sound like a wild animal." Obvious amusement dances on the curve of her lips.

"After the noises you made last night, the shoe fits."

She chokes on a laugh and slaps my arm. "I don't remember you complaining about anything last night!"

I catch her hand and press it to my chest. "I'm not complaining now. Just stating a fact. Poor Niles has been scandalized."

"Oh God." She buries her face in the pillow—*my* pillow. "I hope he didn't hear us."

If he did, he definitely believes in our relationship now.

The trouble is…I might be starting to believe in it, too.

61

IVAN

We're still lying in bed a few minutes later when my door bursts open and my sister comes barreling in.

"Where in the hell have you been all day? I've been calling and—" She careens to a halt in the middle of the room. Her mouth curves into a dizzying smile. "Oh," is all she manages. "*Oh.*"

Cora scrambles to pull the covers over herself. I reach down and grab the comforter, throwing it over her body as I glare at my sister. "Do you fucking mind?"

She crosses her arms and grins. "Not at all."

The bubble pops, just like that. The cone of silence that has been around my room for most of the last twenty-four hours evaporates. As quickly as it disappeared, all the noise of my life comes racing back in.

I need my phone.

Yasha has probably texted me.

My father will want an update. If I don't assure him I'm tracking down the people responsible for this, all my plans are for nothing.

And Anya…

My sister is thrilled right now. Which is exactly why she is the last person I wanted to see me like this. As if her delusional hopes weren't already misplaced, her matchmaking will be insufferable now.

I throw a pillow at her. "Get the fuck out, Anya."

"You two are really taking this charade seriously," she teases. "I don't think you need to pretend even in the bedroom. Unless…you aren't pretending."

Cora pulls her knees to her chest and mumbles, "it's just practice."

It's not believable. We dropped any pretense about what this was and what we were doing hours ago. But still, hearing the words…

The fantasy fades.

I didn't even realize I'd been creating one. But with Cora's body warming the sheets next to me, my mind began to spin a tale.

A world where she and I could be together. Where assassins weren't after her every time we left the house. Where my father kept his mouth shut and his nose in his own goddamn business.

A reality where I could wake up next to this woman and fall asleep next to her and I didn't have to worry about her being ripped out of my grasping fingers in every minute in between.

This could never be my life. It *will* never be my life.

It's better to accept that now and focus on what truly matters.

"If you need something, spit it out," I growl at my sister. "I'd like to put my clothes on."

Anya wrinkles her nose and shoots her gaze up towards the ceiling. "Neither of you were answering your phones. I've been texting you all day."

"Oh, shit!" Cora pats the bed as if her phone might be hiding under the covers somewhere. "I completely forgot about—"

"About the world beyond that bed, apparently," Anya mumbles.

Cora flushes. I shift forward to move between her and my sister. "You could have texted Yasha."

"I did!" she argues. "He told me you were both busy."

"And yet…" I gesture to her with both arms. "Here you are."

"Yeah, but only because I have a surprise and it's timely. I didn't have time to wait for you to come crawling out of your room whenever it pleased you."

"I loathe surprises."

"Which is why it isn't for you," Anya says smugly. She leans around me to grin at Cora. "It's for her."

"Me?" Cora asks.

"Yep. Unless there's another woman hiding in that bed somewhere…?"

"If there was, would you leave?" I growl.

She rolls her eyes. "Are you feeling up to it, Cora? I ask, but given what you've obviously been doing..." Anya circles a finger around the two of us and the bed, forming a heart shape in the air. "...I'm guessing you're feeling a lot better than when I left yesterday."

"Anya..." I warn.

She holds up her hands in silent surrender. "I've planned a little night out for me, Cora, and—"

"No." The word is out of me almost before I can comprehend what Anya is saying. "Cora has left the house twice in the last week and been attacked both times. She isn't going anywhere."

Anya's brows arch nearly to her hairline. "Okaaay. Or we could let me finish what I was going to say before jumping to rash conclusions."

Cora lays a hand on my shoulder and slides closer to me. Her bare thigh brushes against my hip and my entire body tightens.

I don't want her leaving this house, but it is painfully clear she has to leave this bed. One of us has to, anyway. All this time with Cora has my head spinning. I need to get back on solid ground immediately.

"I'm not sure I'm up for going out again so soon," Cora says carefully.

Anya watches me with something like concern in her eyes before she shifts her attention back to Cora. "I completely understand that, but I think you *both* should hear me out. I've taken precautions."

"*I* took precautions," I remind her harshly. "It wasn't enough."

Cora's hand slides from my shoulder to my elbow and squeezes. A silent comfort. An attempt to ease the storm inside of me.

She has no clue she's only making it worse.

I shift away from her, leaning back against the headboard. She pulls her hand back into her lap.

"Okay," Anya says, ignoring my protests. "So I set it up at The Coop."

"The Coop?" I snort. "Abso-fucking-lutely not. That place is massive and—"

"And closed for a private event tonight." Anya bats her lashes at me rather aggressively. "*My* private event. But Rooster said he'd double security as a personal favor to our family."

It's Cora's turn to snort. "You guys know someone named Rooster?"

"He's a really nice guy," Anya reassures her. "Totally trustworthy. He's been a friend of ours for years and he's doing me a huge favor by closing the place down tonight for the event."

"What kind of event?" Cora asks.

Anya hesitates for only a second and then sags with a groan. "I wanted it to be a surprise, but it's obvious that is not going to fly."

"It won't fly no matter what you tell us."

She narrows her eyes at me. "I told you I've taken precautions. Yasha said he could figure out security in addition to what Rooster has planned. That place is going to be covered, and I won't take my eyes off of her all night."

Cora raises her hand. "Hey, hi, hello. Still no clue what you're talking about over here."

"Oh, right. Sorry. I'm planning a…" Anya slaps her own thighs in a sloppy drum roll. "Bachelorette party!"

The silence is weighted, expectant. Anya was clearly anticipating more of an enthused response from us.

"Come on!" she urges. "It will be fun. We'll get ready at my house, have dinner, and then go straight to the club—which will be surrounded by security. Only family and friends allowed inside. It will be perfectly safe."

Cora sighs. "But we aren't even getting married."

"Right, but people are supposed to think that you are." Anya snaps her fingers. "We're maintaining a ruse here, leading people astray. Keep up."

"Who would I even invite? I don't have any friends here."

Anya jerks back like she was physically slapped. "First of all, how dare you."

"I didn't mean you!" Cora insists in horror.

Anya waves her away, already smiling. "Forgiven, but not forgotten. Second of all, I'm inviting Francia and Jorden. Those gals need to get out of the house, too. They haven't been nearly as…*occupied*…as you have been."

"They also haven't had a close brush with murder," I remind her. "Cora hasn't been on some vacation. If they're complaining, then they're ungrateful."

"I haven't spoken to either of them in a while," Cora says softly. "I…forgot about them, honestly. God, I'm a shitty friend."

"You've been preoccupied," I growl.

"And now, you're not preoccupied," Anya bursts in. "You have nothing but time, and I think we should make the most of your continued survival and celebrate a little bit."

Cora is chewing on her lower lip. I know she's only mulling it over because she feels bad about ditching Francia and Jorden. And she's probably worried about not considering Anya a friend, even though my sister is made of much tougher stuff than that. Still, Cora would literally throw herself on a sword for the people in her life.

It's an admirable quality—even if it makes me want to encircle her in plastic wrap and shove her in a padded room.

She leans in close to me. My body presses back into her on sheer instinct. "Will you come with me?" she whispers.

Before I can even open my mouth, Anya chimes in. "Nuh-uh. No soon-to-be-but-not-really husbands allowed. It's a bachelorette party. There will be debauchery he should not see. Penis-shaped gummies and such."

"I've seen worse," I drawl.

Anya sighs. "But how is Cora supposed to flirt with guys and dance with strippers and get free drinks if you're too busy throwing her over your shoulder like a caveman?"

"No cavemen and no debauchery." Cora jabs a warning finger in my sister's direction. "If an unclothed man comes anywhere near me, I'll punch him in the balls. I mean it."

"No strippers? Really?" Anya pouts. "Lame."

There's a rather large part of me that wants to shove my sister out of the room, lock the door, and stay in here with

Cora for the rest of forever. Life would be a lot simpler if nothing beyond this mattered.

But too much shit matters for me to do that. I can't be distracted, but the longer we spend in here, the more at risk I am of losing focus in a way I may never be able to gain back.

It's long past time to cut the cord.

62

IVAN

I need more than a shower to wash Cora off of me.

Her smell is everywhere. She has invaded every fiber of my bedroom. Every thought in my head. I'm stripping the sheets in a desperate attempt to exorcize her from the space when there's a knock on the door.

"Come in." I wad up the bedding and toss it towards the closet. I might have to burn it to get rid of the strawberries and cream smell of her.

I expect it to be Niles checking to see if there's anything he can help with, but Yasha pokes his head in. When he sees me, he manages to look even more smug than Anya.

"Long time, no see, partner."

"Could be longer." I wave him towards the still open door, hoping he'll take a hint and leave. But he doesn't budge.

"I can't remember the last time you didn't have your phone on you. This might be a first, actually."

I rip Cora's pillowcase off the pillow. Then I see a long strand of her hair tangled in the threading and think better of it. I throw the entire pillow into the pile. I'll buy new ones.

"A lot of firsts are happening here," Yasha continues. "According to everyone I talked to, Cora is the first woman you've ever brought into your bedroom."

I whip around. "Who is 'everyone'? Who did you talk to?"

"Niles."

I narrow my eyes. "Bullshit. Niles isn't a gossip."

"Yeah, but he's also a shit liar," he says. "I asked him if Cora was the first woman you'd brought to your room and he tried to dodge the question. But I could tell. She was, wasn't she?"

Change of plans. Stripping the sheets won't be enough.

I need to strip memories. I need to turn back time and rewrite the past twenty-four hours.

Anytime anyone mentions her or this weekend, I'll remember what she felt like underneath me. The way her calf wrapped around my thigh. The scrape of her nails on my shoulder blades and the whispered moan of her breath against my chest as I filled her.

Even amnesia won't be enough. My *body* remembers hers.

I'm not sure I'll ever fully be rid of her.

"If you're such a good reader of people, go ahead and tell me what this means." I hold up two very specific fingers, one on each hand.

Yasha laughs. "That's a 'yes,' obviously. Considering the two of you spent the entire day in bed—another first for you—I'm guessing it went well?"

I throw the other pillows into the burn pile and drop down onto the mattress. Somehow, the smell of her still surrounds me.

Yasha pushes himself off the wall. "Why are you acting like this is a bad thing? You had a good time. Revel in it. Share details."

"I'm not telling you a fucking thing."

Mostly because I don't want to encourage him when he gets in this kind of mood.

But also because what we just did feels sacred. Personal. If I tell Yasha, I might as well actually set up a webcam. Let the internet share in the deepest, darkest desires of my heart.

"Fine. But at least look like you enjoyed yourself. I know you did." He leans in, voice low. "We could hear you."

I grimace and turn my face away. "It was a distraction."

"So?" He shrugs. "That's fine. We all need them from time to time."

"Maybe. But we don't all have time for them."

"That's what I'm here for, Ivan. You can pass some of this shit to me. Let me handle it so you have time to…to fucking *breathe*, man. You need that."

"I'm fine."

Yasha sighs and leans back against the wall. "That's a bad attempt at a lie. But you're a good man, Ivan."

I hear Cora's voice. *You are a good man, Ivan Pushkin.*

"Why the hell does everyone keep saying that?" I mutter.

"But," Yasha continues as if I hadn't spoken, "you're a good man who has too much weight on his shoulders. It turns you into an asshole."

I snort in surprise. "Thanks, Yasha. How uplifting. I feel so much better."

"You would feel better if you let yourself enjoy the pleasures of life every now and again. I mean, fuck," he says, "it wouldn't be the end of the world if you took a weekend off every once in a while to pile-drive some woman into the sheets. A random woman…or Cora…" I shoot him a warning glare and he holds up his hands. "I'm just saying, it wouldn't kill you to have some fun."

That's all I was doing the night I met Cora. *Having a little fun.* I was trying to distract myself from the reality that I was going to have to marry a woman I could barely stand.

Fun might be the death of me. Of *all* of us.

"Tell that to the man who held a gun to my head last night. Having a little fun almost got me killed."

"I would, if he wasn't already dead," Yasha deadpans. "Or if I had any clue who the fuck he is."

I snap my gaze to him. "You found something?"

"Yes. Er—no. It depends how you look at it. The man has no connection at all to the Sokolov Bratva."

I frown. "That's not possible."

"He's never even taken a stroll past their headquarters, as far as I could tell. Nothing." Yasha shakes his head like he can't believe it, either. "I was positive there would be something, but this guy came out of nowhere."

After overhearing the two Sokolov guards talking at the restaurant, Yasha and I both assumed the Sokolovs were behind the attacks. It would make sense—my connection to Katerina and the fallout of our engagement. Plus, Konstantin made it clear at my party that he would still love for me to marry one of his pre-teen daughters. The sick fuck.

"The Sokolovs have the clearest motive."

"Spoken as someone who wasn't running interference between you and all the women at your party," Yasha says with raised brows. "When you pulled Stefanos off of Cora and then followed her upstairs, I thought there would be a riot. Whether they saw it firsthand or not, people were whispering about Cora all night."

Shit.

"I thought we were discreet."

"You were the belle of the ball. There is no way to be discreet when all eyes are on you."

That whole night, all I could think about was how much I didn't want to be there. How much I didn't want to get married to a woman my father chose. How much I wanted to be anywhere but that party.

And then Cora was there.

I drag a hand down my face. "It could be anyone from the party who saw Cora and I together. Someone who felt like I brushed them off, someone who wanted more time with me and didn't get it."

"Exactly. I'm thinking we conduct some unannounced drop-ins on our allies and see if anyone has heard anything."

"Yes," I agree. "Waiting for someone to attack Cora again so we can question them isn't a plan. Fuck what my father says—she isn't bait."

Yasha wisely keeps his comments to himself. But I notice his mouth twitch into a smile. "Who should we visit first?"

"Let's start on the outside and work our way in—someone who has a leg in both worlds. I want to talk to Rooster and Legs. Tonight."

Now, Yasha can't help himself. He grins. "You want to drop in on the owners of The Coop, tonight of all nights? How surprising. I can't imagine why."

I ignore him. "I want you to oversee security at The Coop. That way, you can be close if I find anything. Otherwise, I want your eyes on Cora the entire time."

"Sure. Either my eyes or your eyes will be on Cora at all times tonight. I'll make sure of it."

I glare at him. "*Your* eyes. I'm not going to interrupt the bachelorette party. I'm there strictly for business."

Yasha shrugs. "Business, pleasure—who can really tell the difference these days?"

I pass by him on my way to the door and shove him in the shoulder. "I can."

I have to.

63

CORA

"These are 'your closest friends and family'?" I have to yell to be heard over the blaring music and the massive crowd stuffed into the club.

From the outside, The Coop looked like any other club. A neon marquee, blacked-out windows. There wasn't a line at the door, which made sense considering the place was supposed to be closed for a private event. *My* private event.

Now, I see that there wasn't a line because anyone who would possibly want to be here is already inside. It looks like Anya invited half the city.

She leans in and screams, the words still getting lost in the noise, "Only the people I trust are here. You're safe. I promise."

I'm less concerned about being murdered and more concerned about long-term hearing loss.

Music booms through speakers affixed to every corner of the room. I can feel the vibration in my feet. It rattles my bones.

When Anya mentioned the bachelorette party, I imagined sitting around a table with fancy drinks and shiny dresses and conversation. I wanted to catch up with Francia and Jorden in person, maybe get to know Anya a bit better.

But it might be hard to find a table here—considering women are dancing on most of them.

The table closest to us is holding two women in sky-high stilettos and barely-there dresses. They both blow a kiss in Anya's direction and continue dancing, a gaggle of interested men thronging at their feet. One of the men notices Anya, too. He must not be a friend of Lev's, because he's staring at Anya like he wants to eat her.

Jorden shoves through the crowd. The colored lights flash on her pale skin and her teeth turn a vibrant shade of blue when she smiles. "I never would have guessed you'd have a club bachelorette party, Cora. This is amazing!"

"It is?"

She nods enthusiastically. "I've been cooped up for way too long. I need to let loose!"

"I've been cooped up, too," Francia shouts. Her lip curls in disgust as she surveys the scene around us. "So coming to 'The Coop' is not how I pictured my first outing in a week."

Francia and Jorden joined us for a pre-party dinner at Anya's house. It was obvious by the look on both of their faces that they were shocked by the personal chef and the driver Anya sent to pick them both up. Apparently, their temporary lodgings aren't quite as extravagant as mine.

"I forgot this whole arrangement meant you were living in a mansion." Jorden elbowed me in the ribs after she arrived.

"*That's* why we haven't heard from you. You're too busy living the high life."

"I've just been normal busy," I mumbled.

Busy being fucked up, down, and sideways by my fake husband. But they didn't need to know that. No matter how well it would sell our little game.

Francia stayed quiet. She stayed quiet most of the night.

Until now.

I reach for her arm, grounding myself in the crush of people. "I'm sorry. This is not what I had in mind. I thought it was going to be…intimate."

Suddenly, an arm is around my shoulders. I turn around to find Yasha surveying the crowd. His hair looks white in the neon lights. "Get as drunk as you want, Cora. I'm the designated driver tonight."

"No, you're not," Jorden says. "That old guy with the mustache is our driver."

"Fine. I'm your designated…something that starts with a 'D.'" He waves it away. "Doesn't matter. Have fun."

Jorden's mouth curls into a flirty smile. "I won't be able to focus now. I'll spend all night wondering what the second D could stand for."

Her eyes take an obvious dip below the belt and Yasha actually chuckles. *Hook. Line. Sinker.* He doesn't even know how fast Jorden is reeling him in yet. Poor guy.

"She hasn't even had a drink yet," Francia grumbles to me.

The music is making my ears numb, Francia and Jorden are already at odds, and my head of security is going to spend most of the night fending off advances from people within my own party. And we haven't even made it past the entryway.

"Let's find the bar!" I yell, urging us all forward. "Let's dive in and see where the night takes us."

My enthusiasm wanes moments later when I'm trying to navigate through the herds of people. By the time I get to the bar, I'm sweaty and Yasha is the only one still with me. He stayed purposefully close; I suspect Ivan is responsible for that. But Francia and Jorden got lost in the crush.

"Do you see them?" I ask him.

"Jorden just put a dollar down the pants of a man who is definitely not a stripper." There's a tinge of jealousy in his voice. "And Francia snagged an open table. She's under the projector ordering from a waitress."

I should have gone with Francia. One glance behind the bar is all it takes to see that it is going to be a long wait for a drink. Besides, I'm not even sure if I'm allowed to drink here. Going to the bar was just the only thing I could think to do.

I tug on Yasha's arm, tearing his eyes away from where Jorden is already busy making new friends. "Anya told me yesterday not to drink anything unless you'd checked it."

"You should be safe here," he promises. "Rooster and Legs know what's going on and they told me they personally vouch for the safety of everything."

I watch the bartender closest grab two bottles, twirl them, and then fill a line of shot glasses. In that same five-second span, another bartender next to her fills a beer and slides a pink mixed drink down the length of the countertop.

There are so many bottles and glasses and different drinks. Even if I start off paying close attention, I'll lose my edge by the third or fourth drink. Besides, I have a feeling I should stay sober if I'm going to navigate the social waters I'm in tonight.

"I think I'll be safe rather than sorry," I tell him. "Maybe just a bottle of water?"

He reaches into his back pocket and pulls out a plastic water bottle. "Have mine. I already tested it for you. Definitely not poisoned." He grabs my shoulders and points me towards the table. "You go sit down. I'm going to go wrangle your friend before she gets herself into trouble."

Jorden doesn't look like she's in trouble. She is somehow already toasting a round of shots with a group of people I've never laid eyes on before.

Ivan should have chosen her, I think.

He wouldn't have to work so hard to make people believe he was into Jorden. She attracts people. It's some kind of magnetism in her that draws everyone in.

I've never been good at that part—meeting people, staying in touch. I bounced around from my Dad's house to shelters to my stepdad's house to my shitty apartment… Needless to say, scraping and clawing to put food in my mouth and a roof over my head doesn't leave a lot of time for me to make close friends.

It's part of the reason I hold Francia and Jorden so close. They're the closest things I've ever had to best friends.

Yasha sees me to the table and then dives back into the crowd after Jorden. Ivan would probably remind him that Jorden is not his priority, but I love that he's taking good care of my friends, too. Even if his motives fall more in line with keeping Jorden away from other men than protecting her from harm.

I drop down next to Francia. "No drink?" she asks.

"The bar was way too busy."

She eyes my water bottle and then turns back to the crowd. "I talked to a waitress and ordered everyone something." If she's trying to hide her grimace, she's doing a terrible job.

Francia has always been a little… proper. Jorden would say *stuck-up*, but that's because she didn't know the girls I was a debutante with. I saw them shun lifelong friends because they wore the wrong kind of dress to a tea party.

Francia just knows what she likes and she's honest about what she doesn't. It's a good quality in the right circumstances. Right now, though, it would be better if she had more of a poker face.

"I really am sorry about this," I tell her again. "I know this isn't your scene, but—"

She waves me off. "No, I'm sorry. I'm being an asshole. I'm like a cat, I think. Leave me in a room alone for long enough and I start to go feral. I forgot how to interact with other humans."

"I'm sorry about that, too."

"I haven't been killed by one of Ivan's crazed ex-girlfriends, so I count myself lucky."

I blow out a breath. "He's really doing everything he can to take care of me—of *us*. All of this. He's trying to figure out who might be after me, and as soon as he does, you'll be perfectly safe."

Before she can say anything, a waitress returns with a tray of drinks that are miraculously upright. If I'd been forced to carry them through the dance floor, they would have ended up on the sticky floor.

Francia offers me the same pink drink I saw a woman at the bar drinking, but I wave it away. She leaves it in front of me just in case and takes one for herself.

"Is he worth all of this?" she asks. Her voice is almost quiet enough that I don't hear her. "I don't mean to pry. "I just mean, you could call off the engagement and be safe, right? Someone is only after you because they don't want you marrying him. So if you don't marry him…"

"Then there is still someone out there trying to manipulate him. If it isn't me, it will be some other woman being attacked. I feel like I owe it to him to help him figure out who the threat is, at least."

"How noble of you." She gives me a teasing smile. "He seems to be taking great care of you. I can see why you would stay. I just wanted to make sure this is what you want."

My heart clenches. Her words hit a spot far too close to home.

This *is* what I want.

Not the assassins and masks…but Ivan. Anya. Niles. Yasha.

These people who love in their own unique ways. Who care about and support each other. I've never had anything like it before.

"I want it." I clear the sudden hoarseness from my throat. "He's worth it. I've never felt so…cared for. So safe."

"That's nice." She squeezes my hand once before she pulls her own back. "You have what we all want. Or…what I want, at least."

Jorden told me she wanted a sugar daddy. Some rich man to lavish expensive gifts on her and take her away from her minimum wage days. Francia's desires seem to run deeper than that. There's a shadow looming over her I've never noticed before.

"What *do* you want?"

"Someone who wants to take care of me." She shrugs. "My parents were always busy—working all hours of the day and night to scrape by. They did it for me, but they weren't around. I was alone a lot. Then they sent me to a private school. They were trying to give me the best education they could, but I felt more alone than ever. Growing up rich-adjacent without actually being rich was…lonely."

I can remember how isolated I felt at some of the parties my stepfather sent me to when I was a teenager. That's where I learned that you can be lonelier in a crowd of people than you can when you're all by yourself.

"I can relate to that."

"I just want to *fit*," she says. "I want to find a person who makes me feel like I've found my place. It seems like you've found that. I'm really happy for you."

It's strange to feel like we're bonding while, at the same time, Francia doesn't understand a single thing about what I'm going through right now.

I *do* feel like I've found my fit. It's like Ivan and I are matching puzzle pieces. The trouble is…we're in the wrong puzzle box. We go together, but nothing around us makes any sense.

I'm not sure it ever will.

Tears well in my eyes. I blink them back hurriedly, hoping Francia won't notice.

"And in celebration of that fit…" Francia grabs one of the other drinks she ordered and holds it up to me. "A toast! For you and Ivan!"

I grab my water bottle, raise it in the air, and smile meekly. "To me and Ivan."

64

IVAN

I told Rooster the moment I walked into the back room that I was here strictly on business. But the burly bastard won't hear of it.

"You're getting married!" He throws his arms wide like he wants to hug the world. "We need to celebrate. Legs, crack open the champagne!"

"Already done." A tall, skeletally thin woman—the exact opposite of Rooster in every way—walks into the room with three glasses of champagne held deftly between her fingers. "When you called, I put the bottle on ice. I knew this old softy would want to toast you."

Rooster looks affectionately at his wife and then grins at me. "There is nothing wrong with loving love. People deserve to be happy. Even rotten bastards like us." He elbows me in the side and hands me a glass. "Take this and drink to your good fortune. I saw your little lady out there. She's a beaut."

I glance at Legs, but there's no sign of jealousy on her face. She nods in agreement. "She's a little short for a dancer, but

I'd be willing to make an exception. We'll slap some platform heels on her and she'll be the star of the show."

Rooster almost chokes on his champagne. "We're not going to ask the future queen of the Pushkin Bratva to be a dancer! Good God, woman. Ten years we've been married, and I still can't take you anywhere."

"There is nothing wrong with being a dancer." Legs pinches her husband's shoulder. "Need I remind you how we met?"

He pats her hand, shushing her gently. "No, darling. I remember."

Rooster started the club ten years ago; Legs was his first hire. She started as a dancer, but within weeks, she was his bride and co-owner. They've been doing it all together ever since.

He got his nickname from the bright red mohawk he wears all the time. She got hers from—well, that origin story is obvious. They've been my friends and allies for a long time.

Legs smiles at me. "But of course we won't ask her to work here. I'm just saying she *could* do it. If she wanted."

The image of Cora on a stage, long leg hooked around a bar as she bends herself backwards, dressed in nothing but…

I clear the image from my head.

I set my glass down and lean back, one leg crossed over my knee. "Do you have any information for me?"

The Coop is Rooster's largest club and his favorite, but he has dives and small bars all over the city. Plus, he's friends with everyone—even his enemies. There isn't much that goes on in this city that he doesn't know about. It makes him an invaluable resource.

Instantly, the broad smile and relaxed posture are gone. Rooster shifts into his business persona seamlessly. His eyes burn like coals.

"I wish we had more," he grumbles. "Your second sent me photographs of the men you've captured so far. We don't know them."

"They've never stood around one of my tables," Legs chimes in. "I never forget a face."

Rooster hangs his head. "I'm sorry. I wish we had more to share."

I shake my head. "Don't sweat it. Yasha hasn't found anything on them, either. It's like they came out of nowhere and they refuse to tell us a thing. Whoever they're working for, they're scary enough that these men know failure to complete their mission means death. They're killing themselves before we can even question them."

"Must be someone powerful, then," Legs murmurs.

She and Rooster share a look. So much passes between them in those few seconds.

Rooster turns back to me. "I didn't think it was relevant, but…maybe I have something."

He tips his head at Legs. She joins us at the rickety table. "It was a few months ago," she begins. "I see a lot of men come in here with different women. I'm no prude and I won't turn away anyone's cash. Especially if they're good tippers. I have to make sure I can pay my dancers. That's how I keep the best."

Rooster gives me an apologetic smile. "The short version, darling."

She narrows her eyes at him, but nods. "Yeah. Okay. I saw Konstantin Sokolov here with a woman who was not his wife. They sat together for hours."

Given when I overheard at the restaurant—the Sokolov guards making it clear their leader isn't pleased with what he considers to be me backing out of our deal—I'm still counting on Konstantin Sokolov being somehow involved.

But I'm not sure how this fits together.

"I know that sounds like nothing. Gossip, at most. But there was something about the meeting that didn't sit right with me. Konstantin met this woman here, but they didn't touch. They didn't dance. He didn't even order a drink. They just talked. At the end of it, money was exchanged."

"Did they leave together?"

She shakes her head. "The woman left, but Konstantin stayed and held court for another hour."

"Who was the woman?"

She sighs. "I have no idea. She had dark hair and she looked young. Younger than Konstantin, for sure. I don't think they were together." Legs gives me a tight, apologetic smile. "It's not much to go on, but I hope it might help down the road."

So many scraps of information. Theories and snippets and half-hints. But nothing solid.

It's not enough. Not nearly enough.

I turn to Rooster. "What do you know about Marcus St. Clair?"

I didn't plan to ask about Cora's family. But I can't stop myself. Just in case.

His face creases in thought. Then he shakes his head. "Nothing. I don't recognize the name. Should I?"

"What about Alexander McAllister?"

"That one rings a bell. He's a regular, isn't he, Legs?"

She nods. "Tall, skinny guy. Pompous. He usually comes in with a group of men in suits. They drink and watch the girls, but they don't tip." She wrinkles her nose in obvious distaste. "One of them grabbed one of my dancers and I set the bouncer on him. They haven't been back in a while."

It's not exactly news that he's an asshole. Cora made that clear with the bits and pieces of her story she's shared.

"I'll keep my eyes open," Rooster offers. "I'll ask around, too."

I want to tell him that Yasha has been looking into Cora's family for me, and he hasn't found much of anything. Nothing useful.

That should be a sign that all is well, but I can't shake the feeling that there is something I don't know. Something important.

"Thanks," I tell him.

"It's our pleasure. We're always here to help you, Ivan. Whatever you need." He dips his head in a show of respect, grinning again. "We're lucky to count you as a friend."

"Go to the bar and get yourself something to drink," Legs says. "On the house."

I shouldn't.

I know I shouldn't.

I told Yasha I wouldn't.

But the reminder that Cora is in the club just behind me chips away at the little bit of willpower I've managed to muster.

"You can drink for free from now until kingdom come," Rooster says, sensing my hesitation. "With all the business your sister brought in tonight, we owe you all."

I frown. "Anya made it sound like you were doing her the favor."

He laughs. "A private event this big makes double what we're usually pulling. Your fiancée must have a lot of friends."

Fucking Anya. I should have known she'd do too much. Now, I have no choice but to check it out for myself.

At least, that's the excuse I'm going with.

"Point me to the bar," I grit out. "Time for me to make an appearance."

Rooster has one of his men guide me through the back hallways of the club. When I emerge into the main belly of the place, I see it's absolutely crawling with people.

"I'm going to kill Anya," I mutter to myself.

The only benefit to the mass of people is that I'm able to blend in easily. I slip into the mayhem and carve a path from the bar towards the dancefloor.

Yasha should have told me what I was sending Cora into. The moment he got here, he should have told me how many people were here. But now that I'm in the club, I can see security at every entrance and lining the walls. Plus my own soldiers sprinkled throughout the revelers.

She *should* be safe here.

I *should* leave.

But now that I'm here, I can't go without seeing her. Without seeing for myself that she is fine and having fun.

As I approach the dancefloor, flashing lights twirl, momentarily blinding me. Then I see them.

Anya. Jorden. A few of my sister's friends. They're dancing in a circle in the middle of the floor.

No Cora, though.

I scan the crowd for her face. There's no possible way she would blend in, I know that. The day we spent in bed together has made me a bloodhound for her. I'm positive I'd be able to pick her out of a crowd…but she isn't here.

Just as a knot forms in my chest, I feel a hand on my arm.

I turn and look down at Francia. She's holding a drink in one hand. Unlike the other women in the group, who I can see are glistening with sweat from here, Francia looks like she hasn't spent much time on the dancefloor.

"I heard you were barred from the festivities tonight."

"I heard this was supposed to be a small gathering," I retort.

She grimaces. "So did we all. Your sister knows how to throw a party, that's for sure."

I don't want to chit-chat. The last thing I need right now is to entangle my life even further with Cora's. Once this is over, she and Francia and Jorden will all be out of my life. I don't care whether they like me and I don't need to get to know them.

I'm about to ask Francia where Cora is when she hands her drink to a passing busser and turns to me. "Care to dance?"

I arch a brow. "I'd tell you I'm engaged, but you already know that."

"I didn't figure that would matter," she says. "It didn't stop your fiancée."

I frown as Francia points to the opposite side of the dance floor. To one of the private alcoves that ring the main space.

It's a dark room, especially since it's tucked behind the lights that strobe down on the dancefloor. But I can still make out the familiar shape of Cora. Her golden brown hair. The curve of her hip.

And a hand touching that hip…

My eyes sear up the arm of the man with his hand on my woman. When I see his pale face, practically translucent in the flashing lights, I don't hesitate.

I tear past Francia and make my way across the room…

On a collision course with Mikhail Sokolov.

65

CORA

FIFTEEN MINUTES EARLIER

"I haven't seen a waitress in way too long." Francia grabs her clutch and stands up. "I'm going to brave the line at the bar."

I start to stand up. "I'll come with you."

"That's okay. I don't want to lose this table. If we stand up, someone is going to jump on top of it."

She's not wrong; I'm just not sure I care anymore. Maybe the people on top of the tables have the right idea. It sure looks like they're having fun. The ground floor is a touch less exciting.

"Maybe we could go dance or something. I'm tired of sitting here—"

"Okay, thanks! I'll be right back!" Francia shouts, giving me a thumbs up. I can tell she didn't hear a thing I said.

She heads towards the bar, and I slouch down in my seat.

When Anya first suggested the idea, I didn't imagine dancing the night away in a crowd of strangers, but I didn't imagine babysitting the table by myself all night, either.

I can see Jorden and Anya laughing and dancing in the middle of a circle of people. I should have suspected the two of them would hit it off. They're birds of a feather, for sure.

Even Francia is having a better time than me. At least she's drinking.

I'm sober, alone, and bored.

I wish Ivan was here.

Francia was the only one smart enough to bring a purse, so she is holding everyone's phones. Maybe when she gets back, I can ask for my phone. I won't text and ask Ivan to come. That would be pathetic. But I could tell him how boring it is. How much more fun it would be if he was here. I could allude to the idea that he should come and rescue me.

Rescue me from what, though? From a night out with friends? The Coop is hardly a horror show. I could be having a good time. I just…don't want to be here.

A couple breaks away from the dancers and swirls close to my table. They almost crash into one of our chairs, but they hardly notice. It's hard to pay attention to your surroundings when your mouths are fused together. Their hands roam over one another, lips teasing and tasting. They are lost in the music and each other. Free.

That could be us.

I'm still lost in the fantasy when a dark figure glides in front of me. For a moment, I think my prayers are answered.

Then I realize how wrong I am.

"You look like you need a dance partner."

He's tall and towering over me. His face is completely silhouetted by the strobing lights behind him. "No. Thank you. I'm here for my bachelorette party."

Number one, I have no interest in this guy.

Number two, it's giving me nauseating flashbacks to the night Ivan and I met.

"Then you *definitely* need a dance partner," the man replies with a wicked grin.

I smile tightly and turn back towards the bar. Francia has only been gone for thirty seconds, but I wish she was back already. "I don't need anything. I'm just fine."

"You are fine indeed." His words take on a sinister edge that has me snapping my gaze back to his face. He's still obscured by the lights, but I catch the familiar angle of his jaw.

And just like that, my stomach bottoms out.

No. No, it's not him. He's not—I'm imagining it.

Then he leans down, giving me the first clear view of his face.

"Mikhail." His name rushes out of me in a breathless gasp. It's like the sight of him knocked the wind from me.

"Bachelorette parties are supposed to be fun." He holds out his hand. "Come on, Cordelia. Let's have some fun."

Adrenaline pumps through me at the sound of my old name. The name of another girl from another life. A life where my stepfather had me betrothed to this slimy, snarly, sadistic lunatic.

I have no idea what he's doing here, but it can't be good.

I dart out of my chair and try to lunge for the bar. But Mikhail is there before I can take a single step away from the table.

"Dance with me," he hisses in my ear. "Or I will make things painful for you."

Yasha is here. He'll find me. He'll stop this, just as soon as he realizes what's happening. Until then, I just have to play along.

Mikhail holds out his hand again. I slowly lay my fingers in his palm.

It's a familiar position. We've danced together before. When we were engaged, I was trotted out like the show pony my stepfather wanted at weddings and benefits and things like that.

But this time feels different.

Because I now know what it feels like to actually *like* the man you're touching. To surge with electricity when he's around. To be bowled over by sheer physical chemistry.

Compared to that, touching Mikhail leaves me nothing but nauseous.

Mikhail pulls me onto the dance floor and spins me against his body. He has an easy smile plastered on his face. No sign of the monster that lurks just under the skin.

"What are you doing?" I ask.

"Dancing. Shut your whore mouth and follow along," he growls, still smiling.

His hands slide to my waist and then my hips. He pulls me hard against him and twists and turns.

I lose track of where the table is. Which direction the bar is in. I know Anya and Jorden are out here dancing, too, but I couldn't find them if I wanted to. Every time I try to get my bearings, Mikhail spins me again.

Then I look over and realize how close to the wall we are. How far from the center of the floor we've moved.

He's leading me into the shadows.

I try to pull away, but he holds me with a crushing grip. "No more running away. Not this time."

"What do you want?" I hate the edge of panic in my voice. I hate it even more when Mikhail smirks.

"I want what was promised to me." He drags me against him and holds me firmly by the hips. His fingers dig into my skin. "Don't even think about fighting."

He glances back towards the dark alcove behind him. It yawns open like a cave. I have the feeling that if I go in there with him, I won't be coming back out.

So I hold still and meet his eyes. "I never made you any promises, Mikhail."

"Didn't you?" He grabs my left hand and holds it up, twirling my ring around my finger. "I put a ring here once, too. Does Ivan know that?"

"It hasn't come up."

Lie. Ivan as much as asked me earlier today in bed. I told him as much of the truth as I was willing. Now, I wonder if I shouldn't have told him everything. Yasha could have been on the lookout for Mikhail and my stepfather. He could have protected me from this. The way he has protected me from everything else.

I'm an idiot. I thought the past would stay behind me. I should've known it wouldn't die so easily.

His jaw clicks. "How long have you even known him?"

"It doesn't matter."

Tell him nothing. I hear Ivan's voice in my head. *Tell him not a fucking thing. Keep him calm. Get away.*

Mikhail glowers down at me. "It does matter. It matters a lot. Answer the question.'

"I'm engaged now. I shouldn't even be talking to you."

I try to take a step back, but Mikhail glues our bodies together. His cologne cloys my senses. "Are you worried you won't be able to control yourself around me, Cordelia? Are you worried your fiancé will find out your heart belongs to someone else?"

"I'm just worried you're delusional and I won't be able to stop Ivan from killing you."

I expect him to get mad and lash out. Instead, Mikhail trails a finger over my neck, tracing my jaw. I jerk my head back. "Ivan is the one who needs to watch his back. He took what was mine."

"I was never yours! Whatever we had is over."

I'm not Ivan's, either. Not really. Not in the way I want to be.

But Mikhail doesn't know that—and I have no intention of telling him.

He leans his head to the side and studies me, but when I look in his eyes, I see…nothing. They're dark and vacant. Just black disks, as empty as deep space.

He drags a hand over my hip. "It's not over, Cordelia. It's just getting started."

I shake my head. "What are you—"

"Now that I've found you again…" He pulls me close. "I'm not letting you go."

I shove off of his chest, trying to get some space between us. Trying to find some room to breathe.

"You're insane."

He laughs viciously. "You were promised to me, Cordelia. The deal we made is still on. You are my fiancée no matter what lies Ivan fucking Pushkin has put in your head."

There's anger there. *Rage* in the way he says Ivan's name.

"Do you know him?" I ask.

He snorts. "Everyone knows Ivan. For better or worse."

"How do you know him?"

"I'm much more interested in how well *you* know him," he says. "Have you met Boris yet?"

Mikhail might as well be reading from a notecard. It's obvious he and my stepfather only want to know how much trouble they might be in with the Pushkins for stealing me away. How deep has this relationship gone? How invested is Boris in the idea of me?

Maybe they'll decide I'm not worth the trouble.

Or maybe they'll feed me to the sharks.

"I've met him," I say evenly. "Boris approves of our marriage."

Another lie. Can Mikhail tell? Does he know Boris? If he does, he'll know there is no way the man could approve of me. But if he doesn't…

"Has he fucked you yet?"

I go rigid against him. "How dare you?"

"Don't act so precious, Cora. There are rumors going around about you. Nasty, nasty rumors."

"And you won't get any of them confirmed by me," I snap. "I'm not telling you a fucking—"

He grabs my arm with bruising force and hauls me close. "You'll tell me exactly what I want to know. I'm the one who might be receiving used goods," he hisses. "I have a right to know who my future wife has been with. What kind of filth she's going to bring into our marriage bed."

I stretch onto my toes, getting as close to him as I can. "Fuck. You."

Then I haul my free arm back and throw all of my strength into punching him square in the face.

66

CORA

No one ever told me how much punching someone would hurt.

It feels good for one split second to punch this smug asshole in the face, because my god, I've been waiting to do that for so long.

But that thrill is followed almost instantly by blistering pain in my knuckles. I'm still shaking out my hand when Mikhail turns back to me.

He turns slowly. Slowly. *So, so slowly.*

His cheek is barely red from the hit, but his eyes are blazing with rage. A vein in his neck throbs as he rises to his full height. "You little…fucking…*bitch.*"

He lunges for me. I throw my arms up to shield myself—from a blow that never comes.

Seconds that feel like minutes later, I crack my eyes open, just in time to see Mikhail thrown to the floor by a massive blur of black motion.

He's crash-lands flat on his back. When his eyes refocus, he's staring up at Ivan in unholy terror, who looms over him like the specter of death.

I stagger back against the wall. Relief and dread pulsing through me in equal measure.

Ivan is here. He's going to save me. He's going to end this.

Ivan is here. What will Mikhail tell him?

I press myself against the wall and try to catch my breath as Ivan swoops down and picks Mikhail up off of the floor. Apparently, he isn't finished with him yet.

Mikhail is a stick figure compared to the rippling muscles of Ivan's arms and legs. He wraps a hand around Ivan's wrist, but he can't pry it loose. Can't escape. It's nice to see the tables turned. To watch him squirm while he's manhandled by someone else.

The music is so loud that I can't hear much of anything. I have no clue what they're saying to each other. But I don't have to hear to know it's heated.

Mikhail's eyes are narrowed. His gaze cuts to me a couple times before Ivan twists him away.

"Don't look at her!" he barks over the thumping bass. "Look at me."

Before I can discern anything else, Yasha steps between me and the two men. Guilt is written all over his face.

"There was a threat detected outside," he yells over the music. "I went to investigate. It was another fucking distraction. I'm…I'm sorry."

My hand is still shaking when I lay it over his. "It's not your fault. I'm fine."

His frown twists. I can tell Yasha won't forgive himself for this slip up anytime soon.

Then Ivan barks his name. "Yasha!"

Without hesitation, Yasha turns to his friend and leader. Towards his duty.

Ivan shoves Mikhail towards Yasha, who intercepts him. He grabs my ex-fiancé by the back of the shirt and drags him towards two waiting guards. The three of them escort him out.

When they're gone, Ivan steps in front of me. Only now is the shock starting to wear off. I want to bury myself in his chest and cry. "Ivan, I—"

The words are ripped out of me when he grabs my arm and jerks me into the nearest alcove.

The space is dark. Even though the door stays wide open, the noise from the club softens inside the thick walls. The air is cool and damp. It feels like we're in another world. I'm hit with another wave of gratitude that Mikhail did not get me alone in here.

I don't even want to think about what could have happened if he'd succeeded. About what he would have done to me…

The entire time we were engaged, I knew Mikhail was an asshole. But he never *scared* me quite like this.

Not until tonight.

"Ivan," I start again, my voice shaking. "Thank you for—"

"What in the hell were you thinking?"

The faint glow of the colored lights highlights his cheekbones and jawline on one side; the other side bleeds into shadows.

He shakes me hard. "You could have been killed. You shouldn't have been alone with a motherfucker like him."

Him. He says it with familiarity. Does he…does he *know* Mikhail?

This could be a test. Maybe Ivan already knows about my broken-off engagement. Maybe he's giving me the opportunity to come clean.

But there is nothing for me to come clean about. I haven't done anything wrong. There's no need to tell him anything. The woman who was engaged to Mikhail doesn't exist anymore.

Cordelia is dead.

"I didn't want to be."

His nostrils flare. "Could've fooled me."

For the second time in as many minutes, I'm about to hit a man. "I punched him in the face!"

"Not soon enough."

"Oh, I'm sorry." I snort. "I didn't realize I'm supposed to assault every man who even approaches me."

"Not *every* man, no. But any man who corners you in a club. Any man who puts his hands on you. Any man who isn't me."

His amber eyes practically glow in the dark. I try to squirm away from him, if only to draw some more oxygen into my body. "I asked you to come with me. And I think punching him in the face made it perfectly clear I didn't want to be here with him. I don't know why you're mad."

"Because I wasn't even supposed to be here tonight." He bites his lower lip. When he looks at me, I don't think he's seeing me. He's replaying the scene in his head—Mikhail cornering me against the wall, the shadows beckoning. "I'm mad because you were supposed to be safe here, but you always seem to find yourself in trouble."

I swallow down angry words. Mostly because I don't think I have the energy to speak to them. Not when it's taking every ounce of strength just to keep from shivering. "I was taking care of it."

But my voice sounds as weak as I feel. It isn't true.

This altercation tonight isn't like the night Ivan and I met at his party. That man, Stefanos whatever, was a drunk nuisance, but one I could handle. But tonight... with Mikhail...

I was in trouble.

I didn't have a choice. He forced me away from everyone like it was easy. He made it look like we were dancing. Anyone who saw us together probably thought I *wanted* to be there.

I was helpless.

And then what? Would anyone have seen us leave? If I turned up missing, would Ivan think I ran away from him?

There are worse questions, too. *Mikhail found me.* I ran away. I changed my name. But he found me anyway.

Which means my stepfather won't be far behind.

My head swims with fear. I'm split between the urge to sprint out of this room and run for the hills or collapse into a pile on the floor.

What am I supposed to do?

"Cora." Ivan's voice is firm. He plucks up my hands and places them flat on his chest. "Breathe."

My inhale is raspy. I want to do it better, but I can't. I can't breathe. I'm going to suffocate here, drowning in uncertainty.

Who can I trust?

Will I ever be safe again?

"No one is going to hurt you," he growls. "No one is going to lay a hand on you while I'm around."

His hands on my body feel so right. So real. He is the only person I want near me right now. The only person I trust.

He ducks his head. "Tell me you're alright."

I can't. I'm *not* alright. But I want to be. At least for a little while.

I grab his arm and arch against him. "Dance with me."

His dark brows pinch together. Concern flickers across his face. But I pull him towards the alcove door and back into the main club. He comes willingly.

When we make it to the edge of the crowd, I turn around. I feel his body against my back. His breath on my neck. "Cora…"

It's a question. A warning. A promise.

I reach back and hook my hand around his neck. "I just want to be here with you. For a little while."

He hesitates for a second. Then he grabs my hand and twirls me around so we are face to face. "We can stay here as long as you like."

Forever, I think. *How about forever? Forever sounds nice.*

67

IVAN

I hold Cora in my hands and try to forget the look on her face when I found her. The deep well of fear that opened in her eyes.

It was more than the fear of a woman cornered by a man. She looked *terrified*.

What did Mikhail Sokolov say to her? What did he want with her?

Cora is clinging to me, spinning and swaying as the music blasts through the speakers. It's so loud that I can't think about anything beyond the beat and the rhythm of her body against mine.

I hold her tighter after every song, reminding myself that she is here. She is safe. She's breathing and alive in my arms.

For now.

But even now, I feel eyes on us. On *her*.

We keep to the edge of the dance floor. The crowd of my sister's thousand closest friends give us a wide berth out of respect for me, but I feel them watching. Wondering.

I grip her waist and slide my hands around to the exposed skin of her lower back. I curve her against me, urging our hips together.

The chestnut waterfall of her hair catches the light. Her skin ripples with shifting colors. She's a kaleidoscope in my arms.

I run my hand up her spine and then pull her back against me. My mouth finds her shoulder, her collarbone. I kiss my way across her skin while she drags her nails across my neck and tugs on my collar.

I know her body almost as well as my own at this point. The curves and edges of her. The places she likes to be touched. I want to revisit all of them now.

Yet there is still so much unexplored. So much I don't know about her and her family. Too much.

I need to know this woman inside and out. For my Bratva and my future, yes—but for myself, too. Otherwise, the questions will drive me crazy.

Where did Cora come from and how did she tear down my walls so easily?

"Ivan." She whispers my name in my ear as she draws a hand down my chest. Her fingers trail over my abs, scraping lower with the promise of more.

Oh, right. That's how.

Amongst everything I don't know, there's one thing that is undeniable: I want her.

I grab her hand from where it's resting near my waistband and tug her off the dancefloor. She doesn't ask where we're going. Doesn't resist. Cora just twines her fingers through mine and follows as I lead her out of the club, through the empty room where Rooster and I just met, and into a service hallway beyond.

The hallway is dark and empty. Silent, except for the consistent bass of the music from the other room.

We fall together instantly. Forehead to forehead, we grapple in the darkness—for each other, for a wall, for hope that this might all end in a happily-ever-after.

She circles her hands around my neck. Her fingers play in my hair. Her thumbs stroke the muscles that curve down to my shoulders.

"I should have stayed in bed with you." She speaks softly, breathlessly, but her voice still sounds loud after the noise of the club. "Things were better there. Just the two of us…"

To force down all the words I can't speak, I lean forward and press my lips to hers.

She gasps against my mouth and then leans into it. I smooth my hand down her back to the base of her spine. The curve of her ass beneath the flimsy fabric of her dress is soft and pure.

I should stop this.

Mikhail Sokolov was here. Who knows who else could be lurking nearby? We're alone in a dark hallway, compromised and vulnerable, and it would be so easy to sneak up from any angle.

But the more of her I touch, the more I need. Stopping is not an option. When I look down at her, the hunger in Cora's eyes mirrors my own.

"I want you," she whispers with kiss swollen lips. "Right here. Right now."

That makes two of us.

In one movement, I pin Cora against the wall and wrap her legs around my waist. It's nothing like the slow, lazy tour I took of her body last night. The way I laid her out on the mattress and mapped every inch of her.

This is half-crazed and furious.

She unzips my pants and wraps her soft hand around the hard length of me. I drop my forehead to her shoulder and release a bone-deep groan.

"This is just like the night we met," she murmurs. "The two of us against a wall in a dark corner. Me…not wearing any panties."

I push her dress even higher up her thighs and swipe my hand over her exposed center. Over the evidence of how much she wants this, too.

"You came out with no panties on?" I circle a thumb over the sensitive nub between her thighs. She gasps, biting on her lower lip to keep a moan inside. "I thought you said no debauchery."

"Hm. I do recall saying that."

"Then what do you call this?"

She grinds her hips against my hand. "I meant no debauchery while I was out. While we were apart. But I… I…"

I slide a finger inside of her. "You what?"

"Oh, God." Her green eyes are hazy with lust. "I wanted to think of you. While I was gone. I… I wanted to come back home to you tonight… Ready."

The beast inside of me practically purrs.

"But I'm ready now," she whimpers. "Don't wait. Take me now."

I couldn't wait if I wanted to. I pull my hand away and Cora is quick to position me at her opening. She works me into her warmth so all it takes is one shift of my hips before I'm filling her to the hilt.

I drive her against the wall while she clings to me. I pump every ounce of fear and rage and lust and desire in my body into this moment.

The weight of the night disappears while I'm inside of her. Nothing matters beyond her breath on my neck. The weight of her in my arms.

And when she cries out, clamping down around me as her orgasm pulses through her, I'm convinced she's the single most important thing in the world.

So I close my eyes and give her everything I have, too.

68

IVAN

"I say we break through the gates. Just plow the car straight through the wrought iron." Yasha has a wicked grin on his face. "After what Mikhail pulled last night, it would serve him right."

"It would also start a war."

He shrugs. "Even better."

"As much as I would love to be in a room alone with Mikhail Sokolov"—*if only to figure out what the* fuck *he was thinking attacking my fiancée at The Coop*—"I'm not interested in fighting a war on two fronts."

"Maybe we wouldn't be. I mean, if the Sokolovs are the ones behind the attacks, then it would still be only one front."

"Which is why we're going to drop in on them. *Without* crashing through their gates," I add. "We'll feel them out. See if anything is out of the ordinary."

Legs said she got a bad vibe from Konstantin Sokolov, which isn't surprising. It's hard not to get a bad feeling around his creepy, anemic-looking ass. With his pale face and ghost-blond hair, it's like he just crawled out of his own grave.

But I don't want to discount her lead. Rooster and Legs have always been trustworthy before. I just wish there was a way to follow the lead without leaving Cora home alone.

"Who is on duty back at the house?" I ask.

"Aleksei is in the security shack and Dima is on the monitors." He glances over at me. "Are you expecting trouble?"

"Trouble is all I expect these days."

Every time I turn around, Cora is in the crosshairs of some attack. I can't remember the last time I felt stretched this thin. No matter where I am, my head is somewhere else…

Unless I'm with her.

"Yeah." Yasha sighs. "I sense trouble coming, too."

I tense. "Back at the house? If you have information, you need to fucking tell me right—"

"I'm not worried about Cora. She's taken care of." He peeks sidelong at me. "I'm worried about *you*, man."

I blow out a harsh breath. "Fucking hell, Yasha. Don't say shit like that. I'm fine."

"I think you forget sometimes that my entire job is to gather intel. It's to be observant and pay attention to people. Even you. I know you too well to ignore what I'm seeing."

My skin prickles with sudden awareness. "But you know me well enough to know you should shut the fuck up right now."

Anyone else would back down, but Yasha just laughs. "That's true. And I will… but not until I say—"

"Nothing. We need to prep for what we're going to say to Konstantin when we—"

"—Don Pushkin is never going to approve of Cora," he finishes, ignoring me. "He'll never agree to her joining the fold."

I snap towards him, fist clenched. "No one is asking him to approve of her. She's part of a plan. Nothing more."

Yasha presses his lips together, staring straight ahead at the road. He might be even less convinced by my words than I am.

We wind through the hills up towards the Sokolov property for several quiet minutes before Yasha speaks again.

"Transitions of power are messy, Ivan. Even when they're planned. Even when the passage is from father to son." He drums his fingers nervously on the wheel. "Sometimes, no matter how much people want a peaceful changeover, the old guard has to be dead and gone before the crown fits right on a new head."

My second is talking around the point, but it's still impossible to miss.

A coup. Against my father.

If anyone beyond me heard him say it, he could be killed. He knows that. And yet…

"You've always been loyal to me, Yasha. More loyal to me than anyone. My father knows that and he has tolerated it. But if he hears even a whisper of something like that from you," I warn, voice low, "even I might not be able to stop what he'll do to you."

Yasha makes a final turn into a long drive. Black gates like prison bars mar the otherwise pristine landscape ahead. As the car slows to a stop, he turns to me. The mischievous smile is back on his face. "Whatever you say, *boss*."

We park and get out. "Overcompensating," Yasha whispers as we walk toward the front door.

It swings open as soon as we're on the porch. Konstantin's middle daughter, Kira, stands in the doorway.

"Mr. Pushkin!" She smiles up at me, her adult teeth still too big for her thirteen-year-old mouth. She ushers us inside the way she was no doubt trained to do. "It's so good to see you. I wanted to go to your party with my dad the other night, but I couldn't make it."

"Because it was after her bedtime," Yasha mutters to me out of the side of his mouth.

If she hears him, she does a good job of hiding it. It would be rude for a polite young lady to defend herself, after all. Quiet submission is the name of the game in the Sokolov household. In most of the underworld, really. If it was up to Konstantin, he would hand his middle schooler over to me as a bride, and she wouldn't even know how to begin to fight the sick deal off.

Even the thought of it turns my stomach. What kind of twisted fuck looks at this little girl and wants to marry her off?

She smiles, her lips coated in a purple gloss. "I'll go tell my father you're here."

"No need. I know the way to his office."

Kira stops in the middle of the hallway, her eyes wide. "Oh. Well… I'm supposed to tell him when people—He might be in a meeting."

"It's alright. He'll make time for me."

We turn the corner and see Konstantin's office door closed. I rap one knuckle against the wood before I shove the door open.

Konstantin is sitting behind his desk, one leg crossed over the other. Much to my surprise, Mikhail is here, too. He's standing in front of the private entrance to the office at the back of the room.

"I guess I shouldn't be surprised you didn't wait for me to receive you," Konstantin drawls, a sense of forced laziness in his tone. "You aren't one to follow the rules of social etiquette."

"I don't like to bother with etiquette. Not when I'm amongst friends." I take a pointed look around the room. "Your little girl thought you were in a meeting."

"Kira has grown up a lot since the last time you saw her."

"Is she finally out of her booster seat?" Yasha asks with a sarcastic smile. "Good for her."

Konstantin's gaze turns icy as he stares at my second. "To what do I owe the pleasure of your company, gentlemen?"

"We didn't expect a visit," Mikhail adds. "Word on the street is you're spending all your time with your new fiancée."

For the first time, I turn fully to Mikhail. There's a bruise on his right cheek—evidence of the time *he* spent with my fiancée.

I open my mouth to warn him I'll kill him the next time he touches her, but Konstantin interrupts.

"Mikhail told me he had the pleasure of meeting your woman last night. Cora, was it?" He looks to Mikhail for confirmation. His son nods once. "Well, Mikhail tells me Cora is lovely. As your *friends*, we both wish you nothing but the best."

"How generous of you both."

Konstantin dips his pale blond head. "But of course, I believe if you want *the best*, then you would marry a Sokolov daughter."

"We tried that once before. It didn't work out."

Konstantin's smile falters. "The details of our alliance were written down. I kept a copy, and I'm sure your father did, as well. The verbiage makes it clear that you agreed to marry the eldest available Sokolov daughter. That would make Kira—"

"A child bride," I grit out, unable to hold back my disgust. "Does the *verbiage* explain why a father would hand his child off to a grown man?"

Konstantin's neck reddens, but he doesn't react. "She is mature for her age. If you spent any time with her, you'd see that."

"Unfortunately, I don't spend a lot of time with middle schoolers."

Mikhail leans forward like he is going to do something. What that might be, I have no idea. I made it clear last night that I could more than handle him by myself.

But Konstantin clears his throat.

A look passes between the men. A shared expression that sets off alarm bells in my head.

"Perhaps we're not ready for that discussion yet," the man demurs.

My father would instruct me to keep my cards close to my vest here. Even though I want to chuck my cards out the window and wring both these men by the throat.

Fuck Konstantin Sokolov. And fuck his creepy son, too.

"It'll be a cold day in hell before I give it a second's thought," I snarl. I give each of the Sokolov men a withering glare. "Keep your fucking hands away from my family."

Without another word, I turn to leave. Yasha follows.

"We didn't learn anything," he warns as we march down the hall.

"We learned enough."

The Sokolovs approached Cora last night at the club. Their names have popped up too many times for it to be a coincidence. If they plan to make another move on Cora, I'm going to beat them to the punch.

"Okay. So what's our move now?"

"We exterminate these fucking cockroaches."

69

CORA

"I cannot believe you live here." Jorden kicks back in the deck chair and surveys the sprawling grounds.

We've been sitting outside since she arrived. Niles brought out a tray of fruit and cheese, and you would have thought it was a lobster dinner the way Jorden oohed and ahhed over it.

"Like, a couple weeks ago, we were just two randos milling around with all of Ivan's other guests on this same patio. Now, I'm here as *your* guest. Isn't that wild?"

"Too wild to comprehend," I tell her truthfully.

When Jorden first showed up, I was relieved. I wasn't sure when, if ever, I'd get to have her or anyone else in my life here to visit me. But after the chaos of The Coop, Ivan decided his house should be the site of all future social engagements. At least until I'm not actively being targeted anymore.

Now that Jorden has been here for an hour, though... I'm exhausted.

Exhausted with all the pretenses and the lies. I thought it would be easy enough to avoid talking about the wedding or my relationship with Ivan, but there's almost nothing else to talk about.

"Did Ivan ever tell you why you stuck out to him?" she asks. "Aside from your obvious beauty and charm and wit and voluptuous ass."

I laugh and shrug. "I don't know. Being naked in his office probably made me stand out from the crowd."

"Right. Probably. But how much would that *really* stand out to him, you know? He has to have seen more naked women than the average Joe."

I've honestly never thought about it. And as it turns out, I never want to. The last thing I need to do is think about how I stack up with every other sexual encounter Ivan has ever had.

"I wouldn't know. We haven't exchanged that data yet."

Jorden gives me a knowing look. "Every woman at that party wanted to jump his bones. You can't tell me some of them haven't whipped out their birthday suits to get his attention."

My stomach twists. I know Ivan has been with other women; I'm not an idiot. But it's the thought of him going *back* to that meat market that is more upsetting than anything.

"I'm just saying," Jorden continues, "that there must have been something about you that stuck out. Something special."

"Maybe. I don't know. He hasn't said."

"You should ask. You're living the fairytale, girl. You might as well get the full experience, romantic insights and all."

"We don't really do that."

"Don't do what?" she asks.

"Romance. It isn't really our thing."

If Jorden had a drink, she'd be spitting it out right now. "Are you insane? You're engaged to a kajillionaire right now. This is literally the setup to half of the romance novels I read."

"Those are fiction. *This* is real life. I mean, we've been so busy that we've barely gone on two dates."

She waves a dismissive hand. "You don't have to go on dates to be romantic. It's all about chemistry and sexual tension. And I saw plenty of both when you two were dancing at your bachelorette party."

"I can't believe you saw anything. You were dancing and shoving dollar bills in unsuspecting people's pants all night."

She cackles at the memory and gives me a mischievous smirk that reminds me a lot of Yasha. "Luckily, I'm a good multitasker. I saw plenty. Like, I saw Ivan swoop in and pull that guy off of you. Then I saw the two of you practically go at it on the dance floor."

The photos Anya sent me flicker behind my eyes. My face flushes hot and red. "We were just dancing."

"Puh-lease! There were legit flames coming off of you two," she argues. "It was *hot*. I don't even want to know where the two of you disappeared to when you left... Actually, just kidding. I do want to know. Where did you go?"

I shake my head. "Nowhere. We were just talking."

Jorden wags her brows. "You spoke the universal tongue of body language, am I right?" I have to bite back a smile and she squeals. "I knew it!"

"Shut up."

"Never! I need to know everything so I can use the same tricks to find me a guy like that. I mean, you're raking them in. First, Ivan. Then that guy at the club. Who was he, by the way?"

"Who?"

"The guy Ivan pulled off of you," she says. "He was cute. A little *Addams Family* looking for my taste, but handsome-ish."

Mikhail. She has to be talking about Mikhail.

She says she saw me with him, but if she saw the full extent of that interaction, she wouldn't be talking about it so flippantly.

"Oh. Yeah, I guess he was okay." My voice sounds far away in my own ears. I can hear blood rushing through my veins.

"Okay?" she snorts. "Ivan has destroyed your standards. But whatever, more for me. Maybe I can ask Anya about him. She told me she'd introduce me to some of her friends and—"

"No."

Jorden freezes, shocked for a second before confusion shifts over her features. "No, Anya can't introduce me to her friends?"

I should drop it. Jorden probably won't ever see Mikhail again. Even if she did, he's made it clear he's fixated on getting me back. I doubt he'd go for Jorden.

Yet the thought nags at me.

What if Jorden got involved with Mikhail? In some ways, he can be charming. And if Jorden is serious about looking for someone who can take care of her financially, Mikhail fits that bill.

I know firsthand how hard it is to get out once they suck you in.

I blow out a long breath. "You don't want to know that man. He's... You can do better than him, believe me."

"Did something happen between the two of you last night?"

There's so much I can't tell Jorden. So many things I have to keep hidden from her for her own safety.

But this is something that will make her safer.

"Yes, something happened," I confess. "But last night wasn't the first time."

She frowns. "You're freaking me out."

"I'm not trying to freak you out." Then I think better of it and chuckle. "Actually, maybe I am. But it's only because that guy is an absolute creep. You don't want anything to do with him."

"Okay. I believe you," she says. "But how do you even know him? I thought you and I were the outsiders to this whole world. Francia is the one who knows these people."

I bite my lip. "I don't want you to get mad..."

"Then don't stop talking," she says. "I've been without human contact for the last week, and this is the most riveted I've been since the last season of *The Bachelor*. Spill the beans, girl. All of them."

So... I do.

After keeping so many secrets and navigating the murky waters of my not-really-on and off again relationship with Ivan, it feels good to speak the truth.

I walk Jorden through my mom getting remarried to my stepdad and his expectations for me. I tell her about my forced engagement to Mikhail and how, in the final weeks before what would have been our wedding, I ran for it. I took what little money I had, packed a few changes of clothes in a bag, and left in the middle of the night.

"...Then I got the job at Quintaño's and met you and Francia. And now, I'm here."

By the time I'm done, Jorden is full-on gawking at me, jaw unhinged like an anaconda. She blinks, shaking her head slowly. "That is unbelievable. Honestly, if you'd told me all of this two weeks ago, I would have said you were full of complete and utter shit."

"Thanks for your confidence."

"It's the truth." She shrugs. "I would have thought you were delusional or something. But now, you're engaged to Ivan Pushkin. If that can happen, anything can happen."

"Hey!"

She laughs and reaches for my hand. "I didn't mean it like that. You're a catch. I just mean…well, you know what I mean. One minute, we were working the opening shift and now, you're engaged and being targeted by assassins. It's wild. The shit with Mikhail doesn't sound nearly as crazy compared to that. Even though that dude is obviously a straight-up psychopath."

I sag. "Yeah. He might be."

The look in his eyes last night as he towered over me... It sends chills down my spine just thinking about it.

"And your dad was just going to marry you off to him?" she asks.

"Stepdad. But yeah. He still would, I'm sure. If I went home, they'd put the announcement in the paper the minute I stepped through the front door."

"This just doesn't make any sense. We're women in the modern era. You don't have to marry anyone you don't want to."

I look down at my lap. "It's more complicated than that."

"How? Explain it to me, because I'm lost. Why can't you just call the police on these people?"

"Because they *are* the police," I snap. I take a deep breath to try and soothe my racing heart. "I'm sorry. I just... I haven't thought about any of this stuff in a long time."

Jorden lays a hand on my shoulder. "What happened?"

"Before I left, I tried reporting my stepdad to the police. He was basically planning to lock me in the house until the wedding. *'Then you'll be Mikhail's problem,'* he said. So I called the police and said I was being imprisoned."

"What did they do?"

I grit my teeth together, the memory as fresh now as it was that day. "They sat around the dining room table and had a cup of coffee with my stepdad. Then they shook hands and left."

"Nuh-uh." Jorden shakes her head. "That is not how that works. They can't do that."

"They can when my stepdad is one of their biggest donors. His company bought them a fleet of new squad cars a few years ago."

"But that's not right! They're paid to protect people."

"They're paid for *loyalty*," I fire back. "People like my stepdad have enough of them in their pockets that they get away with whatever they want. It's how I know, if they catch up to me, I probably won't get away again."

Jorden slides to the edge of her chair, her knees touching mine. "Then don't let them catch up to you."

I throw my arms up. "If they're willing to come after me when I'm engaged to Ivan, then nothing will stop them."

"Ivan will!" she says. "Does he know who Mikhail is?"

Guilt rises up in me. I should have told him about Mikhail days ago. I definitely should have told him that night at the club.

Jorden sighs. "I can tell by that look on your face that Ivan doesn't have a clue. If he did, Mikhail would probably be dead right now."

I snap my gaze to her. How much does she know about who Ivan really is?

Then I realize she didn't mean it literally.

"He would have wiped the floor with that scrawny man," she continues.

"I thought you said he was handsome."

She wrinkles her nose. "That was before I knew the truth. Now, he's a disgusting creep who deserves whatever is coming for him. If I had my way, I'd say Ivan is what is coming for him. But that's your choice."

"So you aren't going to tell anyone?" I twine my fingers together nervously in my lap.

She sighs. "No. No, I won't. But *you* should. If Mikhail knows where you are, then Ivan should know about him and your history. Even if it's just so he can better protect you."

"I know." I stare down at the ground, nodding my head. "I know you're right. I would just rather forget that part of my life ever existed. This time with Ivan has been a fairytale. I don't want it to end."

"Aww, honey." Jorden pats my arm. "It won't end. You and Ivan are going to get married and live happily ever after and have so many beautiful babies. Mikhail will fade in the rearview. Trust me."

I give her a tight smile and do my best to make it look convincing. It's hard, though.

Because she has no idea how wrong she is.

70

CORA

Jorden and I are still out on the patio when I hear voices coming from inside.

There's so much security monitoring the property at all times that I'm not really concerned, but I still turn to Jorden with a frown. "Weird. Ivan isn't supposed to be back yet."

I could be wrong. It's not like he tells me where he's going. I don't even mind; I'd really rather not know. As it is, I can pretend he's safe and cozy in an office somewhere with his feet kicked up, as opposed to facing off with his enemies in dark alleys, wielding menacing weapons and dripping in blood.

"Hm." Jorden purses her lips, doing her best to look confused… and failing.

"Are you expecting someone?"

"Me?" She lets out a loud, barking laugh. "Why would I be expecting someone at *your* house? That doesn't even make sense."

I arch a brow. I can almost literally see the cracks forming in her performance. "What's going on, Jor?"

She shrugs. "Your guess is as good as mine. I bet it's nothing. Maybe it's your manservant—"

"Niles," I correct. "And he'd throw you over the security wall if he heard you call him that."

Something that sounds like a busted shopping cart wheel squeals from the kitchen. For a moment, I imagine how I would explain to Ivan that I was sitting on the patio, completely unconcerned, as burglars broke in and wheeled all of his belongings out to their waiting van.

I start to sit up. "I'm just going to make sure everything is okay in there. I can get you a sparkling water or some juice if you—"

"I'll do it!" Jorden jumps out of her chair before I can even finish. "What do you want?"

I look up at her, squinting against the sunshine haloing her head. "What is going on?"

"Nothing!" she insists. But her eyes shift nervously towards the kitchen.

My heart stutters. I trust Jorden. She's my friend, but…

If the last week has taught me anything, it's that I'm not nearly as safe as I think I am. What if Jorden is working with Ivan's enemies?

I try to shove the idea down, but it won't budge. "Jorden," I say evenly, sliding to the edge of my chair, "if you know what is going on, you need to tell me."

Her gaze darts past me to the kitchen door. The voices are still soft. I thought it was because they were deeper in the house, but now, I realize whoever is inside is whispering.

My heartrate ramps up. "Jorden…"

"It's fine," she insists. Her cheeks are flushed. It's rare to see her this rattled. "Everything is fine."

If someone is in my house, it either means the guards let them in or there are no longer any guards. Neither option is great, but there's nothing I can do about it now.

"You know what? I'm not going to sit here and wait for someone to bust in and—"

I'm shoving past Jorden just as the double doors to the kitchen burst open.

And Anya and Francia burst out.

"SURPRISE!"

I stumble back into Jorden, who wraps her arms around my waist in a tight hug. "Sorry."

Relief washes through me. "I thought—I don't know what I thought."

"They wanted it to be a surprise," she explains.

Anya grins. "Was it a surprise?"

"She heard you all squeaking around in the kitchen!" Jorden reprimands. "I could barely keep her out here."

"Was *what* a surprise? Why did I need to stay out here?"

Anya skips over to me and plants her hands on my shoulders. She walks backwards, leading me through the kitchen doors and towards the private staircase on the right. "I had big, grand plans for you, Cora. There were going to be multiple attendants, endless bottles of champagne—"

"And those little finger sandwiches with the cream cheese and cucumber."

Anya chuckles and rolls her eyes. "Niles can still make those for us. I'll put in a request."

Jorden cheers behind me, but Francia doesn't say anything. Aside from the initial surprise, she hasn't said a word.

"Anyway, it was going to be an affair in the most lavish hotel room money can buy. But plans change and I am nothing if not adaptable. So here's the backup plan." Anya pushes open my bedroom door and ushers me inside…

To a room of wall-to-wall wedding dresses.

Movable clothing racks are arranged around the perimeter of the room, each one stuffed with lace and silk and velvet, all in varying shades of bridal white. Heels are lined up under each rack. I don't even need to check to know they're in my size.

"Wow."

It's all I can say. The only word I can muster as I stare at the room overflowing with dresses that I'll never wear to the wedding I'll never have.

As it turns out, Anya ordered dresses in everyone's size so we could all try things on.

"I knew Cora wouldn't love being the center of attention, whereas I live to be the center of attention." Anya laughs at her own joke. "So we're all putting dresses on. It will be fun!"

Ten minutes later, it turns out she was right—at least in the sense that my friends all wearing gowns of their own does make me feel less ridiculous in my puffy-sleeved monstrosity straight out of the 1980s.

"Fun" is a loose word, though. Francia looks like she's in as much pain as I am.

"Some of these are from the designer's vintage collection." Anya steps behind Francia in the mirror, admiring the frilly sleeves. "It's right out of a fairytale."

Francia grimaces. "Am I the evil stepsister in this fairytale?"

Before Anya can answer, Jorden steps out of the closet with both arms wide, walking with her hips pressed forward and her shoulders pressed back. "I look incredible. Now, all I need is a groom."

Anya wolf whistles. "The trumpet silhouette is perfect for you."

The gown is fitted through the middle and down her thighs, but flares out in a whirlwind of ruffles and lace at her knees. It balances her out nicely. She looks gorgeous.

"You really do look amazing," I agree. "Bookmark that dress for when you finally marry your sugar daddy."

"A sugar daddy?" Anya raises both brows. "Tell me more."

Jorden shakes her head. "There's nothing more to tell. Every man I meet is flirtatiously incompetent."

"What does that even mean?" Francia pinches the tulle skirt of her dress between her fingers and drops it. No plans to say yes to that dress, apparently.

"It means they don't know how to *woo* me," she sighs.

Anya nods. "A girl needs to be wooed. It's important."

Is that what Ivan was doing when he studied my naked body up and down before finally handing me his suit jacket to cover up? Was that *wooing*?

If so... it worked.

"I thought you wanted a sugar daddy," Francia mutters.

Francia's inner feral cat is coming out a bit today. She's been on edge since they arrived. Too much time locked away in the safehouse by herself, I'd imagine.

Jorden shoots a sharp look her way, but quickly schools her face into a lighthearted smile. "I'm a complex human, Francia. I want both."

Anya plucks a short, edgy veil from the top of one of the racks and tucks it into her hair. "Based on what I saw at the club the other night, you want a certain friend of my brother's."

"Huh? Who?" Jorden is playing dumb, but her cheeks are pink.

I know where Anya is going with this. Even while Jorden was shoving dollar bills down another man's pants, she was watching Yasha.

"You know who! Don't play coy with me. You two were dancing around each other all night. Not literally," Anya adds. "Despite my best efforts."

"Your *best efforts* were not very subtle. Yasha probably knew you were trying to ship us. That's why he wouldn't talk to me all night."

Anya waves her off. "That was not my fault. Yasha wouldn't talk to you because he's bad with women."

A laugh bursts out of me. "Yasha would be so mad if he heard you say that."

"Of course he would," Anya says. "All men would. It's just because they can't admit that they don't have a single fucking clue how to talk to a woman. Even Lev didn't know how to talk to me until at least a year into our marriage. Men need to be taught. Trained."

"That must be why I can't find a man worth dating," Jorden ponders. "Because I'm looking for one that has already been trained. Or because the only men I have been in recent contact with are just there to watch my apartment."

"You're hitting on your guards?" I ask. I don't know why I'm even surprised.

She winks. "They're cute. And I think they could do a better job of guarding me from *inside* my apartment. It is not a crime to lure them inside with fresh-baked cookies and whiskey."

"No, but it is a crime that none of the guards sent to watch over me have been handsome or shown any interest in me whatsoever," Francia chimes in. She laughs, but I remember the look on her face when we were talking at the club.

She's lonely. I can see it.

"Yeah, sorry about that," Anya winces. "The apartment building where you're at is usually staffed with the family guys. Men who need a set work schedule so they can get home to their wives and kids."

"Just my luck," Francia grumbles.

"Well, don't feel too bad for yourself," Jorden says. "I'm not faring any better. The men you meet are married and the men I meet are hopeless. Which probably means I should stop daydreaming with these dresses. Maybe we should get some nun habits in here to try on for size."

I drop down onto the bed and kick my legs out from under the skirt of the dress. I've only tried on three dresses, all of which have been atrocious. Mostly because I'm afraid if I take this seriously, I might find a dress I actually like.

Then it would be even harder *not* to picture myself standing at the altar with Ivan.

"My view of men isn't so bleak," I say. "There are plenty of nice, handsome guys out there who know how to hold a conversation."

None that my stepfather tried to set me up with, but "a functioning personality" wasn't high on his list of must-haves. That fell squarely after wealth, connections, and a girthy stick up their butt. The last one wasn't official, but I can only assume it was as mandatory as the rest.

"Says the woman engaged to a walking, talking sex god," Jorden mutters.

"Ew!" Anya plants her hands over her ears. "Please never say that in front of me again."

"Sorry, but it's true. Ivan is a higher breed of human. I mean, he had an entire party full of women wanting to marry him. Who gets that kind of response?"

"Rich guys," Francia suggests.

Anya points to Francia. "She's right. Money covers a multitude of sins. Believe me, my brother has his fair share of relationship mess-ups and faux pas. If you don't believe me, ask Katerina."

The air seems to get sucked out of the room. Or maybe it's just *my* air.

"Who is Katerina?" Jorden asks.

Anya's smile looks suddenly strained. "No one. Just trust me. My brother has made his fair share of mistakes."

"No time like the present to spill the tea. Every woman wants to hear about her fiancé's exes while she's trying on wedding dresses."

I honestly can't tell if Jorden is joking or not.

Anya drops the veil back on the rack and slips out of her dress. She lunges for her trousers and sweater like there's a fire. "That may be true, but there isn't a sister on the planet that wants to talk about their brother's love life. I've learned my lesson where that is concerned: mind my own business."

"Since when?" I chuckle before I can stop myself.

She turns to me and I see something pleading in her gaze. Whatever she let slip, it was a mistake.

Drop it, her eyes say. *I'm begging you.*

Jorden is taking a deep breath, ready to launch into what will no doubt be a long-winded argument for why we deserve to know everything about Ivan's past. As supportive as she has been the last few days, I know she's still worried Ivan might be trouble.

Before she can, I step in.

"I'm starved. Do you think there are any snacks ready?"

"Yes!" Anya says a little too quickly. "I bet the finger sandwiches are ready. I'll go grab them." Then she is gone, only the ghost of her Chanel perfume hanging in the air.

Jorden watches her leave and then does a slow turn back to us, eyebrow arched. "That was weird, right?"

"Anya is flighty. That's just how she is," I lie.

"No. No, that was a different level of weird. She was being evasive. What isn't she telling us?"

I stand up and start sorting through the dresses on the racks. "She doesn't want to talk about her brother's personal life. We should respect that."

I know the words coming out of my mouth are the sane, rational thing to say. It's responsible to respect people's privacy and let them divulge whatever secrets they may have to you when the time is right.

Like the way I'm keeping Mikhail from Ivan until the time is right. Even if I have no idea when that time will be.

"Do you have your phone?" Jorden holds out a hand and wags her fingers at me.

"Why?"

"So we can get our Google on, obviously. We need to figure out who this Katerina bitch is."

"She's probably no one. And probably not a bitch, either! She might be just a friend or—" I turn to Francia, knowing I can count on her to be sane. "You probably know something about Katerina, right? You know more about these people than we do. Tell Jorden that she isn't important."

Francia gives me an apologetic wince. "I wish I could, but I don't know anything about her."

"Ooh, intrigue," Jorden hisses. She curls her fingers in my direction again. "Get your phone out."

"Get your own phone out," I snap back.

"I left it downstairs on the patio. Why can't I use yours?"

"Because…" I scramble to think of a good reason. "We're on Ivan's WiFi. What if they can look at my searches?"

"You aren't living in a police state. It's your own damn house!"

If only she knew the truth.

"I have a VPN," Francia blurts suddenly.

Jorden spins towards her, her dress splaying out around her legs. "A what?"

"A VPN. It keeps my searches private. It's for my job."

"You're a waitress," Jorden deadpans.

Francia pulls out her phone. "My *other* job. What do you want me to look up?"

"Nothing," I say.

At the same time, Jorden rattles off what she wants Francia to type in the search bar. "Katerina Ivan Pushkin Los Angeles."

Jorden hovers over Francia's shoulder as she types. Both of them stare down at the phone as Francia scrolls through the search results.

"You two do whatever you want. But I don't want to hear a thing about it," I lie. "If Ivan wants to tell me about her, he will."

Lie, lie, lie.

Ivan doesn't owe me anything. Honesty about his past relationships, least of all. Maybe if we were in a real relationship I'd demand more information from him, but as it is… The fact he is keeping me alive is enough. It *should* be enough. I won't ask him for more than that.

Then Jorden gasps.

I can't help myself. I spin towards them. Jorden is looking down at the phone, eyes wide. Francia is looking at me with something like fear in her eyes.

My willpower crumbles under the weight of my curiosity. I'm about to nosedive off the moral high ground and wallow in the mud of internet gossip.

Then the door opens.

"We have a visitor," Anya says, peeking her head in to be sure we're decent.

Ivan follows her. "I can't be a visitor in my own house."

His voice is gruff, but there's a smile on his face. He has no clue everyone in front of him was just poking their noses into his personal business.

If Jorden and Francia can wipe the shock off of their faces, maybe it will even stay that way.

71

IVAN

Cora's face is pale, her eyes wide. She looks like she's seen a ghost.

Or maybe she just caught a stray glimpse of herself in the mirror.

"What," I ask, looking her over from frilly head to bedazzled toe, "in the hell are you wearing?"

Anya elbows me in the side. "It's a wedding dress, asshole."

"Sure, but which corpse did you strip it off of? It looks ancient."

There is an ungodly amount of fabric draping off of her shoulders. She looks like she is drowning in it. Throw her out on a windy day and she'd probably take flight.

"Apparently, the designer has a vintage collection." Cora tries and fails to flatten the volume around her waist. "You don't like it?"

There's a playful edge to her voice. She knows I don't like it. And I know she would rather get married naked than in this.

Come to think of it, that's not a bad idea.

"I've never been more eager to get you out of an item of clothing in my entire life."

"Then maybe it's a winner," Jorden suggests. She was tucked up behind Francia, but she steps away and folds her hands behind her back. "That's the kind of energy a man should bring to his wedding night."

Francia is still standing off to the side, her nose buried in her phone.

Anya holds up her hands in surrender. "Okay. If you all are going to be gross, then I'm out of here."

"Maybe that's for the best," I drawl. "I think I'll take over the wedding dress hunt from here." I turn to Cora's friends. "But for now, I'd like a moment alone with my fiancée."

"What about the dresses?" Anya protests.

"Wear them, sell them, burn them. I don't give a fuck." Whatever gets them out of here the fastest. I don't even care; I'll eat the cost."

Jorden looks at me warily as she hugs Cora goodbye. Francia doesn't even look at me. She just hugs Cora and then pulls back, holding her by the arms. "Be careful."

Then the women leave and Cora and I are alone.

I circle around her, twisting my head from side to side to capture every angle. "I thought I was vicious, but my sister is heartless for putting you in this dress." I lay a hand on her arm and have to compress six inches of material before I feel her body underneath.

"Believe it or not, I chose this myself."

I arch a brow. "If your goal is to get abandoned at the altar, then I'd say it's perfect."

"There won't be an altar to leave me at, remember?" She turns back to the racks of dresses, the gown swishing around her with every step. "Why take this seriously if the wedding isn't real?"

She's right. I know she's right.

Yet something inside me rages against the idea.

"I remember someone telling me that we needed to practice."

She ducks her head. I can see a blush creeping up her cheeks. "That was different."

"No, it wasn't. No one will believe we're getting married if we don't touch each other in public. You learned that lesson. And no one will believe we're getting married if you don't choose a dress. Same thing."

"If you say so. I've never been married before," she says with a forced nonchalant shrug. "I don't know how any of this is supposed to go."

I step up behind her and slowly pull the zipper of the dress down the length of her spine. "Then let me teach you."

Goosebumps spread across her shoulder blades. She snorts. "You don't know anything about wedding dresses, either… do you?"

She's asking something else. A question beneath the question. But I'm too focused on exposing more of her skin to worry about it.

I push the sleeves down her arms. "I know what I like. I know what I'd like to see you in."

Nothing at all.

As hideous as this dress is, I can't think of anything more beautiful than the way it slides down her body.

What would it be like on our wedding day? How much more would this moment mean after hours spent ogling her in her gown? After vows and cake and dancing? Would I peel her out of the dress slowly like this? Or would I rip the expensive layers to fucking pieces just so I could get at her, touch her, claim her… *my wife.*

Suddenly, Cora spins around to face me. The gown is hanging low on her arms, the top barely covering the twin swells of her breasts. "You aren't supposed to see me in my wedding dress before the ceremony. We're breaking all the rules."

I pull her closer. "Do I strike you as the kind of man who gives a damn about the rules?"

She laughs quietly. "No, I guess not."

"Didn't think so." I pluck her hands away from the fabric she's trying to hold over herself and let the dress cascade into a puddle around her long, toned legs. She's wearing a strapless white bodysuit that covers just enough of her to drive me mad.

I swallow down a groan. "Put something on. Anything."

"As you wish." She riffles through the rack and pulls down a slinky satin gown.

And thus begins *my* torture.

I sit on the bed and watch Cora slip in and out of dress after dress. Again and again, she twirls in front of me. And again and again, all I can think about is shredding through the gowns like a gift box on Christmas morning so I can devour her.

She comes out in the fifth dress and it's a struggle to stay seated. I have to clench my fists to keep myself from grabbing her around the waist and hauling her towards me.

The dress is sheer, nothing but meticulously overlaid lace covering her chest and the space between her legs. I can see the shadow of her body through the tulle. Light dances around the curve of her hip and her thighs. She looks ethereal. Like a dream.

"What do you think about this one?" Long lashes bat at me. There is no goddamn way she doesn't know what she is doing.

I rise slowly from the bed, eyes locked on her. "I hate it."

She starts to smile, but then stops. Her brows pinch together in confusion. "What?"

"I hate it," I repeat, moving towards her, "because every set of eyes in the room would be locked on you. I'd have no choice but to claim you as mine in front of everyone."

I snag her waist and pull her close. Her back arches over my arm so she can look up at me. "How would you do that?"

"I could show you," I whisper, pressing a kiss to the hollow of her throat. "Consider it a rehearsal."

Her phone vibrates on the dresser behind us, but Cora doesn't even glance at it. Her throat bobs as she swallows. "Yes. Show me."

I take a gentle bite of her jawbone, her earlobe, then I press the flat of my tongue to her skin and taste her.

Her phone vibrates again, and I feel her turn towards it. But then I grab her hips and circle her against the length of me.

"If seeing you in the dress is bad," I breathe, "then fucking you in it must be unforgivable."

"Straight to hell," she agrees with a strained laugh.

I press her back against the dresser. "I'm already going to hell. What's another sin on the way down?"

Then her phone vibrates again and again. A nonstop series of messages that are impossible to ignore.

She reaches for it with flamed cheeks. "Sorry. I'll turn it off." But when she sees who's texting, her smile falls.

She scrolls and scrolls, her expression growing stonier by the second. When she finally looks up at me, I feel like the last few minutes were a dream. I must have imagined them.

"You said you've killed someone before."

It's a statement, not a question. But it comes from so far out of left field that I can't get my bearings. I shake my head. "What?"

"You told me before that you killed someone."

"You *saw me* kill someone," I remind her. "That *mudak* tried to snipe you. I killed him to—"

She shakes her head. "Not him."

I step away. "Most people have the 'how many people have you slept with' conversation. This is a new one."

"I'm not talking about your enemies," she says. "I'm not talking about taking out people who attack you. You told me when I first got here that you had killed another girlfriend. Is that true?"

I remember it now. Cora and I were arguing. She wanted to leave. I wanted her to stay.

What are you going to do? Kill me?

It wouldn't be the first time, I said.

"Why are you asking me about this now?" I ask, the heat inside of me turning to solid ice.

Her eyes narrow. "Tell me who Katerina is."

And just like that, the other shoe drops.

72

IVAN

Cora gets out of her dress and into normal clothes faster than should be possible. I still haven't said a word.

There isn't a word to say. Not if I'm going to keep my promises.

She turns to me, her lace bodysuit tucked into her jeans. "Are you really not going to say anything?" she hisses. "Defend yourself! Explain this to me!"

"There's nothing to explain."

She holds up her phone. The screen is black now, but I can guess what the text messages were. The way Francia and Jorden acted when I showed up makes a lot more sense now.

They were digging up dirt on me.

"Your last girlfriend is missing. No one has seen her," she says. "And when I asked if you were going to kill me, you said, 'It wouldn't be the first time.' I thought you were just saying that, but now... Now, I don't know."

"It looks like you know enough." I gesture to where she's slipping into her shoes. "One text and you're ready to sprint out the door."

"Because you aren't telling me anything!" she cries.

She shoves her phone in her pocket and presses her hands over her eyes. When she pulls them away, there are tears gathering there. Emotion threatening to overflow.

She takes a deep breath and whirls towards me. "You and I are in a weird, not-really-a-relationship where we don't owe each other a lot. I'm doing you a favor and you're keeping me alive. It's quid pro quo. This is different. You owe me an explanation, Ivan."

I know I do.

But I can't.

"Katerina has nothing to do with you."

There isn't even a comparison. I was forced to be with Katerina despite having no interest in her. With Cora, I want to be with her more than anything, but I can't. They're opposites in every way.

"She has a lot to do with me if I'm going to end up like her," she snaps.

I take a step towards her and she shrinks back. Actually wilts in front of me.

It's been a long time since she's been scared of me. I forgot how it feels to see her flinch when I approach.

I retreat and fist my hands at my side. "You don't know what you're talking about."

"Then tell me," she pleads. "Tell me what is going on. Trust me with the truth. Tell me that you're the man that I think you are."

My life is built on a foundation of lies. Cora wants the truth, but it isn't my truth to tell.

"I'm not the man you think I am."

Her face falls. "What—"

"You're looking at me like that." I jab a finger in her direction. "You're looking at me like I'm the monster under your bed and that's not who I am. Not to you. Whatever you're thinking right now, it's worse than the truth."

"Okay." She blows out a breath, but it doesn't do anything to calm her. She's still shaking, pacing back and forth in front of me. "Okay, so maybe you didn't kill her. That's what you're saying. But she's still missing. Something happened to Katerina." I don't say anything and Cora seems to fold under the weight of her own misplaced expectations. "If you won't tell me what happened, then it has to be because it's worse than I think. Did someone attack her the way they've attacked me?"

"No one attacked her."

"Then where the fuck is she?!" she screams. "People don't just disappear into thin air! Something must have happened to her. And I know how you are with me. I don't think you would hurt me. We're just pretending, but you've sworn to protect me. Did you swear to protect her, too?"

For a brief moment, I'm once again in the back of that car. The divider is up and Katerina is huddled in the seat next to me. She's wearing a fur coat and huge sunglasses. When she speaks, her voice is barely more than a whisper.

"I trust you, Ivan," she says. *"Whatever happens, I trust you."*

Which is why, standing in front of Cora now, I bite my tongue. I swallow down the explanations that are clawing at my throat.

A tear rolls down her cheek and she swipes it away. "If you couldn't keep her safe, then why should I trust you to protect me?"

It's her doubt in me more than anything that snaps my self-control. I take a jerking step towards her. "I took care of her!"

Cora scrambles back against the wall. Her skin goes pale—*so pale*—and her thoughts are written plainly on her face.

She thinks I *took care* of Katerina. After everything, Cora thinks I killed her.

"Oh, for fuck's sake, I didn't mean—"

"I want to leave." Cora crosses her arms over her chest like armor. "I know you have other safehouses and more than enough guards. Put me up somewhere else."

"No."

She frowns. "Then chain me up. Lock me in a dungeon. *Take care of me.* The only way I will stay here with you is if you force me to stay."

A dark part of me wants to strap her to the headboard and not let her leave until she understands.

But nothing has changed. There is too much I can't tell her— too much she doesn't know. And in the end, it might be for the best if she leaves. She's been a distraction since the moment she arrived.

Out of sight, out of mind. A man can hope, at least.

Cora is glaring at me, preparing for the worst. So when I nod in agreement, the fight drains out of her.

She sags, her shoulders drooping. "I want to stay with Jorden."

I scrub a hand through my hair. Jorden's apartment is a shithole, but the location makes it surprisingly easy to guard. Plus, the private parking garage in the alley is a good entry and exit point. It's not where I'd like to put Cora, but it will do.

"Fine. Yasha can take you. I'll arrange it."

Her knuckles turn white from clenching her phone so hard. She nods and looks down at her feet and mumbles something I don't catch.

Fifteen minutes later, Cora is gone.

The car disappears down the drive, a fog of dust trailing behind it. Once she's out of sight, I walk back into the silent, distraction-free house.

It's never felt emptier.

73

CORA

His last girlfriend disappeared.

She is still missing.

There are rumors he killed her to end their engagement.

Even with my phone turned off and tucked into my purse, I can see the text messages Jorden sent me against the dark backdrop of my eyelids. I can't get the words out of my head.

Ivan's last girlfriend is missing and he couldn't tell me what happened. Couldn't or wouldn't? I'm not sure anymore. I'm not even sure it matters.

The car takes a sharp turn and I press against the back door. My limbs are weak. The fact I'm sitting up right now instead of curled in the fetal position feels like an accomplishment.

Jorden reaches over and squeezes my knee. "Are you okay?"

I look over and try to respond, but the moment I open my mouth, tears fill my eyes. I slam my mouth closed and shake my head.

No. No, I'm not okay at all.

It's not as if I thought Ivan was a saint. I've seen him kill a man. I know his world is violent and bloody.

But I thought he was honest. I thought he was honest about who he is and what he has done. I didn't think he would lie to me about something this important.

I'm an idiot.

"Men are trash," Jorden says. "Worse than trash. They're germs."

"Hey," Yasha complains from the driver's seat. "Not all men are germs."

"Please be quiet, driver. We're trying to have a private conversation back here." Jorden looks to me and rolls her eyes as if to say, *Can you believe this guy?* "All men are germs, Cora. Every last one of them. Especially the ones that make you cry."

I didn't realize tears were rolling down my face again. I groan and swipe at my cheeks. "I'm so stupid. I knew this was—"

All pretend. Those are the words poised at the tip of my tongue.

"I knew this was too good to be true," I say instead. "I let myself have hope, anyway. I trusted him and I thought he would trust me enough to confide in me, but—"

"Ivan doesn't confide in people," Yasha interrupts.

Jorden elbows the back of his seat hard. "This is a *private* conversation."

"Well, this is a *small* car," Yasha fires back. "And you're talking about my best friend. I feel like I have a right to defend him."

"Which goes to show how little you know. You don't have any rights in this situation."

"I'm your driver, not a robot. I can talk if I want to—"

"Now is not the time to hear any arguments in defense of Ivan. Now is the time to berate his character and sympathize with Cora. Later, if and when she's ready, we can be reasonable. *Maybe* you can have sixty uninterrupted seconds to defend your germy best friend. Until then, it's venting time."

I give Jorden my best version of a thankful smile. Though right now, it feels more like a grimace than anything else.

I press my temple against the car window and watch the city pass by in a blur. Staying with Ivan wasn't an option. I couldn't sleep in the room next to his and act like nothing was wrong. Passing him in the halls and making polite conversation would have killed me.

The problem is that leaving feels wrong, too.

It's just all I could think to do.

My dad left. One day, he was there, padding around the house in a pair of worn-through slippers. The next, he was moving in with Crystal and raising a baby that I share half of my DNA with.

Why bother with the old, busted model when you can create your own upgrade?

Why stay when you can go?

My mom stayed physically close, but she left me in every way that counts. She stood by and let her new husband pimp me out to all of his friends' sons to see if they were interested. Alexander McAllister never had a nice word to say about me unless he needed something—an alliance, an investor, a connection. Then I was the most precious tool he had at his disposal.

My mom never said a word. She stood silently by his side, letting him mold and shape me into whatever he needed at the time. Because she was too scared to leave. Letting your only daughter be used as a bargaining chip was better than being a poor, single mother, apparently.

The one thing it all taught me is that when the going gets tough, you run as fast as you can and never look back.

People abandon you.

You abandon people.

It's the twisted, knotted-up circle of life.

In all likelihood, Ivan would have been done with me soon enough, anyway. Like everyone else, he would have left me behind, too. All I did is bump up the timeline.

Yet all I can see when I close my eyes is Ivan's face as he lowered his head and nodded. The broken way he agreed to let me leave.

He didn't even care enough to fight.

Jorden squeezes my knee again. I have no idea how long it has been or how far we've driven. I look over at her, blinking back into reality.

"Do you need anything?" she asks. "My apartment is a grocery deadzone right now. We can stop and Yasha can get you some ice cream."

"I'm not your delivery boy," he protests.

Jorden ignores him, her eyes on me. "Maybe chocolate? Vanilla? Both?"

"Thanks, but I'm okay," I mumble. "I'm not very hungry."

"I'll put in a grocery delivery order just in case you change your mind later. You never know what the Bad Boy Blues will demand."

"The Bad Boy Blues?" I ask.

She gives me a tight smile. "I coined the term. It's when an asshole breaks your heart like the asshole he is and then you need to fill the hole left behind with snacks. Mine usually calls for a bottle of wine and a bag of salt and vinegar chips."

Jorden is trying to distract me—or, at the very least, keep me from going catatonic—but I don't have it in me to joke or pretend. I just want to cry 'til I fall asleep and then sleep until I'm dead.

"Ivan is not a 'bad boy,'" Yasha argues. "Ivan is a good guy. This whole thing is a major misunderstanding."

It hits me all at once that Yasha has been friends with Ivan for years. They are close. He's his best friend and his second in command.

He probably knows things.

Jorden slaps the back of his headrest, jostling the seat. "Pipe down up there. We don't want to hear anything from the help."

"Says the waitress," Yasha mumbles, earning another slap to the headrest from Jorden.

I wave her off. "It's okay. Actually... Yasha?"

He's been trying to talk to me the entire drive, but as soon as I address him, he tenses. "What?"

"What do you know about Katerina?"

"Me?" he asks nervously. "Oh, um...not much. Nothing."

"Which is it?" Jorden bites. "Not much or nothing?"

God, I love her. I don't have it in me to fight right now, but Jorden is in a take-no-prisoners kind of mood.

Yasha sighs. "I know her family is... They're the fucking worst. Katerina was raised like a horse for breeding."

"I can relate," I mumble.

Yasha doesn't hear me and keeps talking. "Ivan and her family have never gotten along. It was always tense because he didn't like the way they did things. They still don't see eye to eye on most things."

"Why did they get engaged in the first place if their families didn't get along?" The words are out of my mouth before the likely answer comes to me. "Did he...did he love her?"

The knife twists in my gut. *Ivan in love.* What a sight that would be. What an experience to be on the receiving side of that.

"Ivan and I are close, but we aren't *that* close. We don't talk about love."

Jorden clicks her tongue in disappointment. "Classic men. God forbid you show your emotions."

Yasha sits up and looks at her in the rearview mirror. "I express my emotions just fine, thanks. I'm not afraid to bare myself to the world."

Jorden rolls her eyes again, but I notice the blush creeping up her cheeks.

Yasha pulls down a narrow alley and then into the private parking garage beneath the building. The pillars are crumbling and covered in layers of graffiti. Trash overflows in the trash cans and litters the cracked cement. But there's a guard waiting at the back door with a gun strapped to his hip.

As Jorden gets out of the car, she wiggles her fingers at the man and grins. "Hi, Leon."

Yasha looks between the two of them and frowns. I know exactly what Jorden is doing, even if Yasha doesn't.

My friend loops her arm through mine and pulls me towards the door, saying loudly, "You're going to love it here, Cora. So many handsome men hanging around to help you get over this little hurdle."

Then Leon leads us wordlessly into the building as the door closes on Yasha.

74

CORA

Despite all Jorden's smiling and flouncing, Leon doesn't say a word to her all the way up the elevator. When we reach her door, he assures us the apartment has been swept and tells Jorden to call if she needs anything.

"What about a backrub?" she hollers after him.

Leon doesn't answer.

"No sense of humor," she grumbles.

She hurries around, tossing clothes over the back of a chair and sweeping up a mess of mail and papers spread across her counter. "Sorry. I haven't had anyone over in a couple weeks. I let regular housekeeping get away from me."

"No problem. I haven't had to clean a thing in weeks, so you're doing more than I have."

She stops and stares at me, eyebrows raised. "Was that supposed to make me feel better or are you trying to brag?"

"I…I honestly don't know," I admit with a chuckle. "It's just the truth. But it's not much of a brag now that I no longer have a maid. It's back to the real world for me."

I didn't even say goodbye to Niles. Or Anya. Though maybe neither of them would want to say anything to me considering how I left.

"Oh, girl." Jorden throws the armful of junk mail into her trash can and then drapes an arm around my shoulders. She leads me towards the couch. "This sucks and I'm sorry. But—"

"I thought it was a nonstop venting session until I'm ready to hear counterarguments."

She forces me down onto the couch and then sits next to me, tucking her feet underneath her. "I said that to Yasha because his loyalty will always be with Ivan. Whatever he says cannot be trusted. But I am a fount of endless love and concern for you, dearest Cora. You can trust that what I'm saying has your best interest at heart…which is why I have to say that I did not send you those texts because I wanted you to call off your engagement and run away from Ivan."

I do a double-take. "You texted me that my fiancé might have killed his last girlfriend. What did you expect me to do?"

"I expected you to soak in your ginormous jacuzzi tub, drink some ridiculously expensive wine, and mull over your next move," she explains. "I wanted you to be armed with all the information to make a thought out, well-considered choice."

I stare at her, blinking slowly. "I've seen you throw a mug of hot coffee in a man's face because he whistled at you."

"It was lukewarm coffee!"

"I have seen you throw your entire phone into a trash can because you got a text you didn't like."

"I dug it out of the trash five minutes later," she argues. "And besides, those things were minor. They were bad experiences with men I barely knew. It's not the same as ending what could have been a lifelong relationship!"

Jorden would have a point…if my relationship with Ivan ever had a chance of being lifelong. But it didn't. We were headed down a path that was always going to end with the two of us parting ways.

"So, what, you think I should have stuck around and heard him out?"

She shrugs. "I'm not here to shame you for what you did. I'm going to support you no matter what. But I just think we owe it to the possibility of your Happily Ever After to consider that maybe we're misunderstanding something."

"The woman is missing. The last person she was seen with was Ivan. What is there to misunderstand?"

"Nothing. Or… maybe everything," she offers. "I just know I've seen the way Ivan looks at you. He doesn't look at you like he wants to kill you; he looks at you like he wants to *devour* you."

I slump backward. "Having great sex does not mean that someone isn't a murderer."

Jorden jabs a finger at me. "Finally! You admit it! The sex is amazing."

I groan. "This is not about that, Jor."

"I know, I know," she says. "It's just nice to hear my theory confirmed. I've never seen you so relaxed around someone.

No wonder it's because you were getting your world rocked on a regular basis."

She's only saying that because she wasn't there when Ivan killed a sniper in front of me. Or when a suspicious bottle of champagne showed up at our table during our date. Or when I was drugged in a bakery bathroom.

Wow. The last few weeks have been a whirlwind. Even worse than I thought.

All of that was incredibly stressful.

Then again, everything in between was nice. My mind wanders to the full day Ivan and I spent in his bed after the bakery incident. We spent hours tangled up together, talking about everything under the sun. I can't remember the last time I felt like that.

So cared for. So safe.

"Being with Ivan felt like a fairytale sometimes." *Evil stepparents and poison included.* "But real life isn't a fairytale. Ivan wasn't honest with me, and I'm not going to live in a lie. I've done enough of that for a lifetime."

Jorden frowns. "I hear you. But maybe he'll call. Maybe he'll explain everything and—"

"It's too late." I cross my legs and sit tall. "I think it's time for me to start over."

"Start over how?"

"Entirely. A new town, a new job." *A new name, maybe. New fingerprints, if I can get them.* "I know this sounds drastic, but it isn't just about Ivan."

"Mikhail," Jorden infers. For once, her voice is serious. "You're really scared of him, aren't you?"

I consider denying it. I don't want to be someone who runs away because they're afraid. Then again, I want to be someone who knows their limits. And I'm pretty sure I've reached it.

There is too much in this city for me to face it all down on my own.

"I don't want to be sucked into his orbit again. Mikhail, my family, Ivan—they're all here. Which is enough reason for me to be somewhere else."

Jorden stares at me for a long moment. I'm waiting for her to argue or try to convince me to stay. Instead, she says, "Fine."

"Fine what?"

"Fine, I'll go with you."

My mouth opens and closes. Finally, I reach out and grab her hand. "I wasn't saying all of that to convince you to come with me. You have a life here. I don't want to—"

"*I* have a life?" she blurts, looking around melodramatically. "Where is it? Point me towards it and I'll gladly stay."

"You have a job."

"Quintaño's is closed for repairs and I'm not naive enough to think Q will hire us all back. He has hated me ever since I told him I'd rather dunk my head in the deep fryer than sleep with him."

I gape at her. "You did *not* say that to him."

"Word for word." She beams with pride. "He's a creep and I'd love a new job. Do you have any other reservations?"

"You have friends here."

"You and Francia," she says. "And don't tell Francia, but I've always liked you more. You get me. So, forget the job and friends. Don't even mention family. You know I have a tragic, utterly heart-wrenching tearjerker of a backstory that isn't even worth going into." She squeezes my hand and then reaches for the other one. Her fingers are cold against mine. "The reality is, Cor, you are my best friend. I know it doesn't always seem that way, but having my entire life flipped upside down because of you made me realize that you're one of the most important people in the world to me. Like, I haven't been able to walk out of my house without guards tailing me for weeks, yet I'm not mad at you at all. If that's not love, I don't know what is."

I laugh, tears once again brimming in my eyes. "I'm sorry."

She shakes her head. "Don't be. Seriously. I've realized what's important to me through all of this and I've decided something: wherever you're going, I'm going, too. I won't let you take off on this adventure alone."

"Adventure," I say softly. "I like that. It sounds a lot better than 'running away.'"

"We're not running away from something; we're running *towards* something," she clarifies. "We just don't quite know what that is yet. But we'll figure it out!"

I've been "figuring things out" my entire life. I can figure this out, too.

I nod. "Okay. Deal."

"Deal." Jorden flops back on the couch and lets out a cackle. "God, this is going to be fun."

"Agreed," I say, even as some deep part of my brain is shouting that this is a dumb idea.

I ignore it. This is the same brain that convinced me it was a good idea to hook up with a billionaire in the middle of his Find A Wife party. This brain makes mistakes. Leaving is the right call.

This time, I'll just have to do a better job of covering my tracks.

75

IVAN

I hear the front door open, but I don't get up.

I'm too busy drinking. The cognac I drank with Cora the night we met seemed like a morbidly appropriate choice. I don't bother with a glass; I just slug it straight from the bottle.

The alcohol is still burning down my throat when my sister appears in the doorway. For the first time in a long time, there isn't a hint of a smile on her face.

"Well, this is every bit as pathetic as I thought it would be," she remarks. "I never thought I'd hate to be proven right."

"Go away, Anya."

She marches over to the sofa and holds out her hand. I know she wants the bottle of cognac, but I ignore her.

"Ivan," she warns.

I glare up at her. "Anya."

She drops her hand and takes a step back. For a second, I think she's going to leave. Anya hates when I'm in a mood—a mood that alcohol inevitably makes even worse.

"Fine. Be a booze-soaked asshole. Call me when you're sober," she shouted at me the last time I got drunk after a brawl with our father.

But she surprises me this time. Instead of storming out, Anya kicks off her heels and curls up on the end of the sofa facing me. "I know you're not really drunk."

I scowl at her, refusing to say anything else.

She's right, of course. I just sat down with this bottle five minutes ago. I've had the equivalent of two shots, maybe, and I'm already ready to be done. With everything going on right now, I can't afford to get shitfaced. No matter how pleasant it would be to forget the events of tonight in a haze of liquor.

I sit up and place the bottle on the coffee table. "Why are you here, Anya?"

"Because someone has to talk some sense into you and I'm the only one qualified for the job."

"That is too depressing to be true."

She shrugs. "Such is your social life. Yasha lets you get away with far too much shit, so he's out of the question. And, well, you know why Cora is no longer an option."

My stomach twists at the sound of Cora's name. It's only been a few hours since Yasha drove her away, but it feels like days. Having her out of my world was supposed to help me focus on what matters.

Why, then, has walking through this house been like fumbling through a dense fog? Nothing feels familiar anymore. In a matter of days, Cora showed up and turned my life on its head.

Now, I don't know which way is up.

A hand lands on my shoulder. I flinch and look over to see Anya is watching me with concern in her eyes. "Tell the truth."

I pull away from her. "About what?"

"About everything."

"You already know—"

"Not to me." She gives me a sad smile. "Cora wants to know you, Ivan. After she was drugged, I was there when she woke up. The first thing she wanted to know is if *you* were okay. She also wanted to know more about you. She had a lot of questions that I couldn't answer…" Her voice trails off.

I narrow my eyes. "What did you tell her?"

"I told her my story," she says, sitting tall. "I told her she needed to ask you about a lot of things, but I told her about myself."

"Fuck, Anya." I drag a hand through my hair and snap my gaze back to my sister. "You told her about Lev? You told her about the deal?"

She nods. "I told her what you did for us. For me."

"Fuck," I growl again.

I told Cora from the beginning that our relationship was just a facade. She knew it was going to end. But I never told her why.

I wanted her to think I didn't care. It's easier if she thinks I'm some heartless bastard who can fuck her and toss her aside when I'm done.

Now, she knows that it isn't about not wanting to marry her or having no interest in her. It's that I *can't* marry her. I can't be with her—because of my own bleeding fucking heart.

"What's done is done, so don't even bother trying to work yourself into a fuss about it. Better yet, drop it. *All* of it. This mask that you put on, this bullshit facade—just cut that shit out. *Tell Cora who you really are.* Tell her what you did for me…and for Katerina."

I shoot a warning look at my sister. She is the only person who knows about Katerina. About the truth of what I did.

Anya looks me in the eyes. "I know it's hard for you, but you really can trust me, Ivan."

"I know that."

"Good." She reaches out again and grabs my arm. This time, I don't pull away. "Because I love you. You're my brother. And, as depressing as it is for both of us, you're one of my best friends, too."

I wait for her to continue, but she doesn't. When I look over, she's blinking back tears.

I shake my head. "No. None of that. No crying."

"Sorry. Now, it's almost like I'm trying to scare *you* away." She laughs and dabs at her eyes. "All I'm trying to say is, I want you to be happy. And I can't remember ever seeing you as happy as these last couple weeks. Cora is—"

"A prop," I interrupt. "She's here to help us catch whoever is going after our family, and then she'll be gone. It isn't any deeper than that."

She sags, staring at me with obvious disappointment. "I don't believe you."

"I don't care," I say flatly. "You don't have to believe me. It's the truth."

"No, it isn't."

"Anya—"

"No!" She stands up and plants her hands on her hips. "You're lying to yourself. Even worse, you're lying to me. You can hide from everyone else, but I'm your sister."

I stand up, towering over her. "Exactly! You're my sister. Which means you know better than anyone the kind of pressure I'm under."

"I *do* know how much pressure you're under. And I…" She wilts slightly. "I know that some of that is my fault. A lot of it, probably. Which is why I can't let you walk away from this woman without a fight. You can't just give Otets what he wants."

"I'm not *giving* him anything. He *takes*," I hiss. "All he fucking does is *take, take, take*. I won't be like that. That is why I let Cora go."

Anya frowns. "You let her go because you don't want to be like Dad? I don't…"

Cora looked me in my eyes and asked to leave. She told me she didn't want to stay here. She said I would have to tie her down against her will to keep her here.

I am a lot of things, but I am not my father. I'll never do to Cora what he did to my mother.

Anya seems to understand all at once. She sighs. "Ivan, this is different. It's not like that."

"I know it's not," I say quickly. "Because I let her go. She wanted to leave, so I let her. It's not like it matters anyway. She would have left sooner or later. Might as well be sooner."

"Don't do this. Don't deny how you feel because—"

Anya cuts off the same moment the front door opens.

There are only two people on this planet who barge through the front door like they own the place. One of them is already in the room. And the other…

"Ivan!" my father bellows.

Anya groans. "Just what this moment needs: *two* sullen bastards."

76

IVAN

"You let her go?" he snarls. "You *let her go?* This woman was on my fucking payroll and you let her waltz the fuck away?"

"That's what I said."

My father's eyes narrow. "Don't talk to me like that. This plan was *your* idea and now, you've let it go completely off the rails.'

"The plan is still on," Anya cuts in, trying to help. "Ivan is still looking for the people responsible for—"

"Enough, Anya!" Otets swipes a hand to dismiss her and focuses on me. "I want to hear Ivan explain himself. I hear that you barged into Konstantin Sokolov's office unannounced yesterday. Now, you're cutting your bait loose without any leads. Make it make sense."

I arch a brow. "I didn't realize you kept in touch with Konstantin Sokolov."

"I have to, when my son decides he wants to start a fucking war," he hisses. "I built this Bratva from nothing and I won't stand by and let you drive it straight into the ground."

Anya is sitting on the very edge of the sofa, chewing on her nails. Her leg bounces with nervous energy.

Strangely, I feel completely calm.

"So what are you going to do?" I ask.

Otets' scowl deepens. "What?"

"If you won't stand by and watch me make the decision, then what are you going to do?"

"I'll take back what is mine, you ungrateful little bastard. I'll force you out. I did it to one of my children already; I can do it again."

Anya inhales sharply. She was forced out of all Bratva business the moment she chose Lev. Usually, our father has just enough tact not to bring it up.

I nod. "You can try."

His lip curls. "*Try?* I can do more than try."

"Maybe. There's a chance more of the men are loyal to you than to me. But I wouldn't bank on it."

"Are you suggesting I don't have control over my own soldiers?" His face is going purple with rage. "You don't want to start a civil war with me, son. It won't end well."

"I don't want a civil war," I admit freely. "But I also don't want your approval. The only thing that matters to me is making the right calls and earning the loyalty of my men. That's what I've done."

"You sound sure." His tone is mocking, but he's fishing for leverage. He's trying to figure out how confident I am. How sure I am that I can take him.

"If you're not, then feel free to challenge me," I say casually.

He opens and closes his mouth a few times, at a loss for what to do. We've toed the line of decorum over the last few years, even as his bitterness about being forced out has risen. But now, I'm saying, *Fuck the line.*

This is my Bratva now.

"So what's the grand plan, son? Your little wife isn't much use if she won't even talk to you." His eyes remain cold and hard as he takes me in. "I shouldn't be surprised. You never could keep a woman around."

I stand my ground. "I guess I should have taken notes from you and locked her up. Maybe I should have slapped her around a bit to take the fight out of her, right?"

"You little fucking—"

"Raise your hand to me and see if it ends well for you, Father. I think you know it won't."

His hand flops back by his side, though it stays knotted in a fist. His jaw works as he grinds his teeth. Finally, he says, "Good luck, son. You're going to need it."

My father walks out of the room with his head held high. But he might as well have a tail tucked between his legs.

The balance has permanently shifted.

Anya waits until the front door clicks shut behind him before she turns to me, mouth hanging open. "Are you the fucking don now? Is that—Is that what just happened?"

"It was a step," I tell her. "A lot of formalities need to happen between now and—"

Anya throws her arms around me, squeezing my middle. "Thank God. It's about damn time."

Reluctantly, I pat her back.

When she pulls away, Anya smiles up at me. "So…?"

"So what?"

She rolls her eyes, frustrated by my obtuseness. "Now that you have that off your back, you can start making plans. Arrangements."

I know what she means. Of course I do.

My father wanted me to marry before he handed over the leadership role. That's the only reason I attended the party where I met Cora. It's the only reason Cora isn't under my roof right now—in my bed.

Now, I'm in charge. New leadership. New rules.

"I don't have any arrangements to make," I say.

Anya stares at me for a long time. So long that I almost say something, just to break the silence. It's like we're in a play and I've forgotten my line.

Finally, she speaks.

"It was really noble of you to make that deal with Otets for me," she says softly. "You don't like big emotional displays, so I've tried not to make one, but…it means everything to me that you wanted me to be happy. You handed over your opportunity for a happy marriage so that I could be with Lev. I'll never be able to repay you for that."

"You don't need to repay me for—"

"But," she interrupts sharply, "if you sacrifice yourself now, when it's no longer necessary, you aren't a hero—you're a coward."

With that, my sister, who never knows when she's overstaying her welcome, makes a timely exit.

77

CORA

Jorden's pull-out bed is a torture device.

The mattress is more iron springs than foam padding and it squeals like someone is slaughtering a pig every time I roll over. I'm positive the guards are going to bust in any second to check for ax murderers.

After an hour of tossing and turning, I give up and go lie on the lumpy couch cushions instead. Jorden is snoring up a storm from the master bedroom.

But I still can't sleep.

Maybe I've gotten used to higher class living. Maybe I'm a snob now. Top-of-the-line memory foam mattresses and gajillion thread count sheets are the only way I can get comfortable.

Or maybe spending nights with Ivan asleep next to me has ruined me for the rest of forever. Maybe I'll never be able to forget him. No matter how far I run.

That thought is scarier than any nightmare I could imagine.

I bolt out of bed and grab my phone. I don't even know what my plan is until I type in Francia's name.

It's late, but she answers right away. "Cora? Is everything okay?"

"Hi. Yeah, I'm okay. I'm sorry." I blow out a breath. "I shouldn't have called. It's late, and I just…I guess I needed someone to talk to."

"Don't apologize. I wasn't sleeping, anyway."

"You either?"

She huffs out a laugh. "I've had a lot on my mind. Ever since we left Ivan's earlier…"

Her voice trails off and I realize I don't know how much she knows. I have no idea what happened after they left the room. And based on the way Francia is waiting for me to say something, I assume she doesn't know what happened, either.

"Jorden told me what you all found."

She exhales. "I figured she would. I'm sorry. I should have texted you, but I didn't want to ruin things. You seemed so happy. I didn't want to be the one to wreck that. And I guess I feel kind of guilty."

"Why would you feel guilty?"

"I'm the reason you were introduced to him at all! If I hadn't dragged you out…"

"Oh, Fran." I shake my head. "No, no, no. I used your name to get through the front gates, but I made my own choices once I was inside. Please don't feel bad."

"Thanks for saying that, but... I don't know. Some part of me just wants things with the two of you to work out. Then I could be a matchmaker instead of a life-ruiner." She chuckles humorlessly. "That's probably stupid. I mean, I knew who Ivan was before all of this. I should have known better."

I keep forgetting that Francia has a foot in this world. That she has access to information I don't have.

"I know you said your family's law firm helped out Ivan's family at one point, but was that the only contact you ever had with him?"

"Well, I didn't have any contact with him directly," she explains. "My family knew his dad, but I knew some of his friends' friends from school."

"Wait—you guys went to the same school? How has that not come up before?"

"Oh, no," she says quickly. "I didn't go to school with him, but a lot of his rich friends went to the same private school I went to. So I knew all about him. Mostly from all of the girls who had their hearts broken after they tried to date him. He was a real heartbreaker back then. Apparently, he still is."

"Are you still in contact with anyone from the school? Maybe there is someone who knows him and might be able to tell me—"

"I wish I could help, but I haven't been in touch with those people in so long. The invitation to Ivan's party is the first contact I've had from that world in years. I went to an alumni brunch a few years ago and caught up with Georgia and Kat, but nothing since—"

"Kat?" My radar is pinging. "Who is Kat?"

Francia catches her breath and holds it. She is quiet for a long stretch before she exhales. "Earlier, back at the house, it all caught me off-guard. I hadn't heard a word about Katerina in years. I certainly didn't know she'd gone missing."

"Oh my god…"

Kat. Katerina. Kat is Katerina.

Francia knew Katerina.

Francia was friends with Ivan's ex-fiancée.

I repeat the facts to myself again and again like I'm afraid I'll forget them, but I still can't wrap my head around it.

"I'm sorry," Francia breathes. "When I first heard her name, I didn't even think it was the same Katerina. I always called her Kat. We all did. I didn't even know that she knew Ivan. I mean, it was possible, but they weren't friends when I knew her. But then I saw the article about her missing and there was a picture… I should have said something right away, but I was processing."

"It's okay," I tell her. "I'm still processing everything, too. It's a lot."

"Yeah, it is. It's why I was going to take the night to think and then call you in the morning. I guess Jorden beat me to it."

I snort. "She texted minutes after the two of you left."

"Her processing time is faster than mine," she chuckles. "But I think I've fully processed, and Cora… I just feel that you should get out of that house."

"Francia—"

"Hear me out," she interrupts. "I know that there is a lot going on between the two of you that I don't understand. Everything is complicated and you all have something going on behind the scenes, but whatever it is, your life isn't worth the risk. If you have even an inkling that Ivan hurt Katerina, you should get out of there. I can try to help you get away. Maybe we can—"

"I'm at Jorden's house," I interrupt. "As soon as Jorden texted me, I told Ivan I wanted to leave."

"And he let you?" She sounds surprised.

I still am, too, honestly.

Again, the look on his face as he resigned to let me leave flashes in my mind. I blink it away. "Yeah, he did. Yasha drove me to Jorden's, so I'm staying here until... Well, until I don't know what."

Someone out there has to know something about Katerina. Ivan won't tell me anything, Yasha wasn't forthcoming, and Francia doesn't know enough to be helpful. But maybe someone else...

Maybe my mom?

I file the thought away as a last resort. Reaching out to my mom for anything is a risk. She may promise to keep things secret from my stepdad, but I know where her loyalty lies. And if I'm serious about getting out of the city, the less contact I have with her, the better.

Still, I'd be dumb not to consider her if I get desperate enough. She spends so much time standing silently by her husband's side like the arm candy she is that she probably sees and hears a lot. If she can't be a decent mother, she might at least be a decent source of information.

"Well, I want you to be safe, which means that hiding out with Jorden is probably the best call right now. Still, this is a big decision. You need to know what your choices are."

"How am I supposed to do that?"

"Don't get your hopes up, but I'll reach out to some people from school. Maybe someone knows something about Katerina's disappearance or her relationship with Ivan. I'll see what I can dig up and we can figure out where to go from there."

For the millionth time today, tears well in my eyes. "You are too nice, Francia. Especially after the way I've turned your life upside down."

She snorts. "No one has ever accused me of being too nice. Feral cat, remember?"

"Well, you're the sweetest feral cat I've ever met. I'm not really sure how I can repay you for—"

"You can repay me by keeping me in the loop," she says, cutting me off. "And whatever scheme you and Jorden have planned to flee across the country, make sure you save a plane ticket for me."

I grin. "How did you know?"

"Because I've worked with both of you for far too long," she chuckles. "Or not long enough, I guess. Because I haven't had enough yet. I'll follow wherever the two of you go."

I squeeze my eyes closed, refusing to sob on this phone call. Finally, I force a word out of my clogged throat. "Deal."

78

CORA

Jorden slams the fridge door closed with a groan. "What did I tell you? Grocery deadzone. There is nothing to eat here. It's a tragedy."

"There's toast." I had to pick a tiny bit of mold off of the bread, but I've had worse. Besides, I forced myself on Jorden without asking. I'm not going to complain about the accommodations now.

"We are growing girls. Toast alone will not satisfy."

I snort. "Well, I'm fine with toast."

"That's only because you never want to go to coffee shops with me. A five-dollar latte will not bankrupt you, Cora. You need to learn to enjoy the finer things in life. Like pastry. And croissants. Maybe a muffin."

I roll my eyes. "Just call Yasha and ask him to take you to a coffee shop."

She sighs. "Well, I would do that, but he told me yesterday that I'm 'taking too many risks' going out every day. But that's ridiculous, because I've basically been a prisoner here. All I've been doing is going to the bodega on the corner for a sandwich at lunch, visiting the coffee shop a few blocks over for my afternoon caffeine hit, and then hitting the gym every evening. Oh, and the taco shop across from the bubble tea stand. Oh, and—"

"He might have a point," I laugh.

She grumbles something I don't hear and drops two slices of bread into the toaster. "Well, now that you're here, I'm sure the walls are going to close in a little more. *Adios*, hot sandwiches. *Adios*, hot guy squatting in the gray sweatpants."

She's joking, but guilt washes over me. I chew on my lower lip. "I'm sorry…"

Jorden whips around. "No! I didn't mean it like that. You being here means I won't need to go scrounging around for human connection. I'll be happier in my four-hundred square foot apartment than I ever could be out in the big, wide world."

"Very convincing," I drawl. "I know I'm imposing. And really, if you need me to stay somewhere else, I can—"

"Girl." Jorden points two fingers at her eyes and then jabs them in my direction. "Listen to me: *I. Want. You. Here.* Okay? *Comprende?*"

I still don't fully believe her, but there is no point arguing about it. So I nod. "Okay."

"Okay, good." She leans back against the cabinet. "Besides, how else are we going to plan our stunning new life if we aren't together?"

"Good point. Do you have ideas?"

I haven't been able to think about much of anything beyond Ivan and Katerina. Thinking about my future feels like staring out an opaque window. I can't even make out blurry shapes on the other side.

I don't want Francia to be burdened with my problems, but I hope she's able to find out something about Katerina. Something that helps give me a peek into what the hell I'm supposed to do next.

Jorden doesn't share in my uncertainty.

"I'm thinking somewhere cold," she muses. "My aunt used to live in Montana. I never went, but she sent pictures and they were pretty."

I muster up a half-hearted grin. "Is this the part where you start waxing poetic about the many upsides of dating a lumberjack?"

She laughs. "I wasn't thinking that, but you won't catch me protesting. Flannel, manly forearms, swinging axes, building us, like, a log cabin in the middle of a pasture... Okay, I'm sold. Where do we sign up?"

Suddenly, Jorden's front door smashes open.

It happens so fast that I can't even react. My heart lurches and I spin around, but my fight or flight instinct is frozen solid. I just stare as Yasha crashes inside, eyes wide and frantic.

"Are you okay?" He's breathless, his chest heaving.

I've never seen him like this. He's always joking around, lighthearted, so seeing him panicked sends a bolt of fear through me.

"Of course we're fine." Jorden scoffs. "What happened to knocking before you—"

"Why aren't you two answering your phones?" he growls. Yasha stomps into the room and spins in a circle, searching. "Where are they? Why haven't you responded?"

Jorden lifts her chin. "I'm on a digital detox."

"You weren't on one last night."

Jorden flushes. I have a feeling I don't want to know what they were texting about last night. Not if I want to look at either of them directly in the eyes again.

He waves her away before she can respond and turns to me. "What about you? Have you heard anything? Where is your phone?"

"I haven't looked at it this morning." I cross to the couch and dig between the cushions until I find my phone. It's vibrating. The alarm I set last night has been going off for the last thirty minutes, but Jorden's couch absorbs everything, including both sound and my will to live.

I silence the alarm and check my notifications. "I have a bunch of missed messages from you."

"Anyone else?"

I double-check and shake my head.

"Shit." Yasha pulls out his own phone and fires off a text. He drags a hand through his hair and curses again under his breath.

Jorden steps closer, a hand reached towards him before she thinks better of it. "What is going on, Yasha?"

Cognac Villain 467

"I haven't been able to get in touch with security at the building where Francia is staying. No one has responded all morning. I also couldn't get in touch with you all, and I thought the worst. I got here as fast as I could, but still no word from Francia's building."

I inhale, trying to fill my lungs with air before they can drown in panic. "I talked to her last night."

Jorden whirls on me. "You did?"

"I called her. I couldn't sleep, so we just talked. Everything seemed fine."

"But that was last night?" he presses.

"Yeah. Like… seven hours ago." Might as well be a lifetime. Anything could have happened to her between now and then. "Have you sent anyone over yet?"

"I don't know what I'm sending them into. I'm not going to send them in blind."

"Cameras!" Jorden suggests. "Look at the cameras and—"

"Down. They haven't been working since midnight. The guards on duty should have informed me, but they're MIA." He nods to me. "Call her."

I type in Francia's name and press my phone to my ear. She picked up immediately last night. It was late, but it was almost like she was waiting for my call. I pray for that to happen again.

But the line rings… and rings… and rings.

"She isn't answering." My voice cracks. "We can go. I'll go in blind; I don't care. If something is wrong, then—"

"Then sending you in will only make it worse. Jorden, you try to call her."

"If she isn't answering for Cora, she won't answer for me." But Jorden still dials her number and waits.

She glances over at me as it rings and chews on her lower lip. Finally, she shakes her head and hangs up.

"This is my fault." My legs practically give out as I drop into a kitchen chair. "Francia was going to look into Katerina's disappearance. She told me she'd ask around. What if she asked the wrong person? Maybe they went after her and… Shit. Shit. *Shit!* This is all my fault."

Yasha lays a hand on my shoulder and squeezes once. "You two stay here. There are still guards watching you. I'm going to go check things out."

"You can't! You said it wasn't safe," Jorden protests.

At the same time, I stand up. "I'm coming with you."

He looks between us, unsure which to respond to first. He starts with Jorden. "If the men are in trouble, it's my fault. I have to get them out."

Jorden's face creases with worry, but she stays uncharacteristically quiet.

Yasha turns to me, finger raised in a point. "And there's no way in hell *you're* coming with me."

"I can't just sit here while my friend is in trouble!"

If he is walking into trouble, someone should be by his side. Plus, whoever has Francia is probably after me. If I have to hand myself over to protect the two of them, then I will.

"Taking you with me is a death sentence," Yasha says. "Even if I survived, Ivan would kill me."

"He doesn't care."

Yasha snorts. He doesn't buy it and, truthfully, neither do I. "Stay here. Both of you. I'll call with updates."

Then another horrifying thought occurs to me. "Does Ivan know about this? Is he going with you?"

Guilt clouds Yasha's expression. "I'll tell Ivan when he needs to know. This is my failure to fix."

With that, he leaves.

In the silence, Jorden's toast pops out of the toaster. The sudden noise makes us both jolt. Then Jorden plummets down into the chair next to me. "Fuck."

"This is all my fault," I whisper. "I shouldn't have used her name at the party. I shouldn't have called her last night. She said she wanted to come with us wherever we decide to go, and now, she might be…"

"She's going to be fine." Jorden pats my hand. Her own fingers are icy cold. "Francia is one tough bitch. She'll be okay."

I try to nod along in agreement, but my hand shifts towards my phone.

If I want Francia to be okay—if I really want to make sure I do everything I possibly can to save her—then I know what I need to do. *Who* I need to call.

I just have to sift through a whole lot of pride to pick up the phone and do it.

But if there is any way I can help, I have to try.

There isn't another choice.

IVAN

I slept like shit last night. I have no one but myself to blame.

That didn't stop me from trying.

As I tossed and turned, I first started to blame Anya. It was her voice that kept ringing in my ears, after all. *If you sacrifice yourself now when it's no longer necessary, you aren't a hero—you're a coward.*

I drag a hand down my face and reach for my coffee.

I decide to blame my father next. His personality ruled the house when we were younger. Anya and I were just kids and my mother's soft, sweet nature didn't stand a chance.

"You have to take care of yourself before you can take care of others," she said to me once. She was cutting back the peony bushes in the backyard, preparing them for winter. Elbows deep in dirt is where she was always happiest. Outside of the house.

Away from my father.

"That's why I come out here every morning," she continued. "I breathe in the morning air and feel at peace before the day starts. Which is why you need to get inside and back to bed."

She wrinkled her nose, grinning as she swept six-year-old me back towards the patio.

I dug my heels into the ground. "But I want to help with the garden! I need to feel peace, too."

My mom planted her hands on her hips and looked down at me. She couldn't keep the smile from her face. "Just this once. Do you hear me? After today, you need to figure out your own way to find peace. *In your room.*"

I managed to cut back just one of the dozen peony bushes before my father stormed onto the patio and called me inside. Being six was no excuse to busy myself with "a woman's work," he snarled as he dragged me in by the scruff of the neck.

I look out over the lawn now. It looks so different than it used to. When Mom got sick, the bushes became overgrown. The lawn devolved into a tangled mess of vines and overflowing garden beds. Otets didn't hire a gardener until after she died. The first thing they did was rip out the peony bushes. He never explained why he had them ripped out, but I knew.

They reminded him of her.

Now, a line of neat hedges borders the fence. I never gardened again after that day when I was six, but I think I managed to find my peace.

And then I let her walk away.

"God damn you, Anya," I mutter.

The moment the words are out of my mouth, my phone starts to ring. I'm positive it's my sister somehow sensing that she won this round and calling to gloat.

Then I pick up my phone and see her name instead.

Cora.

My instinct is to let it ring. I'll call her later. Once I've figured out what the fuck I want to say. Better yet, I'll talk to her in person. I'll show up at Jorden's and explain things.

I've almost convinced myself to let it go to voicemail, but then I snatch the phone up and answer.

Before I can say anything, Cora's voice comes over the line. "Ivan?" My name comes out in a tremble, broken in her desperation.

I stand up on instinct. "Are you okay?"

"I'm okay," she says. "Have you talked to Yasha?"

I haven't seen Yasha since he left yesterday. I asked him to drive Cora to Jorden's apartment, but he knew better than to show up back here while the wound was fresh. Unlike my sister.

"Not today. What's going on?"

"Yasha showed up and he can't get in touch with the guards looking after Francia. Jorden and I both called her and she isn't answering. I talked to her last night; she was fine. But then... I think something might have happened to her."

Blyat. Yasha should have told me. He should have informed me of all of this immediately.

"Are you and Jorden safe?" I demand. "Where are you?"

"Yasha told us to stay at her apartment, but I wanted to call you. If I can do anything to save Francia, I want to do it. You were the only person I knew who might be able to do something."

"Where did Yasha go?" I ask, even though I already know.

"He went to Francia's."

"Shit," I hiss, shifting my phone to speaker so I can send a text to Yasha.

Don't you fucking dare walk in there without me. That's an order. Stand down.

"Are you worried?" Cora asks.

I want to lie and tell her it will all be fine. I want to ease her worries and keep her calm, but I can't lie to her. Not anymore.

"Your friend goes missing one day after you leave my house and my bubble of protection… It's a trap," I say flatly. "Someone wants to draw you out. I don't know who or why, but—"

"I might," Cora squeaks.

"The more information I have right now, the better. Tell me everything."

"I want to, but you have to promise you won't be angry. Francia didn't do anything wrong," she says. "Whatever happens, you can't do anything to her. It was all my fault. I asked her to do it."

"Do *what?*" I growl.

"I asked Francia to look into Katerina's disappearance."

I frown. "What the fuck would she know about that?"

"Francia went to school with Katerina. Some rich private school. They were friends once, but she said they had a falling-out. Francia said she could ask around and try to figure out what happened." Cora's voice catches. "She probably asked the wrong person the wrong question—but it wasn't her fault! She was doing it for me, so I'm the one you should be mad at. If someone has to be punished, let it be me. But save her. *Please.*"

The desperation in her voice wrecks me.

"Cora, I'm not going to hurt you. Or Francia. For fuck's sake, that's not who I am."

"But Katerina…"

I made Katerina a promise. But I promised Cora something as well. I told Cora I would keep her safe. Right now, to keep that promise, I have to come clean. I have to reveal the secrets that drove her away from me and put her in danger. I have to do anything I can to get her back under my roof and in my arms.

"Katerina is fine."

The line goes perfectly silent. I can feel Cora waiting on the other side. So I tell her what she needs to know.

"Katerina and I were pushed into an engagement by our fathers. It was a business relationship more than anything. After the deal I made with my father on Anya's behalf, I was ready to hold up my end of the bargain. Until Katerina told me she didn't want to marry me."

I can still see Katerina trembling as we danced. We were taking our relationship public at some idiotic charity function, and she was a nervous wreck. Every time I touched her, she flinched away. All night long, she kept tossing nervous glances at her father. Konstantin was on the sidelines, scowling at her, threatening her to do as she was told. I pulled her aside and, after some coaxing, she confessed everything.

"Katerina didn't want to get married to anyone," I explain. "She didn't even want to be part of this world, but her father wouldn't let her go. She was the oldest of three girls. Her next sister was ten years younger, so it would be a long time before she was marrying age. Her father wanted to capitalize on every shot he had of securing his family's status."

"That's disgusting," Cora says in horror. "I didn't even think people still thought that way."

"A lot of things about this world are backwards," I admit. "Katerina's family most of all. I told Katerina I would call off the engagement. You might not believe this, but I had no interest in marrying someone who wasn't willing. I never expected to find love with someone, but I wanted a partnership. I wanted someone who understood what I was offering and was prepared to offer the same in return. Since Katerina wasn't, I was ready to end things and face whatever consequences came from ending the deal. But Katerina begged me not to. She said that her father would just force her into a marriage with someone else, someone worse. There was only one option: she needed to escape. So I—"

"You helped her," Cora says quietly. "You *took care of her.*"

She finally understands what I meant yesterday.

"I took care of her," I confirm. "I paid for Katerina to disappear and I haven't told a soul. Except for Anya. And now, you."

There's a long pause before Cora blows out a breath. "I'm so sorry, Ivan. I should have trusted you."

"You had no reason to trust me."

"You think I had no reason to—? Ivan, you've saved my life over and over again. You made that deal with your dad to protect Anya. Everything you've done has been a reason for me to trust you, but as soon as I heard one thing that seemed suspicious, I ran."

"And I let you." I squeeze the phone tight, wishing more than anything that I was with her right now. That I could hold her. "I could have told you the truth right then and there, but I didn't. I let you leave. And that is on me. *All of this* is on me."

"You can't take on the weight of the entire world by yourself."

"It's too late." I shake my head. "I told you I'd keep you and your friends safe, but I let you leave. That was easier than letting myself trust you."

"Why? Why don't you want to trust me?"

"Because it isn't safe for you. The closer you are to me, the more danger you're in."

She chuckles miserably. "Funny, because the only place I've ever felt safe is close to you."

I grimace. I can't stand when she says things like that. It makes me feel things in places I thought were long since dead. It's almost enough to kill a coldhearted bastard.

"I should have listened to that part of me," she continues. "I should have followed my gut and stayed with you. I'm so sorry, Ivan. For all of this."

"Don't apologize."

"I know you want to take all of the blame, but some of it belongs to—"

"Don't apologize yet," I clarify. "Later, when this threat is neutralized, I'd like to hear you say it…on your knees."

I can perfectly imagine the way she's biting her lower lip. The fire that is burning in her green eyes as she says, "It's a date."

"First, I need to find your friend and get you home." *Home.* With me, in my bed, in my house. "And Cora… you know I didn't murder Katerina, but I need you to know something: I will kill anyone and everyone who gets between me and you. Any soul that lays a hand on you dies. I won't hesitate and I won't ask questions."

I expect her to argue. I wait for her to tell me not to kill anyone for her.

But she doesn't say that.

"I know you will, Ivan," she says softly. "Please be careful."

I can't make that promise, so I don't say anything as I end the call.

80

IVAN

I hang up with Cora and call Yasha.

"Let me go in," he pleads as soon as he answers. "This is my mistake. No one else should die because I didn't protect Francia well enough. Let me go in alone. Right now."

"Not a fucking chance."

"Ivan," he growls.

"*No*. You're not going in there to die for this. We had no reason to believe Francia would be a target. Not after every attack for the last two weeks has been aimed directly at Cora."

"I should have anticipated it. That's my fucking job."

"Your job is to be my second. To do what I ask," I retort. "You carried out the security measures I ordered."

"But I should have—"

"Your job is also to do what I fucking say, not argue about who is at fault," I snap. "Shit hit the fan, and it's not time to figure out who threw it; it's time for us to clean up. *That's* our job."

He lets out a frustrated breath. "Okay, but someone has to go in. The place is like the fucking walking dead. No one is answering calls and the cameras are down."

"They could be holding the guards and Francia hostage inside the unit."

"Maybe. But people with hostages are looking for someone to talk to. It implies negotiations. Whoever did this, they aren't talking."

I nod. "You're right. This is something else."

Something worse, I think. Though I don't want to say that out loud.

"Where are you?"

There's a long pause. I know Yasha is trying to decide whether he should tell me or not. Following my orders has never been an issue for Yasha… until his honor is on the line.

"Yasha," I bark.

He sighs. "I'm at the parking garage one block south. I wanted to get a vantage point on the building and come in on foot."

"Stay there and wait for me. We go in together."

I hang up and turn to walk inside…

Only to find my father standing in the doorway.

"Our fearless leader is going to get himself killed on his first full day on the job," he sneers. "What a legacy."

He looks worse than he did when I saw him last night. I take it our conversation didn't sit well with him.

"If you don't have a good reason for being here, then get out of my way. I'm busy."

"I'm not sure why I'm here just yet." He shrugs and meanders casually across the patio. He runs his finger along the back of a chair as he walks. "I might try to convince you not to make a huge mistake. Or I might let you run into an unknown situation, get yourself killed, and run the Bratva into the ground…which would serve you right."

I snort. "Who told you about what's happening?"

"Some of the men still know where their loyalty should lie. They thought the *pakhan* ought to know what was going on."

"Then you know I'm busy."

I start to walk towards the door, but he shifts into my path. "You aren't going to waste time and money on a woman of no consequence. I sat back and let you shack up with your little girlfriend and protect her friends, but no one is going to die to save them."

"You didn't *let* me do anything," I growl. "And the fact that you don't see that this is a direct attack on us and our credibility is just another reason in a long list why you should have stepped down years ago."

Angry wrinkles fan out around his narrowed eyes. His jaw works back and forth. "Our job is not to protect individual people. It's to protect the Bratva—the legacy of the Pushkin name and what I've built. You're not ready for the job if you're going to let some no-name *bitch* distract you from—"

"Talk about her like that again and I'll kill you."

He arches a brow, but doesn't say anything. He knows I mean every word.

"Francia was under the Pushkin Bratva's protection," I continue. "An attack on her is an attack on us. Someone is trying to undermine our authority and make us look weak. She has to be rescued."

"Spoken like a soft-hearted fool. If you refuse to sacrifice anyone, then you'll get yourself killed and you'll take the Bratva down with you."

Maybe he's right.

Maybe I'll walk into that building and die today. Maybe this is the end of me.

But if I die to protect Cora, then I'll die keeping my promise. I'll die as a man of my word.

"The people around you are not pawns you can sacrifice for your own ambition, *Otets*. But when you treat them that way, eventually, you run out of pawns. Then you're left alone."

I leave my father standing on the patio and go inside to prepare.

81

IVAN

Yasha and I approach the building from the rear. Guns are concealed under my shirt, at my waist, and tucked at my ankle. Bratva men are stationed in a perimeter around the building, but they're further out than I'd like. If someone is inside the building with Francia, I don't want them to see us coming.

"Do you think anyone is in her apartment?" Yasha asks quietly.

I scan the windows and balconies. There are potted plants on ledges and lights hanging from rafters. A black cat sits in front of a screen on the second floor, watching us closely.

"I don't know. It depends who is doing this. It could be a small outfit—people looking for a ransom or to boost their credibility. But if it's anything organized—"

"The Sokolovs, you mean."

"They're the most likely. But we don't know until we get in there." I see an emergency door propped open to our right and turn towards it. "It's time to find out."

Yasha and I position ourselves on either side of the door. But just as he grabs the handle, my phone vibrates.

I pull it out, expecting to ignore it. But it's Cora.

"Hold on," I grumble. I turn away and answer the call. "I'll call as soon as I have an update. Just stay at Jorden's and wait for—"

"Ivan," Cora whispers. I can barely hear her, but she's sniffling. Her breathing is coming fast and heavy in the speaker.

I go rigid. Every cell in my body is on high alert. "Cora, tell me what's happening."

Distantly, I hear banging. Loud, echoing sounds coming from her end of the phone.

"Cora," I growl. "What is—"

"I don't know," she quietly sobs. "Someone is—I think someone is inside the—"

Sound explodes through the speaker. It's like a bomb went off in her room.

Then the screaming starts.

I can't tell whether it's Cora or Jorden or both of them, but there is so much fucking screaming. Yasha is next to me, his gaze murderous as we're forced to stand here and listen to it.

Then the noise fades. The sounds move further and further away…

Until all is quiet.

I'm electrified with rage. My body is trembling and Yasha has to pry the phone out of my hands before I can turn to him.

"Trap," I growl.

His eyes close as he shakes his head. "Was it—"

"It was Cora," I grit out, my voice growing louder with every word, "and we fell into a *fucking trap.*"

I spin around and kick the emergency door closed. The metal door bangs back into the frame, and I don't feel an ounce better.

I won't feel better until I see Cora. Until I'm holding her—warm and alive—in my arms.

And I will. I have to believe that will happen. Otherwise, I won't be able to put one foot in front of the other.

"What's the plan now?" Yasha asks.

I snatch my phone out of his hand and stomp down the sidewalk. I hear him walking along behind me. "We find whoever took them and we eradicate each and every one of them from the face of the fucking Earth."

82

CORA

For a second, I don't remember anything that happened.

Then I pry open my bleary eyes and see my surroundings.

Shadowy corners. Dripping pipes. The air smells dank, like we're miles below the soil. I try to lift a hand to push my hair out of my face, but I can't. Because my wrists are bound.

"Shit," I hiss, jerking my arms against the chair I'm tied to. The metal rungs cut into my forearms and the rope burns my skin. "Shit, shit—"

A pale leg catches my eye. I turn and see Jorden slumped in the chair next to me.

My stomach roils, threatening to upend the toast I barely nibbled on this morning. "Jorden?" I keep my voice low. I have no idea who did this to us or where they might be, and I don't want to alert them. "Jorden? Hello? Are you—"

She's alive, I tell myself. *She's alive, and we're going to get out of this. Whatever* this *is.*

I'm still trying to talk myself back from the ledge when there's movement to my other side. I spin around, moving so quickly that my shoulders twinge painfully against the bindings.

A sob wrenches out of my chest. "Francia."

She's in a chair facing me, her hands wrapped behind her chair. Her dark head is hanging forward. There's dirt on her arms and a rip in her shirt. But she's moving her legs.

"Francia, can you hear me?" I whisper. "Are you okay?"

She blinks slowly, opening her eyes wider each time. Finally, she lifts her head and looks around the room.

It's strange to watch her shuffle through the same emotions I did. The confusion, the panic. Her eyes go wide, and I see her chest hitch like she's going to scream.

"Francia," I whisper again.

Her gaze slams into me and I feel every drop of her terror. "Cora, what is—Where are we? Who—What is happening?"

I take a deep breath and blow it out, hoping she'll follow suit. Nothing is going to get any better if we panic. I need her to stay calm and help me figure this out.

Francia nods her head and takes a few deep breaths. When she's calmer, she takes in the room again. She looks to Jorden and then to me, noticing the rope around my wrists.

"Wh-what happened?" Her voice is hoarse. I wonder how long she has been down here. Since our phone call last night?

"I don't know," I admit. "You went missing, so Yasha was trying to find you. Then these masked guys came into

Jorden's house and..." I gesture around. "I woke up down here. Do you remember anything?"

She tugs against her restraints and then sags into the chair with a huff. "I don't know. I remember talking to you. I guess I fell asleep, but I don't remember it. Then something was over my head. There were voices, but they were quiet. They grabbed me and...and I... They..." She shakes her head, fighting back tears.

"I'm so sorry." The apology is dredged up from the deepest part of me. "This is all my fault. I got you both into this and I'm so sorry."

"Ivan is behind this," she says matter-of-factly.

I didn't expect her to forgive me immediately, but her words still surprise me. The shift from panic to theorizing was whiplash quick.

"Well, I mean, we don't know who is behind this. I haven't really—" I haven't thought about it yet. This is why I needed Francia to be clear-headed and not panicked. I may not like her theory, but she's already trying to think about what is happening here and how to get out of it. If there's anyone I'd want to be trapped in a prison with, it would be her.

"Of course he's behind this," she insists. "I thought it was strange that he let you walk out of his house so easily. Now, I know why. Because he always planned to get you back. No matter what."

A few hours ago, I may have believed her. But now...

"Ivan isn't what you think," I tell her. "He isn't what I thought, either. He's different."

"Come on, Cora. Look around. Who else could organize something like this? You've seen how much power he has. Who else could have gotten through the security measures he put in place but himself?"

She's making good points and my mind is still so muddled from whatever knocked me out that I'm tempted to believe her. Ivan is strong. He's powerful. He set up security around all of us—around Jorden's apartment and the building where Francia was staying. It would make sense if he was the one who breached his own barriers. If he made us feel safe, only to yank the rug out from under our feet at the last moment.

I shake my head. "I can't tell you everything, but I know Ivan didn't do this."

"You have to tell me something!" she cries. "Because none of this makes sense. If you know anything, I need to hear it. Otherwise, we might not make it out of here."

I glance over my shoulder and see that Jorden is still slumped in her chair. Now that my eyes have adjusted, I can see that her chest is rising and falling. Relief pulses through me and I turn back to Francia.

"Katerina isn't dead," I say quietly.

Francia frowns. "What does that have to do with this?"

"Ivan is a good guy. That's what it has to do with this. The last time we talked, I still thought Ivan might have killed Katerina, but I know now that he didn't."

Francia is quiet for a second. Then she shakes her head. "How do you know Katerina isn't dead? Did he tell you that?"

I nod. "He did. And I believe him."

Francia blows a dark strand of hair off her forehead and sighs. "I guess it doesn't really matter either way."

"Why not?"

She tries to gesture around and then lets out a humorless chuckle when she can't raise her arms. "Because we aren't getting out of here."

"Don't say that. We just have to think and try to—"

"Try to break through steel?" she snaps. "Because you can't see the door from where you're sitting, but I can. That door is steel and there's no lock on this side."

I turn my head as far as I can, but the only thing I can glimpse in my peripherals is more shadows. I rock back and forth, but all it does is make the metal chair legs scrape against the concrete.

Francia winces. "Stop. Just give it up, Cora. We're trapped."

I whirl back to her. "No. No, I won't *give up.* I'm the reason we are all here and I'm not going to sit back and let you all suffer for me."

Francia and Jorden are going to die down here with me. Ivan is going to get killed trying to save me. Everyone I care about is going to die.

And it will all be *my fault.*

"What do you plan to do?" Francia asks. "What have you done so far?"

"What do you mean?"

"When you were almost sniped at work, when you were poisoned, when Mikhail cornered you at the club—"

Cognac Villain

I frown. "Did Jorden tell you about that? I didn't think anyone else—"

"What did you do all of those times?" she asks, lowering her eyes to meet mine. "*Nothing.* That's what. You did nothing and waited for Ivan to save you."

I press back into my chair and stare at her. I'm too stunned to say anything.

She's right, a voice in the back of my head says. *You've never been able to save yourself. You won't be able to save yourself now. It's over.*

But I shake the thought loose and try to drum up a response. Before I can, Francia releases a sudden sob.

She wasn't crying before, but now, she's shaking. It came on suddenly. Shock, probably. A delayed response to the stress we're under.

"We can't save ourselves," she cries. "So who is going to save us?"

"I told you, Ivan is going to—"

"What big, muscled man is going to burst through the door and take us in his arms?" she continues. "Who is going to put us on his white steed and gallop us out of danger?"

Something isn't right.

The feeling comes over me suddenly. The hair on the back of my neck stands up. Goosebumps prickle against the ropes around my wrists.

"Francia, what are you talking about?"

She looks up at me, all signs of tears gone. Her cheeks are dry and her face is once again flat. Emotionless. "I'm talking about you taking some fucking initiative in your life, Cora. For once."

Then Francia stands up.

No ropes around her wrist. No bindings tying her to the chair. *She was faking.*

She stands up and walks across the room towards me, and I can't process what I'm seeing. Now, I'm the one in shock.

It's Francia.

She did this.

She toes at Jorden's limp leg. "She got a stronger dose than you. So she'll be out for a while."

"Let me go," I beg. I'm still tangled deep in my denial. "Untie us."

Francia grabs the back of Jorden's chair and drags her through a doorway I didn't notice before. The sound is shrill and piercing. I want to cover my ears, but I can't. All I can do is watch.

Then she returns, her eyes dark and fixed on me.

She smiles. I feel the cruel curl of evil slip down my spine.

"No, Cordelia," she says, sauntering towards me, "I don't think I will."

83

IVAN

Yasha screeches to a stop in the parking garage. Leon separates from the cement wall, leaving his post next to the back doors. His brow is furrowed like he has no clue why we're there.

I fly out of the car, already running towards the building. "You haven't been answering your fucking phone," I bark.

Leon's expression filters through every emotion before he digs his phone out of his pocket. His jaw clenches. "No signal. *Fuck.*"

The signal was jammed. Whoever did this planned ahead.

Yasha comes running up fast behind me, but I get to the back door first. I throw it open and head inside as Leon calls, "What should we do?"

If Yasha responds, I don't hear him. I don't hear anything.

My entire focus is on getting inside. Getting to Jorden's apartment. Getting to Cora.

Even though some part of me already knows she won't be there.

What I heard on that phone call told me enough. They were dragged out of the apartment screaming.

We skip the bank of elevators in favor of the stairs, leaping up them three at a time. We exit on the third floor landing and immediately, my stomach drops.

Jorden's door is open.

More specifically, it's open because someone kicked it in with enough force that the trim ripped off the wall.

"Shit," Yasha spits.

I hear his gun slide out of his holster, but I don't even reach for mine. I know I won't need it.

They're already gone.

I push the door open and storm inside, stomping over spilled papers, an overturned stool, and the remnants of someone's burnt toast.

"Careful, Ivan. Let me clear the apartment before—"

"They aren't here."

There was a struggle, I can tell that much. The closet in the hallway is open and hanging off its hinges.

I imagine someone dragging Cora down the hallway in my mind's eye. I envision her fighting, helpless to stop whoever had a hold of her.

My fists clench at my side as I move back to the bedroom.

The blankets are hanging off the bed and the nightstand is knocked over, but my eyes are locked on the closet. On the clothes and hangers piled in the middle of the floor. At the closet rod ripped from the wall.

"This is where they were when she called." I know it's true. I can feel it. The scene is playing out like a horror movie in my head, and I know I'm right.

I should have been here.

As soon as Cora told me Francia was missing, I should have brought her back to my house.

Better yet, I never should have let her leave in the first place.

That's when I see Cora's phone on the floor. It's the phone I gave her when she arrived at my house. The one I had a tracker installed in. It's useless now.

I pick up the phone and slide it into my back pocket.

Yasha has cleared the bedroom and the bathroom already. Now, he is moving back into the living room.

"Ivan! In here," he calls a minute later. I follow his voice into the living room. He's standing by the window next to the couch.

"The window was unlocked and cracked open. I think this is how they left."

I peek out the window and see the rusted remnants of a fire escape. "Do you think someone could have carried them down this fire escape?"

Yasha looks out the window, assessing. Finally he nods. "Yeah, I do. Why?"

"Because if I was in charge of getting two women out of this apartment without being seen, I would have drugged them inside and carried them down the stairs myself. Fewer variables that way."

"You think it was a two-person job?"

I nod. "That's a possibility. Or…"

Yasha spins around, brow furrowed. "You're not really saying what I think you are, right? I watched that girl around you for two weeks. If she is guilty of anything, it's not spying; it's being in love with you."

I shake my head and grit my teeth. "Or she was just a good fucking actress."

"This is ridiculous. Look around, Ivan. Look at this place!" Yasha throws his arms wide. "I don't think you're seeing this clearly. The place is trashed. We both heard that screaming."

The sound of it is still echoing in my ears.

So is the thought that something isn't right.

"Francia went missing. As we were checking on that, Cora and Jorden go missing. And all three of them are gone without a trace. Without any witnesses. Without anyone seeing anything." I shake my head. "How could someone do this without help them from the inside?"

Yasha snorts. "Who exactly would Cora be working for? Need I remind you, we found her when she was a waitress in a diner. I've been looking into her family and the biggest bombshell I've found is that her stepdad shares a few acquaintances with you. Not exactly surprising considering you know everyone."

As Yasha is talking, a thought occurs to me.

"What's her stepdad's name?"

"Alexander McAllister."

"Look for a connection between him and Mikhail Sokolov."

Yasha pulls out his phone, but I can tell he thinks I'm just jealous and overprotective. Mikhail cornered Cora in a club one night—so what? It's not a big deal.

I'm half-convinced that he's probably right. Maybe it's easier for me to think that Cora left of her own free will than to face the fact that I failed her.

I watch Yasha scrolling and typing away. Then, suddenly, he goes still. The blood drains from his face.

"I—" He swallows and starts again. "I kept searching for Cora's name alongside Alexander's, but nothing appeared. No one had any clue who she was and there were no red flags with her stepdad. It all seemed normal…"

I bounce on my heels, waiting for the "but."

Yasha shakes his head. "But you're going to want to see this."

He holds his phone out to me, and I reach for it with numb fingers. I'm operating on autopilot. I'm floating outside of my own body, watching myself move through the motions.

The screen is lit up, filled with some throwaway article from a boring socialite-style gossip rag. But there's a photo in the center.

Of Cora.

She's in a frilly pink and white gown that makes her look like Little Bo Peep, and she's standing next to a man. She's standing next to…

"Mikhail Sokolov," I grit out. "How the fuck didn't we catch this earlier? *She knew him.*"

And she didn't tell me.

I dragged Mikhail off of her and had him thrown out of The Coop, and Cora didn't breathe a word. She never told me she knew him. Mikhail didn't mention it either when I was at the Sokolov Estate. Konstantin said that Mikhail *had the pleasure of meeting* my fiancée. He didn't mention they'd already met.

"Like I said, I searched for *Cora's* name," Yasha repeats. Then he tips his head to the phone. "Read the article."

Beneath the photo, the first paragraph of the article reads: "Earlier this week, Konstantin Sokolov and Alexander McAllister announced the engagement of their children. Mikhail Sokolov, the oldest son of the elder Sokolov and heir to the Sokolov fortune, is marrying a relative unknown. All we were able to dig up about Alexander McAllister's stepdaughter is her name: Cordelia St. Clair."

I look up slowly, and Yasha is shaking his head. "I didn't know it was a fake name. Cordelia didn't appear as Alexander's stepdaughter anywhere and there was nothing at all about Cora before a year ago."

I stare down at the picture. At the woman who is clearly Cora—Cordelia, I suppose—with a beaming smile on her face and her arm wrapped around Mikhail Sokolov.

If she lied about her name, what else did she lie about?

If she did this, *what else has she done?*

84

CORA

"I don't understand," I say, even as the horrible truth is taking shape in my mind. "What are you talking about? What did you start?"

She sighs. "It's a long story, Cora. You've been falling for my shit for so long now that I have to take it way back to make this clear for you. It's going to be, ugh, *so* annoying to rattle off all the details. Do I really have to?"

She sounds bored, but I can see the excitement brimming behind her eyes. Francia is lit up in a way I've never seen before. She's practically glowing. "Radiating" might be more accurate, because the shit coming off of her is pure toxic.

"You made it clear I can't get out of here, so what else are we going to do?"

The thought of what else we could do down here is not something I want to think about. I have a feeling Francia doesn't intend for me to walk out of here alive.

She sighs and twirls her hair around her finger. "This all started... fuck, I guess this all really started when I was a teenager at that godforsaken prep school. I was never enough for the 'cool girls.'" She sneers. "I'll give you three guesses who the Queen Bee of the cool girls was, and the first two don't count." I stare at her silently, but Francia waves me on. "Go on. Make a guess."

I gulp. "Katerina?"

"Ding, ding, ding!" Her upper lip curls. "Katerina Sokolov ran that place. If you wanted to be anyone, you needed to know her."

"Katerina...Sokolov?" I frown. "Was she—"

"Mikhail's sister? Yeah. Fucking keep up," she snaps. "How were you engaged to a guy and you didn't even know his family?"

Because I wasn't really engaged to him, I want to say. It was all for show. Our fathers set it up, and then suddenly, I was going to parties with Mikhail and picking out a ring. It all happened in a matter of weeks, and there wasn't much discussion in between. Mikhail didn't care who I was and I knew it was a waste of time to get to know him when I had no intention of going through with the marriage.

Francia continues on. "Anyway, everyone thought Katerina was God's gift, so I got to know her. She treated me like her servant. Anything she wanted—*'Fucked-Up Franny will do it!'*"

I shake my head but it won't settle into place. "Last time we talked, you said you wanted someone to take care of you. You said you were lonely."

"God, you really ate that up, too." She laughs cruelly. "I told you what you wanted to hear. It's called strategic bonding.

You wear your miserable backstory on your sleeve and I parroted a version back at you. *Help me, Cora, I'm sad and lonely and I just want to be loved.* Fuck that—I'm going to save myself."

"How is this saving yourself?" I ask, gesturing around the dank room. "You are going to murder the only two friends you have? For what?"

Her face splits into a menacing grin. "For *everything*."

"How? I don't see how—"

"Then shut the fuck up and let me finish. I'm telling the story here. All you have to do is sit back and listen." She huffs and continues. "So, I graduate. Katerina goes her way and I go mine. We never speak again, but I see her engagement announcement to Ivan Pushkin. I watch as her life carries on exactly as it was always gonna: high-profile marriage to a connected man, shit out his little brats, and live richly ever after. Every woman's dream. But then something interesting happens." She snaps her fingers dramatically. "Katerina disappears. Bam! No trace of her. Here one day, gone the next. Her father is desperate to find her and I see my chance. I call Konstantin Sokolov, I offer my condolences, and I tell him my plan."

"What plan?" I ask, unable to keep the question inside.

"My plan to worm my way into Ivan's life and figure out what happened to Katerina."

My stomach drops. That's why Francia had so many questions about Katerina. That's why she wanted proof.

I just told Francia what happened to Katerina. Or, what didn't happen to her, at least.

She didn't die.

And now, Francia knows that.

"Konstantin loved my idea and he paid up front for it," she says. "He gave me money for clothes I could only dream about, an apartment with a view, and access to every party I could ever want. All I had to do was hook Ivan Pushkin." Her face sours slightly. "But Ivan didn't bite. The bastard didn't even recognize me when he showed up at Quintaño's to find you."

I frown. "If you wanted to meet him, why did you send Jorden and me to his party?"

She groans. "You don't listen. God, you really are stupid. *Ivan wasn't paying attention to me.* He wasn't interested, so I had to pivot. I had to come up with a new plan and I knew that you and Jorden were my best chance. If there's anything men like Ivan love, it's a couple of empty-headed skanks to flaunt around in front of him."

I want to defend Ivan. She doesn't know him at all. That is everything he *didn't* want in a woman.

But I keep my mouth shut. The longer Francia talks, the longer I stay alive.

"Just like I thought, Ivan made a beeline straight for you. But what I didn't anticipate," she says, that unsettling smile curling the corners of her mouth again, "is how upset Mikhail Sokolov would be about the whole situation."

My heart is thundering in my chest. All the buried threads of my life—the past I hoped I would never have to unearth—are being laid bare in front of me.

Francia.

Knows.

Everything.

"Mikhail was upset because his fiancée had disappeared on him." She pouts dramatically. "She ran off, leaving him jilted…only to pop up again under a new name on the arm of Ivan Pushkin."

Realization dawns. "That's how Mikhail knew we were at The Coop the other night. *You told him.*"

"Genius, right?" She laughs. "When Ivan showed up, I hoped he would see the two of you together and get jealous, but you had him wrapped too tightly around your finger by then. He threw Mikhail out without asking any questions. He wanted *you*. God knows why, but he did."

The venomous rage running through Francia's words is obvious. No matter how powerful she claims to be, she hates that I caught Ivan when she couldn't. She despises me for it.

"Naturally, I realized I was being presented with yet another opportunity," she continues. "In an attempt to find one missing daughter, I'd discovered another. And I wanted my due. So I called your stepfather."

My head throbs. Everything is falling apart. The fragile life I built is crumbling under my feet and I'm not sure what hell is going to swallow me whole. But I know it won't be good.

"So who are you delivering me to?" I ask bitterly. "My stepfather or Mikhail?"

"The Sokolovs gave me more than enough to search for Katerina and I'm sure there will be an even bigger payout when I tell them what you just revealed. Thanks for that, by the way." She winks at me. "And your stepdad was a bit cheap, to be honest. I figured he'd pay a bit more to find out where you are, but you must not be worth that much to him. Either way, I got my money there, too. Those deals are closed."

I frown. "So what's the point of this, then?"

"That is *your* problem, Cora. Oh, wait—do you prefer Cora or Cordelia?" She waves a hand through the air. "It doesn't matter. Your problem is a failure to think creatively. I mean, you had so many powerful men at your disposal, and you ran from all of them. For what? To be a waitress? To live in a shitty studio apartment and scrape by? It's pathetic how you wasted every opportunity thrown your way."

"One woman's opportunity is another's prison," I deadpan.

She rolls her eyes. "Well, your *prison* with Ivan looked pretty fucking nice. Over and over again, he put himself on the line...*to save you.* He risked his position as *pakhan* and all his connections...*for you.* It would have been romantic if it hadn't been so pathetic. But it gave me an idea." She paces back and forth in front of me. "If you weren't going to appreciate what you'd been given, then I would take it for myself. By any means necessary."

"Ivan?" I ask, not quite able to believe what I'm hearing. "You think that you are somehow going to trick Ivan into...into *wanting* you?"

"He doesn't need to want me. I'm not naive enough to think something like that is important. But if Ivan shows up here and finds me clinging to my life after a brutal, heroic fight to save you and Jorden from death—a fight I'll unfortunately lose, sadly for the two of you—then he'll marry me out of convenience. He'll marry me to keep this story quiet and as thanks for trying to save you."

It's terrifying how much her plan makes sense. Ivan has told me multiple times that he wants to marry someone who is well-connected. *Check.* Someone who isn't emotionally invested. *Check.* Someone who knows what they are getting into with him—money and protection, but no love. *Check.*

Francia could give Ivan everything he wants.

"You're forgetting something," I tell her. "You have to pin this murder on someone. Ivan is going to want to know who is responsible and it will all come back to you."

She wags her finger. "Konstantin won't breathe a word to Ivan. Not when he has a spy living in his enemy's house. I'll keep delivering information to Konstantin until he finds Katerina and our business together is done."

I snort. "Good luck getting that past Ivan."

"I've gotten everything else past him so far," she says simply. "He already knows someone is after you. Your stepdad is in bed with a lot of bad people. Could be any one of them who came after you, honestly. Ivan may never be able to puzzle it out."

My stomach is in knots. I'm trying to poke holes in a plan I'm hearing about for the first time, but Francia has been plotting all of this since the moment we met. Every second of our friendship has been a scheme and I had no clue.

Francia has thought of everything.

"You're insane," I breathe. "Actually, clinically insane. None of this is normal. You understand that, right? You're a crazy fucking bitch."

Francia walks around my chair. I try to angle back to see her, but I can't. The ropes are too tight. Then she squeezes my knuckles painfully and yanks on my finger. Something cracks. Pain flashes. Then a weight disappears.

My ring.

She walks back to face me. Slowly, she slips the huge diamond onto her finger.

"Maybe I am crazy." She holds out her hand, letting the diamond reflect the muddy lights of our dungeon. "But you're about to die in a dank basement while this crazy bitch gets everything she has ever wanted."

My fear vaporizes in an inferno of rage.

"Ivan will never be yours," I spit. "He is and always has been *mine*."

Francia opens her mouth to respond…just as something loud shudders upstairs.

She turns towards the door. For the first time since she revealed her loyalty, Francia looks scared.

"Looks like my big, muscled man has come to save me," I spit.

I'm hoping like hell that I'm right.

85

IVAN

"This is a waste of fucking time."

Yasha doesn't say anything, but I know he agrees.

We swept Jorden's apartment again for clues, but found next to nothing. So we are back at Francia's apartment building, once again approaching the emergency exit door on the side of the building.

"Are you going to let me clear the building this time?" Yasha asks bitterly.

"Fuck no." I wrench open the door and step inside. A few feet ahead is another door. There's a doorbell to the right of it with a speaker attached. But when Yasha pushes the button, nothing happens.

"It's disabled," he says.

"Then we'll have to do this the hard way."

I lower my shoulder. Yasha steps up next to me, bracing himself. Then we both charge at the door. It takes a few hits before the wood around the handle splinters. It takes a few more before the door shears away from the handle and the bolt and flies open.

An alarm should be sounding at this point. We've made enough noise that there should be guards waiting for us on the other side.

But there's nothing.

No lights. No alarms. No sounds.

The building sounds abandoned, even though I know there are people living here.

Yasha points towards the front of the building. "We can check the front lobby first. I doubt anyone is manning the desk given what we're seeing, but we could check and—"

Somewhere nearby, a hinge squeals.

Yasha stops talking. His eyes narrow as he drops into a crouch and eases forward. I take up position behind him.

Maybe this won't be such a waste of time after all. Maybe the kidnappers are using this building as their home base.

Maybe Cora is here.

Footsteps sound from the hallway up ahead. Yasha throws out an arm to stop me. "Who the fuck are you?" he roars down the corridor.

A second later, a figure appears at the end of the hallway with their hands raised.

"Don't move!" Yasha yells. "Don't take another—Francia?"

Sure enough, she lifts her head and as her dark hair parts, I see Francia's pale face. When she sees us, she sobs. "I'm so s-sorry."

I shift around Yasha and kneel down next to Francia. "Who did this?"

"I don't know." She swipes at her nose with her sleeve. Her shirt is torn and she's dirty, but she looks otherwise unharmed.

Suddenly, Francia grabs my shirt and hauls herself against me. She presses her face into my chest and cries. "I'm so sorry, Ivan. I tried. I tried."

I glance over my shoulder, and Yasha's face is creased. "Sorry about what?"

Yasha asks the question, but Francia looks up at me. "I couldn't save them."

Our eyes meet. Dread pools low in my stomach.

Suddenly, it doesn't matter if Cora is a spy. It doesn't matter if every word out of her mouth has been a lie. Nothing at all matters...

If she's already gone.

Francia buries her face back in my shirt. I can't formulate the words to ask her what she means.

But Yasha can. "You couldn't save who?"

"Jorden." She sniffles, trying to gather herself before collapsing into more sobs. "And Cora."

"Fuck!" Yasha bellows. He slams the palm of his hand against the wall, then wheels back around. "Who took you? Tell me everything that has happened. In as much detail as you can. Now."

There isn't time for Francia to gather herself or calm down. She's telling us Cora and Jorden are dead, but Yasha is going to keep working until we find bodies.

Bodies. The term feels so cold. So callous. Cora can't be just a body. She can't be gone.

She can't be.

I close my eyes and sense around me for some sign of her. I don't feel anything. But maybe that's good. Because if she was gone—really gone—I'd feel a whole lot worse than nothing.

Francia sits up and curls her body into mine. She's leaning on me like a crutch, her arm clutched around my bicep. "They put a bag over my head while I was asleep. I never saw their faces. Then it all happened so fast. Jorden and Cora were there, but it wasn't long before…before…before I didn't hear them anymore."

Did she suffer?

Did she scream?

Did she cry out for me?

Questions that will haunt me until the day I die ring out in my head, but I don't ask them. I can't ask them. Not yet.

"Why did they leave you here?" I ask.

She turns to me, her eyes wide and watery. "I think they wanted you to find me. Like…like a message."

"Unless they gave you a message to send to me, that doesn't make any fucking sense."

She lays her head on my shoulder, her breath humid against my neck. "The only thing that makes sense to me is that you're here. I knew you would find me."

I look to Yasha. He circles his hand in the air. We need to check the rest of the building. We can't leave without making sure Jorden and Cora aren't here somewhere.

I extricate myself from Francia and press her against the wall. "Stay here. We're going to do a search."

She bites her lower lip. "By myself?"

"Scream if you need help," Yasha says.

Then we both continue down the hallway, Francia disappearing into the shadows behind us.

We turn a corner up ahead and I stop.

"Something about this isn't right," Yasha mutters.

I nod. "Why would they go to the trouble of kidnapping Francia just to drop her back off unharmed?"

"She heard what was going on. She'd be a loose end," he says. "If it was me, I'd kill her to be safe."

"Agreed." I beckon Yasha into the room to my right and close the door. Something occurs to me. "When you put the women in the safehouses, you cloned their phones, right? Can you still see Francia's texts?"

He nods. "Do you suspect something?"

"It would be foolish not to. She's a victim, an eyewitness, *and* the sole survivor? We have to check her out."

Yasha pulls out his phone and opens an app. He inputs a fingerprint and facial recognition before a new phone screen appears on his. This one has a burgundy red background with a black rose in the center.

"This is a mirror of her screen," Yasha explains. "Right now she isn't doing anything, so it's just—"

As he's speaking, the screen changes.

A text thread appears. The number is unknown. A second later, words appear in the box below.

Ivan and Yasha in the building. They're searching the rooms now. I told them I couldn't save Cora and Jorden.

I see red. My vision pulses with rage. "She's part of the plan," I growl. "*She* did this."

I fucking said it seemed unlikely anyone would be able to pull a plan like this off without someone on the inside. But I suspected Cora. Francia flew under the radar. She never stood out to me.

By design, I realize.

I thought she was Cora's friend. Cora thought she was her friend. And she betrayed us all.

"What's the plan?" Yasha asks.

I grab the handle and pull the door open. "She dies."

I retrace our steps, turning down the long hallway where we left Francia. She's still standing against the wall, but her phone is in her hand now. She lowers it as we approach, sliding it into her back pocket.

"Did you clear the building already?" she asks.

I shake my head. "Turns out it wasn't necessary. We already found what we're looking for."

I pull out my gun and aim it at Francia, but she doesn't blink. Doesn't flinch. She stares down the barrel…

And smiles.

"Kill me if you want," she says, her voice suddenly flat and sociopathic. "It won't save Cora."

My finger is poised over the trigger. It's itching to retract. To wipe this waste of space off the face of the earth. "Is Cora alive? Fucking tell me the truth. *Now!*"

Francia's lashes flutter. "For the time being. But whether you kill me or not, she'll be dead before you reach her. Or rather, she'll wish she was dead when she finds out who's coming for her."

That's haunting, but at least it's a flicker of hope in the darkness. A spark of light at the end of this horrifying fucking tunnel.

"What do you want?" Yasha asks. "We protected you. We gave you everything. Why do all of this?"

Francia barks out a laugh. "*Everything?* You think an apartment in some second-rate shithole downtown is everything? I want to be in the mansion. I want the ring on my finger."

She lifts her hand and I see a very familiar ring gleaming there. She didn't have it on before, but there it is, unmistakable: Cora's wedding ring.

My lips pull away from my teeth as I snarl. "Where did you get that?"

"Cora handed it over," she says. "She was more than happy to trade places with me. Turns out your fiancée isn't as committed to you as I'll be."

Liar. She's lying. Cora would have fought to her last breath to never give Francia the satisfaction of seeing her wilt.

"You want to marry Ivan?" Yasha asks in disbelief.

She tips her head to the side, grinning. "Actually, Ivan wants to marry me."

She's insane. I can't believe I didn't see it before. "Not a chance in hell."

She shrugs. "If you refuse me, hell is your only chance of seeing Cora again. Because she'll die. Before you can wrap those deliciously meaty hands around my throat, she'll be gone."

"What do you want?" I growl.

Francia steps forward as if I don't have a gun pointed at her head. She reaches out and strokes a hand down my chest, Cora's ring glistening on her finger. "It's simple. I want *you*, Ivan. Marry me and Cora lives. Refuse me and she dies. So what's it gonna be?"

TO BE CONTINUED
Ivan and Cora's story concludes in Book 2, COGNAC VIXEN.

CLICK HERE TO START READING

Printed in Great Britain
by Amazon